Across the Sands of Time

Across the Sands of Time

A Novel

Nelson Riverdale

iUniverse, Inc.
New York   Bloomington

Across the Sands of Time

iUniverse books may be ordered through booksellers or by contacting:

iUniverse
1663 Liberty Drive
Bloomington, IN 47403
www.iuniverse.com
1-800-Authors (1-800-288-4677)

ISBN: 978-1-4502-3894-6 (sc)
ISBN: 978-1-4502-3895-3 (ebk)

Printed in the United States of America

iUniverse rev. date: 10/27/2010

Acknowledgements

Special Thanks/Military
Former BT2C Lubic Collins, USS Sellers
Petty Officer 1C Mike Thomas, USS Normandy
Former CPO Carlos Rivera, U.S. Coast Guard, Fort Wadsworth, NY
Former Army Sgt Jose Centeno, Panzer Kaserne, Boeblingen, West Germany
Ms Judith Whipple, Historian USS Lexington

Special Thanks/Technical
Renard Martin, PC Guru
George Mota, Former Hacker

Special Thanks/Medical
Dr. Derek Suite, Full Circle Health

Special Thanks to:
Ann Martin, Michael Rivera, Darcel Dillard Suite,
And most important—the publishing staff of iUniverse

Your dedicated support made this book possible—N. Riverdale

Ribbons are for heroes

Chapter 1

For the first time he sat on the pillow-top bench of a Steinway baby grand; its glossy black surface reflecting the big, iron-made object in his clammy grip. Pianos were marvelous instruments. Its black keys reminded him of the striking plumes of a male raven, while the whites, the healthy teeth of a young, Ethiopian prince. His elbows, pressed against the solid wood frame of the music stand, felt raw as he pondered on how many octaves there were, where the middle C was located, what an A chord sounded like, and what bass clef meant. He had heard of these things but never gave them much thought. Only now as he toyed with the fluted revolving cylinder did he even think of playing a note. However there was no time. Not today. If he tickled the ivories, its acoustic energy might cause him to change his mind and he couldn't allow that. His chief delight this moment was caressing the brass loop of the trigger guard as the flesh of his palm wrapped around the slip-proof grip.

Like a pair of sledgehammers his tired elbows slipped on the ebony/ivory keys, creating a monstrous tone that resonated off the soundboard. Its ominous stroke frightened him but it should not have. The jarring chord was his life.

With the piston beat of his heart, his hands' dorsal veins shrunk and a phantom voice called: Get it over with.

The only way to kill the thought that danced in his head like a graceful ballerina was to sneak up on the man he had a gut feeling, was distracted.

Avery moved with haste to a Monticello wood-burning fireplace. Its masonry facade meant nothing without a blazing flame. It had gone out years ago and was never rekindled. "Mom," he said. "Please, forgive me."

He wished the woman in the regal mantel photo was recognizable. Even her voice was forgotten. It was so long ago he felt her protective embrace, he wondered whether the intimate scenes in his head happened at all.

A blast from a muzzle awakened him to his surroundings: a white, blood-soaked carpet; a dark pair of eyes staring back. Nothing in the world had ever changed those menacing features—not love, marriage, or a lucrative job. And nothing would change them now. Not even the bullet that smashed into the back of the man's skull.

Avery stumbled from the Colonial master bedroom into the marbled bath suite with his head pounding from the sulfur smell of gunpowder that rushed up his nostrils and clogged his throat. The abstract pattern that dotted the clean fabric of his designer shirt and slacks, like red paint spattered on an artist's canvas, sent him to a mahogany-framed mirror where he shook without relief. He coughed volcanically into his twin, creating a circular smear of breath. When he wiped away the thin layer of fog with a sleeve he discovered something else was on him, too. On his thick, chestnut-brown hair parted even to one side, on his trembling hands and ghost-whitened face, bits of gray matter looked like dabs of pale plaster.

A quiver-filled cry made his fingers curl against his will to drop the Smith & Wesson to the floor, so he waited with ragged breath until a stormy surge of adrenaline ebbed. When it did, he dragged himself to the square-tiled living room, and in a freefall, collapsed on a big, brown, plush leather chair with all the weight guilt could apply. No matter how high the vaulted ceiling or spacious his surroundings, a hemmed-in feeling began to crush and another thought danced in the aisles of his brain—suicide.

He pointed the revolver over the bridge of his nose, looking down at its blue, nickel finish. There should have been five, gold, hollow-point rounds remaining within the chamber. There were none. A moment ago the muzzle's mouth stunk of brimstone. Now it smelled of clean lubricant.

Finally, with a loud grunt of disdain, the weapon he thought he would cherish slipped free and clattered on the slate-blue floor. His rampaging anxiety would not be so quick to loosen its grip, though, unless he found a sedative, something to numb him down to the bone. He hoped what he was about to do would work. He plucked at the crown of his watch and turned the tiny knob between thumb and forefinger as fast as he could, sending the minute and hour hand racing twelve hours—counterclockwise.

As soon as he straightened up, a pair of gold-sealed master's degrees on a wall, one in psychology, the other in counseling, reminded him where he was and where he sat. Disorientation took flight but not the other things. He pushed down on the watch's crown with an inaudible snap. "You must wonder why I do that."

A young woman in a ruffled, long-sleeved, breezy, white camisole blouse and pleated, short skirt, simply listened; her pupils—like two dots of music notes in settings of dime-size blue irises—studying him.

"It … helps," he said.

Across the office, a painting of a steeple-crowned church amidst an autumn-speckled countryside captured a perfect image of the township he knew well. In it, leafy trees and cumulus clouds took him to a better place, a happy time, a home with quiet rooms so different from where he sat now. Here in his present surroundings he could never relax his taut lips, never blink the harsh feel out of his eyes, never be at ease knowing he was vulnerable before the woman whose name was Karyn.

"You always stare at that painting," she said.

This time when Avery looked at her, he saw something other than her professional demeanor. He saw an unguarded moment that parted her lips and stilled blinking eyes, shooting from him to a corner of the room.

He looked along with her, wondering what it was about him she fancied.

On an aluminum coat rack, a double-breasted dress-blue service jacket hung lifeless like his posture. At the cuff of each sleeve, a prominent double row of braided gold stripes matched the grade of twin silver bars on the collar of his khakis; the ones he wore the day he first shuffled in.

Fastened over the jacket's left breast pocket, three horizontal rows of military decorations were arranged in order of precedence. Among them were those given for pistol and rifle sharpshooting, Arctic and Antarctic service, and a foliage-green, gold-yellow, scarlet-red bar—a Navy-Marine Corps ribbon. Pinned above them he wore what every submariner strove for: the fleet's gold dolphins.

Those were his credentials; the measure of his career. But despite the high-gloss of Navy issue shoes, the impressive uniform, and silver eagle perched over crossed gold anchors on a black-billed white wheel cap, he was aware he didn't act much like a military man each time he dug a pinky in his ear and wiped the excavated waxy gunk on his trousers.

"Your hand was clenched as though you were holding something," Karyn said. "Why haven't you told me everything?"

"Too much to tell."

"So why are you here? What do you want?"

He forced a smile he knew did not come out right. "Flowers."

"Flowers?"

"That's what I said."

"For who?"

"For …." He was stopped by images of faceless pallbearers; those who would help him carry it. There should have been a wake, followed by a slow march to a spot where a mahogany casket would be fed to the hungry earth. There should have been a place where he could come yearly; a granite gravestone where he could lay lilies. But the ongoing, restless desire of such things were like the remains of a man only a stranger seven years prior. "For the one whose dusty ashes were scattered in the wind," he said.

A patch of square sunlight brightened the floor and he crossed the comfortable office to an open window. There, a row of flowerpots rested on the sill: yellow begonias, lavender coleus, pink geraniums. He lifted a pinch of dry potting soil, worked it into his fingertips and brought it to his nose, sampling the dirt's earthy scent. He thought of Mama's black hands. She'd take a generous sip of raspberry tea from a tall glass of floating ice cubes and get to work. Moist soil always clung to her plump fingers each time she repotted sprouting greenery.

Above, the sky was cloudless, a watercolor blue he raised a smile at each time he leaned against a mighty oak. Now what he raised were heavy eyes, sweeping over the wide, flat vista of a military base: its operations facilities and administrative buildings, its historic 110-foot-tall control tower, and the slate-blue bay with long concrete piers that stretched like incomplete runways throughout North Island, the home of the Navy's state-of-the-art computerized fleet. Massive, battle-gray vessels that possessed the strength to plow through the beastlike oceans they were made to conquer. If the office had a window facing west, he would see the great Pacific, always moving but never changing. And if he listened closely and quietly, he would hear it calling ships and sailors to cross it.

The man waited for someone to appear among the military pedestrians milling McCain Boulevard below; someone who passed that way often. When he saw no one, he lowered his head, siphoned a stream of mucus back to its starting point and cursed the monstrous agony he wrestled with. Avery lived in a private world of pain, and except for the woman who sat facing him, he invited no one else to touch the shape and size of his grief.

He lost himself in another painting: A rowboat on a peaceful lake. A man and boy sitting together fishing. A father with his son.

"A new one?" His raw voice rose above the quiet.

"Norman Rockwell. Like it?"

The office displayed several paintings. He could tell they were chosen with care to bring comfort to those who came to see her.

"Nice," he said in a dead tone. "When did you put it up?"

"Months ago. Surprised you didn't notice it till now."

He stopped noticing things long ago: sunny days, clear nights, full moons, star-spangled skies. "Shows where my head's been. Up my six." He fought the temptation to reminisce, but its power swept him away to the pitching deck of a phantom ship caught in a nautical storm. If he didn't hold on to something he would be thrown overboard.

The sound of her voice was the lifeline he held on to. "Remind you of someone?"

He wished she hadn't asked whose face it was he saw in the painting. So he gave no answer.

Karyn typed something into the computer. Last notations of the day, he thought. She swiveled toward him in her chair and he caught a reflection of her in a square mirror by the plants. He guessed at her age. Thirty-one? "Do I embarrass or frighten you?" He gave her a look.

She pushed back the waist-length blonde hair that draped over slender shoulders. "You could never frighten me."

"Then why did you hide your eyes from me before?"

The silence he created gave him a moment to jerk a stiff handkerchief from his back pocket and wipe dirt-stained fingers into it. When he regarded those familiar eyes, he knew in a little while she would be seeing someone else.

"I'll be transferring out of North Island in ten days," she informed him. The officer's eyes sunk, and from within something followed, forcing him into a deep, dark hole. He was as the biblical character Joseph from the book of Genesis, struggling with feeble might to claw his way out of a mud-slippery pit. "You'll be referred to another grief counselor. Is that all right?"

He shrugged. Avery didn't care how Karyn looked at him as long as she saw what he allowed her to see: an unblemished face and tailored body he hoped resembled the handsome males on recruiting-station posters.

A woman laughed in the hall and the sound annoyed him. He swiped his raw nose with the rough handkerchief and walked away from the window. On Karyn's cherrywood desk, a daily calendar revealed a day, a month, a year: Tuesday, May 30, 2062. He sank into a leather chair with hands folded, head hanging, shoulders drooping. She got up and handed him a note written on Navy stationary. He opened it. A flowery script filled the introductory letter he would deliver to the new therapist when his ship returned to San Diego from its six-week-long deployment in the waters off the Galapagos Islands with its assigned, carrier-qualified airwing. Afterward, the *birdfarm* would tie up at the naval shipyard for a six-month overhaul, followed by an extensive standdown period at North Island, five, sea-trial days later.

"Lieutenant?" Her voice drew him. "May I call you Neil?" A surge of blush tinged her cheeks.

"Where did the year go?" he said with searching eyes. "Months pass on the way people do."

He knew the gap in silence was her cue for the next question.

"Are you afraid of being trapped in your present state of mind forever?" He barely nodded.

"You never did tell me why your wife divorced you?" She seemed to lock in on his left ring finger—a white band of skin. Everyone he knew did that.

Avery looked at Karyn and saw *her*. "Leave it for the next counselor." But the next counselor would no doubt do to him what the previous ones had done: walk out on the incurable man.

"Don't let tragedy's power keep you imprisoned." She handed him a pocket-size Life Bible laying on her desk. "Don't you want to remarry?"

It was up to him to accept that bible, or turn away from God. He chose the latter, giving his attention to Rockwell's man-in-the-rowboat painting.

"Was he the one cremated?" she asked.

He let her stare into his silence; a silence deep and vast as an ocean.

"I've never recommended this as a form of therapy to anyone. But maybe you should visit a cemetery. Read gravestones. Maybe—"

"Maybe I should just—"

"What?" she jumped in. She laid the green-covered bible down. "You wouldn't hurt yourself, would you?"

Hurting was the only thing he knew how to do. "Forget it," he said. "It's nothing."

"It's you who's forgetting what I asked to memorize the first day you walked in here."

That day was like going to school for the first time. His gut felt queasy. What will she think of me? The thought intimidated him. She would learn of him before he learned anything about her. There was more to a woman than just her striking legs and good looks. "How did the mantra go?" When it came to him he recited it:

Grief—a human experience,
a natural emotion,
one of many given by God.
While some trod its pathways too early in life,
and others linger long in it,
God by his grace will rise above all pain,
and help me stand on solid ground again.

"I wrote that in memory of my father," Karyn told him. "Weeping out pain is how I survived."

"You're too late."

"What do you mean?"

"Doesn't matter." His gold Quartz beeped. "Time to go." But he knew wherever he went he really wouldn't be going anywhere.

"I've failed you, haven't I?"

Failure wasn't how he would have described it. Abandoned was more like it. A little dog abandoned by its owner; no one to feed him; touch him; left to die.

Take heart, he heard her say. All was not lost. If he prayed hard enough and long enough, things would change. And someday, she added, he would meet someone to remarry. He didn't believe that, though. He didn't even believe the gaping hole in his chest would ever heal, or that good would happen to him again. What he believed was this: he would never stop asking why it all happened.

He closed tired eyes until a long silence passed.

Karyn rose to her feet. "Will I …?" Her chest swelled with the intake of a ragged breath. "Will I see you again next week?"

"You always ask that." He found that forlorn mask and put it on again. "Like one more visit would make a difference."

"Why do you say it that way?"

"What other way is there?" He tried to interpret the message that lingered in her eyes, but was unable. "You're moving on and … so will I." He couldn't believe he said he wanted to move on.

He rose with a limp and shuffled to the corner of the office like a soldier with a leg prosthesis. He lifted his jacket and wheel cap off the aluminum rack and pulled the walnut door open, ready to leave. On the Plexiglas, he read a name: Karyn Engle, USN. Department of Psychiatry

He was gone before she could utter another word.

Back in his quarters, Avery turned away from the faces that smiled at him within photo pockets magnetized to the bulkhead. He rolled out a desk drawer to a full stop, and strangely it beckoned as though calling him by name. There beneath a stack of bundled letters and cell phone lay a 9mm Glock.

The compact weapon. Sooner or later, someone would come looking for it.

The first Glock he held was at a Naval Academy pistol range as a midshipman. The touch of its cool, dark metal and initial jolt up his arm, excited him as much as the glowing projectiles he launched at a silhouetted target a hundred yards away.

Another bull's eye, the range instructor said. You're the damn best shot I've ever seen.…

Avery pushed everything aside, scooped up the lightweight firearm and pointed the barrel at the bridge of his nose. No, I have a better way, he thought. He put the weapon down.

His dizzy mind swum in a quandary of images. Of high places. A long, plunging fall.

"I'll jump!" he said with a determined shout.

He planned it out. When the right moment came, when he could no longer ignore the ticking and when no one was standing watch, he would scramble up ladders and length of p-ways like a football player on a touchdown play. Then with a spectacular leap off Vultures Row, his body twisting and tumbling from the fifteen-story fall, he would slam into the deepest part of the bay with accelerating speed. At that height, water becomes concrete, he thought.

Chapter 2

Atlantic Fleet Headquarters: Norfolk, VA.

In the court-like building's lobby, a tall military policeman snatched a red phone off its cradle in mid-ring. "Security."

"Have they arrived?" someone said through the receiver.

The MP lifted a clipboard and skimmed over the first few names: Hobbs, Evans, Rivera, Yancey, Lee …. There were no forgeries and every ID had been checked. He looked to a surveillance monitor. On the screen, thirteen uniformed men sat waiting in an octagon-shaped room at the end of a broad wing. "All present, sir."

"Good. Send them up one by one. Remember, one by one."

"Aye, sir." The MP signed off, hung up, and gave an order to a stout, white-gloved MP to escort everyone out.

The lobby phone rang again, and the tall MP lifted the receiver. "Security."

"Are they coming?" the voice said.

From ceiling cameras in the adjacent wing, a line of surveillance monitors now showed a group of men leaving the octagon quarterdeck. They paraded through a broad, L-shaped marble corridor until they reached a back elevator, and a big, round insignia at their feet.

"They're standing over the eagle now, sir," the MP confirmed.

"Fine, but remember my instructions."

9

"One by one, sir. Aye." He lowered the phone onto its cradle as he studied the overhead image of dark-haired, broad-shouldered servicemen on the monitors, and waited. With the shrinking pack, the impressive blue-white-and-gold round trademark insignia, obscured by the standing men, appeared on the diamondized marble floor: United States Navy

On the third floor, a tall man—clutching a Navy briefcase—pushed open a fine-grained oak door, and a black military policeman received him with a grim look. He had ushered everyone into the hushed boardroom, one at a time, and with the arrival of the last individual, a wall of men parading through corridor links had been avoided.

The man entered the conference room where every officer and sailor waited; garrison caps and Dixie-Cup hats on a long, polished table. To each man, a clear, cold glass of water lay within hands reach. The thick door closed with a click of its brass lock and everyone stood tall to their feet. Those present comprised of five seamen, three petty officers, a CPO, an ensign, two lieutenants, and a senior officer. The briefcase man would make this their final meeting. He went to the front and motioned for everyone to sit. When they did, two armed MPs swept past each window, lowered all blinds, and the room became dim.

The man fitted black glasses over his eyes. "Gentlemen, it has come to this." Water pulsed in every tall glass when he dropped his glazed leather briefcase—monogrammed with a gold letter "J"—on the long, boardroom table. "Homeland security has gone lax, our president is laid back, and the Pentagon is gearing to pony-up a huge chunk of the military's budget on the Vanguard-3 Global Intelligence Antimissile Space System. Damn them!"

"What makes them think this one will be a winner when the first two flopped?" the senior officer asked.

"Trust me, it won't." The briefcase man shoved back his glasses with a tense finger. "Under our proposal, the House and Senate came up with a plan to channel money where it really belongs. But the president vetoed it, Congress adjourned, and for the umpteenth time the bill was killed." He tightened his lips in disapproval. "This mustn't continue, gentlemen." He rubbed the side of his briefcase; fingers over the gold letter "J". This was the right moment to announce the new plan. "America is asleep. Their apathy a malignant disease that will kill us all if we let it. What this country needs is a wake-up call. And we're the ones who are going to do it."

The speaker opened his fat briefcase, extracted a stack of navy-blue file folders—thirteen of them—and passed one to each man. *The New Proposal* was the title on the cover.

Everyone opened their folder and followed along.

"With a single stroke of the keyboard the story on this page will spread across the country. The sentence in bold letters will be the headline every newspaper will carry and every newscaster will shout from every radio and TV station. But all will be safe for us. *They* have guaranteed it."

The AC system droned like a colony of worker bees hiding within the walls. Other than that, the quietness in the boardroom meant no one would interrupt him to ask a question. "Notice that the remainder of the proposal outlines the plan. It's a simple one: steal the Project Black Files and place them in the wrong hands. With that knowledge, they will inevitably topple this haughty nation, gaining for themselves the superior technology they've been craving for."

He regarded the servicemen with a critical eye. Every groove of flesh on each of their faces spoke of the sleepless nights they spent since joining the board.

"Gentlemen." He cleared his throat. "Our meeting will now conclude. But first, are we in agreement? Are there any objections to putting the new plan into effect at the time and place prescribed? By show of hands, do I have your absolute approval and support?"

He scanned the hushed boardroom again.

One by one every hand went up, and the disgruntlement he felt gave way to a long-awaited satisfaction. "Soon the terrorists will be a superpower," the briefcase man said.

Chapter 3

Neil Avery stood astern over the fantail where he reread her letter. There would be no more romantic greetings at the pier; no more goodbye kisses when her ship left port. Just the numbing emptiness of knowing that this time she would not be coming back.

He stuffed the old letter back into his pocket, tossed a flat stone over the fantail, and timed its fall. Three seconds. The weight of the stone kicked up a baby geyser in the water below, followed by a dimple, and rings of spreading ripples. It was a familiar sight. Those same shapes were on the folds of her slept-on pillows and in his thoughts like tree rings; the ones that counted off the nineteen years he had been in the Navy. Now as chief engineer in his chosen mainstay, away from his apartment in Mariners Cove, San Diego—a place of spacious rooms and too little furniture—Avery's surroundings were with men like him in a nuclear-powered supercarrier whose titanic shape and size were as grand as its name suggested—the USS *Man Of War*—CVNX-7. Homeport: North Island, Coronado.

Military history in Annapolis had taught him that in 1940, the entire fleet at San Pedro—against the livid objections of FDR's Chief bureau-of-navigations man, Admiral James O. Richardson—moved to Pearl Harbor as a deterrent: to dissuade an Imperial threat from expanding farther. But that move was a costly one. The surprise attack on Oahu's tropical paradise by the Japanese on December 7th, 1941, decimated the U.S. fleet, jeopardized national security for all Americans on the west coast for six months, and deemed it necessary for Naval Air Station North Island to be the principal homeport of mighty warships and Marine, land-based aircrafts neighboring it.

Avery graduated from Independence High in Brentwood, California, after transferring out of two schools and expelled from another. He enlisted in the service and knew right away he would have to shape up or ship out. He shaped up, enduring eight tough weeks of boot camp at RTC—the Recruit Training Command in Great Lakes, Illinois. He was ambitious from the start; compelled to make something good of his pathetic life. But fear fueled his motivation, driving him to the edge of insanity. Much as he tried to run from it, he could not escape the nightmare that chased him with vengeance: the blast of a revolver; a white, blood-soaked carpet.

With "A" school under his belt, he moved on to a nuclear technology program. Then, it was off to NavSub school in Groton, Connecticut, for more intense training, this time in Damage Control, followed by his first *boat* tour which launched his career. Upon graduating from Naval Academy, he was assigned to submarine duty as an engineering officer in Norfolk; the jump-off point from which he traveled to see the world. For young Neil Avery, life was a welcome doormat at his feet; the world in the palm of his hands. Abroad, he took pride in what a sub could do to the savage seas: tame its thunder, sooth its rumbling. This is what anesthetized him. But one day it awoke—the raw void—and when it did, he learned to cram its emptiness with duty and drown it with spirits until he returned to his primeval beginnings and understood what it was that kept him up night after night for so long. It was the one thing the Navy could not give him to help him tame it.

Back home, he was the envy of his peers: he had youth, good looks, and a fine future. But in the course of time the years passed, and like the changing seasons, his life also changed. Gone was the excitement of being in the Navy; the sense of adventure at the sight of the boundless sea; the thrill he got when a stiff wind and chilled ocean spray kissed his face. Gone was his heart: Hi, my name is Neil. What's yours?

Liberty sent leisure-seeking men of the *Man Of War* off the ship and off the base for forty-eight hours. It was during this intermission of duty in which he found himself in the foreground of parked fighter jets that crowned the carrier's massive deck. He was alone to read her letter; isolated the way he wanted to be. To that day, crewmembers found it difficult responding to the tragedy. He didn't have to wonder why this was so. The secret of what he had done was out.

Overlooking the slate-blue expanse of San Diego Bay, carriers *USS Pentagon* and *USS Ronald Reagan* stood watch over the base with steel-gray eyes. He removed his Navy ballcap and shielded his eyes from a welder's glare reflecting off the water at the foot of the colossal vessel. The sun was at its zenith, and the stone-made ripples were now replaced by a sweeping breeze that flapped his work khakis and played with his chestnut-brown hair.

A squadron of nine, first-class *Grotons* lay within sight at the submarine base; SSBNs loaded with Trident III E-5s. He felt secure in knowing the

Navy's stealth, ballistic-missile technology could not be obtained by foreign madmen. If they could, the game of mutual world power would come to an end and the United States would be threatened by a superior navy.

Floating above the rocky humps of the Laguna Mountains, silver-bellied clouds, set against the pristine backdrop of a cobalt-blue sky, created a panoramic view of eternity. The young serviceman imagined peering into another world where time, wars, and death had no meaning. Is heaven as real and beautiful as all the sermons I've heard described it to be? he thought.

In the quietness, he closed his eyes, and suddenly, a shift in the breeze blew a gust upon him. Harsh and haunting ….

"I told you to do your homework." The brawny man drew on a lit cigarette, churned its tip ember red, and blew an angry-gray mist in the small boy's face.

"I did," the boy responded with quiet terror.

"You're lying." Evil lurked in those bloodshot eyes. "You know how I deal with liars. No dinner. Kneel and beg forgiveness!" He unfastened the snaps of his suspenders, removed the strap, and held it from the center so that it dangled like a Roman cat-o'-nine scourging whip.

The boy's knees buckled, and for a moment he thought he would fall. "Honest, I'm not lying."

The man's features became rigid to the sound of metal smacking in the palm of his big hand. "Don't talk back to me. I hate it when you do that."

"But I wasn't—"

"And call me *sir*. How many times must I tell you to call me *sir*! You'll never amount to anything. You're too damn stupid. Thank God your mother is dead. As for you …." *Whack*

A meaty hand sent the boy face first to the slated, red oak floor. When he looked up expecting to be flogged, he found nothing over him except the wide open sky.

Searching for answers in the cumulus clouds, the gentle flight of a seagull in an aerial ballet caught his attention. The bird's graceful moves stirred him. If I could don its carefree wings and soar as high as it, he thought, I'd be able to see their faces once more ….

"It was great seeing you again, son," the man with the clergy collar said. "Can't tell you what it means to me and Beulah each time you two visit."

"We love being here more than you enjoy having us." He took his fiancée's hand, feeling the 14-karat, white gold's princess-cut sapphire stone with the epidermal sole of his thumb.

"Next time you come, I'll whip ya again at chess."

"Not if I beat you first."

The clergyman and he exchanged laughter, and Avery's face grew warm.

"Give Beulah and me a call, soon as you get home."

"Roger wilco, over and out," the serviceman said. "I know Mama worries."

"So do you, Daddy." The leggy woman with long, soft hair, hugged and kissed her father goodbye. "Love you."

When the couple turned to leave with luggage in hand, the minister called out to the naval officer. "Neil!" He loved to hear the burly man's voice. It was like the air that fanned his face; bringing comfort; taking away fear.

He looked down at the bay, eighty feet down, someone once told him; its dark color, the oily skin of a sperm whale. The fantail wasn't the lofty balcony pilots called Vultures Row. Still, if he jumped now, the fall would be like a bird shot in flight—plummeting.

"Neil, didn't you hear me?"

Jolted from his thoughts, he slapped his ship cap on, made a swift, about-face, came to attention and snapped a perfect salute: fingers straight and rigid, eyebrow level, elbow cocked. "Commander Valentine, sir. Need me for something?"

The man brought a Sherlock-Holmes pipe to the corner of his mouth and took in a few smooth puffs. "Didn't know you liked living on the edge." He breathed out a gray wisp and it took to the air, disappearing like a departed soul.

"I was just … skylarking." He waited for a return salute.

"Seems more like you've been reminiscing. And when will you stop doing that?" He forced the young man to drop his arm.

Avery moved away from the fantail's edge. "Nothing wrong with showing respect." He wished Valentine had not showed up.

"Calling me respectable?"

A rare grin invaded his weary face. It felt strange to grin.

"Is that a smile?"

Someone asked him the same question once at the Academy. Two female cadet students passed him in a corridor leading to Bancroft Hall. "It's a shame he doesn't smile," one of them said. Later, they passed him again in the hushed rotunda. "Was that a smile?" he heard one of them say.

"That a penlight in your pocket?"

Valentine put in a quiet pause. "You know, I don't believe I've ever heard you laugh. Not once since you were a child."

He frowned at the commander's easy-going appearance; his confident gleam. Nothing bothers him, he thought. Every time they sauntered together through the ship's mazed passageways and over knee-knockers, men would lift their eyes to meet the commander's gaze first. Tanzanite green. Those intelligent eyes had ancestral history in them. William Nesbitt Valentine was of English stock with Scottish blood in his veins whose last name in Latin meant valor. He came from a long line of physicians and Ivy League grads, and eventually became a senior GMO—general medical officer.

The commander had the look in a photo Avery kept treasured in his top pocket; the first person in the world he sought love from—his dear mother.

"How come we don't play chess anymore?"

"Sir?" He gave the penlight another look.

"There you go again calling me sir. Where did you get that?"

The lieutenant didn't care to answer. All lower echelon said sir to a superior officer. But he had turned stranger and in doing so became rigid.

Valentine faced an F/I-190 *Bird Of Prey*; one of the jet planes left over from the festivities of fleet week. "So, what's it like in one of those?"

Avery didn't want anyone knowing more than he cared to volunteer. "What're you talking about?"

"How you got a hotshot pilot to take you up on a dare during the last qual."

That qual was the only carrier qualification period he could remember done solely at night to test every nugget straight out of naval aviation school until their raw nerves became like hardened steel. "Where'd you hear that?"

"From 'J'." He shook his head in disapproval; hair-rug muscular arms over his chest. "I heard it from him."

"J" was Jarvis. Frank Jarvis. Pry-Fly's Air Boss: a crass-looking captain with a curled chin, thin nose, and thinner mouth, and who wore aviator sunglasses morning, noon, and night. He intimately knew his flight officers and everything on their fitness reports like the cluster of ribbons he occasionally petted on his uniform.

Valentine said, "That was a stupid thing you did. One more stunt like that and you'll be drummed out the service for sure."

Avery pitched a stare into the sleek, blue-black aircraft's tandem cockpit. A pair of helmeted pilots offered a salute as revving jet engines whined to an ear-piercing shrill. When the catapult launch officer, housed in the deck's steel bubble, pressurized deck pistons with sufficient superheated steam, he triggered a mechanism and the twenty-two ton *Bird Of Prey* shot up the vaporous-hissing, ski-jump flight deck and soared into the air with a thunderous roar. "I had something to prove."

"Like what? That nobody would recognize you in a flight suit at night?"

That night, the sea and sky were black-hole dark. It was a miracle he handled the aircraft like an expert, slamming it down where the arresting cables kept him and the backseat pilot from executing a bolter. The experience was a heart-pounding shouting thrill. Until the next bird approached. As it came in for a landing, it dipped below the seesawing deck of the carrier and slammed into the fantail's structure, creating a JP5 supernova that ignited the cosmic night. Both the pilot and his RIO were killed and Avery never flew again after that. "I wanted to know if doing zero to one-seventy in three flat could straighten out my ransacked courage."

Valentine pointed the mahogany calabash pipe at the empty aircraft. "That isn't a rollercoaster. It's a hundred million-dollar bird. What were you trying to do, kill yourself?"

He didn't want to die in a fiery jet crash. He would have been content jumping off the edge of the flight deck. But he had lost the chance. "Talk about something else, will you!"

Valentine joined him in the horizon-search. It irked Avery the commander mimicked the lethargic idleness he had been stricken with for so long.

"Resting that knee as I advised?" The medical officer stood shoulder-to-shoulder with him.

"You know I need an outlet."

"Outlet is one thing. Tearing a damaged articular cartilage is another. Heed my warning. Stop lifting leg weights and quit fantasizing about playing in the Army-Navy games again. You'll need your knees for when you get old."

He didn't want to be old. He didn't want to end up in a nursing home, with no visitors, no friends, no family; a stranger to the world. "What makes you think I want to grow old?" Avery retreated into his cocoon. He would be safe there as long as Valentine didn't pursue him. But he knew that wasn't going to happen.

"Mind telling me where the quiet takes you?"

He lowered downcast eyes. "Somewhere in time."

"Still finding it difficult getting over him?"

He saw their faces again. "Them," Avery corrected him. "He and his wife. Back to back."

Valentine told him of the tough times he faced. Things he thought he'd never survive: his father's passing when he was nine; his mother overwhelmed with grief; a house filled with eleven depressed kids; relatives adopting him and four older siblings; Avery's mother staying to help with the younger children because she was the oldest. "If it wasn't for Laura, my mother would've suffered a nervous breakdown and died young."

"Laura? Was that my mother's name?" He received a good, long stare from Valentine.

"You really didn't know her, did you?"

He didn't have to say no. He was certain it showed on his face.

"I'm so sorry. What a lonely, isolated kid you were. I could kick myself for not helping."

"Please, no guilt trips. Not here."

Valentine brought up a reminiscing look. "Laura's eyes." He took several popping puffs of pipe tobacco and blew out smoke as though trying to form someone's face. "How I miss those movie-star eyes. Hazel, just like yours. Oh, and she loved to play piano."

Avery extracted a photo from his top pocket. Her eyes were as Valentine had described. Just like a starlet's. On the photo's backside was one word— mom. He turned it over and looked at the grainy image. "Now I know your name." He kissed the photo of the woman and put it away.

The two officers began to walk. Avery discovered long ago there was something about moving feet that made talking easier. "Did you know my father, I mean, really know him?" A mixture of harsh emotions rose from within and the beast he never defeated returned: shame.

"I met Allen when he was dating your mother. But beats me why he was such a stranger."

That stranger and the life he lived were like the secrets Avery kept—closely guarded. As long as he drank, there was no chance of exhuming the past. But the past had a way of exhuming itself, creating ditches in the night, ditches he staggered blindly toward and fell into. "It's best you didn't know."

"He seemed like a good man," Valentine said. "Aloof, but okay. In a way he was like you."

He abhorred the image his father's name created and focused eyes elsewhere, beyond the bay toward the Pacific. From where he stood, ships sailed and returned after their deployments, sailors and marines returned to their loved ones, and he returned to wallow in his vomit.

"I once learned from your mother he studied applied science in aerospace. Was it true your old man wanted to work for NASA?"

ASU. The abbreviation tumbled in Avery's head. "He did. He was the lead flight director at Houston's Mission Control." Arizona State University grad. High honors. But the remainder of his father's commentary died on the tip of his tongue. Who the hell cares what my dad did, he thought.

"What brought him down?"

It was the same thing that brought Avery down, kept him down, would kill him if he didn't change. "The damn bottle."

"Didn't know that."

He hated the empathy in Valentine's voice. "There's more you don't know." He also hated swallowing stinging saliva. "How old was I when mom passed?" He strained to guess, hoping Valentine would supply the missing information.

"I believe you were six."

A clamped mind opened but dormant memories refused to surface. "Wish I could remember her the way you do. But all that comes to mind is the casket … the empty loneliness."

"Know what killed her?"

All he knew was she was taken to a hospital, and because of his age, he was not allowed to visit. Whatever the doctors said to his father he kept to himself. "I don't know much about … Laura. She left home one day and never returned." No one explained to him why she was in an oversized wooden chest. She seemed to be taking a nap. Then when that strange thing was sealed and lowered into a big hole in the ground, something happened to him. In one mighty surge he went from being a six-year-old to a scared man trapped within an innocent little boy's body. "That's when my father began hitting the bottle. Then, he began hitting me."

"Your father should've told you what I knew. What the rest of the family knew."

He listened with burning ears.

"Your mother died at twenty-six from a rare form of gynecological cancer. That was another tragic moment in my life."

He released the question that pounded in his chest. "Did she love me? Tell me!"

"You were her only child. Best thing in her life. Said so on her dying bed."

Satisfaction cascaded over him and his heavy brow felt light. "I always hoped she did. Now I know."

"What about your father?"

A strident memory tightened his face. Drunkards didn't deserve being called father. His deserved a profane name he didn't care to mention at the moment. "What about him?"

"Didn't you tell anyone what he was doing to you?"

No one at school knew of the abuse he suffered and he saw Valentine didn't understand. But the ship's flight deck was long. More than three football-fields long. He had plenty of time to explain. "It would've been like betraying him. He would've killed me."

"Was he really that bad?"

"He was the only bully I couldn't beat." A seagull cried overhead; its wings taking it far. Time healed no one. It only invaded the body and ate its way out from within. Avery believed his father would come to his senses one day, stop the punches, the verbal assaults, and love him. But when the years dragged on with no change, when there were no more places to hide, he hid within himself and became a depressed loner. Loss of self-esteem turned him into a walking time-bomb. "And that's when …."

The pacing men came to a stop.

The older officer took the pipe out of his mouth. "When what?"

The nightmarish carousel that controlled his thoughts since adolescence, took him for another spin. Once more he stood on a white, blood-soaked carpet from where a pair of cold, angry eyes stared back.

"He kept a gun in the house. A Smith & Wesson…." His eyes stung with so much hate it was as though someone squeezed drops of venom in them. For years he planned, waiting for the right moment, and when it came, he took the revolver from its hiding place and walked in on his father. He was drinking from a big tumbler, resting a meaty hand on a wall, broad back facing his son. Young Avery's heart beat like the punishing blows a training boxer gave to a heavy bag, but justice needed to be carried out. The drunkard had gone too far, turning the once-decent boy into a want-to-be executioner. From up close he pointed the weapon at the back of the man's buzz-cut head, and without a second thought, pulled the trigger. Blood splattered and gray matter flew, but the man did not crumble to the floor. He just stood there defying death.

"The gun…." He felt defeated. "When it clicked, my father spun a backfist to the side of my head, landing me against a wall. Then he yelled, 'You think I'd keep a loaded gun in the house? I'm not stupid!'"

Tarnished guilt came to a boil and the memory stirred to a stormy pitch. He was so consumed with hate that day, the thought of holding an empty gun in his hand never occurred to him. A moment later he ran away, leaving everything except the horrible scene of his father lying dead on the floor like he had planned. It was his eighteenth birthday, and homelessness forced him to join the Navy. But depraved thoughts followed wherever he went.

"Two years later I saw him—in a hospital. Liver cirrhosis. It put an end to his angry fists and the hope I had for a relationship between us. A chance to learn about love. But before he passed, he said something that sounded strange to my ears."

"What did he say?"

He shut his eyes. "Wish I could forget." Lobotomy would help, he thought.

Now that the two men had paced the roof from stem to stern, they ambled back, past shadows of silent jets. Those jets when revved up became human vacuum cleaners. Avery knew a "green shirt" flight-deck worker who came too close to a catapult-ready plane and was sucked whole into the intake. The lacerated man lived to tell about it. What a good way to die, he thought.

Valentine excused himself and engaged a group of airwing maintenance officers in casual conversation; each man with expert eyes on an F-22 Raptor. They would give it a final once-over before its return to the squadron in Coronado. The big, stress-prone aircrafts were constantly maintained, kept in combat-ready condition since it was never known when they would be pressed into service.

Avery continued on slowly and went below, head bowed in thought. He didn't care where he went as long as he went somewhere, so he made a stop at the ship's library before incarcerating himself in his steel compartment. His favorite read: *Scientific American*. But between the lines of each glossy page he planned again. This time he would be straddling on the railing over the control tower. Eyes closed. Body leaning forward. Sooner or later, his gnarled will would yield to an embedded death wish.

Chapter 4

Down the quay they came: a camera crew, and a long-legged reporter, all wearing white polo shirts with the Cable News Network logo on them; all marching with determined pace toward a flag-flapping cylindrical beast, the *Groton*-Class *USS Polaris*, one of several submarines tied down at the naval harbor that day. News of what happened reached CNN first, and as soon as the young reporter, with slick black hair, taped an interview with the gallant men involved in the rescue, Navy Secretary Ben Nobleman would present a lieutenant jaygee, an ensign, a master chief, and a petty officer first-class a patriotic ribbon bar in an open ceremony.

Hot air blew over Norfolk, and day two of fleet week's international pageant of ships and sailors was in full swing, bringing in the huge crowds that accompanied the yearly festivities. Here, military personnel milled with family and friends, and before the main assignment, the busy reporter did a few quick interviews: one with a proud seaman discussing with his grandfather the layout of the missile cruiser he was assigned to; the other with a female junior officer snapping pictures of her sisters with a mighty carrier in the background; and the last with a black petty officer third-class explaining to his younger cousin how ballast tanks filled with seawater made a submarine submerge and how reversing the process lifted it safely from the hungry depths surrounding it.

Tied down in the Elizabeth River, the *Polaris*—a 610-foot long, 60-foot wide sub, dark and sleek—was more than twice the length of NASA's retired Saturn Five rocket. The reporter was impressed with the boat's superstructure: a tall sail rising three stories like a tapered anvil with a distinct hull number tattooed on its side.

From a nearby tender, a tall crane lowered a long, fat canister into the open mouth of a vertical launch cell. The cameraman mentioned that within each canister's womb a tall missile stood, waiting to be birthed. When it was inserted into the individual tubular cell, the reporter and his crew crossed the sub's narrow-grated gangway and were greeted by one of three watchstanders. "Welcome aboard SSBN seven-five-seven."

One of the men went down an open tube and after a moment an intelligent-eyed, round-faced, pudgy-nosed sailor in clean whites, emerged from a four-foot-wide forward hatch like a mole out of the ground and approached.

"Gentlemen, I'm Senior Chief Petty Officer Xavier Auleve. Chief of the Boat." He went on to say his father was a tribal leader on the island of Upolu in Samoa, and hoped the Navy would someday allow port visits to the coral-reef port of Apia Harbor so he could showoff the oyster-rich Polynesian atolls of the South Pacific—and the Islanders' ancient cuisine, music, culture and women—to his crew.

"That would make a good feature story. I'm Royce Gold, CNN." He shook hands with the COB, studying two rows of ribbon bars on his uniform. "My crew."

The videographer, soundman, and lighting tech shook hands with the E-8.

"We've been expecting you," Auleve said. "If you would, please follow me."

Everyone got ready to go below.

The cameraman asked, "What does SSBN stand for, Chief?"

Gold knew this would be the first of many questions fired off today by him and his crew.

Auleve seemed to be a man of disciplined patience. "Submersible Ship Ballistic Nuclear. And please, no taping till we get to the wardroom. This is a highly-classified boat. But I'll be more than happy to give you a quick look if you want."

"Fine," said Gold.

One by one the news crew, with all their equipment, descended the same dim airlock the chieftain-looking SCPO had risen from. After the long climb down their feet touched the deckplate. Royce Gold was relieved to find the hot Virginia sun had been displaced by the coolness within the vessel. "I once got a tour of the *USS Hammerhead*," Gold told his guide. "But not a sub like this. Was that the Trident Three being loaded from that crane?"

"Our newest weapon," Auleve acknowledged. "The deadliest submarine-launched missile since the Tomahawk." He walked the crew through a short passage that led to another open hatch at their feet.

The reporter mimicked the senior chief descending a second ladder, followed by his crew toting a bulky HD camera, sound apparatus, and lamps. Soon, they were in an equipment-crammed space.

A well-built man, with nubby sideburns and red chevrons on his left-upper sleeve, stepped away from a row of stacked, dark-eyed monitors and approached.

"Gentlemen," Auleve said. "This is Petty Officer First Class Keith Radley. Rad, these guys are from CNN. They're here to interview our heroes."

"Welcome aboard, mates. How about doing a story on me?"

"Only if you can captivate our viewers with an extraordinary bluenose tale." The reporter took a look at the elaborate compartment of intercept receivers, sonar equipment, and visual display screens.

The soundman said, "What's all this gadgetry?"

"Our eyes and ears," the young petty officer answered. "Dolphins can't swim deaf and blind."

"Gentlemen," Auleve motioned. "Follow me."

Through the belly of the sub, aft of mission control, Gold and his crew followed the chief of the boat to a dim, long space.

"Gentlemen, welcome to Sherwood Forest." Auleve ushered Royce Gold and the news crew through a dim, narrow walkway—passing fat, snaking pipes, bundled cables, hydraulic valves, and 10-foot-wide, red silo columns—one at a time. They stopped about halfway. "Each silo carries a pressurized, forty-five-foot-long canister you saw being loaded by crane. Each canister holds a Trident. Each Trident carries fifteen nuclear warheads. Twelve columns port and starboard for a total of twenty-four Trident missiles or three-hundred-sixty nuclear warheads. Each capable of obliterating an entire city."

The videographer jacked the HD camera onto his shoulder, getting set to peer through the viewfinder.

"Put that down, mister," the hard-faced COB commanded.

"There's no film in it. Just want a peek through the lit eyepiece."

Royce Gold swept past the remaining silos that carried the sleeping giants within, picking his nose in thought. He made sure that before he faced anyone, his hands would be in his pockets. "I hear they're undetectable," he said to the chief. "What're they made of?"

"A classified, radar-absorbent material called RAM. The Trident E-fives can be rocketed through the air from underwater, while their smaller cousins, the sonar-coated E-sixes, are fed through the torpedo tubes. Once they're on their way, a built-in GPS and terrain-finder guides the missiles to their mark. They never miss."

"Why the stealth design, then?" Gold asked.

"With technology's rapid advance, wasn't long ago decoy Tridents One and Two, launched from a point in the Pacific, were intercepted in midair by our own surface warships in the Atlantic, like hunters shooting down fat geese. Skunkworks went back to the drawing board and the Trident Three Nighthawk was born."

"What's the marmaduke weigh?" the soundman wanted to know.

"Armed with multiple nuclear warheads … seventy tons."

The lighting tech, standing behind the chief, let out a long whistle.

"Excuse me." Royce Gold had a question for Auleve. "Should there be concern the missiles' stealth technology could one day be stolen by North Korea, or their terrorist allies?"

"We steal from them."

"Sir, it's documented from history that during the building of the H-bomb, formula-hungry spies flocked Los Alamos to obtain classified info from dishonest men at the price of a hefty bribe."

Auleve gave Gold an empty stare. "… Gentlemen, this way."

Moving toward midship they climbed ladders with haste and arrived at the top level. Gold and his crew followed Auleve into the instrument-packed quarters of the control room. There, a rugged-looking sailor rose from a console station, and the visitors approached, moving past manual plotting tables, a ballast panel, and periscope stand.

"Gentlemen, this is Third Class, Joe Zimmerman. Zee, CNN."

"Ahoy. What questions can I answer for you landlubbers?"

"None," Royce Gold replied. "I'm anxious to meet with the four men and begin taping their incredible story."

"Alright," Auleve said. "Then I'll ask one. Zee, how much submerged pressure can this boat withstand?"

"Below cruise depth, we're talking over eighty-thousand pounds per square foot—approx."

"Won't the hull crack?" asked the soundman with a daunted look.

"If it does, we pray like hell, and …." Zimmerman reached overhead and depressed a big, red knob. Immediately the urgent blare of the klaxon went off. *Ahrooo-ahrrr … Ahrooo-ahrrr.*

Royce Gold twitched from the sudden sound of the sub's diving horn roaring in his ears. He could tell the chief of the boat and the petty officer third class got a hearty kick out of it.

"Thanks, Zee." Auleve stole the TV crew's attention away from the glass-plated gauges they eyed. "Every fleet week we pull off the same stunt. You should see the looks we get. As though someone from the other side of the ocean had shot a nuclear missile at us. This way, please."

Inside the blue-tiled wardroom of cushy-looking couches, settees, and tables secured in place, the audio person prepared for sound and the lighting assistant turned on a bright lamp as four, young navymen in whites and khakis, walked in. Xavier Auleve briefed Royce Gold on the history of each man, and seizing the moment, the reporter approached the tallest among them and introduced himself.

"I understand this is your third year as a submariner," Gold said to the interviewee. "And that your inspiration to volunteer for fleet service came from stories you heard about Admiral H. G. Rickover. Father of the atomic sub."

"That's correct."

"Ready," said the soundman.

The cameraman assigned everyone to their places, slid a tape into the video's compartment, closed it, and began filming.

The reporter faced the round, polished glass eye of the camera. "From the *USS Polaris* in Naval Station Norfolk, this is Royce Gold reporting on the rescue of plane-crash survivors in the frigid tundra of the Arctic Circle, and of the four men considered heroes."

The whirring camera swung from the reporter to the tall navyman. Royce Gold said, "When and where did the C-130 come down?" He moved the microphone wand toward him.

The young officer seemed to hide a modest smile. "Last month in northern Greenland."

"Please state your rank, name, and tell us what you saw and what you and your team did."

"Of course. I'm Lieutenant JG Neil Avery. *Polaris* was on covert maneuvers, when Bix, our radioman here, picked up a Mayday ...."

Chapter 5

His windowless cabin was quiet, a tad bigger than a two-person sleeping compartment on a commuter train. His childhood bedroom was about the same size, except here, there were no GI Joe action figures dressed in astronaut gear. The cosmonaut was my favorite, he thought.

Young Neil Avery liked how he arranged his dresser with plastic models of NASA rockets, one at each end. On the left-hand side stood the tall Saturn Five—the vehicle that took the first men to the moon, and on the right, the Space Shuttle—the design that promised better things in man's quest of space. Between them he set up a toy replica of the Bell X-1 plane. The rocket-powered jet USAF Major Charles "Chuck" Yeager piloted to break the sound barrier.

The boy Neil learned quick how to escape into far-off, quiet places. He often thought of uninhabited islands and uncharted worlds; desert landscapes where camels with no names would take him from his current surroundings to an oasis of his own making. Although he did not understand such concepts as psychological defense mechanisms until later, he was sure something from within enabled him to soar high above the wispy cirrus clouds into the stratosphere when he exerted his will. And when he wanted to go farther, where zero gravity would carry his bruised body and broken heart beyond the orbit of the moon, the wallpaper's starry designs in his bedroom, guided him past the planets of the solar system and into the distant cosmos. In space, no one could hurt him. Alone in the silence of his spacecraft, no one could see his tears.

Every time Lieutenant Avery stepped into his one-man cabin it was there to reproach him: a newspaper article he duct-taped onto the steel bulkhead by a flat-screen monitor. The story was over a year old. But the words, the memory, had not faded.

An In-Port Secure form, laying face-up on his desk, called for his attention and he scanned the long sheet's list: water system, electrical switchboards, gas, oil, engine rooms, fan rooms, turbines, nuclear reactors, machinery, sewage, ventilation ....

Conditions and supplies were good. Now only one thing was needed. A signature.

And a pen.

He patted his pockets. Looked around.

He pulled a desk drawer wide open, picked it up, and immediately pushed the dark-eyed barrel of a weapon against the crest of his Adam's apple. He pinched his lips so hard they felt cold. He scrunched his face and squeezed the trigger ....

Tightness.

No bang. No click. Nothing. He let out a ragged breath.

Someone knocked on the door and his heart galloped.

He stashed the Glock back inside the drawer, slammed it shut, unlocked the door and opened it. There, Commander Bill Valentine stood with that smoky Sherlock-Holmes pipe clenched in a corner of his mouth; he held the latest edition of the *San Diego Sunday Tribune* at arms length. "Knew you were in here."

"Want me to tip you or let you in?"

"What I want is for you to read this. Something right up your alley." Valentine thumbed through the meaty publication and plucked out the science section. "It's in here." He dumped the rest of the paper into waiting hands and an aromatic flavor filled his nose.

Sitting on top of the pile, the world news headline's story covered the whole page.

U.S. and Korean relations had not been this hostile since 1950, and the world was fresh on the heels of another turmoil. Intelligence reported the North Koreans were on the verge of creating a deadly new weapon to add to their growing arsenal—a fifty-megaton Hydrogen Bomb—and once developed, would be tested. But where its projected thirty-mile-wide, forty-mile-high radioactive cloud would mushroom was anyone's guess. While the UN Security Council came up with counteractive measures to keep North Korea in check, the Communists had plans of their own. They threatened to unleash an all-out military invasion against the South if they didn't get the free reign required for their nuclear/biological development program. In the U.S., the Defense Secretary and Joint Chiefs of Staff were working with the president. They devised a plan to prevent the Communists from going too far. What General Douglas MacArthur never envisioned would be considered if a show of strength failed—a massive, tri-pronged amphibious attack by U.S.

troops above the 38th parallel on both sides of the troubled peninsula, backed by naval/air support and followed by a United Nation's spearhead assault from the South. The article went on to state that Navy Admiral Craig Jenson of the Pentagon, was certain the Koreans would abandon their nuclear weapons project, rejoin the Non-Proliferation Treaty, and settle for peaceful terms. No one wanted another president in the Oval Office to say: Disarm or you will be disarmed.

Valentine found the page. "Tell me this doesn't sound like an excerpt from an H. G. Wells' novel. Read it aloud."

The young officer began from the top.

"Yesterday for the second time in his illustrious career, Marcus Jerome Weinberg, the noted physicist and cytologist from MIT, and distant cousin of the great Albert Einstein, was acknowledged by an army of colleagues and university professors at a gala in Boston, and presented with the prestigious Humanities Lifetime Achievement Award for his continued work in his field. Fifteen years ago, Professor "J", a nickname coined by his associates, received the Nobel Peace Prize for his outstanding research in bioengineering. Although much of his work is classified, his theories on cellular restructure could offer the possibility that in the not-too-distant future, man will be able to ...."

Avery put down the newspaper.

Valentine said to him, "Why did you stop?"

"Scary stuff."

"Yesterday's sci-fi is tomorrow's sci-fact. I've always believed that. Remember Captain Kirk's communicator? Granddaddy of the cell phone. I hear they're working on a tricorder. That should make things easier for me."

"The article isn't about medical toys, Bill."

Valentine tossed him a defeated look. "What is it you hate about the science you love?"

"People playing God," Avery answered. He handed the paper back to the commander with silent protest. "Is that the only reason you came? To show me the latest in twisted technology?"

"No. Security is ransacking my quarters as we speak. Searching for a missing 9mm Glock. Know anything about it?"

"Do I look like I would know?"

Valentine explained that throughout the ship, the chief master-at-arms, shadowed by four gunner's mates, were busy enforcing the captain's command—open all storage spaces, lock-boxes, and coffin lockers; dig through everything in them: skivvies, shoes, toiletries, porn magazines .... "MAAs won't quit till they turn the *Seven* inside out."

From the mirror over a stainless-steel sink, a reflection of a man accused him; the one who trained him to hate himself. Avery dropped to a sit on a settee. Shoulders slumped. Lifeless arms dangling.

"You all right?"

The troubled serviceman remained silent.

"Do you always lock yourself up after a soul search?" Valentine closed the door behind him and sauntered in. "Isolation will do you no good. Yesterday's tragedies have radar. Burning memories to sniff your six. Painful reminiscing only serves to shorten the distance between the past and the present."

"Don't psychoanalyze me, I'm okay."

"One would balk to think an experienced naval officer as yourself still can't shoot straight from the shoulder."

"Okay, I admit to reading something before you knocked." He motioned to the article with the bold headline. The one with his name on it. The story everyone on the base knew about. Avery had read it over and over, more than he wanted to until eventually an afterimage of words in a sleepless gaze tossed him on his rack for endless nights: *Navy Investigates Tragic Collision*

"Why do you keep that thing?"

"Because I have to, dammit!"

"Lower your voice, I'm not deaf."

" … I keep it to punish myself."

"That's no good."

He was right. It was no good to punish himself like this. He would only have to do it again. Suicide was still the better option. It was a one-shot deal. "Who the hell cares." He slumped out of the perfect posture he had always been proud of.

Valentine let an exasperated sigh deflate his chest, and with one clever look, began to make a quick diagnosis. "You've been this way too long. Any longer and …." Suddenly he seemed to have the real answer to the problem. "Know what? You're the only one in the world to step on earth sack with spit-shined, Navy shoes. You're a hopeless case. A born loser."

The ground of depression the lieutenant stood on shook, and a sudden release of stormy adrenaline broke through with tectonic strength.

Bill Valentine said, "If I were you, I'd blow my head off right now and get it over with."

"Fine." He worked a look on his face he hoped was a smile, but once again he hadn't gotten it right. Nothing I do comes out right, he thought. "Open the lower desk drawer and toss me what you see."

The commander pulled the drawer open to a banging stop, pushed aside hard-covered engineering textbooks and a stack of letters, and lifted a 9mm out. He gave it a sleuth-eyed once-over, pipe in mouth. The safety lock was in position. "You stole this from the Q-deck, didn't you?"

"What, you a cop now?"

Valentine shoved the fully-loaded weapon into his waistband. "You have two infractions against you. When are you going to wise up?" He yanked open the compartment door. "This is going back where it belongs," he said. "The armory. See you in admiral's mast."

Despondency wrapped itself around Avery when the cabin's door slammed in his ears, shattering the thought that wanted to surface: Ever love somebody so deeply, yet ...?

The long afternoon dragged into evening, and many were winding down. But not he. Avery was restless; a battle stirring within. All his life he fought against something; ran from someone: his fears, his father, school bullies, and an opposing football team; so he knew what he would be facing an hour from now, tomorrow, the day after that—an unending procession of harassing memories that would pound his head the way a storm-tossed sea pounded a ship. In a frozen state of wide-eyed reflection, he predicted anguish would forever be a part of his life. A stalking nemesis that could only be beat one way.

The prisoner wrestled with his demons from the confines of his solitary quarters until he broke free and fled through the ship's empty passageways where he hurdled over knee-knockers like an Olympic runner.

Up a ladder he went, then another and another, all with the speed of a frightened feline. He scrambled aft with legs in piston motion, dashing through the ship—pumping his arms, gaining more speed, right knee pounding. He made up his mind. This was the day he would do what he planned. What's the difference? he thought. Drowning in the sea or drowning in one's sorrows?

Despite the fact he clocked his elbows, rammed his shoulders, and bumped his head in the marathon through sandwiched passages, he kept going, shooting past the lifeless flag bridge, climbing one ladder after another, ascending to navigations and Pri-Fly until he reached the 011 deck. He undogged the big hatch and rushed out to the balcony. It felt good to inhale the brine that would soon consume his lungs.

Crazed determination sent him to the railing where he swung a leg over the side in preparation for the big leap, then he saw it: a mountainous sunburst cloud that brought him to a stop. Over the Pacific's vista, dazzling streaks of beaming rays stretched like the arms of the Almighty.

He stood motionless with the metal railing jammed in his crotch, teetering on its edge—panting, staring, sweating, lungs on fire, expanding and contracting in rapid cardiovascular rhythm.

Held spellbound by the omnipotent arms above him, a crushing guilt began to shift as the steel harbor played below his feet—fifteen stories down.

He limped away from the straddled position and sat on the hard coated surface of the deck, legs crossed, eyes unwavering on the oblong thermonuclear orange disk that dipped below the voluminous silhouetted veil before it licked the sea and melted into it. Time moved on and cumulus clouds floated over him. But the bruised sky still glowed masterfully with beckoning, outstretched arms.

A thought haunted the perfect silence and thrashed him with perplexity. North Korea's Communists could go to hell for all he cared. As for the science article he read earlier that day .... What did it really mean? he wondered.

Chapter 6

The sign on the smooth walnut door was Karyn's handwriting: *Go in. Back in 10 minutes.*

He shuffled into the private office the way he always did: eyes to the floor, hands in his pockets. He stripped off his dress-blue service jacket, loosened his tie, and drifted past the big, brown, plush leather chair to the quiet window. Looking down McCain Boulevard to the pier, past the military pedestrians and the mighty ships, the world seemed at peace. But peace was not what made sailors skillful. What made them skillful was the jarring sound of the general quarters bell; ships tossed by the sea; airmen in their birds. And for a brief moment he was one of those men. A Navy pilot....

It was the closest thing to being inside a computer. In it, he was part man and part machine—and what a machine it was: the F/I-190 *Bird Of Prey*. Avery was in the cockpit's lead seat, and strapped down behind him was Lieutenant Ed "Dino" Vazquetelli. Whatever Dino said, how he said it, and who he conned to sneak Avery into the aircraft for a flying lesson, remained a guarded secret.

The fighter jet bucked like an untamed horse when Dino fired her up, and the want-to-be pilot and instructor were instantly catapulted into the night, over an ocean they could not see.

Dino turned on a ruddy light, and the cockpit had the look of a film-developing darkroom. "How you doin' so far," he said through the helmet mike.

Avery had taken an accelerated training course, practiced in the flight-simulator room behind closed doors, and felt ready. The momentary blast of the thrusters had pancaked him to the seat after the aircraft ski-jumped into the air, pressing his eyeballs into his skull like someone pushing down on them with their thumbs. "I'll survive," he said. Between his legs the control stick moved on its own. Dino was at the helm of the training craft, and when the control stick stopped moving, it meant the bird was in autopilot.

When they reached 10-thousand feet, they donned their oxygen masks. Avery and seat tilted back, dentist-chair position, and the jet climbed higher, like a rocket on its way to the moon. The aircraft reached 20-thousand feet in no time at all.

Jutting out beneath the seat was a ring-shaped object: the ejection handle. He knew Dino would bring the bird safely back home, so there was no need to worry. But he had heard from another pilot who survived a bolter gone wrong what it felt like. He said: Imagine you're a circus clown, sitting in a big tube of a show cannon with a keg of dynamite under your six, when suddenly it goes off and you're shot out. It's like that. Once the ejection handle is pulled, the aircraft's canopy shatters and the seat's rocket thrusters ignite, exploding with force, propelling the seat-strapped pilot into the buffeting air at a speed of 100 MPH.

Now the altitude dial read 40-thousand feet.

He felt obese in flight coveralls and G-suit which weighed at least fifty pounds: a dome helmet, thick leather boots, Nomex gloves, float vest, and heavy, tight-fitting inflatable trousers to keep blood from stagnating in his legs and force it to circulate where he needed it most: in his torso and brain. A bird that could easily travel at Mach 2 could cause any man to black out. But tonight Dino was cruising at a cool 500 MPH.

The tiny compartment displayed numerous rows of knobs and switches, all bathed in a glow of red: the gear controls, transmit buttons, and various system features to the right; airbrake controls, hydraulic pressure, and throttle to the left. And straight ahead, just above all those Plexiglas-covered dials on the cockpit's dash—the altimeter, the artificial horizon and airspeed indicators, the magnetic compass, the gyro, the turn and vertical speed indicators, the course gauge and direction finder, and a mach meter—stood a panel with a cool-green glow: the GPS-E—a laptop-size, electronic night-vision screen.

An hour into the flight, Dino rolled to his left and let the bird fall out of the sky—nose down, tail up—all twenty-two tons of her. He felt like he was falling off a sea-side cliff with the weight of a car strapped to his back as he dropped headlong, guffawing emphatically into the breathing apparatus. But there was nothing to laugh about. He was simply delirious with fear. The plane went from a 30-thousand-foot plunge to a whip-lashing sweep that sent it up five-thousand feet like a supersonic rollercoaster. He let out an adrenaline-induced whoa from the top of his lungs until his chest hurt, and when the aircraft leveled, the ejection seat set the ragged-breathing chief engineer upright.

"Hold on to your helmet," Dino said. He hit the afterburners and the sudden force pressed Avery hard into the seat. The airspeed dial that read a steady 500 MPH, rapidly climbed: 550, 600, 650, 700, 750... *Crack Bang!*

He knew the blast outside the canopy, followed by a reverberating rumble, wasn't thunder. "What was that?" he said through the mike.

"Sonic boom." Dino's voice coming through the earpiece in the helmet was cell-phone clear. "We just broke the sound barrier." He explained they had zoomed 10 miles in under a hot minute.

The airspeed dropped to 250 and Dino flicked off the reddish cockpit light. "I'm dousing the NV." He meant he was shutting off the night-vision screen. Suddenly the space went dark and the word flying took on a different meaning. At night, without the aid of the electronic eye, there was no navigable horizon and the sky was that of a far-off, sunless planet with no moon or stars; the most perfect blackness he had ever seen. The only indications that he was in the air came from the roar of intakes, the kick of the afterburner's nozzles, the motion of the plane—left, right, up, down—and the LSO's voice coming through the flight helmet, like now, directing the aircraft toward a pair of faint eyelash streaks which were the carrier's landing lights.

The bird's altitude dropped significantly—another 8-thousand feet— Dino called "Ball", and the night-vision screen came back on, highlighting a miniscule carrier; a toy boat in an immense ocean. "Okay, *nugget*," Dino said. "Take her down. I've got your back." Avery's heart rate quadrupled and he cursed beneath his breath. They would have a lot of explaining to do to either the Air Boss, CAG—commander of the air group—or the base admiral.

Now a more pleasant thought fancied him and he allowed to be taken by it ....

He ran a black comb through his thick hair, parting it from left to right. A dab of pomade gave it a great look. He seemed to know someone who parted his hair the other way—from right to left. A woman, in fact. But who that woman was he could not recall.

Someone pelted the window with something. It sounded like raw rice. He went for a look and found that's exactly what it was. The woman who stood outside, in a lavish wedding gown, pelted the window again. He opened it and looked out. "What are you doing here? I'm not supposed to see you till the ceremony."

"I came all this way to tell you something."

A car honked and one of the bride's maids called out.

"Whatever it is, I won't change my mind about you, so there's no point in saying it ...."

Thinking of it now, he wished he had allowed her to confess. Things might have been different. How different he would never know. Now he decided it was not too late for him.

Karyn came in a moment later, he let her get comfortable, then gave her an earful ….

"Twelve years of psychological, emotional, and physical abuse is a long time!"

"Do me a favor," he said. "Don't cry for me. I'm not worthy of anyone's tears." So this is how my last day with Karyn begins, he thought. Breaching that impenetrable wall was not as easy as he imagined.

"Why didn't you tell me about the awful things your father did?"

Worn-out eyes felt corroded from anger. "Do you have to stick me under a microscope every time I come here? Prick me till I bleed?" He stilled his breath and waited a moment. "Sorry. Didn't mean it that way."

She typed something into the computer while he retreated behind his seclusion. Progress notes, he knew. Those notations would remain stored within a Navy database until someone else retrieved them. Every bit of personal information concerning him was there, ready to be reviewed for future counseling sessions.

The lieutenant let the message in her eyes do it to him again and he came out of hiding.

"Neil, there's something you should know."

"What, that you're in love with me?"

She gripped the chair's armrest. "That's absurd. What made you think—?"

"You're supposed to ask about phobias." Psychology's rehearsed lines, he thought. I can do this. "And I'm supposed to sit here and let a child's ghostly nightmare resurface." Now he knew for sure prolonged grief did strange things to certain people, causing them to behave in ways they normally wouldn't.

"What are you afraid of most?"

Now he wanted to reveal more of himself; things he denied, lies he told himself.

"The dark. After my mother died I feared the dark. To this day I sleep with the lights."

"You don't strike me as nyctophobic."

"Does my sudden candidness bother you?"

She typed in the new info. "How about regrets? Any?"

A loud somber yes filled the room, rippling with an echo off the walls, and the office grew quiet.

"Where would you like to start?"

36

The start. The end. What's the difference? He winced at the thought. "I regret my father never loving me."

"Never? He never said: I love you, Neil?"

He had no doubt she was hinting of her true feelings for him. "The only thing he loved was booze."

She turned away and typed. When she finished, she leaned in. Hands balled into fists on her desk.

"My father was the last hope I had for happiness. He failed. But someone gave me a second chance by calling me a strange name—son. I waited thirty years to hear it. From the one who'd be …." He closed his eyes and saw his face. "Gil … Roy Gil …."

"Gilchrist?" Karyn's sweet mouth, pink as coral, dropped open. "You knew him?"

"I loved him."

Roy Nathan Gilchrist. Everyone knew or heard of the burly southern preacher, he thought. He traveled the world. His was a household name belonging to a man who was as great and gentle as Billy Graham.

"And when he called me son, he meant it. It was in his eyes. In his voice."

"It helped take away the pain, didn't it?"

"Not right away." The silence that followed created faces in his thoughts. Voices in his head. He tossed a blind stare at the floor. "Roy and his wife Beulah never had boys of their own. Just girls. Four of them. The youngest was adopted."

New images popped into his head. How do I stop this auto slide projector? he wondered. With each fresh memory that surfaced he rode the crest of welling tears. "One thing about Roy. He never let bitterness invade his life over not having a blood son. I was his son. His real son. And the relationship we had was more than he could ask."

She didn't have to inquire how that made him feel. No one could chip away at his stony heart the way the preacher had. But that was long ago and it had hardened again. Being silent about things always did that to him. Spoken words were like stones. Thrown into a pond, rings would ripple, affecting the motion of the whole. Kept to oneself, the shape of things that should have been were gone forever like lost opportunities.

"I'd give anything in the world to have him call me son one last time."

"One last time? You're still searching for a father figure, aren't you?"

She meant hope of recovering, and he shrugged at the thought. He was past expecting things that would bring fulfillment. He learned long ago that hoping was a futile pastime of fools.

"Any other regrets?"

He studied the Norman Rockwell painting. "That awful day."

"What day was that?"

After Roy was cremated like a victim of a Nazi death camp, his ashes were thrown into the air and the dusty cloud became the capstone to Avery's lingering grief. He wanted Roy to have a fine casket, a lavish funeral, a decent burial. "But …."

"Was that the way he wanted it?"

She was gentle with her words because he felt so fragile. He hated being fragile.

"Yes!"

He took a moment to compose himself, all the while bathing in a twisted thought. What would he do if he never recovered, never found closure, never saw the light of day?

"Why would you regret that? You had nothing to do with it. Wasn't your decision. Don't punish yourself."

"I have to."

"Why must you think like a martyr?" she said.

It was a good question, and he had a good answer: because he didn't voice his opinion on the matter; didn't take a stand. No one expected Roy to die at his age. It caught everyone by surprise. But the real surprise came when he was informed the preacher would have no farewell solemnities. "One moment he was with us, and the next …." He hung his head the same way he did when he first got the devastating news. "There wasn't enough time to book a flight. He was reduced to ashes by the time I … we …. It was like he never lived. Never died. How do you have a funeral for someone who was never born?" He tried to get himself to stop, but he was someplace else….

Two men grabbed him from behind as he walked down a street and threw him into the backseat of a vehicle. He was a hostage now, tears filling his eyes as a white hearse, ahead of the driver, led a train of black Town cars into a rural cemetery. He had never gotten the chance to say goodbye. The hearse made a lazy turn and the car he was in followed. Roy had died without knowing what Avery felt for him. The caravan came to a stop and everyone got out. Keeping his feelings secret is what he would always regret.

Among the autumn trees, there were crowds of people. Mourners. And beyond them was the spot where a big mahogany casket would be brought. Avery trudged past rows of fat gravestones to the rear of the cemetery where everyone gathered around. As soon as the casket was brought out by slow-marching pallbearers, a stirring wind blew and he felt his pulse race. He was being summoned to make a brief speech. With effort, he moved his legs, walking past a robed minister holding an open bible, searching for an appropriate scripture. Psalm 23 was Roy's favorite, he thought. Perhaps he'll read that. He stood behind a lectern brought for the occasion. His pupils felt dilated from so much crying. "I should've sent him a card, written him a letter. Something to let him know I cared. Too late now. Dear Roy, did you know I loved you?"

He blinked, and the big casket in front of him was gone. The cemetery grounds, the bare-limbed trees, the cars and people had disappeared, too. The scene had changed. He was back in her office.

"Roy knew you cared. He must have."

"I'll never know." He let Karyn's angst-marked eyes study him. Roy's casket planted into the earth like a seed would have taken care of things. He made that clear to her. He would have said goodbye, wept the ache out, and gone on with life. "But the girls ...."

Karyn begged him not to stop. She told him the more he obsessed over caskets and burials, the quicker it would bring closure. "Maybe." Now she didn't look so sure.

Behind a stiff mask he saw their faces. Their soft, radiant faces. "The girls were only trying to move on, to piece together their broken lives when Beulah died—two months after Roy."

"Grief?" she asked.

"Stroke. But my wife never knew because ...."

"Because ... what?"

He envisioned that colossal beast rising like a blind missile from its watery depth. "She was out at sea when Mama died." It surprised him he wanted to ramble on. "She was buried in her hometown in Warrenton, Georgia." Another surge of tears rose. "Her family requested it be done that way."

"Didn't her daughters have power of attorney? Neil?"

He heard her, but felt himself being transported into the serene setting of the Rockwell painting. Being in a rowboat on a peaceful lake with his father would have made the world right. The line ran, the boat rocked, and Avery battled a combative fish. How exciting it was. He had never gone fishing a day in his life. It was his first catch on his first try and Roy looked delighted, helping him haul in his prize. An eighteen pounder, my boy, Roy had said. But when Avery reached into the thrashing water, he found no prey, no lake, no boat.

"Why do I find the words, I love you, difficult to say?"

She let out a tiny gasp, closed parted lips, and answered. "In order for love to be expressed it has to be experienced, felt, embraced. Was your mother affectionate?"

His mind felt cold and blank. "Too long ago." His voice had sunk. "But she loved me. Wanted me." He pictured his mother pregnant with him, one hand over the oval globe of her abdomen, singing songs to him in a language only he would understand. "Now I know."

"What about your relationship with … your wife?" She was afraid of bringing up her name, which in turn would evoke a memory, create a scent, resurrect remorse. Avery understood she wanted him to forget and move on. She said, "Did you express your feelings for her?"

"Marriage is different. It just is."

In his world he didn't feel the need to show emotion to anyone. Sentiments were better left to babbling fools—poets and writers; the literary skilled who believed that people were not mind readers.

She said, "What's that proverb about the acorn?"

"It doesn't fall far from—okay, I admit I drank like my old man. But at least she got the gist when I proposed."

Karyn blinked. "No wonder the marriage ended in a sour divorce." In the absence of love, she said, relationships died. He had witnessed it firsthand. "When a person neglects the emotional needs of another through rejection, the result is damaged people who undervalue themselves. Like Reverend Gilchrist."

He didn't like her theories and was annoyed she had changed the subject. "What're you talking about?"

"Why do you suppose he chose cremation over having a wake, funeral, burial?"

"Wait a minute." He held up a hand. "Are you making this whole thing a self-esteem issue? That Roy didn't like himself? He was a preacher, for heaven's sake!"

"If he experienced rejection as a boy, all it would've taken to change his view on cremation was for someone, anyone, to say … I love you. Are you listening?"

I'm tired of listening, he wanted to say. "So love makes the world go round, huh?"

"No. Love makes things possible. It gives birth to miracles."

He was dizzy with thought, but that was better than shedding saltless tears. Whatever it was that got into Roy's head to deprive his family of a final goodbye was a secret swept away by the same gale that blew Avery's life off course. He plucked at the tiny crown on his Quartz. It popped up and he turned back the time twelve full hours. He was tired of racking his brain.

Karyn read the time on her watch, the date on the daily calendar. The session had sped to a close. Another year had come and gone, and in a little while she would be, too. Now the unspoken message he had seen in her eyes would remain where it was. Stashed like the memories he had learned to file away in his troubled mind.

"So, where are you headed?" He wondered what her plans for the future would be.

"Naval Station Norfolk. Got a coveted position and a good salary increase. But it was a difficult decision."

"You would've stayed?"

"Only if something better came along." She looked right at him.

"Norfolk's a great place." He worked up a weak grin. "Started there after sheep-skinning the Academy. Spent my second boat tour on the *Polaris* before coming here."

Avery was glad Karyn had what she was after. But he wanted something for himself, too. The sunburst cloud's outstretched arms in the sky held the answer. Yet knowing that, he preferred to look elsewhere for solutions.

He stood to his feet on tired legs. Tired of the lost journey he had walked. An aimless future laid void before him and the haunting feeling that came with it stared him in the face. All he had was the answer to where life would lead Karyn. The question where time would take him. "I hope nothing but good things for you … Karyn."

She shot a hand to her throat as though feeling for a pulse. "That's the first time you've spoken my name." She rose and extended herself.

He dismissed the handshake.

Avery knew the routine. He straightened his tie, got his belongings, and turned toward the door on his way out. He was raw and edgy, but would push on with his life the way the big ships did when they launched out to sea.

He liked the grainy feel of walnut under his fingers. The polished doorknob looked to be made of Satin Nickel. He opened the door and looked at her, and when he did, he felt the urge to ask something she would say. "You all right?" He had never seen her with that look. Frightened was the word that came to him.

"Why, yes. I … I'm fine."

Satisfied, the battered lieutenant shuffled through the doorway into the hall. Clinging to life by the tips of his fingernails was not his idea of surviving. Neither was living under the turbulent power of his mind that flickered with flashbacks and bad dreams. How he hated to think another episode wasn't faraway.

"Neil?" The sound of her voice grabbed him. "Please let me know how things work out with your new grief counselor. I'd like it if … we kept in touch."

He barely nodded, pulling the walnut door closed with a soft click of the lock. Now he was out of her office and out of her life.

He heard a noise and leaned toward the door. From within the office, a grown woman cried like a young girl.

Chapter 7

Someone pounded on the compartment's door. "Caliber, you in there? You're wanted on the bridge!" When he did not answer, the pounding came harder. "Caliber!"

A barefoot Avery rose from his rack in skivvies and white tee shirt, and pulled the door wide open. He narrowed eyes on a tall, thin-mustached sailor, walkie-talkie on his trouser belt. "Slim, that you?" He hoped his breath wouldn't give him away. "I wasn't dead, you know."

"You weren't tits up, either. You were drinking. So why turn off the hailer and butt-phone?"

Avery's head pounded the way Jordan pounded on the door a moment before. He would have to force an inebriated mind to respond. "Where'd you say you were from?"

" ... Detroit. Cal—"

"And your ancestors were slaves in Charleston?"

"Caliber, you coming with me or not?"

"To the brig? Gotta make sure you're not MAA."

The seaman looked unwilling to indulge him. "Okay, my fourth-great-grandfather fought in the American Civil War, I was the smallest of my brothers in a fatherless home, and I wanna be an officer someday. What else you care to know?"

"For an E-tech you're a well-rounded, exceptional sailor, Slim. Just checking. What is it?"

"I-COM patched an urgent visual through to the bridge. Snowman took the call."

"I'll be there, bare with me." He threw on a pair of cotton khaki trousers and boon dockers, laces dangling, and headed out of his quarters, zigzagging

42

behind the square-shouldered seaman and wondering why the p-ways were painted in red florescent.

He entered the dim-lit bridge: a small, steel compartment of consoles, radars, phones, electronic chart tables, telescopic devices, navigational equipment, and communication circuits—the 1MC, the 4MC, the 21MC. Seaman Jordan pushed past the nerve-dulled khaki, getting ready to relieve a man wearing wiry eyeglasses: the chief quartermaster, Petty Officer First Class Carlos Nieve.

"What time you got?" Avery asked. The normally low overhead looked lower.

"Balls plus five." Nieve was getting ready to go to the mess for midrats like he always did after standing watch.

Avery was acutely aware he should have stayed in his rack. No, he thought. I should've never taken the first sip from that damn bottle! Why didn't I hit the beach with my buddies instead and gone—where? It came to him ....

During liberty, he, Carlos Nieve, and James Jordan would often go to Del Mar Racetrack, or to their favorite oceanfront restaurants: the Sandbar & Grill in picturesque Mission Beach and Bellissimo's in Oceanside. Sometimes a Padres doubleheader would lure them to Petco Park. Sometimes a walk through historic Balboa Park and the charming district of Old Town, packed with Spanish boutiques and Mexican restaurants, would fill their day. And when they wanted the glitter of the night, sparkling as jewels, the casinos and the nightclubs were their gambling and watering holes. San Diego is such a great town, he thought.

He, Nieve, and Jordan met during the course of duty aboard the *Man Of War*, and right away became friends. On any big ship, strangers abounded since it was impossible for everyone to know each other. Recruits had their own fraternal order, Enlisteds had theirs, and officers had theirs. But a friendship between an officer, an NCO, and a seaman was a classification all its own—an uncommon camaraderie—and it showed in the nicknames these three had for each other; monikers no one else on the ship used. Nieve and Jordan addressed Neil Avery as Caliber. The story that once circulated throughout the ship was of Avery's plebe year in the Academy and what he had done to make himself popular. On a dare, he popped the head of a .38 caliber slug into his mouth like a pill and chased it down with his favorite beer. Then there was Carlos Nieve. Because *nieve* in Spanish meant snow, he was Snowman. Now Jordan, due to his height, was never called by his given name James. Slim matched his tall, lean appearance better.

Avery swung around the captain's elevated leather chair and squinted into the glare of the Interactive Visual Communication System. The chief QM hit a relay button for him and the drunkard stiffened upon seeing a man's face in the monitor.

"Avery here." He rubbed at his visage with vigorous hands, trying to look presentable.

"Lieutenant?" The voice from the other side knifed through the bridge. The man in the monitor introduced himself but didn't have to. Avery recognized who it was and why he had called. "Better get here ASAP."

His stupor snapped, he came to his senses, and his arms fell to his side. When the face in the IVCS disappeared, the junior officer churned with a harsh mixture of ripe anger, weighty despair, and burning regret fermenting from within. If he didn't leave right away, the urgent message would pound against the inside of his skull like a week-old hangover.

Looking beyond the raw void of the naval air station he saw it. The accident. It took place on a night like this when a dark sea parted and a wandering steel beast rose out of it.

From the thick, big windshield panel his hand rested on, the lieutenant caught their troubled gaze in the reflection; eyes that knew this would be the night.

Jordan walked past the darkened IVCS. Everything that surrounded Avery was dark: the Plexiglas-enclosed compartment, the world outside, the world inside. "Caliber, you're in no condition to drive. I'll take you."

"Okay." His voice now turned raw. "Snowman, if anyone asks, you know where—"

"*Ve tranquilo.* Go in peace. I'll get Brian Mayo to do midwatch."

"I always did like your wire-rimmed glasses," the lieutenant commented.

Avery made his way off the ship and into the night, knowing when he and Jordan returned, however long it would take, the atmosphere aboard the *Man Of War* would remain spiritless for weeks to come.

At Naval Medical Center San Diego, two men were ushered into the antiseptic smell of the Intensive Care Unit where they pushed through one of many privacy curtains in a corner of the ward.

To one side of the bed, a tall instrument with buttons, dials, and green lights blinked on and off every few seconds, and on the other side, a beeping cardiac monitor sent a slow erratic message that all was not well.

A pair of rubber tubes, connected to a vacuum water-valve system, sprouted from the patient's chest while an oxygen tank pumped humidified air into both lungs. The coma had full possession now, and though the ventilator showed TPR measurements—body temperature, pulse and respiration rate— those vital signs were growing weaker.

When tiredness stirred the standing men, it sent James Jordan to a darkened window and Neil Avery to her bedside where he held a limp hand in his and gazed at a broken frame with a love lost and found. He tried to pray, to resist the hands of time. But time was a fast locomotive. They were powerful machines, able to pull thirty freight boxcars weighing forty tons each at seventy miles per hour. Their speed as they hummed over steel tracks made them impossible to stop at will.

His tired mind blinked like a camera aperture and memories developed with a flurry: the day he saw her, that first date, the year he met her parents, the night he presented her with an engagement ring. How happy they were.

Never again, Avery thought.

Never again would he mistreat her, slap her, grab her by the arm, spin her into his reeking breath and make her cry. The discovery shortened their honeymoon, made the gnawing silence on the flight from Hawaii to San Diego, difficult to deal with and made his anger rise like venom. It happened long before we met, she swore. His name was Gerald Morgan. But he didn't believe her.

The emotionless chatter of voices stirred the air and a clan of doctors pushed through the privacy curtain and stood at the foot of the bed. Her bed. Their faces were blank and somber. The chief attending opened a hospital chart. "Here we have a thirty-six-year-old black female. She suffered a cerebral hemorrhage, fractured ribs, double pneumothorax and broken right femur. She was airlifted here where her other leg was amputated."

"Railroad crossing accident?" asked a resident.

"Worse," said the attending.

Avery's heart paused. Where had he heard the story? It was in the newspaper article he kept duct-taped on the bulkhead of his cabin.

"It's a miracle she survived," said another doctor, the tallest of the group.

"This isn't life," Avery retorted. First chance he got, he would trash that prophetic article. "It's a damn machine mimicking life."

The draining wait. It ripped at him from within, mocking him with remorse. He moved in close to her, knowing his voice would sound torn the moment he spoke. "Honey?" When was the last time I called her that? he thought. An invisible hand gripped his throat. It would remain there until he got used to it, or until it decided to let go. "Talking about my feelings wasn't one of my strengths, yet you married me, anyway. And with each hangover, you kept trying to teach me how to love." He smelled his father's breath and cringed. "I should've gotten on my knees and thanked you for not divorcing me. But never did. Too proud. Now I'm hoping you'll pull through so that we could start over ... again." He stiffened when he realized the long, lonely road that lay before him had no end. Beneath a stinking Bacardi breath he blamed God.

He stroked her bandage-swathed head. How easy it was to be gentle when someone's life was on the line. Six years was all she gave him. Now the furnished private house, not far from the base in Coronado, would be empty. The promises he made and things he hoped for were now wasted dreams. But Avery was determined he would keep her memory alive by not changing anything around the house—not the clothes in her closet, nor the toiletries in the medicine cabinet. In time, it wouldn't even seem she was gone.

An unbroken high-pitched noise spun him around, swelling his head with an awful tide.

Jordan jumped to his feet. A team of MDs rushed in. Castors clattered over ceramic tiles and a nurse pushed her way through with a defibrillator.

"Please disconnect her," Avery begged. "She wants to go."

The attending measured the naval officer slumped in the chair. It was he who had called knowing it would end early that morning. "Lieutenant, my condolences to you on your loss." He was formal. Robot-like.

Avery wanted to smash the equipment. Curse at the doctors. He raised bitter eyes. "Thank you all for fighting to give her a second chance," he said instead.

"Okay, call it," the attending said, now that the ventilator and cardiac monitor were unplugged.

"Darah Gilchrist-Avery," said a resident. "Date and time of death: February fourteen—six-ten A.M."

The chief attending wrote something on the medical chart. Avery didn't have to guess what it was. Deceased.

One by one, the group of ICU doctors filed out of the area until their voices trailed off. Avery knew the chart would be plopped in the nurses station for one of them to take care of.

From the window, pale light illuminated an ink-black sky above. The sun would rise in a moment. But Avery's world had been plunged into the deepest blackness he had ever known.

The nurse removed every rubber tube and wired cardiac patch from the body in preparation for the morgue people. She was good at it. When she pulled the white bed sheet over those lifeless features, she stepped out, and suddenly, a sinking feeling gripped Avery. He shot to his feet, but it dragged him deeper. With the antiseptic scent in the room turning acrid, he discovered being a widower had the same crushing weight as being orphaned. He would have to start sleeping with the lights on again. Eyes open, he thought.

He lifted the sheet away from her face, stooped, and planted a kiss where he had once struck her. "I didn't deserve you. From now on I'll try to be different. I promise. No more drinking, cursing, yelling, smashing things. I'm so sorry you didn't live long enough to hear me say it." A walnut clogged his throat and he pushed at it with words that would sound strange. "I loved you. Always did." He slumped back into the chair like he had been shot. His face twisted with anguish, and tear-flooded eyes made everything around him appear like he was looking through clear Jell-O Gelatin . A thought came to him. "One more thing." It pained him he would be the bearer of such bad news. "Your mother passed away last month. Thought I'd ... let you know."

He waited, wanting for the heaviness he carried on sagging shoulders to lift. Instead it doubled.

A black-robed priest pushed through the privacy curtains and shuffled in; dark rosary beads swinging from his side. "Get out of here," Avery told him. "You're too late."

"Son—"

"I'm not your son."

"Lieutenant, please indulge me. One day you'll look back on all this and it'll seem—"

"This isn't grief," Avery snapped, swiping at runaway tears. "It's hatred. For myself."

Something pounded in his head; his chest. It seemed audible enough to shake him from the tears Darah once cried. Payback, he thought.

A hand rested on his shoulder. It was either the priest, a nurse, a ward doctor, Jordan, or ....

"Didn't you hear me knock?" The man retreated a step and closed the door. "And what're you doing on your six? It's chowtime."

Disorientation took over and everything looked unfamiliar to him: the sink, the overhead, his rack. He got his bearings. He was in his quarters, sitting at his desk, daily reports at hand.

Valentine stood tall over him. The empty pipe he held looked like a tiny saxophone. "You look like crap. Hang out all night?" He swung around him.

"I was there," he croaked.

"Come again?"

"I said, I was there!"

"Where is there?"

"The hospital. Darah's bedside. After all these years, I said it."

The medical officer ran a hand over a pouch of skin that drooped under his chin. He seemed more interested in figuring out how to lose the pocket of fat than listening to whatever it was Avery was about to say.

"What was it Darah once told me?" It came to him:
I like you a lot. Actually it's much stronger than that ....
Darah's told us so much about you ....
Mama, he's white ....
My, that's a big word for such a little girl....
Checkmate!...
Wanna read my book?...
Yes, I'll marry you. What took so long? ....
Welcome to the family, son ....
Gimme some sugar ....

"You seem lost," Valentine said. "You okay?"
Okay, everyone. Gather around for the picture ....
What a great day for a wedding, Roy ....
I take this woman to be ....
Till death do us part ....
You may kiss the bride ....
May I have this dance? ....
Anyone want more cake? ....
I want three boys, four girls, and ....
Valentine waved a slow hand in the young officer's face. "Lieutenant?"
Lieutenant, your wife won't be able to conceive ....
Neil, let go. You're hurting me ....
I'm gonna have a good, long life ....
Taffi's on the phone. Daddy's in the hospital ....
Roy passed away, son. He loved you ....
Why didn't he want a funeral? ....
Avery shot to his feet. A pale-faced twin looked back at him from the mirror over the stainless-steel sink. His breathing turned ragged and liquid diamond drops of perspiration sprouted on his forehead.
"Hey," Valentine said. "You having an anxiety attack?"
Taffi had another asthma attack. She's in the hospital ....
Ave, it's me. Mama just died, but Darah doesn't know 'cuz ....
Patch this message to Ensign Darah Avery aboard the *Essex* ....
Ave, Taffi might not make it ....
What do you mean my message didn't get through? ....
Lieutenant, there's been a terrible accident ....
Darah Gilchrist-Avery. Time of death—6:10 A.M. ....
"Neil!" Valentine shook him, and for the umpteenth time the mentally exhausted serviceman returned from the past to the gray reality he dreaded.

Back to the lonely ache that thumped in his chest with the same recoil of a 12-gauge shotgun blast.

Avery let Valentine's eyes probe his like twin searchlights, trying to read whatever it was he knew was there.

"I think I just ...." He made Valentine wait, knowing he would sound crazy no matter how he put it. "It felt like I went back through time. Such a thing possible?"

Valentine shook his head. "You're still grieving. If you'd like, I can give you something to—"

"I don't want a damn thing!" He looked at that penlight. "You think I'm crazy, don't you?"

The medical officer plowed fingers into his light, cropped hair. He was thinking. "When was the last time you were away? And I don't mean standdown periods at Mariners Cove."

"Aside from sea trials, carrier quals, pre-dep exercises, maritime sec ops, port visits and—"

"You've been married to the *Man Of War* too long."

Valentine was right. He had spent more time on the *Seven* than with his wife. "It's been almost three years but feels like ten."

"What're you waiting for? For me to buy plane tickets, slip them in an envelope, tuck them under your pillow, kiss you goodnight?"

He was waiting for the courage to tell Valentine the truth. "Stop jerking me." His throat bobbed with a nervous swallow. "I've been too busy planning my funeral to get away." A strange silence invaded the compartment.

"What?" Valentine studied him the way Avery thought he would.

"Last week I almost deep six'd from the island."

The medical officer let out a long, low whistle. "That would've been one helluva plunge. Frogmen would've had a tough time searching for a bloated corpse. What stopped you?"

Those sunburst arms across the evening sky were tattooed in his mind. "A glimpse of heaven. Of seeing them again."

"Before you kill yourself, do me a favor. Leave this place for a while. Somewhere far. With your record, you snap your fingers and Fleet Command will approve an emergency leave for a year."

Avery fell slumped on a settee and rubbed an achy right knee. He was lost in a brief thought and came out of it. "I'm used to being on this old birdfarm every time she goes out. I'd rather be here."

"And risk having an emotional breakdown?" Valentine sat in Avery's chair and told him he was a damn workaholic.

"It's all I've got to keep me alive."

"You call this living?"

"Got a better name?"

"Yeah—hiding. You're a miserable soul who refuses to come out of hiding."

"Okay, smiley. Let's have your Rx."

"Me? I'd take a transfer overseas, take on a new project. Anything but stay here."

Avery had smelled it, tasted it, rolled with it in his sleep. Whatever dreams, wishes, desires he had remaining were like the ruddy tobacco flakes his cabin guest fingered into the bowl of the pipe and put a match to.

Valentine nursed on the calabash and the chamber came to a volcanic-red combustion. He let out a thin swirl of gray and leaned toward him. "Doesn't anything interest you?"

In the delicate, spice-smelling compartment, Avery sat motionless. Old, broken clocks were the same, he thought. Unless they were repaired, the time on them would remain frozen; fixed in the past.

"Listen," Valentine said. "If I get wind of anything going on anywhere, I'll let you know. In the meantime you're getting the hell out of here. Pack your bags."

"I'll think on it."

"You'll think nothing. You'll do as I say and that's an order, Lieutenant."

Suddenly, Avery dropped his head … and laughed. Its strange loudness was like a corpse springing back to life.

Valentine looked surprised. "I can't believe it. What's gotten into you?"

"What, I can't laugh?"

"Not at me you can't. What the hell's so funny?"

"You! That's the first time you've pulled rank on me." He laughed, louder this time. "Do that dumb look again."

"I'll save you the trouble." He rose to his feet with a joke in his step. "See you later. And if you're still interested in taking a leap off the tower, let me know in advance. The Air Boss is looking to strap a nugget into a bird for the next shot. Might as well be someone with *experience*." He opened the door on his way out. "One more thing." He put the pipe to his mouth. Prowess marked his keen eyes.

"Get out of here and shut the hatch," Avery said. The door closed, and he reached for his face, touching lifted cheeks, a tight chin, curled happy lips. When was the last time my face did this? he wondered. He looked at a photo: Darah. How he wished he had listened to what she had to say the day she pelted the window with rice. But she was a gray memory now. "She cheated on me." The thought of it stole his smile.

Avery picked up a smooth flat stone from his desk the way he did on the night he scooped up a batch in a fit of anger and hurled them into a moonlit, foaming sea. When his arm tired, he snatched another handful, pocketed them in his swim trunks and followed a trail of sandy footprints on a stretch of Hawaiian beach to the hotel, after he was certain she had fallen asleep.

On the bulkhead by the stones were photos of the Gilchrists: Roy with his heavy physique hidden beneath a ministers' black and purple vesture, bible in hand; and Beulah, the woman he affectionately called Mama, looking elegant in her Sunday best. It was her love, a mother's love, he yearned for and found.

There were other pictures also, those of Darah's younger sisters: Taffi, April, and Olympia—whom everyone called Pia because people said she was small as a pea. She was the adopted one in the family. But no one treated her that way. Neil met Olympia after he and Darah had dated for a year. Whenever the child's oldest sister and her boyfriend visited from San Diego, Olympia would lead him by the hand into her splendid little room where an army of dolls in handmade dresses ruled. On her dresser, every inch was adorned with photos of a little girl growing up; most with smiles and pretty outfits. "I've got to have a copy of this one," Avery had said. The photo he held was of a seven-year-old with a broken arm, taken after ER doctors set it in a plaster cast. A fall from a chestnut tree was the cause of the injury, and two months later, Olympia e-mailed that same picture to him. Her devotion to her newest friend at a naval base three-thousand miles away filled his eyes with joyful tears.

"My darling, little sweat pea." He clutched that photo. "The daughter I'll never have."

That strange equalizer: the good times, the bad times. This is what he mused on to make life bearable.

He opened a desk drawer, stone in hand. There, a bundled stack of old letters that belonged to Darah were as crisp as the day she received them. He plucked an envelope out, unfolded the letter and read it. Within its pages, Mama wrote about the day Roy's dearest friend died, how she accidentally cut her finger preparing dinner after she had gotten the devastating news, and of the central air system that went down on what turned out to be the hottest day of the summer. *You were home on your summer break from college when Zack died,* Mama stated in her letter. *What a sad day. But I fought back with a smile.*

That was then and this was now: his one-man, situated in an endless labyrinth within the ship's bowels. It was here in his compartment where the plaster-white shade of bulkheads made him paranoid and where a stiff sleeping rack and low overhead turned him into an insomniac. His cabin was the only comfort he had now, and he accepted it. An anemic balm in a lonely world.

He rubbed the dark stone. Course wet sand clung to it on the day he picked it up; the long, miserable walk to nowhere; the shortened, four-day, stormy honeymoon. "If I sidearm it at just the right angle with just the right amount of rage," he had said, "maybe, just maybe, it'll skip forever on the surface of the water and not sink."

The stone. He looked at it without blinking. Its long, pounding journey through heavy sand and rough sea was a reflection of his own. I'll survive, he thought. Time will prove it. He grabbed a small piece of paper, scribbled a message on it, wrapped it around the stone and set it back in its place. It read: Across the Sands of Time

Chapter 8

San Diego Union Tribune
Saturday, March 17, 2063
Al-Qaeda's Newest Technology Fails
Muslim CIA agents posing as Jihad operatives discovered an abandoned hideaway where Islamic rocket designers of the terrorist organization were at work to create supersonic stealth missiles for their Typhoon-class Russian submarines. If their goal is achieved ....

"Are you listening to Miss Hamilton or not?" asked the chaplain.

Neil Avery snapped to attention in his chair. "Yes, sir." He read the chaplain's rank insignia: captain—a tall, collegiate-looking man who scowled only when he gave a command. Avery apologized and motioned for Elaine Hamilton, the grief counselor, to continue. She bore the resemblance of a Catholic mother superior without the wimple. Before her lay an open medical chart. Beside her sat Lloyd O'Sullivan: senior, base chaplain. If Avery let the newspaper laying face-up on a magazine table distract him again, he would get bawled out.

"Repeat what she said," O'Sullivan ordered.

Avery didn't hesitate to obey. "I was put on this world to complete a mission. Something only I could do."

Elaine said, "That's right. And if you fail to do that, another calamity will come along and knock you on your six again. You need a defensive strategy to keep you on your feet. Something that will last the rest of your life."

The junior officer couldn't deny it. He needed help and nodded in agreement.

She went on to explain that when death claimed his wife's parents, everything about him went with them because they were the center of his universe. And when his wife died, remorse ate him up alive. The abuses he inflicted on her knew his name, where he lived, and came back to haunt him. Those two things were what fueled the raging fires of his emotions.

Elaine Hamilton closed the serviceman's medical chart and put it aside the way he had done with the mask of tragedy he wore for so long. Overcoming grief was not the same as getting over a departed loved one. He was convinced the two were different ordeals. Grief was the daily wrestling match of the emotions, and the "getting over" part was a lifetime pilgrimage whose end was determined by the weary traveler. It was a journey of endurance, she told him, and she commended him for starting that passage. He was too tired to ponder where it would take him, but it felt good to endure, knowing the series of tragedies he went through would have driven others to acts of suicide. "You've come a long way," Elaine said. "Not everyone recovers."

Now he had to be careful not to look back like Lot's wife or the quest was over. "I'm beginning to understand what happened to my father."

"Exactly!" She said that with such emphasis, he knew it was almost time to leave. But to what? he thought.

Elaine said, "Now, before I close this session, I'll list some important tips about managing future grief. Life is like a big-league pitcher. Mean and tough. You never know what he's going to throw, so you've got to be ready."

"I'm in the batter's box. Pitch to me."

"Good. First, keep busy with your job, or find a new project and get immersed in it. It'll give you routine, structure, purpose, and a sense of moving forward ….

"Second, talk out your feelings. Never bottle things in. Find someone who's a patient, nonjudgmental listener and share your thoughts, fears ….

"Third, deal with anger in a constructive manner. Not destructive. Drinking never solved anyone's problems."

"I stopped boozing," he announced. It was just as well. Every drink he put to his lips smelled of rubbing alcohol: rum, vodka, gin, beer….

"Good for you," said the chaplain.

Miss Hamilton looked relieved her patient had taken one more step in the right direction. "Another piece of advice is to surround yourself with good friends. It's great for recovery and will keep you from slipping into the blues ….

"Fourth, when you're ready, take your next six-month leave out of San Diego. It could help change your perspective on things ….

"And lastly, I congratulate you. As of today you're discharged."

"Ma'am?" He heard her, but his newfound freedom seemed strange to him.

"You don't have to come back, Lieutenant," she said. "Your job now is learning to smile."

He took in a breath and let it out. "Is it really over?" He traded a look with the chaplain.

"It is if you want it to be."

Avery sat there deciding whether or not he wanted this freedom. He was used to that dark cloud hanging over him.

Chaplain O'Sullivan grabbed a pocket-size New Testament Life Bible from the counselor's desk and handed it to him. This time Avery took it. "Every navigator needs a compass," the chaplain said.

Avery rose to his feet, bible in hand. He opened to a place where it said: Help Scriptures In Times Of ... Anger ... Danger ... Loneliness ....

"Thank you, sir. I'll read it everyday."

"Don't make promises you can't keep."

"Not a chance."

The chaplain stood with dismissal in his posture. "I hate goodbyes, but in your case I'll accept it. A pleasure knowing and working with you." They shook hands. Avery felt relieved. O'Sullivan looked like he had something more to say. "Heard the *Seven* is due a port visit to Pearl after carrier quals with the Fourth Air Wing. Must be breaking in a new batch of nuggets. Now's your chance to get away."

Avery smiled and turned to leave. His feet felt light as a feather, but not his head. He had practiced smiling in the mirror that morning and now wished he could've had more time to work on it. Did I get it right? he wondered.

"Take care," Miss Hamilton said. "And do yourself a favor." She opened a desk drawer, put his medical chart in it and closed it. "Enjoy the rest of your life. And congratulations. Got the news the promotion board is letting you climb up another rung. Nice going, Lieutenant Commander."

The main electronics shop on the *Seven* was a confined compartment of forgotten spaces on deck three. Except today, where a raucous drew the attention of more sailors. Among dozens of lifeless monitors, old keyboards, power-supply boxes, motherboards, wires, connectors, RAM modules, optical drives, sockets, graphics adaptors, and outdated consoles stacked on metallic shelves along gray bulkheads, men crammed themselves in for the event they were willing to bet a lot of money on.

In the corner of the compartment, a long worktable had been set up. There, a pair of console boxes stood side by side with two flat screens wedged between them. To the left, two more monitors were positioned, and in front of them sat James Jordan, about to conduct his biggest experiment yet. He knew the tournament was illegal. But since he had never been caught he continued to violate one of the Navy's rules: inciting gambling on board. This time it would be a six-game set of cyber Blackjack. While two computers would duel against each other, the long-legged seaman would tangle with an artificial brain until a winner was declared.

Jordan was riding a lucky streak of cyber, casino-game wins. For him this was just a tune-up for what he really had in mind. In the growing tension, the unauthorized tournament got underway while a spotter, a black seaman named Brian Mayo—a square-jawed, pudgy-face, twenty-year-old—made sure the coast was clear of khakis.

Those who squeezed into the small compartment, huddled over one another, and those who stood in the crowded passageway, craned their necks to get a view of the match.

It was the mighty cerebrum versus an electronic opponent—man against machine—and when the last cybercard was flipped over and the chanting crowd grew louder, Petty Officer Carlos Nieve looked ready to make the official announcement.

"Okay, let's keep the noise down to a decibel." The laughter of gambling-hungry sailors slowly subsided and the shop grew quiet. "The match between the two computers ended in stalemate. But we have a winner in the second tournament, and *he's* Seaman James Jordan. Undefeated champion of the *USS Man Of War!*"

The crowd whistled and cheered as Jordan rose tall, waving clasped hands over his head like a triumphant boxer. "Nobody beats the whiz kid."

Petty Officer Nieve brought down the volume of noise with a wave of his hands. He and the young seaman traded looks. "I'm on to your game. Come clean. You rigged these units, didn't you?"

Jordan had never admitted to anyone his ambivalence toward computers and what he could make them do. Disdained pleasure was never so good. "What?"

Nieve turned to the waiting crowd. "Comrades, as official referee of this match, I ask. Should a man be allowed to win through cheating?"

"Cheating?" Jordan yelped. A roar of hilarity rose from the swarm of men. "Are you outta your frigging mind?" He thumbed his chest. "I won fair and square!"

"Not square enough, mate!" Nieve ripped off those wiry glasses, shoved his face into the seaman's, and cracked a gap-toothed smile. The crowd burst into another round of disorderly laughter, followed by an off-key chorus of country singer Kenny Rogers' hit song, *The Gambler.*

Jordan enjoyed the banter and raucous behavior of the sailors. But when all bets had been settled and the shop emptied, he and Seaman Mayo shut themselves in the storage compartment and Jordan got to work on his next project. He began taking down more monitors and computers from the shelves around him.

"What's it going to be?" Brian Mayo asked. "Cyber slot machine, microchip dice, or several units mated to create a super brain?"

He opened up a console box and took the computer apart, one component at a time. "No more cheap victories," Jordan told him. "Next time it'll be something big."

Chapter 9

The call of individual reveille awakened Avery from a submerged sleep and out of his rack like he had done a thousand times before. At 0730 he left divisions quarters—where officers from every department had assembled for a meeting—and returned to his cabin. Opening e-mails, attachments, and checking Message Traffic from Command would be the first priority of the day for the captain, the XO, the ops officer and all engineers. Everyday thousands of naval messages came through, regarding uniform dress, types of drills, machinery maintenance, orders to fleet, and so on. He looked at a schedule on one such message and read it was the *Seven's* last day at sea after four full months of workups, carrier quals, search-and-rescue exercises and missile-firing practice, which ended with a port visit to Pearl Harbor. How good it was to sit beneath the shade of a Hawaiian palm tree and watch rainbow-colored, hot air balloons float over Diamond Head. He dwelled on that thought for a long time, then headed topside.

The view from Vultures Row was that of the immense Pacific, rising and falling like giant lungs taking in and releasing air. A citadel of phalanx domes, gun mounts, and gray steel—the *USS Maelstrom*—was tailing its DD sister, the *USS Trojan Horse*, some four-thousand yards back of her churning ocean tail, while alongside them, the *USS Man Of War* kept watch over both *tin cans* like a caring mother duck on her little ducklings. The slow plow back to North Island began at Pearl, and would continue until all three ships reached port later that evening. If the Combat officer had posted an ETA, he could quickly get that info without disturbing any of the CIC crew who no doubt had their ready-eyes glued to tracking instruments, surface scopes, and sonar consoles. Avery went into the hull and paid them a visit.

CIC's compartment was dark but cool. The only light came from consoles that emitted their pale green and aqua blue hues as shadowy figures tended to their silent work. With little room for movement he stationed himself by a busy petty officer texting a message to the *Trojan* on a laptop. Behind him a sailor in work dungarees and ballcap, charted the ship's coordinates on a standing glass panel using a grease pencil: lat & long; course and speed. The massive carrier was twenty-five miles out, moving toward land at twenty knots, ETA: 2021. On a three-by-four foot display, a satellite image of the West Coast, from the southernmost tip of California, to the border of Canada and beyond showed how things would appear from an astronaut's perspective in space. The text sailor clicked an image of southern California on his console for a sharper resolution and Avery leaned in. Along the rugged fringes of a brown mountain range, the moss-green contrast invading its slopes was that of a national forest. The image looked just like an overused folded map. What appeared to be holes and tears produced by mites on a page from an atlas were actually lakes and rivers. These showed up as navy-blue on the screen. But he wondered about the shades of fiery-red and salmon-pink. He hunkered to the sailor's level and asked in a library tone. Those reddish hues were the result of recent, unforgiving wildfires, altering nature's topography in its destructive wake, like corrosive rust on virgin steel.

One of the visuals went into shutdown as though someone had turned it off. Another followed a moment later, then another, and another. Avery suspected an electrical problem was to blame and called in electrician's mates and electronics techs to inspect and troubleshoot.

At 0755 the lieutenant commander entered the Island and climbed to the primary flight control deck. Whoever designed the original superstructure's glassed-in tower, stacking the flag bridge, navigations bridge and primary flight control over one another, was a genius, he thought. The Air Boss, Captain Frank Jarvis, the fighter-jet vet, was busy looking into the sky through his binoculars. The catapult officer down below had just launched the last pilot and his RIO from the flight deck in the last fighter plane now headed to the VFA base in Coronado. The carrier qualification period turned out to be a good one.

Jarvis gave Avery a look but said nothing, even though he appeared to have something on his mind. He turned away and stooped over a radar console. Avery could never tell what color his eyes were because he had never seen him without those flight sunglasses. He wondered whether or not he slept with them, too.

Finally Jarvis said, "There're no more birds, Mr. Avery. What do you want, my chair? My position?"

Before he could even raise a corner of his lip to reply, Jarvis bawled about having trouble tracking the squadron on his radar. All the instruments suddenly blinked and everything went out in Pri-Fly: the electronic status

board, the displays, the monitors, the radar screens. The Air Boss and his crew grew puzzled but Avery's steel nerves didn't quiver at the thought of what was going on. He simply wanted to know how much more electronic equipment and computers would be taken down through every space, on every deck, in every officers' quarter.

At 0810 he stopped off to see the executive officer, Commander J. Miles. The XO pushed a briefcase out of sight beneath his desk and began his daily routine of coffee and hardboiled eggs. He told Avery the first order of the day for him was to go over the latest reports on problem sailors, then log them in the system before any punitive procedures were administered through captain's mast. He thumbed the computer's power-on button, and after a moment typed in a password. The lit screen went out. But not before both men got a look at a strange message:

—Access Denied—
Screen Name/Password
*** Unknown ***
Zyto
Zyto
Zyto

At main control, Avery had just relieved the watchstander when he smelled it. The throttleman caught the first look of curling streams of milky smoke crawling along the overhead, and when he did, the 1MC ship-wide speakers rang an alarm, followed by a blaring message: Now hear this. Class Charlie Fire. Class Charlie Fire. Away the in-port fire party to bravo-tack, six-tack, one-tack, echo.

Armed with electrical extinguishers, suited-up damage-controlmen in red helmets and breathing masks, hustled down ladders and threw themselves into the swirling, gray haze. Avery grabbed an SCBA, strapped it on his back and followed the crowd, threading his way to the scene on disciplined feet.

The busy space was noisy with heaving CO_2 extinguishers, and very dark, except for fat sabers of fire-team lights. He retreated from the "Main E" as soon as he saw what the problem was and moved through the cavern length of the engine room, a shaft of light guiding him. He ripped off the facemask/mouthpiece in a jungle of tree-trunk-fat steel pipes and tonnage of machinery, and checked every component in the auxiliary space under an oval beam of flashlight. Up ahead, the glow of dueling beams told him he was not alone. Someone on a chattering walkie-talkie approached and shined an exploding star in his eyes. He fought back by illuminating the man's face. It was the damage-control officer who said emergency lights were on in levels 02 and

03. The DCO took a cursory look at the gauges, dials, and meters of all the tanks, feed pumps and reducers, and wagged his head like a surgeon who had lost his patient on an operating table. The ominous silence was worse than the roaring hum of machinery. The two men split up, Avery climbing steep ladders with the twenty-two-pound, high-pressure air tank strapped to him. He cursed beneath his breath. The ship was shutting down, section by section, like the major organs in a dying man, and there was nothing he could do to stop it.

Valentine and Jordan approached the lieutenant commander from the opposite direction as he emerged from a ladderwell. "Tag along." He slung off the self-contained breathing apparatus and pushed it aside. "Going to the bridge." A trace of swirling smoke filled the flickering passageway.

"This is Pratt's bull," Valentine said. "Let him grab it by the balls."

Avery hesitated for a blinkless moment. "Captain Bligh it is." He unclipped his butt-phone, punched an extension, and relayed a message. He clipped the tethered handset back onto his belt. "When this thing's over I'm taking a major-league R&R."

Valentine asked, "What's B-Six-One-Echo?"

Thickening smoke rolled over their heads. It smelled bad. "Main switchboard," Avery said. "Fire punched out some computers and electronic equipment."

"What's the plan to restore the loads?" Jordan asked.

Avery gave it to him. The EMs would have to kick a power transfer from the remaining switchboards to wherever it was needed.

Valentine looked like he expected the worst. "What about propulsion?" he asked as another fire team scurried past them.

That question could only be answered by the pit snipes.

At the bridge, a pair of EMs—electrician's mates—supervised by the Executive Officer Jeff Miles, were busy checking all hardware and wiring, while an electronics crew tested backup systems, reactor-analysis terminals, and warfare consoles. Avery stood over a monitor that showed computers were nonfunctioning in most spaces. A phone clamped to the overhead above him buzzed and he took the call. A generator had fallen silent and another was on the way out. "Copy that, over and out." He hung up, wondering how long the reserve power would hold.

Jordan and a boatswain's mate marched past him and checked a gyrocompass, followed by the global positioning system and the ship's fathometer. The AC was down, and unless the port and starboard wing doors were left open, blistering sunlight pouring through the windshields would turn the navigations space into an uncomfortable greenhouse. "Nothing here," Jordan told the XO Miles. "Same for everything else, sir."

Avery tried activating the IVCS. The officer of the deck, a lee helmsman, and a junior officer of the deck named Rick Baldwin—a head-shaven, eager-looking, Academy-graduate ensign with a football-player body whom everyone called Bald Rickman—stood beside him. "Another dead system," he told them.

The exec pounded his foot on top of a weapons box and blew out a gust of ill breath. "How the hell does a small fire wreak so much havoc?" he asked an EM.

"Sir, that's gonna take some doing to answer."

Valentine leaned against the electronic chart table, arms crossed. "Damn." Befuddled eyes danced. "What a way to say good morning."

"Who the hell said it was good?" someone bellowed.

"Captain on deck!" the OOD called.

"Atten-hut!" Miles responded, and all hands snapped to attention.

"As you were, people," Pratt said.

With the skipper were two armed MPs followed by navs chief quartermaster Carlos Nieve and the men who would have the arduous task of checking and double-checking over two-thousand miles of bundled overhead cables that snaked throughout the giant vessel like the veins in a man's body; lines that started nowhere and ended nowhere.

Normally the bridge team comprised of twelve to thirteen people. But because of the emergency the compartment was crowded with twenty. "Jeff, Bill. Glad you're here." Pratt stood tall and rigid like the gray bulkhead behind him. He looked like he had news. Good and bad. "Fire is out. And half the ship has lost power." He regarded the QM: a slim petty officer first class with intelligent eyes. "Mr. Nelson, make the watch announcement."

The quartermaster went to the 1MC, hit a switch and got ready to speak into the mike that would send a message through the ship-wide speakers. "Now secure reflash at main switchboard. Now secure reflash at main switchboard."

A monitor blinked on and off, and Miles caught the captain's eye. "Sir, how long will it take to restore things?"

"Depends. Nukes are checking the reactors to see—"

Avery's butt-phone buzzed and he answered it. "Captain, reactor room. We're in a fixed scram. Two screws down."

"Why are they calling you?" grunted Pratt. "There's nothing wrong with my phone or any of the circuits."

Valentine addressed the skipper. "Thank God we're offshore, Jake. But can we limp in on two?"

"We can swim in on one damn screw," Miles said.

Pratt frowned. "That's not good enough for me. I want snipes in the shafts." Everyone traded glances. When no one ayed, the skipper said, "I'm talking to you, Avery!"

"Captain, I can't pinpoint blind." He motioned to the darkened monitors. "I need a full visual on the layout."

"I'll give you a visual," Pratt retorted. "I'll throw you overboard and have someone else get the damn power plant at critical!" He looked to the OOD, Lieutenant Patrick Davis: a lanky, baby-faced officer with strabismus: the misalignment of one eye. "Mr. Davis, you will escort Mr. Avery off the bridge to main control where he belongs." The captain gave the chief engineer a disdained stare. "His presence here is not required. And if he refuses to cooperate, secure him in his quarters under guard."

The OOD stared flatly. "Aye, sir."

Avery couldn't tell if Davis was looking at Pratt, at him, or both.

"Sir," the boatswain's mate interrupted. "Main control has been evacuated due to the extreme smoke condition." He had spoken without being asked, and Avery expected there would be a cutting reply.

"Lose the attitude, sailor." He gave the enlisted a sharp eye as though trying to slash blood out of him.

"Captain, I think—"

"Who gave you permission to think, Avery? We're losing power and all you do is think. You should be getting someone on that main circuit."

But the circuit was toast, and the ship didn't have enough busbar panels and breaker parts to replace what had melted.

The sound of the bridge-to-bridge radio came to life.

"Answer that damn call," the skipper said.

Jeff Miles grabbed a handset and depressed a button. "You're on the *Man Of War*."

"Captain Jason Elser here," said a voice over the ship's radio. "Radars down on *Trojan*."

Pratt looked over his shoulder. "What the devil does he want me to do?"

"Talk to him, Captain," Avery urged.

Pratt ignored him, pushed past the XO posing with the starboard-side handset and pointed to a machinist mate. "Get your six with the others in bravo shaft alley. I don't need you here."

All the first-class had to say was "aye" to appease the bear in Pratt. He didn't. "Sir, you know full well we're at the mercy of the sea."

He stole Avery's line. Bravo, he thought. But if someone else punched the captain, a sure mast would follow.

"I gave you an order, petty officer. Every nut, bolt, and gear on this birdfarm is to be looked at before a voltage drop turns her into a floating dungeon."

However, a dungeon is what the *Man Of War* was beginning to feel like: a hulled in city where sweaty crewmen carried flashlights in preparation for a big blackout.

Jordan spoke up and said to anyone who cared to listen that if the service generators aboard the *Trojan* were cabled to those on the *Man Of War*, the needed power could override the KO'd reactors, jumpstart the reduction gears, and the lifeless screws would turn with hurricane force, propelling the aircraft carrier forward. Since most ships went nuclear, steam generators were only used on conventional vessels. It was a circus evolution that was worth a try. However, getting two dancing ships to hug each other in an unpredictable ocean between whatever length the lines allowed meant one thing: it was up to Pratt to test the theory.

He did not look like a man who took sound counsel from someone of the lower echelon. "Don't tell me how to fix my ship, Seaman. I was a decorated naval officer while you were on tits milk."

Jeff Miles, still holding the radio's handset, told Captain Elser that Pratt was in PMS again. Avery overheard the comment he made: a petty, miserable scum. The XO signed off.

Valentine stepped in between everyone in the mutiny-tense air. "Jake, calm down."

But that only made the CO's dark eyes light up, and with one austere look he ignited the bridge. "You dickheads better follow orders or you'll be sweating piss in captain's mast!"

Miles said, "Sir, with all due respect ... what the hell do you want from us?"

"The conn." He looked to the helmsman. "Come down from full speed to all ahead standard," he shouted. "Steady as she goes."

The helmsman ayed the command, but added there was no control at the wheel.

Pratt lashed out at him and proceeded to breakdown the bridge team with humiliating, verbal assaults. His moral conduct was volcanic again, Avery thought, and if it didn't stop....

"Captain, if you break UCMJ's article one-three-three you'll be in more trouble than—"

"Shut up, Avery!"

His butt-phone buzzed again and he answered it, looking through the bridge window. The news from the reactor room was that the last two screws were down. Now the carrier would lose the battle with the rushing, bouncing sea, making a sound like gushing air escaping from a blimp, and soon, when momentum ran out of thrust…. "Captain, no steam for the turbines. We're as good as dead in the water."

"What's the status on the number two?" Miles asked as the damage control officer came in.

"Aft engine room down, sir," the DCO reported. "So's auxiliary one and two—nuclear and diesel."

The OOD unclamped a port phone from the overhead as soon as it buzzed and put the receiver to his ear. He looked troubled. "Sir, number two switchboard down."

Pratt whipped his head the other way. "Get the EMs to redistribute power from the turbos, one zone at a time!"

A caller's voice came over the 21MC's intercom system: "Captain?" It was the CIC officer. "Combat consoles and GPS down. What's your status up there?"

The bridge lights blinked on, then off, and the emergency lamps came on. It was too late to redistribute power on a ship when there were no loads in the circuits, Avery thought.

Again the 21MC: "Skipper, you copy?"

Valentine interrupted. "Jake, do something about your ship, or—"

The patch line droned through the clamor and all heads snapped in its direction. Everyone waited for someone to grab the phone, instead it just kept buzzing and buzzing ….

"Sir," Miles said. "Perhaps you should get that."

The tall captain jousted past the OOD and XO in three, long-legged strides and snatched the phone from the overhead. "Commanding officer, *Man Of War* speaking."

Avery recognized the gruff voice that came through the secure channel and Pratt scowled. "The entire base? ASAP? Aye, sir." The skipper hung up, slow and deliberate. He stood there like a wax figure in Madame Tussaud's museum.

Now a graveyard silence filled the bridge.

"Captain?" Avery said. The pilothouse crew looked on. "What is it?"

The ocean played against the ship's hull, but its sound was not comforting.

Pratt bunched fingers into two, big fists. Avery had never seen him look so pensive. "That was Admiral Fumo. We'll be pushed to shore by YTBs. When we port, all officers are to assemble at the headquarters' conference room. We have a critical situation."

Admiral Fumo's emergency meeting ended as quickly as it had commenced with no one knowing more than what they walked in with. What was known was the code name assigned to the crisis: Black Sunday. The press had a different name for it—the fall of the United States.

Avery learned from news reporters on the base that the Joint Chiefs of Staff met with the Defense Secretary at the Pentagon, and that a three-man team of NSA field agents had been dispatched to North Island. This was followed by an urgent call to the Criminal Investigations Division in San Diego, and the FBI sprung into action. But not without the CIA's involvement. Their news center were keeping the president and senior advisors on top of the latest developments through the PDB—a presidential daily brief of global intelligence info.

He read the newspaper that evening and also learned that while JCS counseled the president on a suitable course of action, the Department of Defense had its own concerns. If satellite and radar instruments at NORAD malfunctioned the way those at Naval Air Station North Island had, all ICBMs housed in land-based silos would fall silent, even with armed crews holding dual brass keys to remote launch panels. This would compromise the airspace over the North American continent, leaving it wide open to power-hungry nations. Yet even under this scenario, the Pentagon had an active triad for delivering a nuclear counterstrike. If Northrop's boomerang-shaped B-2 bombers and surface warships weren't deployed, the Navy would call upon its top prize—their *Groton* SSBNs. If the president gave the command, the Tridents would be launched.

With a North-Island cloudy night blocking out the stars, most personnel had all racked-out when several men in dark suits were secretly escorted aboard the *Seven*. Avery checked the ship's passdown log. Nothing indicated there would be guests and none of the watchstanders knew anything about the visit. Using the night as cover, senior officers hustled the men below deck and the sudden boarding of the biggest ship in the Navy had been kept unobserved. But the number of personnel involved in the urgent visit hinted to Avery as he stood watch at the quarterdeck the true nature of the call.

An imposing-looking petty officer, Mike Ragazzi, showed up to spell Avery for watch duty and told him the visitors were brought to CIC: Combat Information Center. Earlier that day, the lieutenant commander passed through CIC's elaborate room, crammed with navymen, computers, radar instruments, communications equipment and high-definition tactical surveillance screens. He called them the eyes and ears of the ship.

There, North Island's CO—Admiral John Thomas Fumo; the commanders of the *USS Man Of War* and *USS Trojan Horse*—Captains Jacob Warren Pratt and Jason Ray Elser were accompanied by a troop of top brass. Steel-clad hatches were closed and armed MAAs were stationed before each one. They would maintain watch by the jaundice glow of power-failure lamps like the tall, motionless sentinels of Buckingham Palace.

Avery had been informed no one under any circumstance would be permitted in or out of the entombed CIC until the long meeting was over. And no one, for any reason, was allowed to approach the area. Strict orders had already been given to arrest, without questioning, any unauthorized personnel who wandered by.

Now with the identity of the men secured, Avery, Ragazzi, and those who ushered the group from Washington, into the base with quick discretion, knew one thing. Several men with NCIS IDs clipped to their lapels were aboard the *USS Man Of War*.

Chapter 10

As per the admiral's order, naval officers throughout the base reported to the *Man Of War's* large Civic room where he—the commanding officer of North Island, and a keynote speaker—had just marched in. It had been twenty-four hours since all power aboard the ship known as the *Seven,* had been lost, and a new day brought no answers.

With backup generators working, lights shined over the long-faced, balding Texan from Alvin, standing tall in his formal naval uniform. Now that he had the attention of every man and woman, he tucked a gold oak-leafed wheel cap under his arm, checked the time on his watch, stepped up to the lectern and summoned fellow dignitaries and distinguished guests to take their seats behind him.

"I apologize for the tardiness." Rear Admiral Fumo's drawl carried well in the Civic, Avery thought. It would also carry over every closed-circuit TV in every space aboard the ship. "My excuse for arriving at this time isn't a good one. I had trouble managing my socks. The Navy still refuses to approve my having a personal nurse's aide."

A crescendo of laughter instantly shattered the wall of silence created by the large crowd, upsetting the critical mood in the air for a moment.

Fumo took pause until the roaring subsided. "Now without further delay, I'd like to introduce a law-enforcement agent whose job is to investigate crimes within the Navy and Marines. As keynote speaker for this morning, he'll tell us more about Black Sunday. Please welcome, field agent Dauerman."

Navy personnel, civilian tech reps, and members of the media rose to their feet, spilling their loud applause onto the platform as a fine-dressed, well-built man stepped up to the podium as though he would receive the Congressional Medal of Honor. There were no doubts in Avery's mind he drew the attention of female journalists and reporters. But a crew-cut man in a pinstriped, three-piece vested suit, however handsome, meant one thing to the lieutenant commander. Serious business.

The admiral retreated past Dauerman and took a seat by a Marine MP standing guard with a large American flag draped behind him. Fumo greeted Secretary of the Navy, Ben Nobleman; the head of Department of Defense, Luke Driscoll, and Chief of Naval Operations, Admiral Craig Jenson from the Pentagon—briefcase at his feet and black eyeglasses in his uniform pocket. Each man had flown in from Arlington to hear the message the keynote speaker was about to deliver.

Avery had taken a seat upfront. It was easy to give undistracted attention when a man looked you in the eye.

"Good morning." The agent's voice rang like a potentate on a throne. "My name is Hank Dauerman. As your admiral stated, I work for a law-enforcement agency under the Navy Department. We were NIS until an ex-national security deputy jockeyed for the job's top position, and NIS became NCIS."

The history of the Naval Investigative Service morphing into the Naval Criminal Investigative Service wasn't what Avery expected to hear. It was old news. He figured the agent was simply using that tidbit as a launch pad for what would follow.

"My job here at North Island, is threefold: identify, restore, and apprehend. We've already done step-one—identified the nature of the problem. What remains is patching security holes, restoring systems, and apprehending those responsible for the major disruption of military computers and electronic equipment. To put it bluntly, this base has been crippled. Shut down by a new kind of virus that wormed its way through every system on every ship and in every building. But NASNI isn't the only installation under the Black-Sunday cloud."

He opened an attaché case, took a thick folder, laid it down on the lectern and opened it to the inside flap. "Whidbey Island Naval Air Station and McChord Air Force Base in Washington, have reported all systems disabled. Beale, Travis, Castle, Vandenberg, March, Edwards, and George Air Force Bases all report computer lockups. Point Mugu Naval Air Station also reported instruments frozen. And lastly, Camp Pendleton Marine Corps Base has—"

Reporters and journalists in the front row fired a confusing chatter of questions at the speaker and the stunned assembly followed their lead.

"Excuse me, ladies and gentlemen." The information center reverberated with Dauerman's voice and whistling feedback. "I won't tolerate another interruption. Admiral Fumo will hold a Q&A session at the end of this briefing."

Avery hoped the disorderly crowd would permit Dauerman to continue.

"Yesterday, the network infrastructure of our military was compromised when someone brazenly hacked their way through frontline security and emptied the Navy's Project Black Files. A windfall of top-secret information and highly-classified armed forces plans are now in someone else's hands. The loss is staggering. Whoever has gained this sensitive material will eventually leap many years ahead of the United States in naval technology and military capability."

The news was worst than Avery imagined. He gulped down a foreboding thought.

"It's no secret that crackers—criminal hackers—continue to be a great threat to national security. However, evidence of this transgression suggests we're dealing with someone beyond cunning. A sophisticated individual. A cyber genius."

Avery blamed the Navy for what happened. With so many well-trained operators in various fields, it was difficult to weed out friend from foe; determined spies from dedicated sailors.

"This computer worm—a new brand we've termed Smart Virus—performs like a professional lock picker. Once programmed, it can break into any system, enter any database and steal without leaving clues of the intruder."

Dauerman's message pounded with the power of a pneumatic drill.

"It's going to take a great deal of effort to untangle this nightmarish mess. Especially since the signature-name Zyto contains an anti-tracking code. We'll probably not know right away who's responsible, but I'm a patient man with plenty of game time. I know how to find who I'm looking for. Cyber DNA."

There was nothing the agent would not be able to accomplish. Avery could tell just by studying the look in his clever eyes.

"For now it appears we've been outsmarted by a skilled adversary. However, a plan will be underway to disable the crippling virus as soon as the FBI get their feet wet in this matter. Ladies and gentlemen. Members of the naval armed forces. Your admiral will now answer questions."

Standing to their feet, the large assembly, several hundred strong, loudly applauded in unison. Fumo met Dauerman, and the two shook hands. NCIS's investigation was officially underway.

When all the questions were asked and answers given, those from the media, including all dignitaries and distinguished guests, retreated.

Fumo motioned for a group of men seated upfront to join him on the platform as the rest thronged their way out of the Civic like the end of a blockbuster movie.

"Sorry we didn't get a chance to catch up on old times last night," Fumo said as four men lined up behind him.

"Let's get a bite now at the flag mess," the NCIS officer suggested. "I'm impressed with the supercarrier and its unmixed presence. The century's first to smell of testosterone."

"You'll get a tour. First allow me to introduce some of the men." He started with the first one in line. "This is the medical officer, Commander Bill Valentine; executive officer, Jeff Miles; senior ops officer, Ed Urquart, and Lieutenant Commander Neil Avery. Chief engineer."

"So, you're Avery. Grabbed a good seat upfront. Heard about you."

Avery wondered what he had heard. "Give me an e.g."

"Good things." Dauerman flashed a good-looking smile. The others made their way off the platform, joining those in the passageway. "Tom told me some important news about you and a few other men. With your admiral's permission I'd like to interview potential candidates regarding a new program the Department of Defense is offering. Your admiral tells me you might be interested in doing something different. If that's the case, and if you qualify, you could be a part of it. How's that sound?"

Avery looked from the full-bodied agent to the admiral. "That sounds—"

"Fine," interrupted Fumo. He clapped the junior officer on the shoulder. "Hank, when did I see you last, ASU?"

"You two know each other?" Avery asked.

"Sure," Tom Fumo said. "We were in the martial arts club in high school and Arizona State. Me in Judo. Hank in Tae Kwon Do. And when it came to tournaments we were unbeatable. Hank, how many trophies you win?"

"Not many."

"Cut the horse crap," Fumo said with a dismissive gesture. "I've always admired your talents. Now it's NCIS. I knew one day you'd be doing something like this. By the way, do they still call you *Shank*?"

Avery arched an eyebrow. "Shank?"

"Some people do."

The admiral turned to Avery. He told him *Slamming Hank* was the name the frat-rats had given him. He broke a two-inch slab of cinderblock with one punch and the name was shortened to Shank.

"Show the Commander your fists."

"What for?"

"Come on, show him."

Dauerman clamped fists tight, displaying an enlarged pair of hammered knuckles.

Avery grunted as though he had been hit with a blow. "You could hurt someone with those."

"That's the idea," the spokesman admiral said.

The NCIS officer lowered the twin, calloused weapons. He wore a look of admiration for the young Navy officer until he drove his eyebrows together in thought. "Avery—? You wouldn't be related to Allen Avery, would you?"

He retreated a step. There was only one thing he hated more than that man himself—his name. "He was my father." It pleased him the words came out flat.

"Really?" A pleasant smile ruled the agent's face. "I met him at NASA during my years there as an administrator. Lost track of him after I left Houston, though. Shame he died young. Nice guy. Wanted the moon and more." Dauerman rubbed his big, clean-shaven chin. The man chiseled like a Marine drill sergeant was pondering over something. "I'd like to think he got his wish. Did he?"

The unexpected praise abraded Avery. "What he got was a diseased liver."

The agent shook his head and smiled again. "Don't think hard thoughts of your old man. Now that I've made the connection, I'm looking forward to working with you."

Chapter 11

Neil Avery joined the meeting in progress. He squeezed into the Civic, past a pair of Marine MPs standing at attention, went to the back and listened. Here, things were as the world outside where nothing moved. Not the mighty gray ships, not the elevators in the buildings, and not the checkpoint's red-striped crossing arms at the main gate. Everything remained as was after Black Sunday hit—a frozen base waiting to come to life.

"… Takedown of satellite communications and radar instruments was a diversion that allowed the theft as troubleshooting efforts were focused elsewhere. Whoever overrode your detection system, unleashing a properly engineered virus, could also gain access into other networks, moving up to government and business organizations. And whoever could do that, could gain control of the whole world."

Members of the media shot to their feet, and in the floodgate of confusing inquiry, Avery battled his way upfront. "The hell with the questions," he shouted over the clamor. "Are there any suspects?" What he hoped was the question to end all questions left the large CVIC like an empty tomb.

"Yes," said the NCIS officer. "And they're among us."

Groans swept through the Civic from front to back like an oncoming wave from a troubled sea and a return moan made its way upfront.

Dauerman said, "Using a network sniffer, my team discovered clues that have shed light on certain persons of interest, narrowing our investigation to four ships here at North Island. When the time is right, all suspects will be brought in. I regret I cannot disclose more information. However, as events develop we will keep you posted." He turned to look behind him. "Admiral, any last words?"

Fumo stepped to the podium with ending comments and the hungry crowd of officers were dislodged from their seats with a rushed dismissal that sent them away against their will. Hundreds of grim faces, all emerging from a black horizon, left unsettled to return to the virtual ghost town they had come from—a military base running on emergency generators which lit passageways on each ship, supplied electricity to all mess halls, powered dishwashers in each galley, pumped agitators in every laundry machine and made ACs hum in each duct. But nothing more. Except for sound-powered J-phones, all other means of communication were out, and barring cleaning detail known as clampdown, all work had stopped. Most servicemen and women would take the crisis in stride by playing cards in crew's lounges and working out in weight rooms. But not Avery. He had been forced out of the Civic by a wave of men, all of whom no doubt, would retreat below to the silence of their workstations and rehearse in their minds what they had known so far.

Along the passageway he listened to the buzzing all around him: a horde of servicemen talking at the same time of Black Sunday's inside job. When it came to criminal activity within the armed forces, Avery was a savvy individual. Eight years earlier, a knowledgeable pair of money-hungry, E-5 Navy brothers, stole military secrets and sold them to a Russian handler with connections to the Oblast Federation Embassy in Washington, DC, before being caught by the FBI. Two years later, a PO third-class had also been nabbed for passing information on advanced warship technology encrypted on a CD-ROM to a diplomat in the General Consulate of the Republic of Korea in Houston, Texas. Avery wondered whether the latest incident would bring the Navy to its knees. A trained military man turned spy, one who could decrypt the language of classified documents and codes, was a great asset to any foreign power.

Dauerman's revelation echoed in his head as he entered his quarters. He was gripped in disturbing silence, sensing the *Man Of War* was one of the unnamed ships under investigation. If he was right, that meant that those being sought after were individuals he probably interacted with on a regular basis. Who can tell on a ship this size? he thought. There were thousands aboard the *Man Of War*, more than the proverbial mental line-up of suspects he had conjured up.

He mused on what NCIS had done in such a short time. In lightning-like fashion, they had several men in sight, within reach, and soon, the case would be cracked wide open. Dauerman not only earned his respect, the NCIS officer also gained the admiration from the naval community. He and his team had proven themselves, and when the time came, when the Zyto virus was disabled from every system on every ship and every building by introducing it to a new code the agent had created—Pheryl 13—which would be fed into each computer as an antivirus signature, NCIS would bask in the victory of the first arrest.

Avery walked past the tall, bronze statue of the famous, four-star admiral, Hyman George Rickover, and entered naval headquarters: a four-story, white-granite building with a hedgerow of razor-cut shrubs and a six-foot, gold fouled anchor above its tall, clear, glass doors. With a military cadence in his feet, he removed his wheel cap, approached a Marine sentry on duty, and placed an open palm on a desktop glass plate. He waited for the information to appear on duel, flat screens. One in front of the sentry, the other behind him.

On top of the sentry's desk, a newspaper's headline held Avery's attention:

Rival CIA and FBI Merge Against Cyber Thieves

Although the San Diego Union Tribune covered much of the details surrounding Black Sunday, the bulk of information released came from the Civic-room meetings. But one issue Dauerman did not cover was the CIA's involvement in the case. Avery wondered why this was so. He came up with a plausible answer, one that suited him for the moment. It would have to do with violations against its own charter. He was right. The statement was in the third paragraph of the newspaper article. The CIA, busy tracking down known suspects within the fifty states, had struck a deal with the FBI. They would round up every former hacker and rightwing extremist in their felon file, brand them like cattle and lock them up. As long as the feds closed the reopened investigation on the JFK assassination.

His hand warmed and the multi-scan color monitor pulsed in the sentry's eyeglasses. "Avery, Lieutenant Commander," he said.

The inset likeness of himself on the opposite monitor facing him was a good picture. Now the sentry would have to confirm that the image on the screen was that of the man standing before him. He did. "You'll find Mr. Dauerman in room four-twelve." The inset of the visitor's face blinked off the system.

Avery proceeded to the elevators that serviced all executive personnel and Admiral Fumo's staff. The last time he visited HQ, the scanner had been upgraded from its prototype units and identity verification had been revolutionized. Its security prevented those under the rank of ensign from gaining access into the highly-classified operations facility. Spy crimes changed the way the Navy operated.

A chime announced an elevator had arrived. But he was busy eyeballing the Marine and the weapon he carried. Avery loved firearms. Had from the moment he stood poised at a firing range. Each shot he pumped never missed its mark. "Nice side arm," he commented beneath his breath.

He entered the waiting elevator.

In the rising cab he gave himself a once-over, and the stainless steel was the perfect mirror. He adjusted his tie and checked his service jacket's nickel-size gold buttons from top to bottom; fingertips exploring its flawlessly-designed embossed anchors. He made certain each button was firmly attached, for a loose one meant he was out of uniform. A good first impression was in the works but a scuffed right shoe would spoil that. "I'll polish it later," he muttered.

The elevator stopped and its doors opened wide, revealing the first of many private offices: Room 401. He stepped out with a sprinting heart. What am I nervous about? he wondered. Fumo told him to report to HQ. It was best he go at sundown. The admiral said the appointment was a favor, but it sounded more like a command.

Along the deserted hallway were rooms 405, 406, and 407. A left turn at a red, fire alarm box led to rooms 408 through 411. Another sharp left and there to his right, room 412.

A faint, nicotine smell from within seeped into the corridor where he stood. He raised a fist to knock.

"Come in," someone said. "I've been expecting you."

Puzzled, he turned the knob, pushed the door open with a slow hand and peeked in.

"Well?" said a man from within.

Irritating cigarette smoke. It blew at him, rushing up his nostrils like an oxygen-starved combustion in a backdraft. He had always wanted to snatch that coffin nail from his father's twisted grin and grind it into his pudgy face. But there were consequences. He would have been branded with burn marks on his penis and testicles—again.

He took a cautious step into the dark office where a dim glow came from somewhere, and a thought crawled in his brain like a worm: What am I doing here?

Four figures stirred; their ember-lit cigarettes floating above the surface of a desk. From what little light spilled in from a venetian-shaded window, one man's silhouette brought a fearful memory to him of another brawny man. He pushed the image aside.

A teakettle shrieked from somewhere, and tension, mixed with perspiration seeped through his pores. He raked his throat to clear it of the smoky smog created by the men who faced a small, closed-circuit monitor. "Do you always spy—?"

"You going to shut the door or not?"

He took another step, complied, and his floor shadow disappeared. It was darker without the illumination from the hallway. The lights flickered on in the office and Avery blinked. He recognized the other men as having been at the Civic meeting: chief of DOD, Luke Driscoll and Navy Secretary, Ben Nobleman, whom he met at Norfolk during a ribbon-pinning ceremony. A fourth man, wearing an FBI jacket, stood with them.

Dauerman dismissed them and the tall Caucasians pushed past the junior officer with a tail of cigarette smoke trailing them out the door. The agent rose from the fortress of a grand ambassador desk and welcomed his guest. Behind him, a draped American flag partially obscured an aerial shot of CVNX-6—the *USS William Jefferson Clinton*. Before him lay a glass ashtray, a pack of gold-tipped Camels, a black phone, a laptop and an opened roll of Tums in a spiral of tattered wrapping. Dauerman yanked the window blinds up, inviting the night into the office. "Now I can answer your question."

Avery stood there without blinking, studying the agent like a rare, old penny. He once had a one-cent coin with Lincoln's profile hidden beneath corroded copper. He put that penny into a solvent, plucked it out a moment later, and read a number: 1963—the year Kennedy was assassinated. Dauerman had that kind of face: the beardless features of old, honest Abe.

The agent blew a smoky stream at him, and again that image flashed across his mind: I told you to do your homework!

Dauerman flicked off the surveillance screen like a TV set and slid it out of sight in a filing cabinet. "I wasn't spying on you. Just testing a new unit."

"Where's the camera?"

"You tell me." The agent sat down. He looked tired. Beaten-down tired. He had worked against the clock and against a hacker, reversing the fallen-domino effect of crashed computers. That done, most of the FBI left town but NCIS would stay.

Avery resisted the impulse to express how grateful he was that a naval base had been brought back to life. Pheryl 13. "Why do you want to see me?" He was impressed with the man in the Armani suit, Dior white shirt and Versace black tie. He had held everyone at the Civic meetings spellbound and was sure to do likewise with the candidates he would be interviewing. But where were they?

Dauerman flicked tobacco embers into the ashtray. He put the cigarette to his mouth, pulled in a long, deliberate drag and blew out perfect circles of floating vapors until each disintegrated. "That's why I want to see you." He put the cigarette to his lips again and created more smoky rings. He seemed fascinated with the way they appeared and disappeared. "Just like decellularization."

Avery coughed volcanically into a fist. His throat felt sandpaper raw.

The agent gave the serviceman a look. "Sensitive to smoke, huh?"

A quiet yes escaped his lips. Avery had not moved since he entered the office. He stood fixed in the same spot. Feet hammered to the floor. I shouldn't have come, he thought.

"Should've said something. You're no mute." Dauerman extinguished the diminished cigarette in the ashtray crowded with spent butts. He motioned to an old leather chair, ripped in spots and missing all of its black casters. "Have a seat right there."

"What the hell for?"

"I have an interview to conduct." The agent rose, fixing his tie.

"Don't know why we can't do this standing." Avery removed his service jacket and frowned.

"May I take that?" He approached, hand extended. "Get you coffee?"

Despite the fact the lowered chair looked uncomfortable, Avery forced himself to cooperate. "Alright." He sat. "Make it black. No sugar."

Dauerman grabbed the jacket and cover, and moved past him across the office while Avery looked to the distant lights of the base through the night veil that descended over North Island. With his things hanging on the door's hook rack behind him, Dauerman assumed the role of host, pouring coffee for the lieutenant commander, then for himself. He stepped away from the teakettle's hotplate, handed his guest a generous portion and swung around his desk, wispy steam rising from his mug.

A moment later the room became warm. Very warm.

Avery rested the burning mug on the desk. The agent fished a cigarette from the open pack by the black phone and brought it to his rugged mouth.

"Light another one of those and I'll—"

"What?" Dauerman said. "Hit me?" He pinched the gold-filtered cigarette behind his left ear and gave a hard smile. "You don't have the balls."

The office grew quiet. It was the perfect time to get up and walk out, but Avery had something on his mind. "Why am I here?"

"No need to be uneasy, just drink your coffee."

"I said, why am I—?"

"It isn't poison, you can drink it."

The volatile liquid in the mug would take a while to cool off. Just like his temper. "Why must everything be like an oven—this office, the coffee? Is this orchestrated intimidation necessary?"

"Sorry, Commander. I neglected to warn you. I like my brew hot. Very hot."

"How about fire and brimstone? You like that, too? I caught your reflection in the window. You turned on the thermostat, didn't you?"

Dauerman laughed, went to the thermostat and set it to the off position. He strode back to the desk, sat, and powered on the air conditioner in a window sleeve with a remote control. "If you can't stand a warm environment, how do you expect to survive the intense heat of the *cylinder?*"

Avery's throat bobbed, but there was nothing for him to swallow. "Look, mister—"

"Call me Shank."

The mention of a superheated contraption created an enigma, and the serviceman hated enigmas. Such things gonged in his head like a general quarters bell. Avery had to know why he was there. He was convinced he was being led into ultimate peril. "What cylinder might that be? And what did you mean by decell … what did you call it?"

"Priority first, Commander. For now I'll need your paw print on some paperwork in order to begin."

"You're asking me to sign up without knowing what this is about?"

"I can't divulge information if you're not interested in volunteering." He got up, went to a gray file cabinet and opened a drawer. He found what he wanted. "You do want to volunteer, don't you?" A legal form of some sort was thrust into the JO's hands. Then a pen.

Participation in Research Form: I (Volunteer's name), *being of sound mind and….*

He didn't like where this was going. "This job seems risky."

"How long have you been in the armed forces without confronting danger? You've done it before. Why should it stop you now? Or have you forgotten your Arctic and Antarctic assignments with the Navy?"

Avery was unpleasantly surprised. Those assignments were classified. Only the Pentagon and the Navy Department were privy. "How did you know about those deployments?"

The agent took a seat. "It's my business to know."

"And my right to ask about a job description."

"Life without risks is a yawn. What were you expecting you'd be doing when you walked through my door? Grooming puppies at a kennel?" Dauerman huffed out a laugh.

"Something out of harms way," he retorted.

"Your diminishing interest disappoints me, Commander." He took a sip of steamy coffee, tasting it like soothing, warm cocoa. "I thought you were an adventurer. One who'd jump out of his skivvies to be an explorer. But if safety is the issue, I'll give it to you." He leaned to one side of the chair, in a going-to-fart position. Avery wondered what else he knew. "The reason DOD is interested in you is because you have no kids, no siblings, no parents—not even a dog."

Avery leaped to his feet and the arteries in his neck throbbed. "Where did you get that info?" He fisted the desk and the black coffee in both mugs pulsed. "Answer me!"

"Do you always erupt like a geyser?"

"Cut the crap and answer the question."

"But if I did that the game would end. And so would the fun."

Avery frowned. There was nothing amusing about having a stranger tell you your background. "What fun?"

"I need some form of entertainment to tip the scales of this stressful job, Commander. Please indulge me a bit."

But he was in no mood to humor anyone. He was taken aback that the Federal Department had compromised its code of ethics. "How does DOD know about my private life?"

"You sound like a man who wants to walk out."

"Answer me, dammit!"

"They have their sources."

Avery decided it was best if he calmed down. The reason he was there was still not clear to him. "Why me? What's so important about me?"

The agent told him the Defense Department considered him a valuable asset. They had already taken great measures to ensure no one would grieve if something should happen to him. "What could be more safe than that?" he added.

"How considerate of them." Avery didn't want to sit down, but he did.

"I see the truth doesn't satisfy you."

"Nothing satisfies me."

"Perhaps the answer about your service record will." The AC hummed in the background, but its cooling power had lost its effect. "I read your ribbons from here. They tell quite a story. What you've done. Where you've been."

It was a lame answer, Avery thought. Dauerman needed to come up with something better, and he did. His job was to match the project's profile. To recruit an honest, disciplined military man who had twenty years of service under his belt. But the individual had to be an unmarried man.

The thought of being forced into singleness was like having a death sentence imposed on him by a gavel-hammering judge. "You've been misinformed. I'm a widower."

"My condolences. Was it difficult losing her?"

"My wife was my last love." If I really cared, why didn't I say it? he thought. "Don't ask me that again."

"How touching. But from a security standpoint, being romantically involved can put a damper on things."

"How so?" Avery was trying to irritate him on purpose.

"I'll ask the questions." He looked like a detective with the unlit cigarette pinched behind his ear. "Got a girlfriend, Mr. Avery?"

"Thought DOD knew it all?" He crossed arms over his chest, relieved that bit of information escaped them. "What's a girlfriend got to do with anything?"

Dauerman's breathing became heavy. "Part of the interview."

What was the harm in admitting the truth? Avery thought. He was a defeated man. Lying could do nothing to help him get back what he had lost. "No. There's absolutely no one."

The agent smiled. "Good."

Security leaks were serious things, Avery thought. Many a military man ended up in penal institutions because of the power of a loose tongue.

"The project's director, Dr. Weinberg, will be pleased. He'll be flying in tomorrow."

Weinberg. The name rang like the ship's general quarters bell. Where had he heard it? He downed several hot gulps of coffee to give him time to think—to learn something about the agent. He guessed that if one studied a man's surroundings, one could learn about the man. Avery put it to the test. He traced a glance to a water cooler in the corner of the office, paper cups protruding from its side, and Dauerman's eyes followed. A shoulder holster, hanging from a second coat rack, displayed an austere-looking weapon the serviceman had seen earlier. "Nice side arm."

"It's an A-forty-six Barrington. I'm a crime-solving investigator. I'm allowed to carry it."

"That's not what I mean and you know it."

"What do you want, Avery?"

"I know weapons. Never seen one like that."

"The Navy's behind the times. What can I say?"

"That Marine guard in the lobby isn't. How do you account—?"

"You think you've got a connection here, huh, wise guy?"

"You know I have. Those weapons are like a pair of aces. Two of a kind."

"You don't know the first thing about my line of work."

Avery knew that JAG and NCIS were pillars of the Uniform Code of Military Justice and that Dauerman's people—two other agents—were masquerading as Marine guards. It felt good to say it. "Care to prove me wrong?"

"I told you …." Dauerman pointed a fat finger at him. "You know nothing about my work."

"So, it's true."

"This meeting's about you, not me, Avery."

"It's about both of us. If I'm going to work for DOD, you'll have to tell me what this is about. Why you're here. Why I'm here."

"Sign that form, then I talk." The agent turned away in his chair, offering the officer his back. He looked through the window, into the dark distance of North Island. "Why does a floating bellhop want to know about undercover work, huh? You're sniffing my crotch and I don't like it."

"Dogs don't mind. It's how they get acquainted."

Dauerman let out a tired laugh. "You amuse me." Suddenly he spun around. "Let me give you an FYI. I'm here to protect this country from all enemies—foreign and domestic. Like it or not."

It sounded like the Boy Scout's creed, not the mission statement that made DOD and the U.S. Navy a family.

"Why do you find pleasure intimidating me?" In one quick motion, Avery kicked the old chair out from under him and shot to his feet. "And where did you get this wasted piece of—?"

"Commander!" A deriding laugh broke the turbulence in the air. "This is simply a psychological test." He gave a pleasing smile. "Don't you know before the body is tested, the mind and will must first be tested? Has the Navy taught you nothing after all these years?" He sounded like an old, Shaolin monk. "This is my way of finding out if you're the right man with the right stuff. If you can't take a little intimidation, how will you stand up to Project Spectrum?"

Avery had always considered himself to be a renegade full of piss and vinegar—the wrong man with the wrong stuff. "What's Project Spectrum?"

"You, Commander."

"Me?"

"Exactly. You will either make or break man's first attempt at his final achievement."

"You make it sound like I'm going to the moon."

"Where you're going no one's been."

Avery didn't want to hear he was going somewhere without knowing where that someplace was. And he didn't like waiting for a proper response. No matter how long he looked at Dauerman through narrowed eyes, he would not be satisfied with anything he said. Cat-and-mouse games were not exciting. Especially when one was the mouse.

"It's vital you join DOD's team of specialists."

Avery felt hemmed-in. A team of specialists meant the Defense Department was gearing to conduct something serious. "Is that all you're going to tell me?"

"There're other things to explain first. But now that you've passed the first part of this test, I can disclose the nature of the project you'll be involved in."

Avery gulped down the last remaining bitter dregs from his mug and made eye contact with the big, NCIS man. "No more delay tactics?" He fought to relax.

"Soon as you sign that PRF, I'll start." The agent's face showed sincerity. He got up, rolled out his chair and his guest sat in it. Avery looked over the form and scribbled his name on it.

He put down the pen. The legal document was signed.

Dauerman lifted his black drinking mug from the desk and stirred its contents with a plastic spoon. A man addicted to caffeine and nicotine was always stirred. "One day when this is out in the open, the Department of Defense will reward you by throwing a parade in your honor. But none of that will happen without going over the ground rules." He settled his rump on the edge of the windowsill and looked into the coal-black night. "First, I expect you to act like an officer of the United States Navy."

Avery said, "I don't need to be reminded of military protocols."

"Excellent. It's good we understand each other. The success of this program hangs on the hinges of total secrecy, just like any wartime operation." He slurped down a mouthful of coffee and rested the mug beside him. "I am speaking your language, am I not?"

"Just proceed."

"Second, don't do anything without proper supervision." Dauerman explained he would be working with sensitive equipment that could cause injury to himself and others. If he goofed up, he would be terminated. "Clear?"

"You said you were going to get on with it."

"I say a lot of things. What's the hurry?"

A fist-size knot pulsated in Avery's gut. One was terminated from a job when they didn't perform to the employer's level of expectation. But what was that job? he wondered.

"Third ...."

Avery began having second thoughts. Working for the Defense Department was someone else's opportunity of a lifetime, not his. What he wanted was—

"Did you hear me?" Dauerman said.

He was unmasked and had to admit he wasn't paying attention.

"I said, you'll have to work Sunday thru Saturday. No time off."

The young officer had worked everyday for the Navy the past twenty years. What's the difference? he thought. "Any other do's and don'ts?" He wished the admiral had chosen another candidate.

"As a member of Spectrum, you are not to have any association with the opposite gender. DOD doesn't want you screwing up on this program by screwing around."

Avery had a thought: So, the job offer is really a dancing worm. And someone wants a big fish to take a bite.

"Lastly—"

"Dammit, come out with it." He didn't have to tell the agent his constrained presence had run its course. "Don't make me put together a mosaic of tiny tiles from scraps of information. I'm not good at unraveling mysteries!"

"Commander, I was hoping you'd show some patience. But what the hell. Raise your right hand as an oath of confidentiality."

The grim moment left Avery silent. He shuffled his feet under him, unable to keep them still.

Dauerman waited, blinking a few times.

Finally he answered, "I swear on my mother's grave I'll be quiet! What else you want, blood?"

"That'll come later." The agent moved from the window to the front of the oak desk and sat. He took the form from the serviceman and laid it by the phone. He looked ready to talk of something important. "Ever hear of Quantum Nuclear Genetics?"

Avery took a stab at it. "The science of cloning."

"You're wrong, mister. QNG is a viable technology resulting in decellularization. The cell-by-cell breakdown of the human body."

In a heartbeat Avery's world had changed. What would it take to change with it? he wondered.

The morgue-quiet office was disturbed by a trilling cell phone.

Dauerman popped it open. "Shank here. What's up?" He rubbed his stomach and frowned. "A lead like that on Jenson would give the president the runs and blow the roof off the White House. I'll have the FBI pay him a visit. Is that all, Mr. Driscoll?... Good."

Someone was tightening the screws on the investigation, Avery thought, and the first suspect mentioned took him by monstrous surprise: Admiral Craig Jenson. The Pentagon's top man in the Navy's War Department.

The agent snapped the cell phone shut, shoveled a handful of Tums into his mouth and crunched until he swallowed. He rubbed his stomach again. "Damn bleeding ulcer."

The lieutenant commander decided he would walk out—now.

He rose to his feet.

Dauerman chose that moment to keep him where he stood. He told him that thirty years ago in a private meeting much like the one they were in, the theory of reversing cell disintegration was proven and Spectrum was conceived. Over time, a carefully assembled team of top-notch science engineers and biogenetic physicists from around the country, celebrated the painstaking completion of a project they toiled over for so long.

Avery sat, rattled by the thought of his own question. "What does the government plan to do with that kind of technology?"

"Who said anything about the government?"

"You mean—?"

"Not even our president...." He said select members of the Defense Department, including Spectrum's designers, had vowed to take its secret to the grave. The look on his face made that clear. "How's your knowledge of history?"

"Get to the point."

"Ever heard of the Manhattan Project?"

Avery didn't like the sound of it. He prepared himself for an earful.

The Manhattan Project was a classified undertaking just like Spectrum, with an elite group of scientists backing it—J. Robert Oppenheimer, Leo Szilard, and Albert Einstein. Oppenheimer teamed up with General Leslie Groves' Army Corps of Engineers and civilian employees at Los Alamos, New Mexico, and everyone kept President Truman and the rest of the U.S. in the dark until the last moment when the secret was unveiled in July of 1945. The success of that project changed the course of history, ushering in a new era for mankind. And a new fear. One unparalleled since the beginning of time.

Dauerman used the right word—fear. It grappled with Avery like wrestling sumos and wouldn't let go.

"The Manhattan Project was the code name for the plan to end the war against the Japanese," the NCIS officer said.

Images of an old newsreel played back in Avery's mind with Dauerman's voice narrating the horrible scenes of a city in ruins: a desert landscape of flattened buildings, radioactive rubble, and mangled steel girders. The secret weapon was dropped from a B-29 bomber over Hiroshima, Japan, and the monstrous mushroom cloud that developed from the catastrophic explosion still loomed over every person, every city, every nation.

Little Boy. It came to him. Little Boy was the nickname given to the atom bomb that instantly killed over seventy-thousand people. It was delivered in the plane christened after the pilot's mother: Enola Gay. "That secret's as old as its history," Avery said.

"But history's about to change again with a new one."

"For better or worse?"

"You make it sound like a bad marriage, sailor."

The junior officer was irked by the sailor title and would've walked out, but he wanted to know what this new secret was. He was told in a nutshell *Priority First* had developed a complex instrument. Potent enough to defy the laws of physics. However, that did nothing to explain the kind of instrument it was, what it was designed for, and who had built it. "Who's Priority First?"

"The unsung heroes who birthed Spectrum."

He had pieced the bizarre puzzle together. But something was wrong. An all-important piece was missing—deliberately left out. Avery sensed it in his gut. "I'm no Einstein. What the hell you want with me?"

"Phase one of Spectrum involved inanimate objects. Phase two, plants and animals. You will be phase three."

He discovered how startled he was when he stopped breathing. Now that he was aware of his calling he would sit back and plot his way out. "Do you always use deceit to get people involved in human experiments?"

"Please smile when you say that."

Avery glared with flinchless eyes and a speech followed. Someone within the science community of Spectrum wanted to play with little, white mice. But he wasn't about to be their mouse, their toy, or anything else. He jumped from his seat, snatched the form he had signed, and ripped it. Adrenaline carried him across the office without him feeling his feet on the floor.

"Commander, that wasn't mannerly of you." He sounded like a Catholic priest Avery once knew. "Your abrupt behavior shocks me. There's a lot in store for you if you'd just listen."

"I'm done listening." Avery yanked the door open with a whimper of courage—the little he had. Grief destroyed the rest. "Shove the remainder of what you have to say where the sun don't shine." A loud, door bang followed.

"Wait!" Dauerman ordered.

He said something: a pounding phrase that ended with—another? A brother? No. He said something about his mother. About seeing her again.

Avery let the words dance in his head: Wouldn't you like to see your mother?

He heard Dauerman speak through the closed door. "You could be the first man launched from Spectrum's time machine. But ... that wouldn't interest you."

Avery froze where he stood; his head tumbling in a hangover of thoughts. He reeled, but with each step he took it called to him. Time travel.

He pushed the door open and just stood there in the corridor. "Mind repeating what you said?"

"Why don't you come in and we'll discuss it."

He faced Dauerman, closing the door behind him with a snap of the lock. Churning thoughts led him to where he was before.

"If you don't like what I'm about to say in the next few seconds, I'll let you walk."

Avery wouldn't move from where he stood.

"But first you'll have to sit."

Strangely, he complied.

"You're no lab mouse. Wasn't my intention to make you feel like one. And, this project isn't an experiment. Spectrum is man's opportunity to soar to heights never before achieved."

"What makes you think I want to take some crazy ass trip?"

"I knew your father. He told me you were fascinated with the bright, explosive plumes that shot space shuttles into orbit and that you dreamed of being an astronaut. Why else would you be here?"

A hidden strategy was in the works. Avery wasn't stupid.

"Man's final frontier is the cosmos. But DOD is about to do one better. All they need is a willing pioneer to lead the way."

"Don't sugarcoat it, just give it to me straight."

They faced each other like two opponents playing a deadly game of chess. The next move would be Dauerman's.

"Commander …." He took one last swig of coffee and pushed the mug aside. "You have a hunger for adventure despite its dangers. I know you do. Why else would you consider submarine duty? Arctic and Antarctic service?"

He mulled over another thought: Is it possible to travel back through time? He wanted to ask the question that burned through him like a bleeding ulcer but kept it to himself with the many other things he stored. "Who else told you about me?"

"Your admiral. Tom was good enough to disclose what I needed to know and that's the truth."

Now Avery's thoughts led him on a strange journey, where time, space, and the present melted into the past.

Dauerman brought him back. "Where were you, Commander?" His tone was familiar.

"A place you wouldn't understand."

"Is that where you wish to go?"

"I told you, I'm not taking any crazy—"

"So why waste my time?"

The loud silence stymied his thinking for a moment. He was beginning to hate twenty-first century technology. It made it difficult distinguishing fact from fiction.

"No need to be nervous," Dauerman assured. "Once you've completed the necessary training, going back through time should be no different than crossing the street."

An old emotion roiled in his chest and she appeared, looking at him with starlet eyes. "When can I see my mother? Hear her speak, touch her face, feel her hands?" The thought wouldn't leave him alone.

"You amuse me."

"I'm going to keep throwing questions till you stop ducking." Suddenly he realized with stunned madness what a fool he was for believing there could be such a thing as time travel. But that madness became greater with the next thought. "Where do you keep this bad-ass toy?"

Dauerman plugged the cigarette, pinned behind his ear, into the corner of his mouth and lit it with a Zippo. He took a deep drag and blew out a mist of gray. "At a training facility in Coronado."

He wanted to ask another question, but there was satisfaction in knowing he could be better than his father. Spectrum could outdo NASA. What could be more paramount? he mused. A trip to Mars, or a trip back through time? If there was a nobler quest than that, it would be that he could join the ranks of the world's greatest explorers. Immortal pioneers, such as Columbus, Wilkes, Lindbergh, Hillary, Byrd, Glenn, Armstrong. But being a hero is not what he wanted.

The agent took another drag and exhaled gray particles into the air. He got up, served himself a cold cup of water from the dispenser and gulped it down to the sound of air bubbles floating to the surface of the large, plastic container. "You've been in the Navy a long time. How about a promotion?" He walked around the front of his desk again, parked a hip on its squared edge and faced the serviceman. "I can have authorization forms sent to your admiral." He crushed the paper cup in his big fist and arched a shot over his shoulder, sinking it into a corner wastebasket. "Just say the word and you'll have new shoulderboards." He laid the lit cigarette in the ashtray.

Now Avery was aware once everything got underway, there would be no turning back. No squirming out. The project would demand one-hundred percent commitment. He could see it in the interviewer's face.

"I'm having you assigned to the office next to mine. It's yours till the program folds—or until you die. Whichever comes first."

The serviceman wasn't amused. He had come in with dark thoughts and would leave with darker ones.

"Just kidding." Dauerman smiled, unfolding tall to his feet. "Come. You'll like your new workspace."

Avery grabbed his jacket and wheel cap, and both men stepped out into the corridor. Navy personnel were heading out at the end of another long day.

The agent produced a silver-colored key from the side pocket of his suit, unlocked the deadbolt to the adjacent office and opened the door wide. The window's view of the base, with its mammoth ships in the harbor, was a Navy-lover's paradise. But not for Avery. He refused to enter the dark vacancy. "Room four-thirteen?"

"What's wrong, Commander?"

" … Superstitious."

"If I didn't know better, I'd say you were nyctophobic." Dauerman flicked on the lights and the serviceman stiffened. "Now what're you afraid of?"

"I wasn't counting on us being neighbors."

"You wound me, Commander." A grin stretched across that handsome face where every line on his features—the contour of his chin, his build, his temperament—said he was a determined NCIS cop, one who would soon bring down a brood of hackers hiding somewhere within the naval air station. "There's nothing to sweat over. I'll keep the music down." He locked the door with a slide of the deadbolt. "No one can break into these offices. These are high-security magnetic doors. Computer controlled. In the event of a fire, tripping the alarm will unlock them—setting off the waterworks." The look on his face gave Avery something else to think about. "This is classified work we're conducting, Commander."

He was unsure what the agent was referring to—NCIS work, or Spectrum—but sensed he was in for more than he bargained for.

"Tomorrow morning, report to the medical building so we can get the ball rolling."

Things were happening fast. Too fast for him to control. "Eight o'clock?"

"Good enough." Satisfaction put a smile on the agent's face. "Make it fasting. I'll also need to touch on some final details before you can begin."

"Okay." He kept it short, anxious to leave, not wanting to deal with Dauerman for the remainder of the evening. "Is that all?" Avery knew from now on he would never be through asking questions.

"Yeah. We're done. Shove off."

The 0-four officer turned on his heels and started down the hall.

"Hey, Avery!" Dauerman called.

He spun and one-handed a small, gold-colored object hurled at him. His military reflexes were still quick. He opened his right fist and was puzzled by what he saw.

The two men's eyes were locked in a tangle of looks. "How did you get this?" Avery displayed a nickel-size button like a rare coin.

"It came off, Commander."

He ran a hand over the fabric of his jacket and found the bald spot. He marched away to a waiting elevator, rode it down, and exited HQ with one thought on his mind: Mom. I'm going to see mom again.

Chapter 12

Throughout the naval air station, a steady August breeze stirred streams of limp pennants and flags to life. Avery had legged it from the medical building on McCain Boulevard to the pier. His physical went well. He ascended the carrier's gangway and, at the quarterdeck, manning the brow, saw Mike Ragazzi—a bulldog of a man with a thick neck and walrus mustache. When the petty officer of the watch wasn't at the Q-deck with a sharp eye on the flow of personnel leaving the giant vessel and returning, other duties kept the POOW busy.

Avery trudged up to the end of the brow and snapped a salute at the deck flag: Old Glory. "Permission to board," he said as a greeting.

The POOW was glad to see him. "Granted." He fired a salute, elbow cocked, fingers straight and rigid, eyebrow level.

"What's the word, Rags?" He returned the watch officer's salute.

"Calm seas, sir. Now that Pratt's off my six."

"Told you there'd be no more trouble."

The glint in Ragazzi's eye was the thanks for a favor bestowed on him. It was three months ago Ragazzi's wife, who piloted business charters, had been killed upon takeoff in a Learjet crash in Florida. But Pratt would not release the bereaved petty officer to attend the last minute, two-day, closed-casket wake at Heaven's Path Funeral Home in Tampa. "I need you here," he ordered. He tore the chit handed to him and that was that. Despite Ragazzi's pleadings, the captain remained austere, not willing to listen to his executive officer, command master chief, and two ship's chaplains who advocated for the distressed sailor. Pratt's message, resonating off the bulkhead of his at-sea cabin, was harsh. His authority was not to be questioned. That's when Avery decided to take matters into his own hands against the unjust captain, away from listening ears. He got Pratt to respond to a call over the 1MC to report to the third-deck fan room, and when he got there, the door flew open, and Avery pulled him in.

"Sir, if you ever need anything," Ragazzi said, "don't hesitate to ask. Your request will be considered a command."

Avery clapped Ragazzi on the back and went through the quarterdeck where his quick steps reverberated through the vast emptiness of the eighty-thousand-square-foot #2 hangar bay. There, officers were engaging in HTH—hand-to-hand fighting drills. The *straddle* was one of Avery's favorite defense moves, and he had learned it well. It involved one man—the instructor—lying on a mat face-up while an opponent-volunteer stood over him with a fake handgun. The instructor explained that although he was on his back, he had the advantage over the standing assailant, and he demonstrated it. He crooked a leg behind his opponent's, and using the other, knocked him flat with a swift kick to the gut. "Okay," the instructor said. "Let's practice that for a while and later we'll do headlocks and full nelsons."

To the steady hum in his ears, Avery stepped through a hatch, ready to go below. If the ship were cut away like a layered cake, he would see that above the huge hangar bay were decks 01, 02, and 03—where numerous shops and spaces abounded: stowage, squadron, catapult, staterooms, command ops. This was followed by the flight deck on which the eight-story-tall, control-tower island stood, rising up to deck 011. Below him was the second—or waterline deck—then the third, fourth, and fifth decks, going down even farther to A-level, followed by B-level, where the volcanic-noisy, machine-filled engine rooms, auxiliary space, and the nuclear reactors were housed in the ship's bowels.

Descending steep ladders with amazing ease, each step thudded from the soft heels of Navy issue shoes; his feet moving in swift succession over grated metal. The *Man Of War* was such a great ship. Back in the day, before the turn of the twenty-first century, officers on carriers bunked four to a compartment. Sometimes two. Those who had the privilege of their own staterooms were captains, XOs, and CAGs—commanders of airwing groups. However, now that the birdfarms were getting more spacey, some junior Os got dibs on their own quarters, depending on who they were and what they did. This didn't mean much to junior officers, though. They were segregated from senior officers the way men were separated from boys.

Avery marched through long familiar passageways, past the tailoring shop, to his segregated one-man in deck three. With service jacket in hand he got to work.

Someone rapped on the door of his cabin.

"Enter."

He always said enter, no matter who it was. In the ship's steel fortress, Avery felt safe.

A khaki opened the door.

"Hey, Bill." Avery worked a tip of thread through the eye of a needle.

"I know this is gonna sound dumb, but ... what're you doing?"

"Sewing on a button. Popped off." He showed it to him.

"Why don't you let tailoring do that?" Valentine said. "You've got more important matters to attend to."

"Such as?" He pushed the threaded needle and it bit through the buttonless spot on the jacket.

"Tex asked me to track you down. Wants you to skip HTH and meet him at the flag at once."

Avery guessed he looked tense by the manner in which Valentine looked at him when he said: "Something bothering you?"

"What kind of mood is he in?"

"Relax. Our pleasant admiral isn't pissed off ... yet."

"In that case ...." Avery placed the jacket on his rack with the sewing needle protruding through the fabric. "I'd better not keep the Old Man waiting."

"Don't. I'll take care of that," Valentine offered. He grabbed the service jacket, held the threaded needle between thumb and forefinger and looped several stitches through the button hole. "You shove off."

A rare smile lifted his face. "Aye, aye, doc." He slapped on a Navy ballcap, and down the passageway he went.

"You owe me one, mister!" Valentine hollered from the cabin. "And take care of that scuff!"

But the lieutenant commander paid no mind. He was more concerned over what John Thomas Fumo wanted.

Flag bridge: command center for carrier strike group operations. The domain of admirals. Avery wondered how many people had met here with Fumo in private and left muttering expletives. He stood at the opened hatch and knocked. The admiral's back faced him as he stared beyond the mighty ships of North Island. He was dressed in sharp khakis and wore a garrison cap strategically cocked to one side. Avery couldn't blame him for the image he wanted to uphold. He was a *Thor* among admirals with plenty of authority to dispense and had to show it. "Sir? You ... wanted to see me?" He held a salute and waited to be acknowledged. The Old Man still had the concentration of a young fox. But it always snapped like a brittle pencil.

Fumo faced the young officer with that familiar, aristocratic look. "Thanks for coming." He gave a nonchalant salute. "Was hoping we could talk earlier, but the OW informed me you'd be away for a while."

Avery entered the Plexiglas-encased compartment and shut the hatch. The admiral moved away from the varied instruments surrounding him: a GPS receiver, advanced radar screens flanked by an array of computer consoles, communication equipment, and gyrocompass. He passed a chart display and motioned to a pair of cushy command chairs. The only time Fumo wanted to sit was when he knew he would be longwinded.

Wonder what this is about? the lieutenant commander thought.

He sat facing the rear admiral; eyes in carefree contact.

"The reason I wanted us to meet in private is to congratulate you on your move to HQ. You're one of my finest officers. Wish you the best."

"That's it?"

"Were you expecting wings for jet jockeying?"

He and Dino should have gotten chewed out in admiral's mast for the brazen stunt they pulled: a chief engineer, coached by a hotshot pilot, landing a multi million-dollar aircraft on the midnight deck of an ocean-bouncing carrier. It was a damn good controlled crash. Beautifully executed, he had to admit. But Fumo was offering him a dismissal. Avery could leave now and not another word would be spoken on the matter. He refused it. "I'm expecting you'll be upset at my backing out." Now he realized he had gravely complicated things.

Those unruly eyebrows that crowned the ridge of the admiral's forehead dropped. "Care to explain?" He folded big arms over his chest. But Avery felt relieved. If Fumo yelled now, no one was there to witness it.

"What's to explain. I simply changed my mind."

"And pass up a promotion from O-four to O-six?"

"I'm being skipped to captain?"

"It's my understanding you were aware of the new paygrade. Why the surprise?"

He was more than just surprised. He felt bum-rushed.

"Neil, this is an opportunity for you to have a shore billet while serving your country. Time away from the *Seven* would do you good."

"It's not what I want … sir."

The admiral regarded him with steady eyes. "All forms have been authorized by me and copies sent to the board. I'm not good at undoing things."

Avery lifted his cover for a second and plowed into his scalp. His fingernails felt like dull knives. The fallen button from his service jacket troubled him still. "Will the Admiral permit me to ask a question?"

"Sound off."

"Out of thirty-thousand naval personnel on this base, why me?"

Fumo's countenance darkened like the earth's shadow swallowing the face of a sly moon in a lunar eclipse. "Wish I could dress this dilemma in a velvet tux, but I can't. The bare-ass truth is you weren't picked."

Avery lost the nerve to ask. A response would come, anyway.

"Neil, you're being pressured into this billet 'cause you were sold."

He let that roll in his head. It didn't sound good. People were sold at one time. Blacks, during the slave trade. Not now. Not navymen. "Sold?"

"Your position as Cheng." The admiral removed his garrison cap, peeled off his service jacket and draped it over the seat; a regalia of ribbons bedecked his uniform. "About a month ago the Navy decided to hire civilian contractors. They'll be filling the gap left behind by all senior engineers being let go. I'm sorry. Wish there were something I could do."

"Why didn't someone tell me I was being forced into retirement by a bunch of sandcrabs?"

"Because no one wanted to see you, of all people, get another bum break. You've had enough of those. DOD is extending a new job classification to the Navy. If you accept the offer you can keep your commission."

"And if I refuse?" Avery knew he had said the wrong thing.

He received a stern look from Fumo. "You'll be dismissed from the Navy. Permanently."

The young man bowed his head. Civilian life. He knew so little about it. "So this is how my career ends."

"Forget I'm a son-of-a-bitch. Take my advice and the opportunity. I wouldn't do favors for anyone, except you and ...."

Avery's gaze jumped into the admiral's falcon-round eyes—and he saw *her*, dressed in that tailor-made blue uniform that spoke of patriotism for her country. "She was the only one on the base with that strange power over you, sir."

"It happened the moment I laid eyes on her."

Avery hoped an old trick would cure him of the mortal sin he called guilt. He turned back the time on his watch, twelve full hours. If the admiral asked what he was doing, he had a ready answer. He would simply say he wanted to shorten his life so he could die.

"Darah had just entered the Academy with high hopes. She was a bright, young lady. A real go-getter." The years sparkled in Fumo's faraway look, like the silver stars he wore with pride on the collar of his perfectly creased shirt. "I was an O-seven, back then. Seems like yesterday she and I spoke." He seemed afflicted with the same chronic sadness the lieutenant commander had. "Strange how memories vivid with colors fade to gray with the passing years."

The young officer pushed down on the watch's crown. He did not get the desired effect he thought he would.

"An admiral shouldn't go around talking like this, but Darah was like a daughter to me. Dolly and I were fatally fond of her. Adopting her, so to speak."

Fumo had painted on an imaginary canvas a stunning portrait of the woman Darah was: an officer of the United States Navy. She never looked lovelier, a stoop-postured Avery thought, rubbing hands while listening.

"Of course, when you two met and things started getting serious, my heart left me. That's what fathers go through." He looked disappointed over something. "Darah politely declined dinner invitations with Doll and I after that. Except when she brought you over to the house. Seems she wanted you all to herself. If it wasn't for her, I never would've met you. Funny how things turn out." He mentioned one more thing about Darah excelling to the top of her class in plebe year, before his eyes fast-forwarded to the present. "She loved you. And I know you loved her."

Physical abuse isn't love, he thought with disdain. "I never did thank you for being a pallbearer at her funeral. You and Bill knew I couldn't. Too weak from sorrow to lift a casket."

"Why the belated sentiments?"

Avery sighed, keeping his answer locked within. When discreet eyes fell on a gold Quartz watch, he knew by the silence Fumo was nearing the end of his talk.

"Let me say this and I'm done. Fate is a complicated thing to understand. You never know where you'll end up once the journey starts."

"Sir, thanks for the talk." He felt a surge of resolution flow in his blood. "But something's been bugging me. How does NCIS know so much about my military record? My personal life?"

"There's a serial hacker among us. NCIS has been investigating everyone's military and personal life, including mine. Not everything that slithers is found beneath the ground." Fumo dug into his back pocket and produced a pair of black shoulderboards with four, gold-braided stripes. "This is a reminder of your new seniority. They used to be mine, bringing me a bit of luck along the way. Hope they'll bring you luck, too."

"But, sir, with all due respect—"

"Don't butt me, sailor. It upsets me seeing a man out of uniform." He handed him the shoulderboards. "Snap these on, and that's an order—Captain Avery."

He took them and grinned. Losing an argument with the Old Man was not as bad as he thought it would be.

Fumo said, "I've forgotten when it was I saw you sport that confident gleam."

"Thank you, sir." He admired the new boards and thought of how its stripes would look on him. He had taken a leap from junior-O to senior-O and was proud of it. "This could only mean one thing."

"What's that?" Fumo asked.

"I don't have to salute Commander Valentine anymore. Now he salutes me."

He drew a chuckle out of the tall Texan. "You'd salute the world if they paraded in front of you."

The men stood to their feet and shared a quiet laugh.

Avery let a rigid salute fly and turned sharply on his heels. He moved past a row of dark-eyed monitors and grabbed the steel hatch on his way out.

"Captain Avery...." The young navyman did an about-face in slow motion. The admiral said, "It's none of my business how you run your personal life, but I have something else for you." He donned that impressive-looking service jacket and approached, dipping into his pocket for the second time.

"You're full of surprises, sir." He wondered over the sudden change in the admiral's features.

"It's addressed to you." He handed Avery an unopened envelope. "Seems you haven't been replying, so she asked me to play Mr. Postman. It's the least I can do for someone who's close to me as Darah was."

Avery took the clean, white envelope. His name was written on it but nothing else. "Doesn't have a sender's name."

"Doesn't need to."

A long moment passed in which the urge to leave abandoned the newly-promoted captain.

"Don't you recognize the handwriting?" Fumo broke the quiet spell. "That anonymous letter is the other reason I called you in here."

Avery moved past the admiral and ripped at the envelope. A perfumed scent escaped, arresting him. He hopped on a command chair and unfolded the letter:

My Dearest Neil,
By now you must know of the bedroom confessions tucked away in my heart. How or ....

He stared at Fumo's profile, then dropped eyes onto the letter. The smooth paper and the feminine swirls of her flowery script were like a roadmap leading him through a delicate path laid out before him. He resumed reading:

How or why it blossomed I can't explain. I only know it happened and can no longer live with my secret. Now, regret for leaving NASNI is all I think about. I love you and want to be near you. My dreams of you no longer satisfy me, for what I want is ....

He tore himself from the letter and the image of yearning arms reaching for him. He would say nothing of what he was feeling to the admiral. Avery would leave it up to his imagination to discover what his silence was saying.

"Karyn's my granddaughter. Writes often about you."

Avery let the backing of the tall, padded-leather chair hold him up. The letter's sweet fragrance had left him in a drunken stupor, beckoning him to visions of her Cover-Girl face.

"I still recall your wife's funeral. Those sunken eyes of yours." The admiral turned toward him. "In all this time you haven't lost that look."

Karyn's voice whispered in his thoughts. He stuffed the letter back in the envelope and laid it facedown on the window ledge.

Fumo approached him like a sentry at the main gate. "If you don't mind me saying so, I believe love can live again. Karyn's a wonderful, young lady."

Avery waited for the punch line. He felt disoriented. What he heard the admiral say was he didn't want him to rest with a knife at himself. After a nanosecond, he realized what he had actually said was: You don't have to spend the rest of your life by yourself.

"Don't play cupid, I'm not lonely."

"Is that what you think I'm doing?"

"How can I begin anew when I'm still in love with the person whose name is chiseled in white marble?"

"I understand your reason for not staying in touch with Karyn. But you're not grieving now, are you?"

"No, thank God that's over with, but ...." A sigh caught his throat.

"But what?" Fumo asked. Avery knew Fumo was responsible for the mental and emotional well-being of each of his men, whether he knew them or not.

"I'm stubborn. I *want* to remain under dark clouds and old memories."

In the silence, the two men studied each other.

Avery groped for words and found them. "I don't expect you to understand this. But sometimes the past has a way of calling me. As though somehow, by some means, I had the power to change it. To be honest with you, sir, I'm not sure I'm ready for all this. A new assignment, promotion, Karyn."

"You're saying that 'cause you're afraid of what tomorrow may bring. But life's too short to count tears."

The young serviceman turned his face away from Fumo. Away from the truth.

"I felt your loss back then and I feel it now. As painful as it is to grieve, it's important to love. It's one of life's greatest mysteries. Don't allow hidden fears to put love and life on hold."

Finally, Avery faced him with listening ears.

"You weren't afraid of grieving in a time of death. Don't be afraid of loving in a time of hope. For love itself contains in it both common elements. Just as love demands grieving, grief demands loving."

A sea surged within Avery: the froth of white on sand, the rising slam against jagged rocks, the push and pull of an undertow. He stuffed Karyn's letter into his top pocket and locked eyes on Fumo. "When Darah died so did I. Living again never occurred to me."

He waited for the admiral to say something.

"Darah lives forever in your heart. You'll never lose her again as long as you keep her memory warm, and as you do, you'll hear her say it's okay to move on."

Avery decided it was time to accept Fumo's advice. There was no point in dragging any of this further. He would just have to take things as they came. Damn, things were happening fast.

"Karyn will be visiting North Island sometime next month to see me. She has an older sister in Santa Barbara she'll be spending time with. But between the two, I can't help thinking her real reason for coming is you."

Avery stood. "Fine." He and Fumo shook hands. "Just give me a chance to breathe." He stepped through the steel hatchway, waited a beat, then about-faced, saluting Fumo before heading down the island ladderwell.

Now there was more on his mind than hiding behind the pile of memories he had been using to overshadow his greatest regret: not expressing his love to Darah.

Chapter 13

It was stamped Rush Delivery: a legal-size, manila, padded mailer laying on an oak desk. Now there was nothing more for Avery to do except wait with a decorated wheel cap on his lap, knot in his stomach, disappointment in his posture. He was sold to Spectrum.

Dauerman took a sip of steamy coffee. He was dressed in denim Dockers, a gray NCIS sweatshirt, and black, Tae Kwon Do ballcap. "You're a member of the team now, Captain." He sliced open the big envelope with a paperknife in one hurried slash and extracted a dark, Pendaflex file folder. "Once I go over the results, your journey will begin."

Journey. Fumo mentioned something about a journey, too. "Is it the contents of the envelope you're after, or something more valuable?" Avery had never seen anyone's eyes dance over a medical chart. He was told Dr. Weinberg was specific about the maximum requirements for a test pilot. He would accept nothing less.

Dauerman opened the chart. "Your lungs are clear; no tumors or polyps in your intestines; heart and mediastinum within normal limits …." He turned a page. "The CT of your brain and major organs demonstrate no abnormalities. However …." He squinted as though reading small print. "Your blood profile shows borderline LDL and …."

The Navy captain sat up.

Dauerman pored over the page with consternation on his brow.

"What is it?" Avery expected an unusual silence would follow, and it came.

The agent searched through the page as though looking for an explanation. He flipped through the next page and the one after that. Avery sensed the answer had lay in front of him all along.

He seemed to have found something. "Damn, you're fit as a racehorse." He snapped the chart closed and grinned.

"There's something wrong with me, isn't there?"

The phone rang but Dauerman refused to answer it. "You don't qualify. Abnormal white blood cell count."

He told Avery another applicant would be called in and he would be out as a civilian. But he wondered where Spectrum would find another individual bereft of parents, stripped of siblings, robbed of spouse and left childless? There was no time to select a new candidate. The project's director wanted someone immediately, and where would that leave the man bent on staying in the military? Avery didn't see himself as a schoolteacher, a lawyer, a social worker. He saw himself in polished black oxfords, crease-pressed trousers, ribbon-bedecked jacket. He decided, as soon as the meeting was over, he would go into town and find a recruiting station. I'll join the Air Force, he thought.

"There is a way around the problem," Dauerman said with a tone of resolution.

Avery anticipated the answer before it came. He knew too much already. And that's exactly what the agent told him. Now he would have to volunteer for the ultimate project, whether he liked it or not, whether he was fit for it or not. But he was used to mandatory issues. He had a track record for such things: the bleak world of U.S. Station McMurdo in Antarctica; submarine maneuvers beneath the Arctic ice that China and Korea had secretly tracked for years; and now this. Time travel.

Dauerman opened a desk drawer wide, threw the Pendaflex file folder in it and closed it fast. He said DOD could still come out on top if their little secret was kept. He opened another drawer to a full stop, reached in for whatever he knew was there and threw a pair of weighty objects on the desktop.

Avery hated the idea his life was expendable. Even replaceable if something should happen to him. "What're those?"

"Keys, my Captain. Keys to the kingdom."

He tossed one of the objects at the serviceman where it landed cradled in his hands.

"Heavy."

"Made of lead."

He examined the grooveless, twelve-inch long, three-inch wide, rectangular-shaped key, turning it over like a weapon. Dark magnetic strips on its sides were the only visible features. A key this size and shape was a sure sign of stranger things to come.

"You'll be needing that in your travels. It'll give you easy access to the labs—ours and theirs." He banged the drawer shut.

"Labs? What labs? And what kind of doors uses keys like these?"

"Wondered when you'd ask." Dauerman shot tall to his feet and marched to the door. "Follow me." He opened it wide.

Avery sheathed the big lead key in his back pocket and both men left the office and entered an elevator a moment later. The weight of the object felt like a machete handle jammed against his butt.

"This is the only cab you're to use."

"Use for what?"

Dauerman answered by pressing the floor buttons on the side panel in rapid succession. "Four, one, three, two, four, one." The sliding door shut. "Memorize that sequence," he instructed.

The elevator dropped, sloshing nausea in the pit of the captain's stomach as the red numbers on the digital overhead raced across the display like a countdown .... 4 ... 3 ... 2 ... 1 ....

Avery grunted in astonishment as the elevator shot past the main floor like the cable had snapped. It descended deep, silent and long, into what seemed to be the belly of the earth—a forbidden abyss.

When the strange ride ended, Dauerman produced a ring of keys from his side pocket, slid one into the fireman's control panel and turned it. Nothing moved. Except for the two men's airways exchanging carbon dioxide for stale air, dead silence ruled.

The forced elevator stay was longer than Avery desired. Then the silver-glazed backing he leaned against opened without warning and a sudden blast of cold rushed at him.

"What's this dark crypt you've brought me to?"

He waited for Dauerman to say something, anything. Instead, he slapped the control keys in the palm of the serviceman's hand and without a word, stepped past him out of the elevator. A moment later he was gone. Swallowed by the dark.

Avery froze, wondering how the NCIS investigator could possibly see without lights. Despite that, the agent kept going. One echoing step at a time.

After the long walk to nowhere, the crushing silence returned. Avery stuck his head out of the elevator like a frightened turtle peeking from its protective shell. "Dauerman!" *man, man, man ....*

The cavernous echo ricocheted until an evil quiet murdered it.

With the intensity of the lifeless abyss growing stronger, his ability to think was almost stifled. Avery didn't need his thinking prowess to repeatedly thumb the close-door button. But when it wouldn't respond to his jabs he jerked on the cold metal doors until his hands hurt.

"Step out of the elevator!" *vator, vator, vator ....*

He fought with Dauerman's command to break away from the fear that held him in the cab's stainless-steel frame. He had been in worse scenarios, so after a reluctant moment, he proceeded into a long, rectangular wedge of light cast onto a sandy-gray floor. Intergalactic space was just as black as this, and it would get blacker with each step he took as he moved farther away from the only existing light source—that of the lit elevator car behind him.

A vibrating slam, followed by a swoosh of cold air, paralyzed him with a hair-raising rush. Now that the elevator door was shut, his shadow and the wedge of light it was encased in was gone. "Dauerman!" *man, man, man ....* His voice returned to him more distressed than when it left, causing his heart to kick against his ribs. "Where am I?" *am I, am I, am I ....* He fought the reverberating blows of his echo like a gladiator blocking whizzing arrows with a shield. "What's this hell you've brought me to?" *to, to, to ....* Again his cries died out, producing something he dreaded—defiant silence.

Imagined or not, a light winked on and off. Whether it came from someplace near, or somewhere in the abyssmal distance he couldn't determine. Blackness had eaten away his 20/20 vision, making him blind. "What's this godforsaken place?" *lace, lace, lace ....*

Suddenly a thin shaft of light came on, revealing a man standing afar in its measly beam.

"Walk toward me, Captain." *ten, ten, ten ....* The shout was followed by reverberating laughter.

"I'm sick and tired of your gags." *ags, ags, ags ....* "When will you stop?" *op, op, op ....*

"Don't be alarmed." *armed, armed, armed ....* "All good students are tested." *ested, ested, ested ....* The abyss magnified his voice. "Walk this way." *ay, ay, ay ....*

Avery stalked the glowing milky trace, so faraway, echoing footsteps guiding him forward. The floor he walked on was smooth and flat. He didn't have to worry about tripping over anything, but he was cautious and therefore stopped. From everywhere, tungsten lamps flickered around him—2,000 kilowatt strong. Eyes narrowed to welded slits, his face shrunk tight, and his arms flew up, battling a steady rhythm of pulsating lamps that came to an intense crescendo of burning lights. He kept turning away to find darkness, but no matter which direction he chose, someone kept sticking him in the eyes with a phantom pencil. The whiteout blindness took a while to adjust to, and when he was able to see, he looked about and was acutely dumbfounded. There, centered beneath a towering domed ceiling, he marveled through welded eye slits at the splendor that surrounded him; the architectural grandeur that loomed above him, in front of him, behind him.

Dauerman's heavy steps echoed closer to where the senior officer stood and the two were face to face. "Magnificent, isn't it?"

Avery craned his neck as far up as it would go. "How does one get up there to put in new lights?" He was out of breath from his baptism of darkness and knew Dauerman would make fun of that. He let out a clipped laugh and the Navy captain looked him in the eye. "Where the hell am I?"

"This is the world of Spectrum. An elaborate maze of tunnels, caves, and laboratories."

"Down here, beneath HQ?" Avery did a slow, about-face. He took a moment to study the crypt's gothic theme, limestone floor and marbled walls, hoping it would clear his head from a stream of thoughts that disoriented him. "I've never seen anything like this."

"No one has, except for DOD and its small community of scientists and technicians."

He was as plankton in an ocean universe. "This must've taken decades to build." He gave Dauerman a look. "How big is this place?"

"Bigger than your imagination. Follow me."

Avery didn't like the forced camaraderie, but he walked alongside Hank Dauerman, anyway; away from the enormous tomblike dome. They approached a pair of steep, darkened tunnels and stopped. Dauerman hit a side panel and a pale-green light came on. He motioned for the senior officer to take a look.

"Where's it lead?"

"Snakes another four stories down." He pointed to the other one. "Located at the end of that tunnel is a fallout shelter, capable of comfortably housing and sustaining five-hundred people at one time for an entire year." Dauerman's face darkened. "One can never tell when the great bomb will fall."

The two men came to the opening of the main corridor: a wide, lifeless, arched passage filled with demon-faced stone gargoyles and empty, black silence. "This is where I turned on the lights." The agent hit another square panel with his palm and a dim florescent bulb came on farther down the endless-looking tunnel. "The power circuits can also be controlled from my computer and Dr. Weinberg's computer."

"How long is this trip gonna take?"

"Relax, we just got here."

Both men left the dizzying heights of the domed area behind them and ventured through the long, morgue-like passageway.

After a long march, the wide tunnel narrowed down to a small, cave-like path. Avery's gut told him it would lead them deeper into the underground world. He followed Dauerman's unhesitating steps, shifting his weight for balance as they descended. "You're like a mole in its hole."

"The Defense Department has allowed me to have a copy of their blueprints."

Now at the bottom of a subterranean hill, a light from somewhere split the darkness in half. Avery turned both ways. He looked at Dauerman. "Dead end?"

Before them stood a concrete wall.

"On the contrary." He pointed to a dim shaft. "Your journey has just begun."

Stumbling behind the agent, Avery's guide was the sound of plodding footsteps several yards ahead.

Something fluttered over his ear and clung to his right lobe with its spindly legs. It felt like a cockroach and stung like a bee. He swiped it off with a yelp and gulped deep breaths to control his heartbeat. How he once enjoyed Jules Verne movies. Especially the one about the university professor and his colleagues, lost below the center of the earth. Such tales filled his head with exotic dreams—an explorer traveling through uncharted caves filled with rows of hanging stalactites that reminded him of T-Rex teeth. Now what filled him was a dreadful fear of dying where he stood. What he wanted was to get the hell out of there. Someplace where his secret phobia wouldn't manifest itself in ragged gasps and nervous shouts.

Deeper into the oppressive unknown they went, Dauerman leading the way with a laugh. Despite the fear factor that made Avery want to turn and run, he commanded his legs to move forward. Up ahead, a bright light came on and frightened the blackness, chasing it in every direction.

"Who did that?"

"Motion detectors."

They pushed onward, leaving behind the welcoming presence of lights that turned off in the empty distance.

"How far down are we?" He could only guess where the barely lit, narrow tunnel they were in would lead them.

"Fourteen stories. But there're other tunnels that go down farther." He told the serviceman he had to find a way to ease him into this. Not many people liked the idea of being cooped up in an underground rats maze. It was just human nature.

Onward they ventured and the passage widened, leading to a winding, castle-like stairwell going only one way—down.

Around them, shadowy figures moving beneath their feet like escaped convicts, added to the mystery of the seemingly endless journey.

At the bottom of the stairway, a foreboding tunnel split into a fork of shafts. Perspiration had wept through Avery's armpits, stinging him. It soaked through his Navy-issue shirt and dress-blue service jacket. He unbuttoned it and loosened his tie. "Now what?" In the ominous gleam, something scampered across the concrete floor. "What was that?"

"Just a resident." The gloomy corridor mimicked Dauerman's voice.

"What else you got down here?"

"Located through the right shaft is the workout room. Through the left, the genetics lab, with marble-top tables, glassware, centrifuges, incubators. And straight ahead—"

"Wait, let me guess. San Francisco?"

He drew a chuckle out of Dauerman and followed him, deeper into the alien silence. A stench of oil from somewhere sickened Avery. It was too late to turn back now.

At the end of the rock-pitted tunnel they entered what looked like the jaws of a monstrous beast. They walked between its teeth: stalactites and stalagmites that threatened to bite down on them. A few yards ahead was a real dead end. A flat rock wall.

"We're here."

As far as the serviceman was concerned he had reached the earth's core. "This is what you dragged me into this godforsaken place to see? An unexcavated cave?"

"No. What's behind it." With a thrust of the long magnetic key he penetrated a slit in the rock wall barely visible in the florescent gleam of minerals, and like an elevator door, the bedrock barrier spread apart on rails with a rumble. He activated a main switch and the darkness was chased away by a crescendo of halogen lamps that revealed a hidden laboratory and goliath glassy machines, backlit by yellow spotlights that made them appear to glow supernaturally.

An antiseptic hospital smell smothered the captain, and for a brief moment he lost the ability to breathe. "What the hell are those?"

"The cellular time units. Beautiful, aren't they?"

Two vertical cylinders—marked positron and negatron—were embraced by long titanium arms and stood at opposite ends of the loft-size lab on chrome platforms guarded by twin, bulbous, white tanks releasing wisps of gaseous vapor. A curved row of computer monitors the agent called the control station dominated the center of the floor, and behind it as they moved deeper into the lab, a variety of high-tech instruments and other unrecognizable equipment lay before Avery. He inspected a complex system of turbogenerators similar to those on the *Seven*. Augmented electrical power meant the lab was designed to be a very busy place.

He walked beneath crisscrossing steel pipes that towered over him in the high ceiling. The reactor plant aboard the *Seven* pumped superheated steam through a series of such arterial pipes which powered the ship, fed its turbines, and drove the shafts. But there was always the danger of pressurized steam leaking.

Each belch of gaseous vapor from the bulbous tanks behind the cylinders made his exposed skin feel colder. Not many things disquieted him, except a talkative agent and a strange laboratory.

"Those pump a measured amount of chilled nitrogen gas through the cylinder's vents. Helps offset most of the unbearable heat."

"What creates the heat?" He had a gut feeling he knew the answer.

"Nuclear energy."

Avery decided he would study the monstrous machines from a safe distance. But when he stared at them too long without blinking, something seized him and he approached one of them. What the hell am I fascinated about? he thought.

He looked Dauerman in the face. He seemed to be enjoying something.

"Don't mind me. I'll just stand back and let you two get acquainted."

Now he stood close enough to touch the strange contrivance that loomed tall over him. He had never felt repelled from anything one moment and drawn to it the next, except this.

"Would you like to step in and get the feel of it?" Dauerman invited.

He said no without so much as a thought.

Suddenly, he thirsted for instant knowledge and stepped up to the high ramp on which the mighty negatron stood clamped to an O-ring. Again the unit's gadgetry pulled at him. He fought to be released from its hold, but found himself peering through the glassy structure rising from its post. At the base of a power converter that capped the cylinder, a protruding, cone-like device—similar to a dentist's chair-side X-ray machine—pointed to the shoe-shaped fiberglass imprints that marked the spot on an electromagnetic plate where a traveler would stand. Dauerman talked too much as far as he was concerned.

The next introduction Dauerman made was to the ten-ton VSC 9800—an atomic Vector Supercomputer. Its sole responsibilities were to regulate the CTU's time sequencing, quantum pulse, and activation of the particle accelerator while its muscular-circuited counterpart, the Van Allen Troubleshooter, could solve and analyze scientific and engineering problems.

Lastly, he explained the digital piece of hardware that hung above the Vector like an omen: the instrument warning panel. "Now that you've seen everything, aren't you anxious to start?"

He was anxious, all right; anxious to run back the way he came; ready to battle rats, bugs, and whatever else awaited him; hoping to awake in his quarters and find this was just a bad dream. It was all too real, though. He imagined a horrible scenario and blinked, dislodging the thought he knew would later come back to haunt him. "Who else will be training to be a toilet astronaut?"

"You're the only guinea pig," he said with a look that insisted Avery was inferior. "Let me show you your quarters."

The two men walked past the long arch of the computer-cluttered control station where Dauerman motioned to a steel door, hidden behind the positron cylinder.

"What's in there, a dungeon?"

"Captain Avery, you do have a sense of humor after all." He opened the big heavy-looking door, revealing a spacious sleeping compartment with rooms. "I'm certain you'll find our accommodations much cozier than the crawlspace you have aboard that birdfarm you're assigned to."

"Wait a minute. I'm gonna be sequestered in this godforsaken place?" He scanned the luxury suite: there was living room furniture, a flat-screen television, walk-in closet, dresser and mirror. He would have to sublet his apartment in Mariners Cove.

"Don't worry. We'll let the dog out for a walk."

"Should've told me I'd be wearing a leash." He checked out the master bedroom, testing the king-size bed with a few sitting bounces. He laid flat on it and found it comfortable. Now his steady eyes were fixed above him.

"You'll never lose your way around here if you study that. I guarantee it."

Avery couldn't care less about the color-coded map of the entire underground facility that stretched across the ceiling like a painting in the Sistine Chapel. It detailed the honeycombed world he found himself in. From the elevator to the transport chamber.

He sprang to a sit, pensively recalling a weekend he had stayed in a fancy, five-star resort hotel after he graduated naval academy. He wanted a place where he could have 48-hours of R&R, swimming, gambling, and a few drinks. And this place reminded him of that time. Dauerman called it the commodore's suite. But there would be nothing sweet about being locked up fifteen stories below street level.

The agent stepped over to a mini-refrigerator and opened it like a game-show host. It was stocked. "Like what you see?"

In the underground world of Spectrum, Avery was aware he would have everything he needed, except at night when he was alone. "I'll like it better when the program's over."

Dauerman closed the refrigerator. "Spectrum is a lifetime contract. I took the liberty of forging your name on a new PRF. You're in this thing for the long haul, sailor. Till death do us part."

Avery jumped to his feet like he was about to attack the agent, and the agent reached inside the back pocket of his denim Dockers like he was going to pull out a knife. "Got a complementary gift for you." He pulled it out and handed it to him. "Since you're our first candidate, I found it in order to present you this presidential fountain pen." They moved from the luxury suite to the NASA-like control room. Being a time traveler would demand a busy schedule.

The classy, gold-capped pen was engraved in old-English lettering. It had someone's initials: *NSP*. "It's definitely not a BIC." He gave it another look. Gratuity was usually given after a service was rendered. "Why the favor?"

Dauerman told him Spectrum's community of scientists would be indebted to him for his upcoming journey. A simple sign of humble appreciation could help a man like him go a long way.

They clasped hands in a firm handshake. The man had said journey, as in singular. Avery hoped that meant the program wouldn't last long.

"Sure this isn't another one of your gags?"

"You wound me, my Captain. This is on the up-and-up. Try it. Here's a scrap paper."

Blue ink flowed smooth and even as he spelled out the letters of his last name with big, sweeping loops. "Nice." He gave the pen yet another look.

"And you were afraid it would explode."

Avery wasn't worried about the pen. He was concerned over other things, such as wanting to know and not wanting to ask. He asked, anyway. "So, what does NSP stand for? No safety promised?" He stuck the expensive pen in his shirt pocket.

"National Security Personnel. A title that'll one day be worn on the uniforms of future time travelers. What else you want to know?"

There was one more thing. "When do I … start?" He scratched the earlobe where the bug had bitten him. It felt fat and warm.

"Tomorrow at one. That'll give you more than enough time to gather all your personal crap."

Both men marched through the laboratory on their way out. The tumor-like knot that held Avery's gut in its malignant grip began to let go as they walked between the cave's stalagmite teeth.

"Hope you're not prone to homesickness, Captain. It can get lonely down here."

Chapter 14

"Enter," Avery said with little enthusiasm. He was almost done packing his belongings when someone rapped on the door of his compartment.

"*Buena suerte, mi amigo.*"

His back faced the man who spoke. He had heard the phrase enough times to understand its meaning. Good luck, my friend.

"Don't let your departure change anything between us. I knew the moment we met, we were going to be best friends."

Avery grabbed two chocker whites, two dress blues, four khaki uniforms, and two civvy suits from a measly-size storage locker and zipped them in a Wally bag. "Hope it stays that way." He moved to the bunk, lifted open the coffin locker beneath the rack and bagged more stuff. Then he saw it. Staring at him as though it had eyes. It was time to get rid of it. He dug trimmed nails between the gray duct tape and steel bulkhead, ripping the newspaper article away from where it clung for over two years. He began reading the memorized story when he clamped his hand tight into a fist. "No more." He pitched the balled strip of paper into a wastebasket, but that did nothing to discard the memory of verbal assaults and blows he inflicted on Darah. His cruelty returned to visit and that made him glad. Sort of. If I could do it over, he thought, it would be different.

He looked over a small shelf that held his Academy books: Calculus, Engineering, Physics, Chemistry, Nuclear Science .... He bagged them, including all the smooth stones he had scooped up in a fit from the sugar-soft sands of Maui.

Pictures of Roy, Beulah, their daughters, and little Olympia, in an arm cast, no longer decorated the bulkhead over his desk. All his classical CDs were zipped up and ready to go, too. What remained were the years he had spent aboard the *USS Man Of War*. The good times. The bad. He hoisted the army-green duffel onto his bunk, fighting against the strange emptiness surrounding him. "I'll ... miss this place."

"This place will miss you."

He looked at the petty officer's wind-sculpted face, rugged mouth, and pronounced brow. Their fraternal bond was like an Olympic torch. A light of victory. One he couldn't afford to lose. He couldn't just allow their brotherhood to be extinguished by a possible war he read about in the morning paper. Servicemen in harms way needed support and encouragement from comrades back home. He would keep in touch with the chief quartermaster until all was well abroad. But for now his friendship with Carlos Nieve was as the *Seven*. Sooner or later the mighty ship would be deployed across the Pacific with every able man aboard, leaving their friends and loved ones behind. "When you get back, I'll be waiting with my own Harley so we can ride together. That's a promise."

"I ride rough country. Montana, Utah, Arizona. Think you can hack it?"

"Anything you can do, I can do better." He put on a thin smile despite the sinking weight in his gut, and stepped through the doorway. He stayed there for a moment, then turned about for one final look at his quarters. Every single detail of the windowless compartment—the TV, the tiny closet, a long sleeping rack, the mirror over the stainless-steel sink—was suddenly different. CVNX-7 had been his mainstay for nine years and now it was coming to an end. He had once given thought to the possibility that one day he could be the commander of a mighty vessel; one that patrolled the seven seas. That desire wasn't strong enough, though. It was just as well. He had lost command qualification on the night the *Bird Of Prey*, Dino helped him pilot, snagged the arresting cable on the *Seven's* carrier deck. Dino gave him an OK grade for the trap, but Jarvis and Pratt gave him a sharp warning: no more bull crap; no more playing the maverick. Thinking back on that, his true desire was for something simpler; more important. Something he once had but threw away. "Now comes the toughest part about leaving. I'm thankful I don't have to recite my sentiments to everyone."

"You mean Pratt isn't on your farewell list?"

Just hearing the name irked him. "Would he be on yours?"

Nieve sat by Avery's stuffed duffel bag. The overhead lights revealed the thinness of his receding, black hairline. "Heard what happened in the fan room. How you threatened to break his legs in his sleep if he didn't behave."

Avery didn't want to be reminded of the incident. "I did it for Rags." He gave a melancholy shrug, letting the glumness take over. "So he could touch his wife's casket and ... say goodbye."

He wished he had gotten the opportunity to say goodbye, too.

"Caliber…. Beneath that tough exterior you're more sentimental than I thought."

For him, being sentimental came at a high price. More than he was willing to pay. He was glad he would never have another confrontation with the ship's captain. "What's eating the skipper? He wasn't this way when we met." He was convinced something bitter had happened to make the man callous.

"He's an old, army boot. Hard and unforgiving. I'm not the only one who wants to see him go. No one onboard likes him."

"Won't envy you when this birdfarm sails."

"She sails without him on the next deployment," Nieve said with emphasis.

"Who told you that?"

"Word of mouth. Directly from Valentine who heard it from Tex."

"But he's getting ready to slap on new boards after one more tour of duty."

"Seems the admiral rewrote the script."

"How come?"

"Beats the crap out of me."

The news put Avery in a silent spell, but only for a moment. There was no time to think of procedures and regulations. Sometimes the Navy's decision makers did things with no rhyme or reason. "Time for my *arrivederci* rounds." He grabbed a *Man Of War* ballcap from the filing cabinet near the doorway and put it on. "I'll start with Slim." He was usually in the main electronics shop this time of day, he thought.

Nieve said, "He's been spending a lot of free time locked away. Alone with computers. You don't suppose—?"

"Snowman. Shut up."

Avery navigated through the ship's passageways with one grinding thought: If Slim isn't careful, one day he'll get in trouble.

Pratt poked his head out of the stateroom. Two Marine sentinels were in the busy passage. When the way cleared he motioned for Seaman Brian Mayo to step out.

Everyday Pratt's stateroom was guarded by a pair of MPs: each in eagle-globe-anchor fatigue caps and camouflaged utility uniforms; each armed with a weapon. Wherever the captain went—the pilothouse where he took the conn, the officers' mess where he ate, the head where he pissed—two Marine corporals tailed him like twin shadows beneath his feet. Only one man onboard knew the varied launch codes for the arsenal of SAM, TLAM, and Exocet missiles. It wasn't the XO, the weapons officer, or the head of CIC. Only one man could give the order to protect the *Seven*. To bring honor or infamy. That was Pratt's job.

As soon as Brian Mayo disappeared down a ladderwell, Pratt turned to the two Marines. They were like loyal dogs he once had. They would listen and obey. "Someone from electronics will be bringing a new computer at fourteen-hundred. Knock!"

"Aye, sir," they responded in unison.

Avery took a shortcut through an undogged hatch that led to a number of stowage spaces, and proceeded to the main electronics shop, scouting for Seaman Jordan along the way. The third deck was deserted. But there was no reason for it to be that way. The *Seven* was scheduled for battle-readiness exercises and antisubmarine-warfare practice with its task group in another six hours and all hands would need to get ready. He entered a quiet compartment of lifeless computers and comatose monitors on metal shelves. It, too, was deserted. Where was everyone? It wasn't possible for all hands to have gotten libs on what would be a busy day.

He tried to get Jordan on his butt-phone. "Slim, what's your twenty?" No answer. He tried Brian Mayo and got the same response. Carlos Nieve wasn't answering, either.

He went for a phone on the bulkhead to get someone to relay a message over the 1MC. He contacted the pilothouse, the quarterdeck, damage control, and the engine room. The ship was a ghost town. He heard a noise and turned to look. It was Captain Frank Jarvis. He disconnected a laptop from a service module and slipped it in a briefcase. The laptop was probably his, Avery reasoned. He was simply checking to see if it worked, or perhaps he was stealing it. Dino had a right to dislike and distrust the man in aviator sunglasses, and had taken to calling the Air Boss a double-SOB. Boss spelled backwards. Jarvis snapped the leather briefcase shut and marched past Avery on his way out. He looked to be in some kind of nervous hurry.

Someone in boon dockers came in as soon as the Air Boss left.

"Looking for me, sir?"

It was Brian Mayo. On his shoulder he carried a computer. "One of Jordan's toys?"

"Skipper's unit. Died on him. I'll test it when I get back."

"Where're you going? And where's the ship's crew?"

"Can't say, sir. Under orders."

"Mayo, if you don't tell me what's going on, so help me—"

"Sorry, sir. Won't get it out of me."

The seaman placed the console on a worktable and hustled out of the shop. But the words he left behind stirred the air. Skipper's unit. Died on him.

No computers had malfunctioned since Black Sunday. They were reprogrammed and good to go. The tech reps who had been retrained by Dauerman had made sure of that. "Unless …." Avery had a malignant thought. He looked past every piece of hardware, on every shelf, in every corner, and found what he was searching for. It had Pratt's name on it. He unclamped a holding bar, tore away the repair order, slid the unit off the shelf and hauled it onto his shoulder.

One of Pratt's MPs rapped on the fine-grain wood with the bottom of his fist. The captain yanked the stateroom door open from within and frowned on him.

"Sir, your computer's here."

"So early?" There was a sudden pause of silence. The man in the passageway with a console box on his shoulder—face hidden from view—would have to wait until the skipper gave the OK. "You're blocking my doorway. Get in."

The man pushed past the captain and the door closed behind him. He hunkered down with back turned, laid the console box at his feet, then connected the monitor, speakers, keyboard and printer to their ports. When he plugged in the power cord, he slid the unit on its track, secured it with tie-down straps, thumbed the start button and waited for it to power up.

Nothing happened.

"I should have you arrested for sneaking in here." Pratt regarded the man in sharp khakis the way a junkyard dog would an intruder.

Avery rose tall and faced him. "MPs are out front. Be my guest."

The skipper seemed distracted by a thought, his eyes in pensive motion like the ship's reduction gears. "Tell you what. Just leave and I'll dismiss the whole thing." It was unlike him to be in a forgiving mood.

On his desk, wordy printouts carried bold-type logos of the FBI, CIA, ATF, and DEA. "What are those?"

"What are those, *sir*," Pratt corrected him.

"… Sir," Avery gritted. How he hated that word.

Pratt cleared his desk, stacked the printouts into one pile, and stashed them in a briefcase. He sat facing away. "Black Sunday bit the Navy in the ass. Only a fool would deny our Project Black Files are in the hands of a foreign military power, anxious to implement the designs contained in them. But there's one thing we still have we mustn't give them … time. Time for them to build. To test. What the hacker stole might still be retrieved, sparing our nation from grave danger. But since NCIS are moving at a turtles' pace, we owe it to ourselves to conduct our own investigation." He spun toward Avery. "Wouldn't you agree?"

"That story's as crazy as you."

"Shut your mouth!"

They eyeballed each other, dueling in silence for a moment.

"Who appointed you over NCIS?" Avery attacked.

"Don't you want to know the *truth*?"

The young serviceman crossed arms over his chest defensively, giving the skipper a look of ill regard. There could only be one truth. "It's already been established that persons on this base have a hand in this."

"I say it's the admiral and his staff. And they're using Jarvis as a busboy."

Avery had not yet formed a suspect in his mind, and running into the quiet-loudmouth Air Boss carrying a fat briefcase wasn't a sign of foul play. Or was it? He sharpened eyes on Pratt, wanting to curse him out. "Let me tell you—"

"No, let me tell *you* someone's done the clever snooping for me. Corrupt officials in this country are gearing to overthrow our government by upsetting the delicate balance of power from within. But they can't do it without the arm of the military. They need people in uniform. Top brass from every branch of service willing to sell their souls to see the birth of Americanism—a Communist USA. That's how Hitler did it with fascism."

Pratt had often gotten political after downing several cups of tar-black joe. But never this bad, Avery thought. "So you think Black Sunday was an outside job, huh?"

"It's a theory no one's bought yet, but yes. With a little inside help."

The twist in the story twisted Avery's gut. He knew there was more by the look on Pratt's face.

"JAG has launched a separate investigation and opened Fumo's e-mails. He's been playing encrypted ping-pong with Admiral Craig Jenson of the Pentagon. Messages shared between the two were filled with classified info. Why the CIA haven't arrested them isn't a mystery. They've made us think it's against their charter to do so, but I know better. The CIA is involved as well. When I prove that, I'll contact the FBI."

"Tex and Jarvis are too dedicated for this kind of crap. They've got pensions coming that'll fill Fort Knox."

"Knox is peanuts compared to the Black-Sunday payoff."

Avery became stone silent. As much as he wanted to play an ill game of dodge ball with Pratt, he didn't doubt someone had an accusatory eye on someone else on every ship. But what good was that? It was better to let things come to a boil, for in the end, the crime would be solved and the hackers arrested. The question in his troubled mind was—when?

The oval flat screen stared at both men like a big, dark eye.

Pratt looked ready to talk about other issues.

"It's come to my attention you're jumping ship."

Avery didn't like the way he phrased it. "Abandonment is a dishonorable term. I prefer to call it a smart career move."

"People decamp when they're in skunk trouble. I know you stole that Glock. Who were you planning to kill? Me?"

Something roiled within Avery. It felt hot and rose like a mighty geyser. "I wouldn't waste a bullet on you."

Pratt launched himself from his chair into the naval officer's face. "Abandonment, transfer—call it what the hell you like." The confrontation brought into view a résumé of features that added to Pratt's demeanor: a barely-visible, pink surgical scar above his lip; sprigs of hair that peeked from dark nostrils; clawing crow's feet at the corners of murky eyes. "This is the second time you've gone over my head and now it's an undeserved promotion. Don't think for a moment I've forgotten our friendly chat in the fan room. I let you and Rags win that match, but the games aren't over. I'm still in command."

The skipper returned to the dark monitor. Tapping the keyboard didn't help one bit. He snapped a stare at Avery. "Want to know the truth? The admiral's favors are an attempt to cover up something big."

"The only favor Fumo did is get me off this ship." He pulled the stateroom door open and blew past the camouflage-dressed MPs.

He pounded through the look-a-like corridors. At Valentine's quarters he rapped on the door but got no answer.

Someone said, "He's below, on trim evolution."

The haircut joke did not go off well. The newly-promoted captain swiveled into a flawlessly executed about-face. He squared his shoulders at attention. His eyes and the admiral's met.

"Stand easy."

But a twitching facial muscle couldn't stand easy, and he wondered when the admiral would notice.

"Bill told me he wanted to look his best before deployment," Fumo volunteered. "Frankly, I think he's got himself a girlfriend he's trying to … something wrong, Captain?"

"Yes, sir."

"Sound off."

"Sir, I think you'd better keep an eye on Jake."

"What's wrong with Captain Pratt I don't already know?"

"I think he attempted entering a network security site."

"You'd better be certain."

"Sir, his system is non-operative. That could only mean the new intrusion detector activated a shutdown."

"Follow my six," the admiral commanded.

Fumo ordered the Marine MPs to step aside. A sharp knock on Pratt's stateroom was followed by an enter reply from within.

The admiral pushed the dark, fine-grained wood door wide open and looked in.

At the blackened computer screen the skipper sat at his desk, advancement forms in hand representing sailors up for promotion. He fisted each one with a big, red rubber stamp—rejection.

"Your system down, Jake?"

He touched the keyboard, the screensaver gave way, and the monitor came to life. "The power switch on the old one was out of whack, sir." He removed black eyeglasses from his face, packed all the advancement forms together and pushed them aside. "This one's running fine."

Tom Fumo and Neil Avery eyeballed each other.

"Sir, I came from the shop—"

"Let me handle this," Fumo said.

"Did Captain Avery take the Admiral away from his duties?"

"Not at all, Jake. Just making sure everything's shipshape."

"Sir, get Seaman Jordan and Mayo here," Avery advised Fumo. "They'll sing."

"Jordan …." The admiral aimed a junkyard-dog look at the seaman. "Was there a problem with Captain Pratt's computer?"

"I sent Mayo to look at it."

"Well, Mayo…?"

Avery looked on in silence. A facial muscle still twitched from anger.

"Sir, it's the motherboard. The unit shuts off at will."

The interrogation made the young seamen look tense.

Fumo rubbed his big chin in thought. Pratt looked calm. Jordan and Mayo's dark eyes rocked.

"Anyone else you want me to summon?" Fumo waited for Avery's reply.

"Uh, no, sir."

The admiral dismissed both seamen. They uttered an aye-aye and took off.

"Jake, sorry for the intrusion."

"Not at all, sir." He smiled through the side of his mouth.

"Captain Avery, come with me."

"Aye, sir."

Avery followed the admiral's commanding footsteps.

The two men stood at Valentine's cabin. Avery didn't like the way Fumo eyed him.

"Shank warned me there'd be dissention in the ranks."

"Sir, I know what I saw."

"It's the word of three men against yours. And I understand one of them is your best friend." Fumo looked displeased. "Why do you fraternize with that seaman? It'll only lead to trouble."

He narrowed a look on him. "What're you saying, Admiral?"

"Wipe that angry look off your face and I'll tell you." In the silence, both officers studied each other. There was always something to be learned about a man, Avery decided. Even when you knew that man. Fumo said, "We're all under the NCIS microscope. Everyone's a suspect."

It was the distraction that made everyone a suspect, Avery thought. The same kind of distraction that made the theft possible. "Sir, I know for a fact they're dragging their feet on this, waiting for a hacker to drop his trousers and flash a vertical smile. What if it's Pratt?"

"What if it isn't?" The admiral went on to say that being a military hacker carried a punishment of court-martial, dishonorable discharge, or a lifetime sentence behind bars handed down from a Navy tribunal. Jake had a good naval record. He was a former squadron commander who was up for flag rank, and, despite being a pain in the glute, wouldn't piss away a thirty-year career.

"In other words, sir, we're just waiting for the nightmare to begin again."

"Let NCIS handle this," ended Fumo. "We don't need to create more disruption by being involved."

His mind spun to a stop. The last thing he wanted on his last day aboard the *Seven* was a falling out. To leave on a sour note. To get caught up in a matter he knew nothing about. Something that belonged in NCIS's backyard. Avery decided to let the matter lie like a dead dog.

Valentine showed up at the tail-end of their talk. "Is this a private meeting of Navy brass, or can anyone join in?"

"Didn't I tell you," Fumo said to Avery, avoiding the commander's eyes. "He's all primped for his date."

The buzz-cut enhanced Valentine's appearance. He looked more like a commodore than a ship's physician.

"Heard she's a cute lieutenant," Avery added to the joke.

Valentine led them into his twelve-foot-long, eight-foot wide quarters. At one end, a two-man rack, one over the other, were individually draped by thick, bunk curtains. It amazed him still how anyone with the commander's height and build could even get into those coffin-like beds, let alone sleep in them. At the other end of the stateroom, a bolted square table for working and eating, resembled a booth at a cozy diner. The slate-blue floor tiles had a waxy gleam, and a Tibetan handcrafted, rustic, ancient-patterned rug at the foot of a small couch, gave the windowless compartment the comforts of home.

"Okay, you two." They sat on that small couch. "This is supposed to be a happy occasion. What was that serious tone I walked in on?" He leaned against a wooden panel from where a retractable desk could be opened for use.

"Don't change the subject," Fumo dramatized. "Just tell us her name."

Avery let a grin invade his face. Boyish things were strange, but they felt good. "We couldn't resist doing that to you, Bill."

"Wait till you hear what we're going to do to you."

"What's up?" He darted a look between the admiral and the medical officer.

"There's a surprise in store on the roof," Fumo opened up. "We can't let a man of your caliber walk off without some sign of appreciation, can we?"

"Please, not a fancy sendoff."

"Why not?" Valentine seemed puzzled by the request. "This is about your dedicated service to the *Seven*, the Navy, your country. All twenty years. Congratulations, you've earned this."

Twenty years, he thought. Most navymen never received the recognition due them, much less a handshake. For him, however, a noteworthy celebration was in the works. How he would have gladly traded twenty years to be with the woman he still loved.

Fumo stood for the handshake. "No one will be able to fill your shoes. I won't let them."

"You'll be sorely missed," Valentine added.

"Hey, I'm not retiring. I'm leaving the *Seven*, not North Island."

Valentine plucked a medical penlight from his top pocket. "Between here and HQ is far enough." He handed it to him.

"What's that for?"

"You've always liked it. Take it, or you'll steal it."

He took it and clipped it next to his new fountain pen.

Fumo's cell phone chimed a marching tune. "Well, gentlemen." He seemed impatient. Perhaps he had an important matter to take care of. "Shall we proceed to the roof? Presentations should be getting underway."

On the *Man Of War's* massive flight deck, row upon row of sailors in dress whites and polished shoes, stood at parade rest. As soon as the trio of khaki-dressed officers stepped off the *#3* aircraft elevator and were in sight, the men, hundreds of them, simultaneously executed the sharpest group salute Avery had ever seen.

Fumo and Valentine flanked Avery, marching past the ship's eight-story superstructure, and when they did, the thunderous roar of four F-117 nighthawks in diamond formation, sliced through the air above the big carrier with lightning speed and precision, signaling the rising of the American flag on the control tower and the ready band to the glorious tune of *The Star Spangled Banner.*

The young captain responded to the orchestration of trumpets, trombones, and tubas with a clean salute, body tall and erect, heels together, shoes turned out at forty-five degrees, eyes straight. At the clash of cymbals he breathed deep and let it out. How he used to pace the deserted flight deck—eyes sunken, head drooping, shoulders slumped. Now music played, seagulls danced above him, and shipmates acknowledged him. The exhilaration. He couldn't get enough. He would walk off the ship a proud man instead of leaping off it.

Fumo ordered everyone at ease on the last note, and exuberant shouts rang, followed by din cheering, shrilled whistling, and louder shouts of Avery's name. The formation of sailors collapsed and a crowd of well-wishers thronged him in a mighty rush. Nieve was there, Jordan was there, Rags was there, Davis was there. Dino even made a special trip to be on hand. Everyone was there for the farewell presentation. Everyone, except Pratt.

Near the end of the ceremony, when roast speeches had been said and all laughter put aside, the senior chef rolled out a big, carrier-shaped cake from the ship's galley. *Good luck Neil Avery* was written on it in red icing. It was now time to eat.

With so many officers, enlisted personnel, and those of the admiral's staff swarming over a train of folding tables cluttered with food and beverages, it was no wonder the celebration went into overtime.

Avery smiled into the lens of a Pentax 50mm camera. Jordan pressed a release button and a shutter whirred. Every moment, every crisp salute, every color of Avery's ribbon bars had been captured. He snapped away until the crowd dispersed below deck. In a few hours they would push out to sea for antisubmarine warfare practice.

A short time later, he went below. He grabbed his duffel and Wally bag from his compartment and headed to hangar-bay one. There, a group of senior lieutenants were engaged in handcuff-escape drills with a tall, decisive-looking man—NIPD's chief of police. Avery laughed to himself. Getting out of cuffs was a no-brainer. They stopped what they were doing to salute as he went by.

He rode the *#2* platform elevator to the roof once more where an empty stretch of flight deck remained with no one there to greet him. He shouldered the duffel and began his journey. This was it. The gulls were gone, the air was still, and the great, red-and-white flag with stars ablaze in a field of blue had ceased to flap. Strange, he thought. A moment ago a sea of faces surrounded him. They called out his name. Clapped him on the back. He was popular.

Now he stood alone.

He looked below, starboard side. Two officers had stepped off the brow, one of them holding a black briefcase. Fumo and Jarvis. The Air Boss handed the admiral the briefcase and he walked away with it. Avery ejected the thought Pratt planted in his head. It was a Navy custom for someone to carry a flag officer's bags when unboarding.

"Hey, Caliber," Jordan called out. "One more shot!"

Avery spotted him high in Vultures Row, zooming in on him with the Pentax. Anyone with a crazed desire to jump off the ship at that height was a nut, he thought. He struck a masculine pose for the seaman: duffel hoisted over his left shoulder while flexing a hard muscle and holding the Wally bag with his right.

"Take care, sir." He coughed into his fist. "And don't be a stranger. Drop by." He coughed again.

"Will do," Avery called back. "Will do," he whispered.

Chapter 15

One P.M. That was the time the elevator came to a stop from its long, strange descent. With duffel and Wally bag in tow, Avery toured past the high bright lights of the domed structure and directly into the crypt-like main corridor. He was not yet accustomed to the route he had to take through the perplexing labyrinth, so he relied on a printed diagram; a map of the subterranean world. He arrived at the laboratory fifteen minutes later. Its bedrock wall wide open.

He entered, plopped the army-green duffel onto the limestone floor, and looked about. There was no sign of anyone. He stepped around the control station, and right away, the monstrous structures standing on each side of the lab exerted a pull on him. It surprised him he would break a Spectrum rule so soon. He climbed the negatron's high ramp, stepped over a threshold and stood on the electromagnetic plate's shoe imprints, activating the giant glasslike tube until it came down all the way and locked in place. Something hummed and air fanned his face. A light flickered, then flashed, and a pyrotechnic display filled his eyes. He felt himself falling, tumbling, flying without wings. His crotch hairs stood and he took in a ragged breath. Harry Houdini loved death traps like these, he thought.

A big hand gripped the back of his shoulder, jolting him with a start.

"Don't be afraid of it," Dauerman said. "You'll have to get in it sometime."

Avery said nothing. He draped the Wally bag over a cushy-looking swivel chair at the control station.

The agent stood poised with mug in hand. "Coffee?"

"No thanks."

"You'll need it to calm your nerves."

"There's nothing wrong with me," he battled back. "Just get me iced tea."

"You know where it is." He sauntered to a corner of the lab and poured himself a mug of steamy black liquid from a coffee station. The serviceman followed. The agent eased a hip on the edge of a desk, and with back turned, faced the ten-week training schedule written on a large, white board:

Phase I Codes
Phase II Systems/RP
Phase III Diagnostic/Repair
Phase IV Shuttle/TSI

Dauerman's first few coffee sips seemed to go down like soothing, warm milk. Nothing fazed him.

"Operating and maintaining these machines must generate a mega bill." Avery's eyes roamed the lab from corner to corner.

Dauerman turned and put down the mug. He looked interested in giving an honest answer. He said the Defense Department had coordinated with Spectrum's team of scientists, allowing them to supervise the project if they could finance it. After the old Navy headquarters was demolished, DOD got things started by paying off private contractors and architects from their annual budget to build a new HQ and the domain under it, therefore, keeping everything as property of the Pentagon.

Avery noted the agent's explanation, but he told him there was more. Funding came from the Corporation: Private investors. Shareholders with Spectrum. Dauerman gulped down a mouthful of coffee. It was as simple as that.

It didn't seem farfetched. In fact, it sounded plausible. Everything in the realm of government revolved around politics and was backed up by men in power. That power was as diverse and complex as the Pentagon, which controlled national security and all branches of the military. Avery decided to dismiss the inquiry.

"Now, you'll excuse me, Captain, for there's work to do. I have a schedule to keep, a team to supervise, and a brood of hackers to nail." He snatched his coffee mug and sauntered out of the lab, slurping as he went. "Don't touch the gadgets," he said. "And read that manual on the desk. I'll be back."

Footsteps trailed off in the long tunnel. The captain grabbed the Wally bag and duffel, and went to unpack.

Avery stepped out from the commodore's suite into the strange quietness of the enormous lab after a long, two-hour read. Like Mission Control, an army of electronic equipment surrounded him. My dad worked in such a place, he thought.

At one end of the Vector Supercomputer that spanned wall to wall with tracking instruments, graduated gauges, and tiny darkened bulbs, Avery spotted something he hadn't noticed before. In a room cluttered with so many overwhelming machines, a small pair of Geiger counters on a shelf was the last thing he expected to find. Immediately he imagined lethal levels of poisonous radiation seeping through unprotected walls as frantic technicians with gurgling units swept handheld detecting wands back and forth.

He dislodged the unpleasant thought, straining to understand the complexity of the wondrous machines to the sound of footsteps behind him.

"If it doesn't fit your frame of logic, don't force it," someone said.

The unfamiliar raspy voice turned Avery around. There were four men. The fat one, wearing black, Clark-Kent glasses and carrying a glazed leather briefcase, looked like a VIP.

"I'm Dr. Weinberg." He laid the briefcase at his feet. "You were in quite a trance." He loosened his tie, unbuttoned his white shirt from the top and peeled off a honey-brown tweed jacket, flinging it over his shoulder. "You must be Captain Avery. Heard much about you. May I call you Neil?"

He was troubled that everyone seemed to know something about him. "Fine." What else did this man learn? he thought.

The doctor approached with a pleasant look and firm handshake. "No need to be uneasy. We won't be strangers for long."

Avery held his breath. The stench of halitosis on the scientist was bad. As bad as fly-infested dog feces rolled in a wad of rotten tobacco leaves. The fat man stroked a trimmed beard with a manicured hand and fancied the serviceman with a roving look. Avery knew whatever DOD had given Weinberg to work with would have to do.

"Let me introduce the team." He seemed satisfied someone had volunteered for the program and turned to the stone-faced technicians standing behind him like loyal servants; all dressed in neat, camel-gray suits; all armed at the hip with cell phones. He started with the one who had sea-blue eyes. "This is the senior engineer, Karl Jager." Then the one with the cleft chin. "Information analyst, Scott Quinn." Then the man with the czar-like mustache and goatee. "And program specialist, Yuri Stas. Their job is to assist me during lab operations. Get to know them. It's good insurance policy. Any questions?"

Avery said nothing. He realized who these men were and what they were going to do to him.

"Good. Let's proceed. The sooner we do, the sooner you'll see your mother."

The doctor stood his briefcase on the control station's counter and the four men scurried into the next room, emerging a moment later in their white, lab garb. Quinn stacked a pile of black safety goggles near the fat briefcase and called the doctor by name. They spoke in undertones.

Weinberg. Avery gave the name yet another thought. He was right. It was familiar.

A sense of urgency filled the air as Jager, Quinn, and Stas began the task of going around the large laboratory—flipping switches, pressing knobs, turning valves, getting the generators and mega computers to emit a stream of colored, pulsating lights.

Avery got wide-eyed and his heart began to jog. "Am I being sent now?"

"No," chuckled Weinberg. "The techs are just running diagnostics. These machines haven't been used since the Defense Department selected me to head the program, so we need to make certain everything's in tiptop shape before we start."

He relaxed but tensed again. "And if there's a problem?" He knew he was being childish and hoped Weinberg would work up a tolerant smile.

"Not to worry. If we find one we'll let you know."

But he wanted to know now. "What I mean is …." His eyes followed the technicians moving about. "That warning panel." He pointed to it. "Don't tell me you're not concerned about radiation leakage."

"You've been watching too many submarine-disaster movies," the doctor said in complete calmness. "If you're worried about a nuclear accident, you can forget it. The reactors are housed in a primary-coolant compartment beneath us to maintain safety." Weinberg powered-on a line of computers at the control station and a moment later the monitors glowed green. "Gone are the days of Chernobyl and the sudden meltdown that spewed lethal levels of alpha, gamma, and neutron particles into the air by the careless ignorance of those men. All these walls are made of thick lead and the floor is water-tank shielded. We're perfectly safe down here, my friend." He opened the fat briefcase and extracted a folded copy of the San Diego Union Tribune. "There's nothing for you to do around here now." He handed it to his guest.

He took the newspaper, and upon opening it, realized who the doctor was. "You're Marcus J. Weinberg. The Yale graduate and Rhodes scholar from MIT."

"From the cytology and bioengineering department," he confirmed. "So, you've heard of me."

"Read a column on your research over a year ago that mentioned the Nobel Peace Prize you were awarded."

"Great," he said with a broad smile that showed tobacco-stained teeth. "It's good to know someone's interested in my field."

125

"It's my background as an engineering officer that landed me here, Dr. Weinberg."

"Please, call me Marc." He sat by a control module and pushed back those fat, black glasses over a sloped Roman nose as a 3-D human image slowly turned on a computer screen. "Did you know our bodies are made up of a hundred-trillion cells, and that the blueprint of our physical structure is packaged in our genes?"

The captain realized there was a lot he would have to learn.

"Don't worry over the genetics. I'll teach you the lingo and everything else you'll need to know." He ran a hand over a commanding waistline. "After I get something to eat."

Avery relaxed and smiled. He was so glad Marcus was cordial.

The doctor gave him another one of those roving looks. The way a mad scientist regarded a white rat. "We're going to get along fine, you and I," he said.

With those words, Avery was very much aware the classified project was underway.

Week One: Lack of freedom, and endless hours at the lab, made the first full day at Spectrum longer than Avery desired. He was tired of the cold filtered air, unaccustomed to being in one place all day long and uncomfortable with the idea his new home was fifteen stories below ground, while at day's end, Marcus and his crew could leave. Compared to life aboard the *Seven*, things were different. There, he could move about at will; leave ship and return. Here, day after day, night after night, he was a prisoner in a cell with no bars. The intricacies of CTU technology, bioengineering, cellular physics and time travel were brain tiring and time consuming. Avery wondered whether he would ever feel at home in an intimidating environment.

Week Two: Marcus sat at a control module with his trainee, Captain Avery. The schedule was now in full swing, and things were getting harder. But Avery was used to being trained hard: boot camp's weapons and fitness course; NavSub's class-intensive nuclear studies; the Academy's football drills. Yet Spectrum was unlike anything he had been thrust into.

Marcus said, "Did you understand that?" He had gone over the pulse magnometer's primary lock-in settings and analog templates for the second time. "I don't know whether anything is getting past that mesmerized, boyish look."

The front worked. But Avery wondered how long he could keep up the masquerade, for the more he looked at everything around him, the more he wanted to run from it all. "Can't help but be a boy with all this gadgetry. Not to mention the maze of complicated tunnels down here."

"Technology and underground worlds are a given," Marcus said. "And I'm not just talking about NORAD's combat op center. Ever been there? Shank and I were given a grand tour."

The captain was torn between learning all he could and knowing too much. Captured frontline soldiers were always tortured for the information they knew. If the feds found out about Spectrum….

Marcus pushed back his glasses. "Then there's that UFO facility in southern Nevada. It's Spectacular."

"Those places are on the map," Avery said. "How has this one remained a secret for over twenty years?"

"Through lies, denials, and constant deception. With this kind of technology it's necessary to hide what we do."

"Will the masquerade ever end?"

"Why should it?" Marcus said.

"Then how will you keep the U.S. Navy and the FBI from making the discovery of a lifetime?"

"With techniques from friends in high places—Area Fifty-One."

That bit of information made him think. Science and technology had become warped ever since it had gone underground. "Is that why Mr. Shank's eyes look eclipsed?"

Marcus heaved out a laugh. "Those aren't just his eyes. He's an ex-SEAL. Ever since surgeons implanted night-vision contacts he's been like a stray cat in the night. Doesn't take much for him to find his way in the dark."

"I see, said the blind man." Avery pushed himself up from his chair and stepped around the length of the control station. Before him stood the twin cylinders. Spectrum's scientists either had not, or would not use the machines on themselves. He wondered which was it.

"You seem skittish. Still troubled by Spectrum's technology?"

He gave Marcus a dull look.

"Whatever's bloating you, Captain, this is the time and place to fart it out."

"I don't understand the partnership between you and Shank."

"What's not to understand?"

"You're the director. Why do you need him?"

"He's the oversight officer. Serves as the project's watchdog." The doctor went on to say that until Spectrum became a recognized agency with the United States government, like NASA, Dauerman would continue to protect its technological secrets and its employees from potential enemies. The last thing anyone wanted was for Spectrum to fall into the wrong hands. If that happened, time travel could easily destroy the world. "Any other questions?"

He didn't have to think twice on it. "The Corporation." He wanted to know more, for the more he knew, the safer he would feel. "Tell me about it."

"Spectrum's rainbow organization of private investors. They're former CEOs of failed companies looking for another chance to make it big. Time travel will be a marketable business one day. If I were you, I'd invest."

It was the stock market advice of the century. But the thought that Spectrum could one day outdo NASA, didn't ring as it did in the beginning.

"What's the matter, Captain? You look bewildered."

"Let me get this straight. Money for every piece of machinery here, including this high-class sewer, was allocated by the ... Corporation?" He was sick of inhaling the doctor's breath each time he spoke.

"They had the bread. We had the technical know-how and top scientists to engineer the program."

It all made sense to Captain Avery. But what would the Navy do to him when they discovered a hidden lab under their feet? Hang him? Shoot him? Imprison him? He lunged away from the control station and marched out of the lab.

Marcus followed. "Hey, where're you going? You aren't supposed to go anywhere unescorted. Avery!" He chased him up the dim-lit cave, dodging in a field of standing stalagmites on his way to a corridor tunnel that led to the genetics lab. "Hey, I'm talking to you." He caught up with him.

"If I'm going to work in that chamber, I've got to be sure of something." The sound of his voice bounced off thick walls. "Otherwise there's no point running my mouth asking questions."

Marcus scooted past and body-blocked him. "Why can't we talk in there?" His voice rushed into the endless darkness. "What's wrong with you?"

Avery waited until silence ruled within the long shaft. "Ever get a feeling about something you can't prove but trust your gut?"

The doctor drew a blank stare.

"Look, I already know too much and that puts my life in danger. I want to know for certain that place isn't bugged."

"Listening devices? You're paranoid."

"I'm not going to prison over a project our government knows nothing about. Do you have any idea what the CIA or FBI will do to us if they get wind of this? They're not nice guys."

"You worry over nuts and bolts, my friend."

The captain turned away. "Tell that to our president." He walked Marcus to the G-lab, opened the steel door and flicked on the lights. "We should be safe in here." They marched past a red phone on the wall and mounted themselves on wooden stools by one of the marble-top tables. "Like I said, wherever Shank goes the feds are sure to follow."

Marcus smirked. "You don't have to speak to me in undertones."

"I don't have a choice."

"Does your gut feeling also tell you I'm a spy?" Marcus laughed it off.

Avery withdrew a pen from the top pocket of his service khaki and wagged it in the doctor's bearded face. "How much are you willing to bet he's sniffing someone out with this?"

Marcus shot to his feet and snatched the pen from the naval officer's grip.

"You're jumpy all of a sudden," Avery said.

"Shut up."

"You're right. If that's a microphone he can hear us from anywhere."

The doctor uncapped the fountain pen and examined its ink flow on a notepad laying nearby. "Seems all right." He unscrewed it, emptied its contents and broke them down into smaller parts, scrutinizing everything with a patient eye. He spread out all the pieces on the table and sighed with relief. "What made you think it had ears?"

Avery looked away from the fragments. "Nothing. Nothing at all." He massaged the ovals of his eyes, trying to work out the tiredness with round measured movements; the same way he did when he checked for abnormal growths on his testicles. He looked at Marcus.

The doctor studied him. "Tell you what. Let's get back to the lab and turn the mother upside-down to make sure there're no bugs anywhere."

He was swallowed up in thought. Bugs of any kind disquieted him. Listening devices and the insect variety. He hoped that thing, whatever it was, would not land on him again.

"By the way," Marcus said. "Have you made out a will? You could die here, you know."

When the technicians searched every corner of the equipment-filled transport chamber and found nothing to confirm anyone's suspicions, Marcus Weinberg and Neil Avery got to work. They flipped switches on the Vector, turned dials on the reactor terminal, and set the commands on each unit at the control station. It was time to introduce the next phase: programming the quantum computer and initiating the RP sequence. The serviceman had been told it was vital he understood RP—Return Procedure. For once thrust back through time he would be on his own. The early stage of the program meant there would be no one to assist him at Norfolk's underground facility.

After a question-answer session with the technicians, Marcus approached Avery. He told him he would like to skip everything on the ten-week schedule and catapult him back to a time when San Diego was inhabited by the Kumiai Indians of northern Mexico, and later by the Portuguese, under Spanish rule. But without the proper training, that would prove disastrous. "Well, anything in your life you haven't done you'd like to accomplish?"

He wondered what made him ask. "Dreamt of being an astronaut. Space exploration fascinates me. Haven't lost the romance in all these years."

"There's a theory that space travel and time travel are kissing cousins. You may get your wish after all." He added that the Indians of Kumiai could wait. His mother was more important.

Week Three—Day Four: Marcus let Avery work on the drive generators that fed the deadly technology, and under the influence of its turbo electric, 180,000 horse-powered whirring engines, the tall, glassed cylinders glowed. It was just a matter of time before he embarked. Laura Avery, he thought. Would I recognize her? Would she recognize me?

The negatron and positron dimmed after an idle period. "Tell me," he said over his shoulder to Marcus. "How's it work? How do these things do what you claim it does?" He knew he had turned on the doctor's professor instincts and he would begin to lecture.

"Familiar with Einstein's special theory of relativity?" An index finger stopped those sliding black glasses.

"I have a scientific mind just like you. Minus the PhD."

He drew a chuckle out of the overweight scientist. "Then you know traveling at, or near the speed of light, slows time down. Dilating it."

He only knew his silence would push Marcus to use simple layman's terms.

"Okay. The cylinders work like a phone. Here, instead of sound being converted into electrical impulses, then back to sound, something different occurs."

Avery moved away from Marcus.

"Relax, we're not flushing you down a toilet. Once you step into the tube, your body will undergo something unique. Show you what I mean."

He keyboarded a series of numbers into the computer, pressed enter, and something whirred, activating a twelve-foot, stainless-steel ram through a four-inch-wide shaft in the high ceiling, lifting the negatron's large tubular body with a slow rise. The electromagnetic footplate pulsated from fiery yellow to neon-blue as though beckoning for someone to step in. Anyone.

Marcus pushed himself out of his chair and marched toward the raised cylinder towering over him. "What an awesome machine." He adjusted some foot dials on an instrument panel. "Your dream of being an astronaut is about to come true." He spun at the serviceman in the silence that followed. "Does my excitement frighten you?"

"It isn't you, it's that thing."

"Then I must convince you of its capability. Take off your shoes."

The odd command puzzled the captain.

"What's the matter, your feet stink? Off with the footwear."

He removed the left one, hesitated, then removed the other, fighting the cold that shot through his feet. He handed Marcus the scuffed shoe first, wondering what he was going to do with them. The tube, as Marcus called it, seemed to look over their shoulders.

"I'll start with these. But next time I expect you to be in them." He placed both Navy-issue shoes on the stationary imprints and the glass encasing above him began descending with a whir.

Marcus backtracked to the control station's quantum computer. "Those plates have sensors," he said. "It's like someone's standing there." He typed away for a moment. "Just logged in time and destination." He grabbed protective goggles, strapped it over his head, and tossed a second set into a pair of fumbling hands. The cylinder came down all the way, locked firmly in place with automatic foot clamps, and began to rotate. "Shield your eyes."

A loud humming sound filled the lab, and rows of flashing red, green, and yellow lights strobed wild across the face of the accelerator panel. The turbogenerators and gas-handling system hissed with excitement, and a spectacular display of sharp colors filled the cylinder in a blinding swirl of nuclear energy.

Avery didn't know what to call it: fixation, captivation. He only knew that the eerie glow of the spinning machines bewitched him more than any foot-fetish moment.

A buzz grew louder, and a bright orange mass filled the encasement in a funnel of atoms that a moment ago were an ordinary pair of shoes. The tornado-like display suddenly shot across the lab from one rotating cylinder to the other with bolt-lightning speed and the serviceman jumped back as though something evil had passed through him.

When the whirring sounds of instruments died to a humming stop, the alternating red and green lights on the particle accelerator faded. All that remained were tiny darkened bulbs on the panel's surface that resembled the end of a Christmas holiday. The transfer was complete. Both cylinders had stopped spinning, returning to their clear, silent transparency.

Avery stripped off the dark safety glasses. Not too many things paralyzed him with astonishment.

Marcus said, "That was a ten-point-four-second transmission with electromagnetic amplitude and quantum at normal wavelengths."

"My shoes!" Avery stared at the doctor like he had never seen him before; goggles pushed onto the top of his head. "Where'd they go?"

"They're in the second tube," Marcus declared with triumph.

The captain crept toward the positron cylinder. He was glad it was only a machine. But it was a strange machine. One that could swallow him whole and not spit him out the other end. He peered in.

"You can't see them 'cause they're in a different time zone," Marcus said.

The cylinder was empty. When his shoes began to materialize, his mind went numb. He wanted to speak but exhilaration had gotten in the way. Or was it fear?

With a buzz, the cylinder lifted, a rush of cool steam escaped, and Avery examined the shoes for irregularities: its leather, its laces, its aglets. He snatched them from the electromagnetic plate and made a quick retreat from the vaporous, hissing unit.

"Feel cold, don't they?"

He nodded with a puzzled grin. That's when he noticed it. "Scuff's gone!"

"Your shoes were in that tube for the past four weeks," Marcus said, "waiting for atomic time to catch up to real time."

Avery took a moment to understand the logic. It was easier if the doctor just lectured.

"It's all about quantum physics. You just witnessed a demo of how objects sent to the past are brought back to the present. If that had been you, Captain, you would've been able to see yourself, but I wouldn't. Just as you wouldn't be able to see me. See?"

"Sounds asinine, but yeah, I get it. Because four weeks ago you weren't in this room. We hadn't met yet."

"Got it. What the CTUs did is a theory that's taken decades to prove. It's called—visible atomic structure versus invisible atomic structure."

With the third week of training completed, Avery knew Marcus would move things up a notch.

Week Four: Avery sat in his HQ office, room 413, poring through thick, hard-covered laboratory manuals until his head hurt. He picked up another textbook and read the opening title of the first chapter: *Shuttling*. It explained a vigorous phase of being shot out of one tube and into another; going from physical state, to floating atoms, back to physical state; broken down and built up again. During the 1960's, NASA's first astronauts had trained for the harsh environment of space—exposure to the ungodly elements of subzero temperatures, searing heat, deadly radiation—and he would undergo the same tortures. He turned to the next page. *Time travel can have serious effects upon the human body much like weightlessness does on long space flights, such as chronic disorientation, bone-mass loss, weakened heart, time lag, and* ....

Someone knocked and the door opened. "Neil, what're you doing here?"

He was so engrossed in his studies he didn't even notice Marcus and another man had let themselves in until he heard the door close.

"I told you to take the evening off and leave the building. You'll go nuts immersing yourself like that. I've never seen anyone look so tired in all my life."

"You should be commending me for the hard work I've put in," Avery rebutted. "I can adjust the gauges on all the equipment, monitor the uranium reactors, diagnose problems with the coolant system, take apart the CTUs' life support and power converters and put it back together like engine parts in an auto shop." He studied the well-dressed older man next to Marcus. "Going to introduce us?"

Marcus turned to the man wearing black eyeglasses. "Jules, this is Captain Avery." He motioned to the Navy officer. "Neil, this is Dr. Jules Ian. We worked together on Spectrum's prototype till his retirement from CIT. There's a matter of importance we need to discuss." He locked the door.

The two men pulled up a pair of cushioned chairs and sat with grim faces. Jules Ian laid a briefcase at his feet, opened it, and extracted an 8-by-10-inch headshot, passing it to Marcus. Marc eyed the photo and handed it to Avery.

He examined every facet of the middle-aged woman in the shot: Clear skin complexion. Brunette, shoulder-length hair. Bright eyes. Pristine smile. "Who's this? And what's—?"

Ian lifted an arthritic hand and halted Avery. "That woman is my wife. Claudia Britney. A brilliant nuclear cytologist with Spectrum. Was, anyway." A sudden, deep-throated hacking shook the old man in his seat. "Excuse me." He found a handkerchief in his suit pocket and brought it to his mouth, readying for something. "The photo you're holding was taken before the project's designers arranged a hasty funeral. It kept local police at bay for a while, but ...." He coughed again, and this time Avery saw something dark on the man's lips, almost black. He wiped it away. "But when the empty casket was exhumed, the FBI was called in. Claudia vanished without a trace during an unauthorized lab test. She took a foolish gamble and transported herself through time. I need to know—"

"Forget it. I'm not playing PI for a broken-hearted, old fart."

"For chrissake, Neil." Marcus scolded him with a sharp look and pointed to the photo with a crooked index finger. "If you thought you signed up for a joyride, you're mistaken. We're dealing with a missing person—and an investigation."

The loud silence awakened Avery. It chased away the weighty tiredness and caused every nerve ending under his skin to spark with anger. "So this is why I'm here." He put the photo down. "This is what I'm training for. As a guinea pig to help cover-up the mistakes a bunch of piss-scared gods have made." It stunned him to have learned the reason he was a Spectrum pilot. Their own, man-eating invention had put them in a corner.

"Truth be told, this isn't about seeing your mom. It's about this damn mess we're in. Claudia is too celebrated to just drop off the face of the earth. She must be located. If Shank found out I lied to him, he'd have the feds raid this—"

"Marc, forgive me for interrupting." Ian turned from the angry physicist to the naval officer. He removed his glasses and narrowed bullish eyes on him. "Young man, as you can see I'm not well. Keeping hope alive has been a difficult task. I don't have much time." He rubbed gnarled hands together and lowered his eyes as a plea for pity. The old man was a bad actor but by no means a pushover. "My last wish is to find Claudia. If she's alive, and I know she is, the missing person's case can be closed and the FBI will be kept from discovering Spectrum." He crossed long arms on his chest. He looked like he wanted to bark out a threat. Instead he said, "I have to know. Her family deserves an answer."

Avery gave the large, glossy color photo one more look. After a long moment he no longer saw a cellular physicist. He saw his mother. "Point taken," he said to Ian. "Marc, how much shuttle practice would I need to prepare for the real thing?" He wondered how the doctor would answer that.

"Hard to say. You're our first trainee." His eyes darted around the office for a moment. "We've never done this before."

"Yes you have," Avery corrected him. "Your lies stink like your breath."

Marcus was not used to driving over 75 mph, but he needed to get to the naval air station on time. Morning schedules and impatient technicians were stressful things.

A dark sedan behind him whooped, forcing his Buick onto the shoulder of Interstate-5. Two brawny men stepped out of the vehicle, flashed their FBI shields, and searched his car. But all they found was a cluttered glove compartment and leather briefcase. They asked him to step out.

"Mind telling us where you were going in such a hurry?" The first agent opened the briefcase and searched through it. It was obvious he was looking for a weapon beneath the stack of navy-blue file folders. The missing person's case must have gone sour and suspicions of murder now followed. But Dr. Ian hadn't killed anyone. Neither did Marcus. He simply had an affair with Claudia and now was left to wonder when the old man would die. If he didn't die soon, there was always the licensed pistol he kept in his hotel room.

"Aren't there enough cops handing out speeding tickets? Now it's Quantico rookies."

"Don't get smart. Just tell us where you're going."

Marcus huffed out a breath and loosened his tie. "Frisco."

"To see who?" asked the second agent. He flashed a photo of Jules Ian. "This man?" The sound of traffic was distracting.

Marcus forced himself to look at the familiar face in the shot. It was only a matter of time before the feds stumbled upon the truth. He had to tell them something to get them off his back.

The first agent, the younger-looking of the two said, "We want to question him about his missing wife. Or we can take you in and interrogate you later. Whatever you prefer."

"Don't know him."

"Certain of that?"

"Look, I'm giving a lecture on environmental science at Lawrence Berkeley at eleven sharp. And afterwards I'm attending a dinner engagement with the national laboratory's director and deputy director." Marcus fought to control his bobbing Adam's apple.

"Can you prove that, Dr. Weinberg?"

"If you're in doubt, follow me." He began to perspire.

Once everyone had gotten into their vehicles and pulled off the shoulder, Marcus kept a sharp eye on the traffic ahead, and on the rearview mirror. The tall plainclothesmen were tailing him from a discreet distance. When he passed the large green highway sign that read San Francisco, the FBI vehicle zoomed past him and got off at the next exit ramp. They were gone. However, the doctor wondered whether they would return to San Diego and wait for him there, or have another FBI car tail him. Whatever they had planned, Spectrum's technicians would have to proceed without him for a few hours more. Maybe the rest of the day.

Dressed in Navy coveralls, Avery busied himself deciphering code numbers the quantum computer displayed on a practice grid. The senior engineer, Karl Jager, approached with a black mug in hand. He looked like an MD in his long, lab garb. "Coffee?"

Avery pushed away from a line of green-eyed monitors. He was tired and needed sleep bad. "Thanks." He took a hearty slurp. "This should keep me awake."

"It's decaf."

"In that case I'll forgo the jog around the base tonight."

Jager rolled out a chair and sat next to him; active computers humming at their feet. "I trust Marcus spoke to you about a will?"

Scott Quinn did something to the particle accelerator as Yuri Stas looked on, taking notes. "He told me about making out a will, Claudia Britney, and the mission. Won't be seeing my mother like I'd hoped."

"Did he ... tell you about the accident?"

Avery put down the mug by the keyboard and looked at Jager. Really looked at him. "What accident?"

Quinn and Stas were distracted with their work.

Jager's sea-blue eyes darkened, and what followed was a tale from the unknown realm of genetic engineering.

Avery kept hearing the story in his head: Shuttled himself ... garbled remains. "What do you mean?" He knew a bizarre answer would follow.

"The man, probably a janitor, had to be euthanized."

He flinched with anger when Jager shrugged it off as though it were a harmless science experiment. "An innocent man was murdered?"

"Can't call it murder if it wasn't human," Jager said with tempered coolness. "He wouldn't have survived in the condition he was in, anyway."

Now Avery wondered what had actually happened to Claudia Britney. Had she really transported herself back through time, or was it murder, dressed to look like an accident? "What happened then?"

Jager told him that Spectrum was abandoned with the possibility of never resuming. But a stubborn group of elite physicists and genetic engineers continued experimenting. Relentless months of trial and error were spent on sacrificing animals, making corrections.

His veins shrunk and something inside his head rolled with violence. Avery wasn't scared of bad dreams. He was afraid of something happening to him.

Now Jager said that the quantum research and new findings produced by those scientists is what paved the way to what he had witnessed last week with his shoes. Without their work, none of what they currently had would've been possible.

He fought to dislodge an unpleasant vision. "What'll happen to me if I die? Who'll bury my garbled remains in a cheap casket, or arrange a hasty funeral? Who'll keep the FBI at bay?"

Jager looked stunned. "Asking unwelcomed questions is *schlecht*. Bad."

Avery jumped to his feet. "It's gonna be bad for you if another accident occurs!"

"Stop pissing on yourself," Jager snapped. "Nothing will go wrong. Not this time."

The serviceman was hoping the program had defaulted due to gross mechanical problems and bad judgment of incompetent technicians. But the raw truth made him aware the clock was ticking down to zero hour and his fears were growing stronger. Even if he came up with a daring plan to desert, it would only bring him back to this: Spectrum had something he wanted.

"These are marvelous machines. They're not the same ones experimented on twenty years ago and their use have yielded nothing deformed. I'd stake my life on this technology," he said to the captain, with conviction.

"Then you go through the damn tube."

Jager got quiet. He jumped out of his seat, hurried around the long arch of monitors at the control station and joined his two colleagues. Avery knew Jager would say something as soon as he turned around. "I can guarantee this. You'll recellurize with no problems. From your DNA strands to your chromosome links."

Week Five: The day Avery dreaded had arrived.

After Marcus Weinberg and his team kicked up their heels and sipped down a hot cup of java, they donned their white lab coats and ran one last diagnostic check on everything in the transport chamber. Captain Neil Avery was to begin the first of many shuttles at 8:00 A.M. If they started now they would be ahead of schedule.

7:46 A.M.

Dressed in drab, itchy dungarees, Avery stepped out of the commodore's suite and without saying a word, strode past the busy men. Every piece of apparatus—the consoles, the particle accelerator, the gas-handling system— blinked at him, hissed at him, stared at him, and under the ceiling lights, the burning halogens seemed lower, brighter, hotter. He sat at a monitor the way he once sat in the school principal's office when he was six years old: weak kneed and sweaty and terrified. The principal told him his mother was dying. What was dying? He knew it was dreadful because his gut regurgitated something awful. On the computer screen the countdown sequence gnawed into his tired eyes and he quivered.

Marcus called to him and he gave him his full attention. "I've been meaning to ask ...." He turned a tank valve and flow knob from right to left on the bulbous coolant unit, crossed the lab and did the same to the other. The flow gauges were now set and the vaporous, liquid nitrogen tanks were

137

ready to go. He marched to the control station and pulled up a seat next to the serviceman. "What would you do if you saw someone from the past you once knew, once loved?"

His deepest yearning was aroused to the highest pinnacle of his emotions.

Marcus pitched forward like he was going to tell him a secret. "Tell you what the right thing to do is," he whispered.

"You're not in any position to tell me right from wrong," Avery countered.

The doctor reeled back in the chair. He seemed to understand that deceiving the navyman had put a splinter in their friendship. "I'm telling you, anyway. You'd better walk away. I'm not sure if that's enough to shake you from whatever fantasies you're holding, so I'll add a word of warning. Spectrum is a scientific venture. You're not here to place your personal Genesis apple back from whence it was plucked, so don't do anything stupid. You listening?"

"... Yeah." His mind was a turning rolodex of tender memories; each one of the woman who had become his second mother. "I'm all ears."

"You'd better be. The laws of physics and nature of time are fixed. If you end up trying what I think you'll do, history's timeline will spin you on a familiar, vicious carousel. Still want to work for me?"

"I'm here, aren't I?"

Marcus turned toward a monitor, and with a few simple strokes of the keyboard, the screen lit to a dazzling blue. He worked fingertips into his neat-trimmed beard, read the information and acted accordingly. The negatron cylinder lifted with a whir. "This is a dangerous phase with many unknowns. If you can accept that, we can proceed."

Avery rose to his feet and faced the threatening cylinder. There were many what-ifs in his mind, too. "What're we waiting for?"

"Good." Marcus looked glad. "Ready for a test drive?"

"All systems go," he said with feigned confidence. The two men shook hands.

Marcus took a badge-like device from the pocket of his lab coat and clipped it to the serviceman's dungaree collar.

"What's that for?"

"To measure radiation. X-ray techs use 'em in hospitals. Get in." He grabbed a pair of welder's goggles from the counter and strapped it over his head.

Avery approached the raised cylinder like a reluctant astronaut creeping toward a doomed, space-shuttle rocket.

"You claustrophobic?" the doctor said.

"Too late to ask that now." He ducked his head, stepped over the threshold and placed his feet on the green-glowing electromagnetic plate's imprints, activating the transparent enclosure into a slow drop.

The technicians applauded, and when the tall, wide cylinder snapped into place at the base of the O-ring platform, it locked a traveler inside and its outer shell began to spin.

A tiny speaker somewhere above him clicked on, and everyone's voice piped in: "Gentlemen," Marcus said to his crew. "Our theories end here. Quantum science will now be taking over." He moved to another monitor. "Checklist time."

The techs readied themselves at the control station's flat screens that flanked them.

"GHS?" Marcus said.

"Check!" Jager answered.

"Power converters?"

"Check!" Stas said.

"Particle accelerator?"

"Check!" Quinn acknowledged.

"Compressed air?"

"Check!" Stas called.

"Radiation level?"

"Check!" Quinn replied.

"Vector?"

"Check!" Jager announced.

"Give it a ride," the doctor calmly ordered.

Marcus logged something into the system and a noisy hum filled the lab. The supercomputer had kicked in, white lights strobed wild across the particle accelerator's panel, the gas-handling system hissed in return, and a surge of adrenaline jumpstarted Avery's heart into a racehorse gallop. He clenched his fists to control the sharp quiver in his body, but nothing could control the thoughts that began to take over, flashing before him like a near-death experience: his mother's funeral; the accident that stole Darah away; Olympia Gilchrist's tiny arm wrapped in a plaster cast; the asthma attack that landed Taffi in the hospital ....

He shoved away distorted images and stared through the double-glassed cylinder. Marcus and the others were frowning with concentration, huddling over the controls, leaning into the glow of monitors shooting a steady stream of data into their eyes with a flurry.

A wave of pressure pushed against every inch of his body when the interior of the cylinder started heating up. His eardrums popped, and a voice piped into the tube: "Air pressure and power level at thirty-five percent, fifty percent, sixty-five percent ...." He was close to the point of cellular breakdown, and with a pyrotechnic display swirling around him like flashes of lightning, a droning buzz from the overhead electromagnetic plate, filled his ears, drowning out everyone's voices.

The thermo-glass enclosure spun faster, and knowing in another minute the experience of being shot across the lab from one tube to the other would change the world around him forever, made his head spin, too.

Quinn sprinted across the lab as though in a stricken panic. Stas and Jager followed in the same manner when the doctor lurched into a pulsating red signal on one of the screens, indicating the cylinders were spinning faster than they were supposed to; creating a pressure that if not checked, would begin to crush.

Marcus hustled to the gas-handling system. He would have to yell in order for his men to hear him over the noise. "Scram the reactors. Probe the Vector. Deactivate the particle accelerator!" He grabbed a big control wheel with both hands, and with teeth-clenching might, strained to turn the air release valve, but its cold, hard steel bit into soft flesh. Now it was the dumbfounded technicians who thumbed at jammed switches and non-responding buttons, throwing Marcus back to the controls in a hurried attempt to shut down everything by computer command. Strangely, the CTUs' monstrous instruments refused to obey.

The doctor shouted another nervous command at his crew and they scampered back to their places. A second red light flickered on his screen, an acrid smell filled the lab—and Marcus spotted it—a jig-sawed silver pipe pissing dense liquid over the Vector Supercomputer. The leak gushed, and an explosion sent streams of electrical sparks at the four perplexed men, forcing them to take shelter behind the control station. It would be safe there as long as nothing else happened, but a sudden bang sent the doctor's crew pushing past him into a corner of the smoky lab. The occupied spinning cylinder had come loose, pounding with a rhythmic shaking that caused hissing gas to jet into the glasslike tube, engulfing the Navy captain in a thick, silver cloud.

Marcus climbed the negatron's high ramp and thumbed an emergency-disengage button at the base of the unit until it hurt. The humming surface of the gyrating cylinder blew wind at him like an industrial fan. When foot clamps refused to release the negatron from its hold, he read a gauge. The temperature within the tube was 42°F and dropping fast, one degree per second. "Gotta get it open."

The instrument warning panel came to life, flashed *Potential Danger*, and an alarm scattered the technicians in every direction. Marcus thumbed the emergency disengage again with no action resulting. He ran down the ramp to the control station and punched new commands into the system. Nothing worked. The machines were the masters.

Avery fisted the immobile inner layer of the tube that embraced him like a sealed coffin and the blank-faced crew tinkered with the gas-handling system as though help were on the way, but the doctor knew better. On energized legs, he shot back to the doomed unit in a desperate attempt to open it. He flung a swivel chair over his shoulder and the centrifugal force of the negatron catapulted it across the lab. "Damn!"

Strain-faced technicians shot from one corner of the lab to the next, one instrument to the other. The warning panel had jumped from *Potential Danger* to *Danger*, and a second alarm rang. If the unnerving rhythmic blare continued, Marcus feared his crew would abandon him.

Avery dropped to his knees within the tube, mouthing shouts from the pain, the cold, the fear. But with all the noise in the lab, there was no way Marcus could hear him. His desperate cries had been silenced.

The warning panel leaped to its last stage—a bright, pulsating *Critical Evacuate*, and a third alarm went off.

"Pressure is building!" Marcus could barely hear himself barking at his team. The sizzling circuitry, clamorous machines, and wailing alarms were just too much. "Get out!" came the final order.

Adrenaline rocketed him to the Van Allen Troubleshooter. When commands to the massive unit did not compute, he grabbed a yellow Geiger counter, clicked the turn-on dial on the box's black face and extended the mini wand for a quick reading. The counts-per-second needle beneath the glass plating failed to jump. "It's damaged!" He couldn't keep his hands from shaking.

At the blast of another siren, Marcus waddled back to the control station. Stas and Quinn scurried past him out of the lab into the mineral shimmering cave and the doctor slipped on wet tiles, landing with a hard thud. The confidence he carried had lifted, and in its place, a chilling specter of what was to come took over.

Doing the only thing he knew would work—save his own life—Marcus pushed himself up with urgent strength and glided to one of the monitors. The last remaining moment on the critical stage read: 20 seconds. If Marcus could not save the trapped man in the time remaining, Captain Neil Avery would die from a body-ripping explosion.

Chapter 16

A silver-winged Boeing 7E7-Dreamliner touched down with a screech, and ten minutes after passengers let out, the tall man saw her appear through a crowd of marching travelers. She cat-walked on stiletto heels to the luggage-claim area of flight 780, where she extracted a pink sweater from her open carry-on, and draped it over her shoulders. With slender arms folded, she searched. Somewhere in the chaos of the moving carousel, her baggage crawled along.

The soft cry of a little girl distracted her, and when she turned to look, a Navy officer in chocker whites, approached.

They smiled and met each other halfway. She looked dazzling in that mid-thigh length, peacock-plume designed, solid bodice dress.

"How are you, sweetie?" Fumo kissed his granddaughter.

"Just dandy," Karyn replied. "You didn't have to dress in whites for me."

"I'm meeting with Admiral Craig Jenson of the Pentagon. He's on the next flight in." Fumo switched a briefcase from one hand to the other.

"Must be important if you're carrying that. Sure you haven't got military secrets in there you're passing on to him?" She teased the admiral with a smile.

He followed with a hearty laugh. "You've been reading too many JAG novels." He read the time on his watch. He was a busy man and it showed. "Sweetie, I hate to dump you after I promised I'd drive you to the hotel, so you'll be riding in my personal cab." Fumo called over his shoulder. "Driver!" The tall man in a short-sleeved uniform blouse, white trousers and matching shoes, squeezed through the crowd and approached. He doffed his wheel cap to her, shielding his eyes. "Take this young lady to her hotel, the base, wherever she wants to go," the admiral ordered.

"Aye, sir."

The driver peeked from under the visor of his cap and Karyn gave the clean-cut man another look. "Neil Avery! I thought so." She flashed an attractive smile. He removed his cap and pinned it under his left arm. She said, "You look like a new man." Suddenly Karyn snapped from the spell, and in doing so, spun toward the luggage carousel. She chased down her travel case, and with one swoop, snagged it and dashed in his direction. Now in a prolonged embrace, his face rested on her soothing hair while her head found shelter between his neck and spacious shoulder.

Avery couldn't recall the last time a woman's fresh presence excited him. He only knew the smiles that once lifted his heavy countenance were few and far apart.

Fumo said, "I made dinner reservations tonight for three." He told them where and when.

The news delighted Karyn. Avery followed with a chiming thank you.

"And I'll even throw in the evening—under one condition," Fumo said. "That you bring her to the Westgate Hotel before the stroke of midnight, or I'll have a truckload of MPs haul you in for insubordination. Is that clear, mister?" A grin filled the admiral's long face.

"You, insubordinate?" Karyn said to him.

Fumo cocked his arm out and brought it back, giving a dress watch a quick look as he shuffled his feet. He transferred the briefcase from one hand to the other and clapped Avery on the back. "Well, sorry to rush off, but duty calls. Carry on, you two." He gave Karyn a parting kiss and disappeared down the long terminal, leaving the two of them alone in the crowd.

Avery enjoyed Karyn's new look. The blonde hair that once draped down to the small of her back, was now a jaw-length, party-style half-up do, windblown to curly perfection. Her eyebrows were long and curved like her legs and hips, and a touch of raspberry gloss on her lips gave them a bold look. She was more riveting than he dared remember.

She seemed impressed with his new shoulderboards. He was a lieutenant the last time she saw him. But he quickly learned that having two extra gold-yellow stripes meant moving on, giving into change, just like she had done with her hair.

He fidgeted with the car keys behind his back. "How was the flight?"

She smiled and took one step forward, standing toe-to-toe with him. "Long."

Her voice rang like music.

He grabbed the large travel case and yanked on its retractable handle.

Side by side they walked through the buzzing crowd. His stride was long; the pomp of a victorious matador. Hers was brisk and smart: businesslike; an eye-pleasing walk to every man who glanced her way.

Near the end of the terminal they entered a coffee shop, sat facing each other in a cozy booth, and ordered ....

A waiter arrived with a triple stack of Belgium waffles, side of sausages and hard black coffee for him, and an etiquette portion of fluffy scrambled eggs, crisp-brown home fries, and a tall glass of orange juice for her. She spoke as they ate. But Avery's mind was on his latest nightmare. What happened at the lab? He heard their nervous shouts again, saw the images of men scurrying about, smelled the stinging smoke. He was in his mother's womb. Coiled in a fetal position. Slowly it came back to him. The rest of the story Marcus had supplied ....

Marcus clutched his chest as the monitor's clock sped to its final seconds like a New Year's Eve countdown. With the lab's sirens wailing, he pushed chairs aside and crawled under the safety of the long control station. "What the hell you doing here?"

"To get you," Jager snapped. "If we don't leave now the blast will kill us both!"

"I'm not leaving without Avery!"

"You're not dying with him, either!"

Jager grabbed Marcus by the collar of his lab coat, he retaliated with a shove, and a prone scuffle broke out: legs kicking, arms flailing, elbows banging against the inside of the thin metal frame that shielded them.

A humming noise kicked in, and an explosion of colors replaced the slit of light at the base of the forward panel where both men lay facedown. From somewhere, another sound rushed with so much noise it forced the hiding scientist and his colleague to investigate. Marcus was the first to peer above the edge of the front panel. With dark goggles shielding his vision, the rotating positron came ablaze with a neon-blue human image: its lungs expanding and contracting in rhythmic sync to a runaway piston heart.

A whole line of lit monitors at the control station darkened and Marcus rushed to the gas- handling system. The needle beneath the glass-plated gauge pointed to zero. He checked the particle accelerator. Its green and red indicator lights had gone off at the same time the warning panel's wailing alarms stopped.

"Loud silence," Jager said.

Gray smoke smoldered behind the Vector Supercomputer, licking the high ceiling and clouding the lab. Marcus was puzzled. "Wonder what caused the shutdown?" He moved with caution on the slippery floor to the monstrous, spinning cylinder. It came to a stop and rose on its own with a mighty rush of compressed air. Avery tumbled out of the machine through a silvery mist and slammed his face flush against the chrome platform. He lay there motionless. "Dammit, Jager. Don't just stand there. Help me move him!"

Each man grabbed Avery by an arm and dragged him down the ramp. They got as far as nine paces when a violent seizure shook the navyman like a combative fish plucked out of water, and they released him.

Jager said, "Remind you of something?"

"The shuttle chimp that died of convulsions," Marcus replied.

Suddenly, the captain's thrashing stopped. Was he—?

Marcus dropped to his knees, flipped the body over, and shot a hand over the unconscious man's nose. "He not breathing!"

Jager pressed fingertips into a jugular. "His heart stopped!"

The doctor pinched Avery's nose with thumb and forefinger, opened his mouth, and repeatedly blew hot breaths down an airless windpipe. When that didn't work he crossed hands over the man's chest and pumped rhythmically.

Marcus was getting tired but didn't quit.

Avery remained unresponsive.

After a long exhausting moment of more chest compressions and lung ventilation, he decided to stop. "Call an ambulance," he told Jager.

The senior engineer gave him a mouth-parted stare. "Are you nuts? We've got to cremate him."

Marcus realized what he had said. The lab felt like a cold, abandoned morgue. Jager was right. The body would have to be disposed of and another candidate sought.

Avery came to life with a jumping jolt, startling Marcus and Jager. He gasped for air, forcing his lungs to accept the stench of smoke that clouded the lab. He coughed until his ribs ached, until he tired of rocking back and forth on his spine. Now as he lay on one side, his coiled body took on a fetal position.

Marcus shot to his feet. Jager did likewise. They clutched Avery's legs and dragged him into his private sleeping quarters. "Let's hope the dry floor and change of scenery help him recover," Jager said.

Someone galloped into the transport chamber. "Professor "J" where are you?"

The cry from the lab spilled into the adjoining room where Avery lay on the floor.

The doorway darkened.

It was Stas, followed by Quinn.

"Is he dead?" Stas asked in a heavy breath.

Marcus rose from his knees and looked at the three men standing in the doorway.

"What the hell happened?" Dauerman said. "And what's that burning smell?"

Avery came around, vomited food, and the lab-coated techs leaned over him. With each nauseous ejection, a surge of pain pounded in his head like a squad of Marines stomping on him with angry boots. The techs hoisted him to his feet and carried him to the bathroom—his head positioned in the pristine toilet bowl for the next discharge.

Marcus left the technicians to play nurse while he and Dauerman stepped into the messy lab.

"The gas line split in two places," Marcus said. "The worst break occurring in the power converter."

"That frozen nitrogen could've shattered Avery's body into a million glasslike fragments." Dauerman inspected the rest of the lab. "How did the VSC blow?"

Marcus led the way, sloshing in pure liquid metal. They approached the burned-out atomic supercomputer for a closer look. He pointed to a silver pipe in the high ceiling. "Cracked right there. Its contents spilled into the unit's electrical panel causing a fiery, short circuit." He hacked out a cough, stroking what was once the smooth enamel surface of the Vector. It was now pocketed with dents and tattooed over with big, round, black burn marks. Marcus stripped off his lab coat, still soaked from the slippery fall, and tossed it aside like an old banana peel. He looked at Dauerman. "Jager and I used the control station as a shield. If it hadn't been for me—"

"No, if it hadn't been for Quinn on the red phone cueing me to shut down the system from my office," countered Dauerman, "this place could've been destroyed."

"What the devil do you want, a half-ass apology?" Marcus wasn't about to let the agent have the last word. He pushed at him. "You knew damn well liquid sodium would eventually corrode that old pipe. That line should've been inspected before allowing us to proceed. The core in a critical reactor will go into meltdown without a coolant."

"That's your job. I'm just a watchdog."

"Don't push this off on me, Shank." He shoved back sliding glasses with a crooked finger. "This lab hasn't been maintained in god knows how long. It was an accident waiting to happen, almost claiming Avery's life. Neglect is what split those pipes. Now who's supposed to take care of this mess and fix the damaged negatron?"

Dauerman pushed out his chest and grinned. "It's your toy. You fix it."

Marcus ripped those glasses off. "Dammit, this is a major derailment. Any suggestions on how to get back on track?"

"Sure, just get on it." His cool tone angered Marcus even more.

The NCIS officer sloshed his way out of the laboratory with an air of indifference and the doctor marched back into the open compartment to check on his sick patient.

"How's he doing?" he asked Quinn.

"His stomach must be stripped by now. He's vomiting blood."

"Ohhh," the serviceman groaned. "Stop the damn rollercoaster."

After a long wait, Marcus and his men helped Avery up from the bathroom floor and carefully walked him to the big, wide bed, edging him comfortably on soft pillows. A gasping thank you escaped his lips. He opened his eyes, but had trouble recognizing who was who by their blurred faces. Except the doctor.

"I figured out what went wrong," Marcus said.

Avery sat up. In the reflection from the dresser mirror at his bedside he thought he saw a big, ugly knot with protruding blue veins on his forehead.

"Lie down, you idiot," the doctor ordered. "You're not well."

Jager, Quinn, and Stas stepped out of the room to begin the massive cleanup in the lab.

Avery groaned. "I'm fine." A new barrage of torturing coughs rolled from within, knocking him flat on the bed, coiling him again. He gasped for air, and noticed blue crescent moons on all his fingernails.

"Your lips and eyelids are blue, too," the doctor informed him. "Lack of oxygen." He hacked out one of his own coughs.

"And that's from too much cigarettes," the serviceman warned.

"Never mind that. Bet you have a headache."

"The size of a watermelon." He sat up and barked out another set of coughs. "How'd you know?"

"You've got a golf ball sitting over your right eye. That, and a nosebleed."

Avery swiped a shaky finger over his upper lip like a kid with a runny nose. He searched for the thing on his pulsating brow and felt its size and shape.

"I'll fetch ice for your head and an air tank to help you feel better. You'll have to wear a nasal cannula, though. I'll also need to check your vitals. Put you on a treadmill and do an EKG." Marcus ran a fat hand over his forehead, mopped off the sweat, and huffed out a breath of relief.

From the lab, the technicians' voices filtered past the open door ....

Quinn: "Almost a repeat of Spectrum's first fatality."

Stas: "We lost funding when the police exhumed Mitchell Braun's garbled remains."

Jager: "Why didn't anyone think of getting a defibrillator for this place?"

Marcus quickly closed the fat, metal door. "I'm glad you're alive, Neil. Damn glad."

Avery realized he was in a soundproof room. "So that you can continue experimenting on your lab mouse?"

"No, stupid." Marcus creased his face in annoyance. "Who else can we push through the tube, me?" An awkward silence fell and both men locked eyes on each other without blinking. "You know my pot-bellied frame can't fit. You and your damn solid physique."

A wave of relieved laughter filled the room, prompting another violent episode of hacking from both men.

Marcus waited until he caught his breath. "You need oxygen. Let me get that tank."

He started to head out.

"What happens now?" Avery hated the sound of his raspy voice. He lowered his head into his hands, hoping to find relief, but the pounding felt worse.

Black eyeglasses crept down the slope of the doctor's nose. He pushed them back with a pensive look. "Hmmm, this is bad. Spectrum will have to be terminated." He stared at the wall like a blind man, then gave Avery a look. "I know someone in Arlington who's looking for a man like you to fill a vacant position with ONI. Think it over and let me know. In the meantime consider yourself on permanent leave ...."

He and Karyn had eaten and paid at the cashier. "You're quiet," she said. "You okay?" They left the coffee shop and headed through the airport terminal to his Ford Taurus.

He was thinking how fortunate he was to still be in uniform. Marcus hadn't said he was a civilian. No one had. He simply said the project was terminated. But what did that spell for him? If he accepted the Navy job in DC, he would have to pack his belongings and leave North Island. "Just wondering what you'll be doing with your free time."

Air fanned his face as they got into the car and drove off. He wished those rolling clouds had not covered over the silver curtains of the sun's rays, leaving a threatening steel-gray sky. "So, where will you be staying?" He focused on the road and traffic ahead.

"Santa Barbara. My oldest sister, Gloria, owns a beach house there. Every year we fly off to some exotic place. But this year we're beach-bumming from her back porch. Maybe do some town-hopping between there and Sacramento."

"Sounds nice. My late wife and I spent a lot of weekends in Santa Barbara, before we married."

Karyn got quiet.

"So, you lied," she said after a while.

He realized what he had said. "I'm sorry. Really. I made up the divorce tale because it was easier than losing her to that horrible accident."

"That's okay," she said with thought. "I would've done the same."

Traffic from a connecting route began to merge with I-5, slowing things down. If the highway were less congested, he would have bypassed the naval base and kept going, riding the Ford until he got to Seattle, maybe Canada. Someplace where he could escape and forget. With his luck, the car would break down before he arrived anywhere. He noticed her studying him: hands on the steering, eyes on the road. She had something on her mind and he knew it.

"I'd like for us to get away for a while. Can you?"

"Funny you should ask." He gave her a split-second look. "I have plenty of time."

The clouds wrung out a gentle rain and he turned on the wipers. Their rhythmic motion was as the swinging pendulum of a grandfather clock, reminding him of the long year they had been apart.

Karyn said, "Did you receive my last letter?"

His silence spoke of the many she had written; the ones he did not answer.

"Yes. Got to admit I was surprised."

A rumbling FedEx truck passed him on his side.

"Why didn't you write back? You had my address and e-mail. It would've been all right."

"Couldn't at the time."

It got quiet again in the car. "I'm sorry." She turned to him embraced in her seatbelt. "I didn't expect you to just stop grieving and start living. That's not what I meant."

He peeked into her eyes like he had done when he first met her. In them was a quiet romance. Another love letter sent directly to him. Traffic was moving a little better now.

She told him she never mentioned about the way she felt because she wanted it to be his choice. For months she trained her eyes not to betray her. She learned at Cornell, it was wrong for someone in her profession to let intimate thoughts interfere. It's risky, they had said. But as the pages of her daily calendar fell away like autumn trees shedding its leaves, the passion subdued her without a fight. "Can't believe I said all this."

He checked the rearview mirror and made a lane change, all the while listening with a sprinting heart.

She went on to say that she wanted to develop a non-formal relationship outside the confines they were both accustomed to. But she kept the secret. The way he buried himself in his pain.

Avery wanted the same thing she did. He would have to force himself to admit it, though. "I always liked you. Just couldn't show it at the time. Didn't know how. The size and shape of my grief disabled me. Still don't know whether I can or not."

He drove through the falling drizzle; each drop kissing the windshield. He let her think that one over.

At the naval station's main gate, he rolled the Ford past a row of leafy Palmettos and came to an easy stop. Avery powered his side of the window down and the Marine on duty approached. He checked the decal sticker on the windshield, then gave an ID card a keen glance. The rain came down in sheets now. Drumming on the car's frame.

"Morning, Captain." The booth sentry at checkpoint-one saluted. "What a gully-washer, sir." His poncho dripped from the downpour. His eyes swept past the captain to the woman in the car.

"She's with me," Avery said. "Admiral's granddaughter."

"Beauty and the beast," the clean-cut Marine murmured. He gripped the rim of his M1 helmet liner in a gentleman's gesture; raindrops bouncing off it.

The gate's wooden, red-and-yellow-striped crossing arm lifted and Avery eased down on the gas, passing through at twenty miles per hour. The sentry standing at attention let the car pull away.

Avery escorted Karyn to McCain Boulevard's medical building where she once worked and studied. She visited all her former colleagues, toured the facility's lecture hall and stopped by her former office. The paintings, including the Norman Rockwell fishing scene, were still there.

She looked out the window. "I'd like to see your world."

"Got just the thing."

As soon as the rain stopped, Avery took her to the *Seven*, high atop Vultures Row. The supercarrier's massive flight deck and the gray humps of the Laguna Mountains in the distance were his kind of view. "Want to go higher?" he asked her.

She looked interested. "What do you have in mind?"

He drove her to the Marine Corps Air Base where a pilot—a close friend of Lieutenant Ed "Dino" Vazquetelli—took them for a brief ride between the hanging clouds and the mushroom-shaped island of Coronado, on a long-bodied, Vietnam-era type Huey helicopter. Avery still loved flying. The beating of the helo's four-bladed rotors and whining twin engines reminded him of that. Now that project Spectrum was over he began to muse on going to aviation school. Surely someone could pull strings for him to remain in the Navy.

It was well past twelve when he drove Karyn to the hotel in downtown San Diego. The Westgate resembled a glass palace of sparkling windows; a glittering facade guarded by tall office buildings, all beneath a powder-puff gray canopy, masking what could have been a clear, ebony night. He turned off a busy street and found a parking spot as the blanket of dark clouds rung out another torrent. With the wipers inactive and the idling engine killed, they spoke without undoing their seatbelts for as long as the rain cascaded over the windshield and the view from within the car appeared dreamlike.

After a while, a gentle wind hushed the skies and chased thick clouds away.

Avery popped the trunk open and got out of the car first. He handed her a light-colored satchel and bulky travel case; her soft hand rested on his in the exchange.

He felt his eyes dance, locking with hers in deep, satisfying warmth.

"Mind if I ask something?" Karyn said.

"Shoot." He closed the trunk, and together, they entered Westgate, strutting on a Persian carpet to the ranks of crystal chandeliers glittering overhead.

"Any regrets?"

The question was a familiar one. "None whatsoever."

The hostess at the check-in desk greeted them.

Chapter 17

Neil Avery loved the way Karyn's hips filled her strapless, red gown: in the shape of an upside-down rose. With one arm embracing a matching handbag and bare feet in slingbacks, the naked luster of her ankles, legs, and neckline beneath her looping, hand-length hair revealed more of her than he had ever seen.

Driving north on State Route 1, a dusk-orange sun stained the blue Pacific in a dancing beam of ocean light. The plan was to spend the evening at Bellissimo's, Avery's favorite dining place in Oceanside, where Admiral Fumo had reserved a table for three. It was the same place the young captain, Carlos Nieve, and James Jordan frequented whenever they hit town for a night out.

Avery parked behind Fumo's burgundy Cutlass Ciera and silenced the engine. He got out first, and like a knight in naval dresswear, opened the passenger's door and ushered Karyn into the extravagant restaurant; her hand around his arm, his wheel cap in the other. "Your chivalry impresses me," she said. "Sure you're not a gallant stranger?"

Fumo mused from a window table at a blazing sky and landless horizon. He waved above the heads of patrons, signaling the maître d' who ushered the young couple to their seats. He rose tall as Karyn gave the interior of the restaurant the once-over with a simple smile of approval. Avery also loved its warm, rustic atmosphere, wine-colored carpet, soft-lit mini chandeliers, and tapestry window treatment. He draped a service jacket over the backing of a chair and sat when the others sat.

In the background, romantic music played. A young server, in a tux-type apparel, approached the trio and handed out three, leather-bound menus. Each with the name and picture of the restaurant.

Karyn looked to Fumo in a moment of indecision. She turned to the young captain who had already ordered filet mignon with rice pilaf and steamed asparagus in hollandaise sauce. Fumo ordered a porterhouse steak platter and convinced Karyn to go for the sautéed duck breast special.

As soon as dinner was served, a second server crowned the center of the table with a tall, chilled bottle of Gallo Nero.

"What's the occasion?" Karyn said to Fumo. Her smile was like the studded chandelier above her.

"You, me, and Captain Neil Avery. How often does this happen?"

"That's a lot of wine," she said. "I rarely finish one serving."

"And I don't drink anymore, sir." Avery handled the bottle with the vintage-gray label. "Especially something called Black Rooster."

"Nonsense. I'll just give you each a fill. Taste it and tell me what you think." Fumo undid the bottle and played host.

Karyn took a quick sip. "Nice." She set her glass down.

Avery swirled the scarlet beverage and let its aroma put him in the right mood. "Good choice, sir."

Fumo had command of the conversation—just like Karyn warned he would do. She said he wanted control over every aspect of naval activity at the base: the tactical and strategic utilization of its ships; security and personnel. He was a power-hungry individual, she said; a man accustomed to being in the center of it all, and tonight would be no different.

He talked up a storm, hands in constant motion, until suddenly he became silent and the spotlight he was in now turned on the young captain. What would satisfy the insatiable hunger for information Avery saw in the admiral's eyes? Ships, port visits, sailors? It came to him. He was sure the Old Man would be interested in other matters.

"So, tell me about your new post."

Karyn asked, "What post?"

"The one that got him promoted."

She engaged Avery with a knockout smile. "I knew you were destined for greatness."

Fumo dabbed his mouth with a big, cloth napkin. "How are things coming along, if you don't mind me asking?"

Avery shrugged those big shoulders. The project was over. "No big deal."

"What is it you do?" Karyn asked.

The question came at him like a torpedo fired from its tube and his appetite drained.

Fumo and Karyn waited. Had the accident at the lab not occurred, the program's success could have been a very big deal. All of NASA's flight directors, civil engineers, astronauts, and scientists would have all resigned and applied for Spectrum. Avery was sure of it.

"Just shoreside duty. You wouldn't want to hear it." The glass of untouched wine beside him resembled a goblet of human blood. He pushed aside an unfinished platter of food and reached for it.

Fumo looked disappointed. "Doesn't sound anything like the national security job Admiral Jenson described to me."

Adrenaline surged to his head, pure and hot. If Avery didn't take a few quick swigs of the crimson-dark liquid, he would have to run a mile to consume the tension building from within. He lifted the big glass and pushed some of its contents past his dry lips. It went down like fermented venom, exploding in his stomach with tremendous heat. "Let's celebrate the evening and leave it at that," he told Fumo. "Shall we?"

The admiral's long face dropped and he put in a sour stare.

"Cheers," Karyn agreed.

Fumo chimed in behind her with narrowed eyes and the three of them clinked their long-stemmed glasses and took a generous sip.

While a busboy cleared the table, Fumo refilled the captain's glass—for the sixth time.

Avery felt an unsteady grin take over.

Fumo said to him, "I understand Shank is moonlighting for the Central Intelligence Agency."

If that was true, Avery thought, it meant the hackers were doomed. They might even be put to death for espionage. "Seem worried, Admiral."

"Just poisoned by curiosity."

The young captain took a gulp of wine, rinsed his mouth and swallowed. "CIA, encrypted messages, secret projects. I don't know a damn thing. And neither does this nation's ruling hierarchy." He put down an empty glass and wiped his mouth on the white sleeve of his shirt. The admiral cocked a thick, sandy eyebrow and poured in another fourth.

Karyn leaned into him. "What're you doing? You'll get him drunk."

"Care to share the family secret?" Avery asked.

Fumo said to Karyn, "He doesn't seem to mind." He shifted eyes on the captain. "Secret projects, huh? Must be something unauthorized if the government is in the dark."

Avery guzzled down several more mouthfuls of Gallo Nero, leaving the rest to sway at the bottom of the long-stemmed glass. "I wouldn't worry. DOD knows what they're doing." He wiped his mouth with the back of his hand—and burped. "It'll eventually come out. Unlike my belch."

Fumo gave Avery a probing stare. "How about now?"

Karyn looked displeased. She leaned into the linen-draped table and cupped her warm hand on his. "Stop drinking and tell him what he wants to know!"

He chugged more of the potent red stuff down his throat, gasping with each gulp. "DOD is experimenting with nuclear genetics." He studied Fumo's wineglass. He had downed only one serving. Just like Karyn.

"If you don't start making sense, mister, you'll be headed to my mast. Am I on your radar, Cap—?"

Karyn silenced him with her touch. She turned to Avery. "Genetics? You mean cloning?" Her face drastically changed. So did Fumo's. In the brief spell he did not recognize them.

"Physics and the ability to create life outside the womb," Avery said. "Now that's an interesting dance pair."

"I've got a better combo." Fumo pricked him with sharp eyes. "A stubborn naval officer who refuses to talk—behind bars. You owe an explanation."

"Don't dig a grave and jump in it, Admiral."

The sudden shift in attitude silenced Karyn.

Fumo pushed aside the empty wine bottle. "I'm responsible for whatever happens on the base."

"It isn't about you, sir, or the base."

The admiral leaned in. "What, then?" The smell of ultimatum ripened on his breath.

"It's okay," Karyn assured him. "Whatever it is, you can say it."

Avery's pulse quickened and his pores released stinging perspiration. "It's … classified."

"Nothing's classified as far as I'm concerned. You have twenty seconds to spill your guts."

A force gripped the air and Avery's features, too. Peer pressure of the highest order, he thought. And that from his commanding officer.

He hoped the truth would sound crazy. "… Time travel."

"What?" Fumo said.

Karyn's eyes rolled to Avery. He couldn't tell whether the look on her face was a worried frown, an incredulous gawk, or something else.

He expected she would remain silent but knew Fumo would not. "C'mon, Captain. I expected you to say something intelligent—but not this. Time travel?" He gave Karyn a blank look.

"It's just an evaluative study on quantum theory. Nothing to concern yourself over … sir."

A server, with bottle of wine in hand, rushed past the trio. The admiral said, "So, where have you traveled to?" He crossed arms on the table. "Back to the days of King Henry the Eighth?"

Avery was counting on the background noise to drown out their unusual conversation. "Of course not." He felt the need to get defensive. "I haven't been anywhere."

"Doesn't sound like your project will, either."

He was right. At this moment, he thought, everything in the lab was being disassembled, torn down, hauled out.

"Well," Karyn said. "I'm ready for dessert." Her soft eyes looked from Avery to Fumo. "How about you two?"

"Not me, darling. An admiral's got to look his best if his men are to look up to him." He hailed the steward. "The rest of the evening is yours."

Captain Avery belched. The server arrived with the bill.

"We should do this again," Karyn suggested.

Avery grabbed the wineglass and took one more hearty swig. He let out a groan beneath his breath.

Fumo stood to his feet. The naval officer in the impressive-looking dinner jacket was hard to miss in the crowd. "I wouldn't skip another engagement like this for the world." He eyed the young captain. "But please, no more science fiction. I'll talk to SecNav in the morning. Get him to keep Admiral Jenson off my six if something should come down the pike."

Fumo leaned over, kissed Karyn on the forehead and headed to the cashier as the tall server passed him on the way to the table.

"Will there be anything else?" The waiter posed with pad and pencil.

Karyn smiled. "Yes. We'd like dessert."

Karyn Engle forked the edge of her cannoli. Between each bite, she tasted a bit of coffee. "Know what it feels like seeing you again?" She reached for his hand and took it.

Avery indulged his palate to a double portion of firm, cold gelato. His favorite was peach. "If it's anything like surfing, the feeling is mutual."

Now Karyn licked off a dab of ricotta cheese from a corner of her mouth as her toes roamed beneath the hem of his trousers. He drew a breath, and eyes darted from the cold gelato on his gums. A sudden rush from within merged into a sweet high, and with parted lips, a cool gasp escaped like a winter's breath.

"I like the schoolgirl in you. Wanna smooch?"

She withdrew her foot and handled the pastry with etiquette fingers for the next bite. "What on earth is wrong with you?"

"Me?"

"Yeah, you, mister. Didn't you realize you drank most of that wine? John was trying to get you to talk." Her face darkened with guilt and paled with apology. " ... And I helped. I'm sorry." She sipped down the last of her coffee, had a final piece of pastry, and sucked dabs of creamy cheese off slender fingers.

Avery's long-handled ice cream spoon tinkled at the bottom of the tall, dessert glass. He wiped the sweet peach flavor from his lips with a big, cloth napkin.

Karyn searched in her handbag. Head bowed. She extracted a compact and popped it open. "Were you serious?"

"About?"

Now she looked for something else. "You know." She found it, uncapped it, and with a twist, a soft capsule rose out of its hiding place; a cool watermelon shade.

"Oh, that." The Italian music in the background lulled and he felt it was safe to talk. "We live in an age where anything is possible. Including the impossible."

Karyn batted her eyes. If she did it to hide the fear in them, it didn't work.

The handsome couple rose and walked away from the table, leaving behind the dark turquoise sea that swayed with rhythmic cadence in the quiet distance. Avery paid for the desserts and coffee, and on their way out he opened the thick glass door for Karyn as he had done on their way in. Now hand in hand he led her to his car. They had enjoyed their evening. They had enjoyed each other.

He approached the Ford Taurus, one arm snaked around her waist. He fumbled for the keys in the pocket of his Navy jacket, and with a clipped laugh, pulled them out. He had trouble unlocking the doors with the remote.

"Neil, let me drive. You're smiling like a jerk." She took the keys.

Suddenly he realized it. I'm drunk. Something he hadn't experienced in two years, slammed into the side of his head. He swayed as though standing on the pitching deck of a ship.

Karyn opened the doors with the automatic and took the wheel of the Ford. He buckled up and the headlamps came on. She guided the car out of its parking space and hit the gas.

"Sorry, Karyn. I should've never let that happen." Funneled lights illuminated the dark road ahead. A sly moon peeked its face through a broken cloud riding with them, and hid again.

"Wasn't your fault. I should've warned you about John."

"What'd I say to make him angry?"

"Forget it. I'll drop you off at the base, then cab it to the hotel."

"Thanks." He was too mortified to say anything more.

Sunlight speared through his eyelids and Avery awakened, recalling the restless dream he had from a lethargic slumber that held him in its grip. He was handcuffed within a slow moving car winding through a surreal-looking cemetery where visitors looked like ghosts. Up ahead was that familiar white hearse leading the way, and within it was a casket. Who had died he couldn't remember, though.

Now he was fully awake. He was in his car, his hands were free, and he was going somewhere.

A woman was at the wheel of the Ford, and the jagged cliffs that rolled by as she drove were those of the Pacific's seacoast on the way to Santa Barbara. Had he the presence of mind to return to that lofty stretch of precipice and waiting boulders below, he would have dove to his death a long time ago. Thinking of it now, he was glad he didn't take the plunge.

Karyn pulled into the driveway of a pastel-colored house: poppy-red shutters, lemon-yellow awnings, warm-blue siding, cream-white roof. There, behind a gray Chevy Tahoe, she cut the Ford's purring engine, met his eyes, and ran a light finger over his ribbon bars. "We're here." She handed him the car keys and described her sister's house: a huge, bay window overlooking Leadbetter Beach, a sleepy back porch, quiet guestrooms, a breakfast nook, and …. She apologized for rambling. "Just excited," she said.

Avery let a catlike yawn work its way out of his rundown body. His side of the window, closing with a whir, made the same dreadful sound as that large cylindrical tube when it closed down on him.

"That was some crash landing, mister. Didn't you sleep well last night?" Her fingers roamed beneath the hem of his sort-sleeved whites.

"Too busy barfing."

He wished a recurring nightmare he wrestled with for the past two nights, had crept away with the monstrous hangover he had conceived and given birth to. Now the thought of the frightening accident at the lab made his chest tighten and knees shake.

He stepped out of the car and followed Karyn up a pristine walkway of interlocked pink paving stones that led to the picturesque, two-story house. He finger-combed his hair in the breeze that flowed over the cream-colored beach and fitted his wheel cap over his brow. Karyn rang the front door bell. She took his hand and squeezed it.

A woman appeared behind a draped window, and with a happy shout, she swung the door wide open. Sunlight hit her face and the family resemblance showed. The woman pulled Karyn in with big arms and inspected the naval officer. She tried to give lift to a limp French roll over her nape. "Aren't you going to introduce us?"

Karyn did, and they entered the house through a tiled foyer which led to a sun-drenched living room where a bay window displayed the steel Pacific.

Gloria smacked Karyn on the fanny.

"Saw what she did? That's her way of saying she's happy I'm here."

Now she fluffed her sister's hair. "Love that curly-layered cut, Missy. Makes you lustfully attractive." The two women sat on opposite ends of a floral-patterned Mansfield couch. It was a nice four-seater. Long enough to sleep on.

Avery sat across from them in a recliner and enjoyed the once-over Gloria gave him.

"I admire a man in uniform. I find them dashing. Tell me about yourself, sailor."

There wasn't much to tell when there was plenty to hide: abuser, liar, drunkard. He gave her a toned-down synopsis in one quick phrase of military jargon, portraying himself as an unassuming man with plenty to accomplish. First impressions are important, he thought.

"Gimme a break. You didn't get those captains' shoulderboards for nothing."

"Twenty years of military service," Karyn announced. "And the next CO of North Island."

"Do I hear wedding bells? This doll-face sister of mine is in love with you, honey."

He gave Karyn that practiced smile. How he wished she were Darah. He would turn away from the past and all his mistakes and learn to laugh with her, cry with her, instead of making her cry alone.

A lascivious tongue mopped his hand and he retracted it with a snapped look. A meaty Labrador Retriever had emerged unannounced from behind the wide-back recliner.

"Here, Champ. Come here, boy." The dog trotted to Karyn's extended arms, clicking the parquet floorboards with his nails. She held his big, black nose and rubbed hers against it. "Haven't seen you in so long. How are you, fella?"

"Champion's fine. Took him to the vet two weeks ago for his annual." The dog tail-wagged his way to Gloria.

"Owning a dog must be nice," Avery said. The women lovingly stroked the beautiful, black animal. He had wanted a dog after his mother died, but his father wouldn't allow it. He hated dogs. Hated life.

"I know a few breeders. It's never too late. Our granduncle at the age of eighty-two adopted three of them. It helped him get over the agonizing hump of being a widower."

Widower, orphaned, only child. I'm cursed, he thought.

Champion strolled to the uniformed guest as though expecting a treat. When Avery reached out to pet him, the dog abruptly pushed a fat, long muzzle into the stranger's crotch and a wrestling match ensued.

"He doesn't mean any harm," Gloria said with an amused look. "He just wants to get acquainted. Big dogs are like that. Their way of shaking hands."

The canine got a whiff of what he wanted and backed off.

"Oh, is that all?" Avery was relieved but hot-faced. "Thought he was after my manhood."

The women let out a hysterical laugh.

Gloria coaxed Champion to sit at her feet.

Avery let the sudden rush of heat drain from his face and put in a thin smile. "I can't have a dog now." Champion made his way back to the visitor. He reached out and stroked him. "They need as much love and attention as a child. That's something I can't do." Never learned, he thought.

"Doesn't have to be now. Maybe when you retire. Dogs make loyal friends and playful companions. With my boys away at college, Champ helped me survive the painful years of divorce. Couldn't have done it without him." Gloria took one glance at the lovable animal and got misty-eyed.

After the three each had a slice of crumb cake and coffee, they left the spacious living room and walked about the house.

In the master bedroom, Avery sat by an open window in a big, brown rocker and swayed as though he were out at sea. A flock of birds sailed past the cotton-candy clouds, and the rhythmic ebb of the great Pacific tugged at him and let go; pulling and releasing.

"Your heart belongs where mighty ships sail, doesn't it, sailor?"

"Been over it, under it, through it, but never been free of it." He rose from the old, rocking chair. "You have a beautiful home."

Karyn stood by the door as though sending subtle signals for her sister to pick up.

"If you're not in too much of a hurry, I'd love to prepare dinner for you and Karyn." The serviceman smiled on the gracious invitation. "And if you aren't planning on heading back to the base, why don't you spend the night, or even several. That's what the guestrooms are for."

"Me, stay?" He caught Karyn in one of her winning smiles. Her body language spoke of beach walks, swaying on the back-porch swing, locking eyes with his. "I couldn't impose."

"What impose? I'm inviting you. What do I care as long as my sister's here. Besides …." She winked at him. "Karyn wants you to stay. She put me up to this. Right, Missy?"

Her creamy cheeks bloomed to a red pastel tint. "You'd better say yes. She won't take no for an answer."

He smiled with silent acceptance.

"Then it's settled." Gloria clasped her hands. "You'll stay for dinner, and you'll stay as my guest for as long as you can."

Champion mouthed a red rubber ball and walked it over to the man in uniform. He heeled at his feet and gave him a look. The dog had the muzzle of a young bear. His jaw looked strong. His eyes were dark and clear, showing intelligence, and the coat on his sturdy body was short and smooth.

"Oh, look," Karyn exclaimed. "He wants you to play with him."

"He obviously likes you," Gloria said. "And he's not the only one." She beamed with pure joy. No one had to tell Avery that joy was for Karyn. Divorced women like Gloria were the type that wanted their younger sisters to fare better than they had. "Now that you two are here, let's head to the beach after dinner. Heaven knows I could use a good, long walk."

Dusk was nearing when the long barefoot stroll on the cool pristine beach turned them all around, bringing them back where they had started, behind the pastel-colored house where a gentle porch light welcomed them like the errant moths that danced over it.

Gloria hurled Champ's rubber ball into the rumbling waves and the large-bodied canine dove after it.

"Isn't it beautiful?" Karyn took Avery's hand.

The last glowing rays of the evening dyed wispy cirrus clouds in the color spectrum of the twilight sun. "Like standing on the edge of the world." He turned to look at her eyes.

Karyn lurched at him with a kiss. Her lips were full. Moist and soft. They embraced, and she smacked him on the fanny. "I'm happy you're here."

"You're cute and you're fresh. I like that."

He made her laugh.

On a large, well-spread, white beach blanket, a bare-chested Avery had the entire real estate to himself, lying face-up in the California sun. He was in his swim shorts: one leg crossed over the other, hands folded behind his neck. His eyes were closed and his hair was slicked back the way his wife used to like it; dark as the plumes of a raven, she once said. He loved to swim and was good at it. The ocean temperature that time of day thrilled him. He never shrunk away or grew tired of the cold water, no matter how long he stroked. And when he reclined too long beneath the sun's embrace, he thought about something Darah once said:

"Better use some of this sunblock unless you want to get stung."

His eyes popped open and he saw an upside-down view of Karyn over his head: the sand dunes above, the bright sky below. "Well, good morning. Or is it afternoon?" He rolled over on his chest. Her toenails were pedicure clean; pink like her tank top and shorts. "Don't you own a G-string?"

"Is my fantail the only thing that interests you?"

"Everything about you interests me, including your wee-hour chirping with Gloria. What did you caged birds talk about?"

She knelt on the thick sand. "What do you think?" She looked surprised.

"Football?"

She threw her hands on her hips and frowned. "I should sack you. Face first in the sand."

"Please do."

Karyn laughed like a woman in love. "Where's my sister?"

"Running errands. Took Champ along."

"I swear, that dog loves riding in that SUV. You'd think he was the owner."

A breeze rolled over the lapping waves, catching strands of Karyn's hair and making them dance in the sunlight. She stripped out of her tank top and shorts, revealing a complete woman in a G-string swimsuit: legs, hips, boobs, brains.

He couldn't resist flashing a grin. "That's more like it."

She gave a pleased smile and sat on his blanket; Ray Ban glasses crowned on her head. "Mind if I rub some of this on you?" Her thin eyebrows lifted with expectation. "You're turning red."

"Be my guest." He positioned himself for the rubdown. "But I like a healthy, reddish tone."

"So do lobsters." She applied the lotion to her hands and explored his athletic body—over every inch of skin, every ripple of firm muscle on his arms, shoulders, back. "Turn over," she said. He laid there, enjoying her touch. "I said, turn over." She slapped his fanny, snapping the serene spell that held him.

"Hey, not so rough. I thought you liked me."

"I do." She looked at him with those dancing blue eyes highlighted by the sun. "More than you'll ever know." Her moist fingers interlocked with his, thrilling him to the rush of air on his face. She leaned over him and stretched her curved body close to his. She kissed the tip of his nose and pinned snips of unruly hair behind an ear. "Let me love you."

Her scent cast a spell over him, and before he knew it, he pulled her close and sealed his lips over hers, making love to her tongue with his. The warmth of her body drove away the cold, empty world he had known, while her mouth over his was as life-giving CPR.

In a breathless moment they embraced; passion flowing like the stretching tide.

"It's a shame." Karyn rose to her feet and walked along the tall sandgrass.

He followed her. "What is?"

"That we hadn't met before. Earlier in life, I mean."

"Wasn't meant to be." He wondered what she thought of his answer.

"Is it meant now?"

"Don't let love make you impatient."

She reached for his hand and grabbed it. "Can't help it."

Music seemed to fill the air. Avery heard it in his head, humming with the tide. It made him want to soar above the champagne-sparkling breakers on the wings of a migrating bird returning from its journey to a place where it belonged.

"Has there ever been anyone in your life?" He lost himself in her eyes.

"What makes you ask?"

"Your kiss. Am I your first?"

"Was it that bad?"

"Just asking."

He drew her breath out.

"There was someone. Once. At Cornell."

Avery waited. They strode forward.

"What happened?" He wanted to know as much about her as she knew about him.

"Didn't work out. All he wanted was someone to have in bed."

Avery knew there was more. He smiled as though it were the first time.

"Okay, I did have feelings for him if that's what you're fishing for." She punched him in the stomach with a light fist.

"What I wanted to hear you say is—you're my first."

Her silence was as the breeze that played with her hair. Karyn met his eyes and held it there. "Yes, you're my first. But only because he was a loser."

"Hard to believe."

"What's so hard?"

"You're a catch. Any guy would desire you."

She leaned into his firm chest, lifted herself up on sandy toes, and planted a moist kiss on his lips. "But no guy could flip me like you do." She cupped her hands over his ear and whispered something that drew him to the fountain of youth in her voice. She bolted away from him, running in the direction they came.

"What did you say?"

"Catch me!"

He felt a throb down there. "And if I do?"

"You can kiss me all you want."

Avery chased after her, kicking up sand with fast, long strides. She attempted to elude him but his Running-Back sprint narrowed the wide gap between them until she was within arms reach. Hungry hands grabbed her waist and she laughed. Her ticklishness began to harden his manhood and he pulled her close to him. Everything about Karyn was inviting.

Water surged at their feet.

"That was too easy," he gasped. "You wanted me to catch you."

"No," she said in a deep, warm breath. "I wanted you to kiss me."

Slender arms curled around his neck and she indulged herself on his lips; wild fingers running through his short, wet hair.

He wrestled her onto the sand, rolled her over him, and a cold wave covered them. Her delightful scream intoxicated him so much that all he wanted was to pin her down and make love to her there. She squealed, trying to escape his grasp, but he held her down until a second, white-capped breaker blanketed them and she let out another potion-filled scream.

The water ebbed and he stood her to her feet. Hair plastered on her forehead and both sides of her face drew a hearty chuckle out of him. "Why does it feel we've laughed before? Kissed before?"

Her contagious laughter subsided. "Because we have." She picked up her fallen sunglasses and reached out to him with appetite in her eyes. Her touch and smile kept him aroused. "In my dreams of you."

Karyn released his hand with a tracing caress and strode ahead, luring him with kisses she blew over her shoulder. Kicking up bare feet, she winked at him and hungry eyes followed her with pleasure. He was more than just captivated by her, he was head-over-heels now, just as she was for him.

Hand in hand they returned to their starting point and discovered Champion lying on the beach blanket. He sniffed at the ocean scent in the air and barked as the couple approached.

"What a life," he said. "Does it get any better?" The big Labrador got up effortlessly and with a vigorous tail and dancing rump, came to him. Between and around his legs Champ went. He grabbed the dog's hanging, soft ears and massaged his wide head.

"Champ learned his beach-bumming ways from Gloria," she said with a knockout smile.

"Looks like she's got him spoiled good."

They enjoyed another laugh.

"I wish we had forever." Champ came to her and sniffed her toes.

"Forever is what we make from all our yesterdays." He allowed her gentle eyes to search his, to learn about him, to love him more. Hungry lips met again and he tasted her, taking in her warm breath.

"Hey, you two," Gloria chimed through her bedroom window. "Don't you ever think of anything else?"

"We do," Karyn said with emphasis. The ocean current carried her crisp voice into the air. "But it can wait till we're married."

His lips formed a smile, and he searched for a word to describe what he felt. Was it wonderment? Excitement? Pleasure?

She rubbed the dog's belly and turned to him. "I love your boyish grin." He sighed with relief. Happiness. That was it. He was happy.

After dinner, he and Karyn kissed under the star-studded sky that shined like a million tiny diamonds on a blanket of black velvet. Cuddling behind the house overlooking the dark, inviting sea, the porch light went out with a pop and the glow that draped them darkened. What remained was the sound of breakers, rumbling like their love for each other. He kissed her hand and searched where an engagement ring had never been. Now she gently explored. In the dark, the white band of skin, tattooed around his ring finger, would not be found.

With a dim lamplight at his side, Avery tossed under the covers of the guestroom bed; his mind on the weekend in Seattle, and the long, scenic drive he and Karyn had taken up the Pacific Coast Highway and back in a rented, two-seat, Saturn Sky convertible. Where did these last two weeks go? He thought about it so long, the sweet insomnia gave way and he shut his eyes. He dreamt of Karyn, sleeping naked beside him.

A slice of dawn climbed over the clouds and lit the guestroom. He rolled over, using the pillow at the back of his head to shield his eyes from the gold streams that seemed to part the long, cottony drapes. A cell phone chimed *Anchors Aweigh*. He grabbed the cellular off the nightstand with a wandering hand, hit the talk button, and pressed the phone against an ear. He let out a groggy hello.

"Neil, that you?" someone said with urgency.

He yawned like a tired bear, wiped a rivulet of drool from the corner of his mouth, then rubbed a deep slumber around his sluggish eyes, but they still felt heavy. He didn't need to look at his Quartz. "Marc, do you realize what time it is?"

"Time to get back to the lab. We're set to go!"

Now he was really awake. "You said it was over."

"Just get your ass here."

Chapter 18

When Avery entered the loft-size laboratory and scanned all the enhancements—the polished anticorrosion pipes, the Vector Supercomputer's new outer shell, the diamondized floor tiles, the upgraded shutdown devices and the gleaming chrome power converters that capped the improved Kevlar-shielded thermo-glass enclosures—the doctor marched toward him. "Like the facelift?"

The walls smelled of fresh paint, masking all the burned spots. "I'm not impressed."

Marc's smile fell. "Who cares what you think."

"So, why ask?"

From one corner of the lab to the other, Marc's crew were busy running diagnostic tests on every piece of equipment. Although the technicians moved with quiet confidence, the urgency written on their faces could not be hid. Lost time needed to be made up, and that placed Avery's life in danger again.

Jager mentioned it was a miracle the captain's broken-down state had not seeped through the gaping cracks in the number-one cylinder Marcus discovered the day after the accident. If it had, every microscopic protoplasmic cell in Avery's body, all one-hundred-trillion, would have floated through the air like dust blown in the wind—scattered and unrecoverable. Quinn said the experience would have meant a new kind of death, bringing an end to the project.

Marcus pulled everyone together for last-minute instructions. The techs listened attentively and conducted a rehearsal of all emergency scenarios and evacuation procedures to help them keep their minds sharp and reflexes quick. When everyone was ready, Avery walked up the negatron's ramp, placed his feet in the cylinder's fiberglass shoe imprints while Stas and Jager shouted a rundown check on each system. It was time. Quinn powered the glasslike enclosure, sealing in the ragged-breathing serviceman.

The doctor gave the signal for all to shield their eyes. "Okay, gentlemen. Let's take the fiction out of science."

It wasn't necessary to demonstrate the improved safety of the monstrous machines now. There was no time. The techs were applauding, the lab's big halogen lights were flickering, and Marcus Weinberg was at the helm of the control station, ready to start the sequence that would begin to tear Captain Avery apart, cell by cell.

The lab looked clearer from within the thermo-glass tube as Quinn fed information into a computer: date, time, and destination of pilot—to the positron cylinder. Avery was used to the procedure. Now with a mixture of nitrogen, oxygen, and argon filling the airtight tube, the doctor and his crew monitored all data displayed on a big, main screen. From practice sessions at the control station, this data appeared on a grid. Small squares shining through a HD panel. If just one of those squares blinked, it meant something was wrong with one of the cylinders, one of the nuclear reactors, or any number of things in the lab. So far, everything was running smooth. Every piece of complicated equipment behaved like it was supposed to.

At exactly the same time, the turbogenerators kicked in and the lights on the instrument panel of the particle accelerator strobed to life, activating the gas-handling and coolant systems, along with the pulse magnometer.

Within the spinning cylinder, the overhead electromagnetic plate gyrated counterclockwise at such an incredible speed, it created an oppressive G-force that squeezed at the subject from all sides. The awful discomfort was worse than the gnawing fear, and just as bad as the fiery red-and-yellow lights that stung his face when his ears popped from the rising pressure of the nuclear-powered machine. Marc's voice came over the tube's speaker, announcing that the power-level bar on his screen climbed to thirty, forty, fifty percent ....

Perspiration wept through the pilot's pores when the cylinder's pressure reached sixty percent. A whirring sound from within deafened him, and Avery closed eyes tight, praying while the power level surged higher: "Seventy-percent, eighty ...."

An alien sensation attacked his body, and his heart raced with marathon speed when Marcus said the indicator bar on the monitor had gone as far as it could go.

Avery began to dissolve with a thrash; glowing cells rising through the cylinder like underwater air bubbles. A floating surge swept through him and time seemed to stop. He was as an astronaut in an out-of-body experience, snatched in the arms of zero gravity. He looked at himself and discovered a world within a world: muscles, organs, pulsating blue veins. Now his skeletal structure became visible to him: hips, femurs, metatarsals, phalanges—all disappearing in a blast of power that shot him across the lab as he let out a rollercoaster scream.

A pair of flickering red and green lights alternated on the particle accelerator, and the positron became consumed by the same display that set the negatron aglow. With the breakdown transfer completed, Marcus, Quinn, Stas, and Jager beamed with an aura of success. Somehow, Avery could see their faces. How he hated looking at their euphoric faces while he suffered.

He reappeared in the second cylinder like a lightning bolt igniting the night, and the pulsating indicator lights on the particle accelerator came to a twitching die out, followed by the diminishing whir of sounds that emanated from the surrounding instruments. Now that everything came to a humming stop, a loud silence filled the lab and the men snapped their goggles off like rubber masks.

Marcus stood over the monitor's clock for a readout. The small speaker within the tube carried the announcement. Total time elapsed: one minute, fifty-seven seconds.

The positron cylinder automatically lifted, and Quinn, Stas, and Jager rushed forward. Avery, dizzy from the fantastic transfer, stepped down from the machine like a drunken sailor emerging from a barroom brawl. With eyes shut tight, he held his head as though it would fall to the floor.

"This is one malady we will never comprehend," Quinn said.

"I wouldn't want to," Stas replied.

"Let's get him in the room." Jager steered the teetering captain into the luxury suite, one step at a time. "Think the effects of the negative polarity will kill him?"

"Only Professor "J" can answer that," Quinn said.

Avery staggered into the pristine bathroom and collapsed on his knees, face first into the cream- white Kohler toilet bowl which caught his stomach-emptying eruptions. It was over. But not the sting he felt throughout his body from the perspiration that gushed out all at once.

He toppled and fell like a corpse on the cold tiles, barely feeling the impact of the fall, much less being hoisted by Marc's men who promptly dumped him on the bed, flat on his back.

The doctor entered the room and ordered everyone out.

"Neil, you all right?"

He felt like he was on his deathbed.

"Can you hear me? Do you know where you are?"

He pressed trembling hands against his temples, feeling the onrush beneath a cold layer of papery skin; blood pumped from a heart beating like a tribal chieftain's African drum. He had never gone skydiving a day in his life, but knew what it felt like now: tumbling headlong through thick clouds without a parachute, gravity mocking him. "Stop yelling!" His vision had blurred and his speech had slurred. "And lee me alone. I wanna die."

"Die?" Marcus flinched. "We're just getting started."

The doctor got his medical implements, and after he took the serviceman's pulse, respiration count and BP, he told him he would need treatment for burn marks on his face and jaundice-yellow eyes. He exited the room and shut the soundproof hatch. Avery would survive. But he wasn't in a hurry to get back on his feet.

At last, after all the waiting, planning, scheduling, and more waiting, the first flawless shuttle had been completed, and later, however long it would take, when all the ill effects had worn away—the headaches, the nosebleeds, the nausea, the twitching body that buzzed from his skull down to his extremities—there would be a second test, followed by a third, then a fourth, a fifth, sixth, seventh ... until he was totally immune to all the nasty symptoms of the breakdown, build-up process. Now if he pushed those thoughts aside he could sleep.

Avery pounded on a whirring treadmill with tired feet. If he didn't fight off the stress and strengthen his heart, the arrhythmia episodes that jarred him up at night would continue—maybe even kill me, he thought. After a grueling week of more training and more cardiac tests, followed by an EEG and lung-function exam, the negative results earned him a day off.

Avery made the four-hour drive to Santa Barbara in three. His plan was to spend the day with Karyn, Gloria, and Champion, before his return trip to North Island the following morning.

Gloria cooked up another superb dinner, and afterwards, only the handsome couple set out for a stroll on the wide, sandy shore.

The vista of the Pacific horizon was striking; a universe in itself. Nature owned a spectacular gallery of picture paintings, each one with infinite colors spilling across the cirrus sky. Yet unlike the perfect heavens, the distant sailboats, and dancing sandgrass, the orange glow of the setting sun was not as picturesque as it once was.

"Seven days without you was too long," Karyn said. She wrapped her arms around his waist, fingernails clawing into the flesh of his back.

"I'm tied to the base. Married to the military."

"And involved in a strange project," she added.

"Does that frighten you?"

A warm breeze fanned his face. Foamy, white surf lapped at his feet. She kissed him. "Not when you hold me."

She pressed a cheek on his chest, and each time she blinked he felt those long lashes brush against his skin. She was quiet now. So unlike the woman he had come to know. A question bobbed in his mind like a buoy floating aimlessly in an open sea: What's she thinking?

Avery jumped into tropical whites and matching shoes, and headed down the hushed stairs. He expected Gloria would be in the kitchen, and he was right. She was jabbering to herself, trying to work a jammed key out of a deadbolt lock from the kitchen door which led to the side of the house where Champ sniffed around a bed of rosy tulips, yellow buttercups, and baby-blue chicories.

"Need help?" Something got Champ's attention and he trotted toward the beach.

"Oh, please. I just had this put in a few days ago."

He gave the back of the turning latch a look. "Got a Phillips?"

She hauled a big toolbox from under the sink, and found it.

He undid the small latch, removed the backing plate, and checked the six-sided screws. Hmmm. They were in too tight and wouldn't budge. He would need something other than a screwdriver or pliers. He asked whether she had a set of Allen keys. She didn't. Now he wondered whether she had a drill gun—with bits. All he needed was a hexagon-shaped bit. Something in just the right size. Luckily, she had those.

He sprayed a whisper of WD-40 into the back of the lock, and with a light buzz of the drill, loosened the two inbus screws. The jammed key came loose and he readjusted everything inside; not too tight; not loose, either. He slapped the round metal plate back on, screwed the turning latch over the cylinder's tail, and he was done. He had worked like a surgeon.

She made him breakfast: a thanks offering of coffee, eggs, hash browns, and sausages.

They spoke while he ate.

Twenty minutes later, Karyn, in a mint-green, terry-cloth bathrobe and long quiet face, barefooted her way down the carpeted stairs into the kitchen and sat at the table with him.

Gloria snuck a kiss on her sister's cheek from behind. "Morning, sleepyhead."

Karyn said nothing.

"What's wrong, honey?" Gloria traded a look with her guest and gently pinned back loose strands of her sister's hair behind her ears. "Not hungry?"

Karyn usually fixed breakfast for herself. This time she just sat.

"Want me to make you something?" Gloria's voice went soft.

The young woman nodded without a word.

Avery dabbed the corners of his mouth with a clean napkin and studied Karyn while Gloria started her sister off with a hot cup of coffee and a touch of milk.

Through the open kitchen door, a barking Champion charged in: nails clicking the Maplewood floor, tail beating against the table's legs. The naval officer was used to the dog's routine and knew Gloria would vacuum up the grainy trail of sand the big Labrador always left behind.

Champ sniffed his way to Avery's side, heeled, and gave him a docile look; his fleshy-pink tongue lolled from one side of his panting mouth.

"He missed you last week," Karyn said.

"He wasn't the only one," added Gloria to the sound of a metal whisk beating in a china bowl.

"They're keeping me extra busy at the base. I've never been so dogged in all my life."

"Hey," Gloria said. "Watch your language around Champ. He's sensitive."

He smiled at the joke, rubbing the dog's large head. "Sorry, boy. No hard feelings?"

The Labrador let out a gentle bark. Avery looked to Gloria for an interpretation.

"He said you're forgiven."

The two had a quick laugh.

Except Karyn. "When will I see you again?"

Her question didn't surprise him. In fact, he expected it. "The way things are going ...." He rolled his eyes in thought, wishing he didn't have to go back to the base. "Maybe the end of next week."

Gloria slid a Lenox plate before her sister. The smell of hash browns, green peppers, and eggs, filled the air. No one could make a meaty omelet like Gloria. She left the kitchen and stepped out the back porch with Champion trailing her. Now he and Karyn were alone.

"Next week?"

He groaned out a sigh, searching for an honest answer instead of dealing out a counterfeit promise. "Okay, I'll see you as soon as I can get a day off."

"See you? I want to spend time with you."

There it was. That strained moment. The intruder that stood between them the previous evening as they walked along the water's edge in silence.

"Alright, I'll get away for several days."

"Promise?" Her eyes danced along with his. She looked hopeful, anticipating the answer that he knew would make her smile.

"I promise." He fortified his oath with a squeeze of her hand. No more lies, he told himself. Not this time.

Week Six—Day Two: There were no signs the punishing schedule at the lab would let up. In fact, the shuttling regimen would have doubled had Marcus not spoken up. "A human life was almost sacrificed." He stood firm against his Russian and German staffers—Yuri Stas and Karl Jager—who huffed down his back because he had not caught up with lost time. "I want to prevent another misfortune from happening, even if it slows things down." Success, Marcus said, was secondary to the captain's well-being, and with that, the doctor ordered them to drop the issue. Now he allowed the young officer two hours of free time every morning to get away, to keep stress from building, to spend time with friends aboard the *Seven*. The opportunity meant the serviceman would begin Spectrum at 10:00 instead of 8:00. But the senior engineer, Jager, and the program specialist, Stas, were not thrilled.

Avery couldn't care less how they felt.

Week Six—Day Three: Two men were in an examination room. A doctor and his patient.

"Your EEGs are normal. Your EKGs are normal. And your lung function results are good, too." Marcus closed the patient's chart. "As for the blurred vision and unexplained deafness—"

"Can't you cannonball someone else out of the tube for a while?" the tired serviceman said. "Why do I have to be the circus clown all the time?"

Marcus looked displeased. "How would it look if something happened to me or my staff?" he retorted.

Rushing up the Pacific Coast Highway, past the jagged cliffs and ocean vista, en route to Santa Barbara, Avery fought with the tiredness that ravaged his body; the secret courtship that weighed on his mind. If the stress continued, he would never get rid of the protruding veins on his forehead, or the sore diaphragm in his abdomen, nor the circles that clung to his eyes. He would be like the victim of a stalker—tension following him wherever he would go. That tension was with him the evening he and Karyn embraced on the beach, and the added stress it created was with him when he returned to the base. There was only one way of dealing with the arduous hours of daily training he had been subjected to, on top of the long drive to see Karyn: Marriage, he thought. We could elope. Change our identity. Never come back.

Beneath the gray cumulus band and gold-yellow sky, the immense ocean played like the Plesiosaurs that once lived in it. A dazzling sunburst cloud had capped off another evening, and in a little while the pearl rays of dusk would yield to the night. Avery loved Gloria's beachfront home. Everyday offered a breathtaking view. Nature was timeless; ageless as the flotilla of clouds in the expanse of the endless sky.

Hand in hand, he and Karyn strolled aimlessly on the thick, cool sand. The rumble of waves seemed louder without conversation. But this is what Karyn wanted. Quiet time alone.

Avery understood she craved to hold him in her arms for the rest of her life, loving him with a Xena-like strength only he had come to know. The angry yearning he saw in her eyes spoke loud and clear to him. Karyn didn't want to lose another moment of what his warm, masculine body did to her. She told him she wanted what all women wanted: for love to last until the world stopped spinning, until the stars stopped twinkling, until she stopped breathing.

Now that things were heating up with Spectrum, he realized this was the moment. If he didn't say it, if he couldn't find the courage, it would forever remain unsaid. He turned her toward him and dropped to his knees. She made a sound, a girlish sound, and fingers twirled tight around his. Her eyes were fixed on him: two dots of black oil in blue opals. He hoped he would not sound awkward.

"Karyn?"

Her cheeks lifted and her eyes turned into crescent smiles. "Yes?"

"Will you ... will you forgive me for what I'm about to say?"

A charging wave smashed into a boat-size rock, creating a curtain of rising water and geyser spray. "Forgive you?" She looked confused. Her fingers twirled tighter around his. "I love you!"

"Will you love me still when I tell you I won't be staying tonight? I only came to talk to you. To see you one last time."

His own words grabbed him, shook him, leaving his ears to ring with the message he knew she was hoping to hear: Will you marry me?

Her eyes had the veins of a cracked mirror, and like a gutted fish she stared back at him, breathing ragged.

"Our relationship isn't going to work," he said. "Not because I don't want it to. But because it's wrong for us to continue in light of what I'm involved with." He gave her a closer look, waiting for some sign of understanding. There was none. "I'm sorry. I had to let it out. The way you taught me to."

"Please ...." Eyes leaked fat tears. "Let's give love a chance." Her voice quivered and his heart sank. "It can work if you believe with all your mind and soul," she added.

He bowed his head, wishing it could be true, wanting never again to vandalize his life. But he felt he had a reason for doing it, despite the fact he didn't understand why. "Stop kidding yourself." He rose to his feet and knocked the rough sand from his knees. He would forever hate this moment. Hate himself.

"You're good at covering lies with promises." Her voice hardened over the quiver. "Aren't you?"

"You're wrong." He tried to find those eyes through wet, bristled lashes. Her eyelids were as the sky: closing into night. "I could be dead tomorrow. And where would that leave you? Broken the way I once was. My job is too risky with no guarantees. The only way for me to be happy is for you to be free."

The disappointment in her flooded eyes bore a fist-size hole inside him. He could feel the blood dripping.

"But I am free!" Her chest heaved and her nose reddened. "I'm free when I'm with you, without you, and even when I'm angry, like now. Why can't we be together?" Avery knew she would ask another question that deserved an answer. But was it the one she wanted to hear? "Why must it end like this?"

"I'm a dedicated military man. I need to finish what I started. To find my purpose."

"I want to be your purpose—to be your wife!"

The possibility of Karyn physically lashing out came to him. He had robbed her of becoming a bride, and would have to disarm her of any intentions of harming him by letting her speak her mind.

"You haven't said it yet, but I know you love me. I came all this way so we could have each other. Think of what you're giving up."

He waited for her to blink, to sob. What would she do if she didn't? he thought. It was no good to bottle up emotions.

She cast scarlet eyes at the ebb and flow of foamy surf at her pink feet and how with each surge the sand darkened. Another wave covered her bare feet, washing over tiny pieces of fragmented shells scattered about. "Fragile things always break." She gave him a dry-eyed look after a long moment of reflection. The effervescence in them was gone. "I wanted so much for this to work."

"Long-distant love affairs are like sorties," he told her. "Can't stay in the air forever."

"Then come with me." For a moment her eyes brightened. "We can still make this happen."

"No," he said. "You can't run away anymore than I can. We'd both regret it." In his mind, a Boeing's engines revved up. Destination: Norfolk, Virginia.

She said, "I should've known I could never redeem a relationship doomed to fail before it began."

He wondered whether her wound would ever heal, whether she would need therapy after this. "Maybe the future has something in store for us. If you can wait that long."

A sharp, ripping silence fell, followed by a chill of dismay. Over the troubled horizon, dusk had yanked clouds of darkness over it. Now the ocean vista no longer looked attractive to him.

"Tonight the stars will refuse to shine." She looked at him with sorrow-shaped eyes and tried to take his hand. He backed up and walked away, leaving her standing on an empty stretch of beach.

Gloria approached with tear-glittered eyes as soon as he walked into the house.

"I saw it all through the window," she told him. "Your body language tells me it's over."

"Did I stab you, too? Bring back images of your own failed relationship?"

"Not your fault. Awful moments are hard to forget."

He would speak no more of pain, or broken relationships, nor anything that wrung up unanticipated tears. "I'll have to be getting back to the base. Tough day ahead tomorrow." He touched her hand. "Thank you for all you've done."

"Don't mention it, sailor." She swiped at runaway tears and threw her big arms around his neck. Her strong embrace squeezed out some of the hurt he had inflicted on himself. But what would he do with the rest? he wondered. "You're welcome here anytime." She tried to smile, but a drooping face wouldn't let her. "Keep in touch. Champ and I would love to see you again."

He gave a tight smile as Champion trotted into the room with that red ball in his mouth. He heeled at the serviceman's feet and waited. He petted the big, black dog. "Sorry, fella. Can't play with you." Labs are so well-behaved, he thought.

"Give him your paw, Champ," Gloria commanded.

Champion released the ball and let it roll away.

The friendly dog stretched out a paw. Avery took it.

"Don't worry about me," he told Gloria. "I'll be fine. Take good care of yourself, and—"

Gloria kissed him on the cheek. "You're not to blame. No one is. Life is just a series of laughter and tears, and sometimes, we cry more than we laugh."

Avery walked out of the house, dragging his feet. How many times had he laughed in his life? He got in his Ford Taurus and drove off.

Keep in touch. Gloria's voice would echo in his head throughout the long drive back to North Island.

"Will do," he promised himself. "Will do," he said with a shadow of doubt.

Chapter 19

Nice hideout you have here." The harsh tone from outside the cluttered electronics shop startled him. "Perfect spot for a cyber crime."

The sailor in dungarees backed away from the lit monitors and ripped black eyeglasses off the bridge of his nose. "Who's there?"

The quiet that followed felt ominous.

"So glad you and I could meet like this," spoke the faceless voice from the passageway.

"I said, who's there?"

A big man stepped into the light.

Jordan went cold. He shot to his feet and shut the monitors off.

"Why'd you do that? Afraid what I might see?"

"Doing my job is none of your business."

"On the contrary. Solving crime *is* my business."

The first thought that came to Jordan was how to get rid of the agent. The next was what he would do when he returned. "No one's allowed down here at night. How'd you get past the watch officer and undog the stowage hatch without being stopped?"

"Let me do the interrogating." The brawny man drew a cigarette from a pack in his pocket and brought it to his mouth, Zippo in hand. "Mind explaining why you're here alone?" He cocked back the Zippo's cap, struck the flint wheel, and a peak of white flame danced as he lit the cigarette.

The question bit Jordan like a venomous snake. "I maintain the ship's online equipment. Troubleshooting and repair never stops on a birdfarm this size."

Dauerman swaggered forward, lurking with every step. He scanned both sides of the compartment where dusty computers and old monitors lay abandoned on long, metal shelves.

Jordan swallowed thick saliva. Behind him, several computers were linked to a pair of LCD laptops, each with enough storage capacity for him to do what he wanted. If Dauerman inched another step, he would notice the tangled mess of cables and other external devices for sure.

"Leave the seaman alone!"

Dauerman looked over his shoulder as Pratt entered the compartment. Normally, the captain closed the door behind him wherever he went. This time he left it open. It was a sure sign he was not alone.

"What brings you here?" The agent looked at him like pointing a gun.

"About to ask the same," the skipper said.

"Don't give me that smug look, Pratt. You know the nature of my business. What's yours?"

"The command of this ship and the men aboard her."

They circled one another like red cocks ready to fight.

"Do you always drop in unannounced?" Pratt's blinkless eyes were harsh.

"Only when I'm looking for someone." The cigarette, tucked in a corner of the man's lips, did a dangling dance.

"Well, you aren't going to find who you're searching for aboard my vessel, mister."

"Let me decide that, Captain." The agent pounced on Jordan with a confrontational stare. "Step aside, sailor."

Active motherboards rumbled behind the seaman.

"Get out, dammit." The skipper snapped his head in the direction of the open door.

The agent just stood there, blowing a mist of gray into the air.

"The next command I usher will be over a phone," Pratt said.

Dauerman spat an abbreviated laugh.

Pratt looked tense and flushed. "We can do this my way or let the MPs handle it. Which will it be?" He motioned for them to come in.

Jordan hoped Dauerman would heed the warning and scram.

The NCIS officer complied and headed out.

At the last microsecond he did an abrupt, about-face. "I'm looking forward to doing business with both of you again."

Pratt and his MPs escorted Dauerman out of the shop.

Jordan flicked the monitors back on, blew out a gusty breath, and wiped a moist brow with the palm of his hand to the sound of clapping shoes trailing in the passageway. He transferred the information he wanted into the laptops, disconnected them from the service computers and stored them in a big, Navy briefcase. Receiving officers' shoulderboards would be just as gratifying.

Avery had trouble concentrating. He made serious errors on TSI's test-screen grid, and no one was pleased. He sat down and performed the task again—with the same results. He wished the chair he sat in rocketed him across the lab. Perhaps that would clear his head. But it would have to go farther than that, and really fast. Faster than a fighter jet being catapulted into the air from a carrier's flight deck. But he tried that before. Nothing helped.

"What's gotten into you?" Marc's patience had run paper-thin, and that brought on added stress. "Slow down and pay attention to what you're doing."

TSI—Time Sequence Initiation. The most crucial part of Captain Avery's training couldn't be fouled up. Everyday the Navy officer practiced to get it right, to commit to memory every last bit of detail and order in the launch sequence. If he got it wrong now, he would get it wrong when he worked alone on his return trip through time and be suspended between two dimensions: the past and the present. Life and death.

Week Seven: Avery and Marcus synchronized watches at 10:00 A.M., and a moment later, the familiar swirling colors of the decellularization process swooshed the serviceman into a kaleidoscope-dimension of strange shapes and warped sounds through which he had to swim. He was relieved the dark trip into the unknown portal would be brief.

An electric-blue flash of light filled the positron and a goggled Marcus marched away from the control station as soon as the spinning cylinder came to a humming stop. Avery stepped out from under the rising tube and came down the ramp. He studied the technicians' faces. History had been made and the world was oblivious to it.

Marcus pushed protective goggles over his head and peeled off his regular glasses, giving the pilot a once-over. "How do you feel?" His hand on Avery's arm tightened.

"Not dead." He smelled a fresh stench of cigarettes on the doctor's breath and clothes.

"Great." He fitted those thick black glasses over deep-set, olive-green eyes. He was satisfied.

Quinn checked the young captain's blood pressure while Stas flashed a penlight into his eyes.

"What time you got?" Avery was acutely aware his life would never be the same after today.

Marcus snapped his arm out and cocked it back. "Ten 0-six. You?"

The watch the doctor sported carried three dials on its face. The serviceman checked the time on his Quartz. "Nine minutes of."

Stas, Jager, and Quinn wore the same euphoric expression. Marcus let out a shout. "Know what this means?" He spun on his heels and jumped up and down.

The technicians shrieked like high-school pranksters.

Avery stiffened like an old, ironing board. "Did I really go back?" He tried to mimic what the others were feeling and doing but could not.

"By fifteen minutes. But that's nothing." The pragmatic scientist pushed back falling eyeglasses. "Wait till we add more time to the chronograph. You'll be traveling back—not days, weeks, or months—but years!"

Avery was gripped by something he wanted to shake loose. It felt like an army of leaches sucking blood out of him, weakening him.

When the number-two canopy clamped down, Marcus and his crew brought out several bottles of Korbel Champagne. Corks were popped and they toasted each other. But in the guzzling celebration Avery remained silent. There was one step left. The real thing.

"Here, take a swig of this," Marcus said. "It'll wash away that worried look."

Avery took the bottle by the neck but wouldn't bring it to his mouth. "So when's the big day?" He looked from Marcus to his team. They also waited for his reply. Everyone had worked themselves to exhaustion, packing nine weeks into seven. With so much more to be done and so little time to do it in, Avery wondered whether the doctor would be able to finish the rest of what was scheduled. But it didn't matter now. They had all come this far and yearned to move on.

The long-nosed scientist took a fifteen-second hiatus to think it over. He gave the serviceman a decisive wink. "Two days from today," he croaked. "Saturday afternoon at one."

With that, Karl Jager, Scott Quinn, and Yuri Stas popped more champagne bottles and poured the sparkling liquid over their heads without a care as they whooped and laughed to the carbonated sting in their eyes.

In the ready room aboard the *USS Man Of War*, a large group of officers caught the first broadcast of the news as it was being reported that morning from CNN. Bill Valentine turned up the volume on the TV set so everyone could hear it.

Live from the South Lawn at the White House, a well-dressed tall man with gray-haired temples and dark, bristle-looking crew cut, marched up to a podium and looked directly into the camera. "My fellow Americans ...."

With one command the United States president cancelled all scheduled Navy sea patrols and port visits. The Democratic People's Republic of Korea had made the first move, making sure their diplomats' chairs were vacant before deploying hundreds of ready tanks and thousands of marching troops to key positions throughout the northern half of the peninsula during the final UN summit meeting. The Communists had kept to their word and would not pull back unless allowed to sell off a fraction of their stockpiled nuclear weapons to Iran, Iraq, and Syria. The ultimatum made the president call upon the U.S. Seventh and West Coast Fleets to respond at once, and in two days, the first of four carrier strike groups, comprised of twelve heavily-armed vessels per task unit, would be deployed to the Sea of Japan as a show of strength.

And scheduled to lead the armada—the *USS Man Of War.*

A strange silence gripped the laboratory the following morning. Spilled champagne had been mopped dry, cork tops were picked up from the floor, and empty, dark bottles disposed of. What remained was a forgotten celebration. Avery wished he, too, could forget....

Jager, Stas, and Quinn were in the genetics lab, analyzing DNA samples before and after shuttling while Marcus was busy in the transport chamber. He stopped what he was doing, and with a look of quiet discretion, pulled the Navy officer aside. Avery had worked his way up to the level of a certified Spectrum tech, and because of that, Marcus said it was imperative he introduce him to one last procedure. They walked to the console-cluttered control station where every monitor emitted a busy stream of light. "You're part of the team now. My fourth assistant, if you will. But heed my warning." Marc's face stiffened like rigor mortis had set in. "You mustn't breathe a word of what I'm about to show you."

Puzzled by his graveness, Avery sat as instructed.

The doctor punched a series of codes into the quantum computer; commands the captain was not familiar with. When he finished, the cylinders' power converters activated, groaning like wounded Grim Reapers, until twitching white lights on the particle accelerator darkened to blood-red and the overhead halogen lamps powered down to a shadowy dimness. The uneasy serviceman hoped Marc's next words would push the sudden strangeness in the air out of the way.

"Wish I had a test-crash dummy I could use as a demo." He held down the keyboard's control button and tapped the letter "X". "Then you'd see whatever is placed in the tube under this template will have its broken-down structure irretrievably lost."

A doomsday message pulsated on the screen—Chill Factor ... Chill Factor—and all warmth drained from Avery's face. He envisioned himself being skinned alive, ripped to pieces, trillions of cells and thousands of atoms racing away at the speed of light with nothing left except empty echoes of dying screams.

Avery began nibbling his lip. Tiny pieces of flesh tore off and he spit-dried them out. "What's its purpose?" Now his bottom lip felt raw like his nerves.

"That's like asking why the H-bomb was created."

Another thought seized Avery. It frightened him to have to ask it. "So where exactly do these particles of matter travel to?" He sensed another horrible revelation of modern technology.

"You could call it a molecular abyss," he said without flinching.

"Where in the name of time is that?" He blind-stared Marcus for a reply.

And with a mystified look, he answered. "No one knows."

Every time Avery studied the *Seven's* soaring radar peaks and mountainous jagged frame, a special pride welled in his chest. He had loved every minute of every year spent there. The Navy was his life. It was in his blood. But like the final hours of a New Year's Eve, time was dwindling. He would not be boarding CVNX-7 much more after this, for on the following morning at 10:00 sharp, the massive, battle-gray ship, carrying over six-thousand men and ordnance within its colossal, twenty-four-story-tall frame, would launch out into the horizon until it reached the Sea of Japan, where every ship involved would wait for new orders from the president.

Maneuvering within the vessel's busy passageways, past crowds of seabag-carrying sailors and duffel-bag-toting marines, Avery wondered what the *USS Man Of War's* fate would be. What his own would be.

He found Commander Valentine in sickbay. Boxes of medical supplies for the long voyage across the Pacific, were stacked to one corner of the compartment. Everyone aboard was busy and behind schedule. Avery was familiar with the routine. It happened to him too many times.

On an exam table, a grimacing boatswain's mate lay face-up; work trousers down to his knees and dungaree top pulled up to his chest. The medical officer poked his fingers into the man's crotch, working his way up a sagging belly, making the patient moan. "That's for getting into trouble," Valentine said. He gave a look over his shoulder when Captain Avery knocked on the door. He motioned for one more minute so he could return to his patient. "Results have come through. No gastro. No hernia. What you've got is a bleeding ulcer. One that's readying to erupt. Get up."

The sailor rose to a sit and hopped off the table, one hand gripping a Navy ballcap and the other rubbing his abdomen. He yanked up his skivvies and trousers.

Valentine snapped off the latex gloves. "I'm recommending a one-week leave of absence. *If* you can get it." He filled out a medical chit and handed it to the ailing petty officer, along with a supply of stomach pills. "Good luck handing that to Pratt. And no more barroom brawling. The next punch in your gut will ignite it with the fury of an active volcano."

Avery stepped in as the boatswain's mate stepped out.

"Don't tell me you've got a bellyache, too?"

He gave Valentine the same look the boatswain's mate did when rigid fingers poked him in a sensitive area.

"Had a feeling you'd be by." He motioned to an empty chair. "Snowman and Slim asked about you. Told them it was a matter of time."

Avery preferred to stand. "Funny. That's exactly what I came to talk about."

"What?"

"A matter of time." He knew his troubled look would give him away. "Got a minute?"

"You look like an insomniac," Valentine said. "Anxious about something?"

" ... No." His eyes danced around sick bay for a moment.

Valentine moved in closer. "Then why is your lip peeled as though you've been biting it?"

Avery dropped to a sit in the chair. Thoughts gathered like thunderstorm clouds.

Valentine said, "A while back you told me R&R was in order. Change your mind?"

"Still brooding over Roy not having a funeral. And the girls not fighting to have Beulah's burial site closer to them instead of a thousand miles away."

"Why did you create such a rift with your wife's sisters?"

"Can't you see this my way?"

"If I did, you'd never stop lying to yourself. This ongoing soap opera of yours is more than a misunderstanding between grieving relatives, isn't it? You and your sisters are pissed at each other over burial arrangements."

His uncle was right, but he chose to deny it. "You think you know so much."

"Don't get testy with me, buddy. Your problem is you don't know how to follow up on your word. Darah's final resting place should've been in North Carolina. Not a Navy cemetery three-thousand miles away. But when the girls failed to make arrangements for Beulah's funeral, you retaliated like a spoiled—"

"I'm wasting your time."

"Neil, what did you come here for?"

The young officer stiffened in the pensive moment. If the FBI sniffed long enough, they would come looking for him, and when they found him, they would no doubt question him about Claudia Britney, Jules Ian, and Mitchell Braun. Braun's garbled remains didn't get that way by itself. "I know something the Navy and this government doesn't."

"What can be more classified than our Project Black Files?"

Avery waited a beat. "You believe in time travel?"

Valentine threw him a slanted stare. "What kind of question—?"

"Just answer me!"

The Navy doctor stepped over to a medicine cabinet. "Do *you* think there's such a thing?" He unfastened a padlock, opened the twin metal doors and found what he wanted: a small bottle.

Avery read the label on the shelf: *Diazepam*. "Valium?" He jumped to his feet. "Why don't you listen first?"

His fiery tone made the commander lean in, and when he did, he got an earful of a bizarre account ....

"Your crazy story is too elaborate to be a lie. You're a sane man after all."

"I'm not finished. Tomorrow afternoon I'll be on a history-making journey of the likes no one has ever accomplished."

"Through time?"

"And back." He was emphatic about the return trip. Ending up in suspended animation between two dimensions was another nightmare that beckoned at his doorstep.

"Using a military base to conceal dangerous scientific equipment is a threat to national security," Valentine informed him. "Know that?"

"What the hell you want me to do?"

"Blow the whistle. If you don't, I will."

"Can't. Sworn to secrecy."

"You just finished telling *me*! What's the difference?"

"The difference is I trust you. At least I thought I did."

He bolted for the door, knowing there was no safe place he could go with the truth. He was a marked man.

"If you leave, I'll report this to Tex."

"You haven't the balls." He squeezed the doorknob like he was going to rip it off.

"Stick around for the matinee."

Avery's back muscles felt hard as steel and his cheek began to twitch.

Valentine snatched a phone off the bulkhead over his desk. "I'm warning you, don't leave."

"You can't threaten me. You're not my father."

"Your father's dead, so shut your lip."

"Shut it for me."

"Neil, you're emotionally unstable. If your plan is to take this trip to fix things, you'll destroy yourself by reliving the past."

"You're no psychiatrist. What the hell you know about emotions?"

Valentine slammed the phone on the desk. "Enough to say I love you, dammit!" He punched a set of numbers ....

A female voice came through loud and clear: "Admiral Fumo's office ...." Silence. "Hello, is anyone there?"

Avery yanked the compartment door wide open and stared into the passageway bustling with sailors and marines.

"Admiral's office. Hello?"

The voice halted him where he stood. He clenched fists so tight he was sure they had white-knuckled. He gave Valentine a look.

He lifted the receiver.

"Belay the call."

After a long silence he hung up.

Avery fought to find relief from the tension that wrapped itself around him like a knotted chain on a fouled anchor. "Sorry, Bill." He reentered the compartment and closed the door, slow and sheepish. "I was out of line."

A frowning Valentine fixed his slanted eyebrow but still looked rouge-faced. "No, you were way out of line." His grin seemed forced. "And so was I."

The air relaxed. Avery would feel better if he explained. "I've been depressed for years over unresolved issues. Sorry it came to an ugly head in front of you."

"It's pent-up anger that's eating you. Plus, you've already apologized. What more do you want?"

He could no longer hide what he wanted most out of life. "Another chance."

Valentine huffed a sigh.

Avery flashed a weary grin and headed through the passageway.

"Neil!" Valentine's voice carried into the crowd, anchoring the young captain where he stood. He turned to find a concerned look tattooed on the medical officer's face, and he understood why. "Stop by tomorrow morning," Valentine said. "It'll give us a chance to start anew."

"Will do," he promised. It was one he knew he could keep. "Still going to—?"

"Report this?" Valentine chewed on the silence for a moment. "I never heard a thing."

Standing on the edge of the concrete pier at 0800, his gaze was fixed on the behemoth-size ship he once called home. The years slipped away quickly, and in another two hours, the proudest vessel Newport News Shipbuilding had ever assembled would push away from its mooring, leaving a great void at the naval base and a bigger gap in Avery's world. Soon there would be no place left for him to go but Spectrum.

In the crew's lounge, long-time friends gathered around him. They shook his hand, clapped him on the back, clamored for his attention, and talked about whatever raised their testosterone level.

When time thinned away, so did the large group of men. They had said their goodbyes and prepared for departure. It would be a long time before Avery saw any of their young, intelligent faces again. And even longer before port visits sent a new batch of sailors to a peaceful part of the world.

The last four men in the lounge were James Jordan, Carlos Nieve, Bill Valentine, and Neil Avery. Over the 1MC, Admiral Fumo made his usual good-luck speech. He made it known that Jacob Pratt, Mike Ragazzi, and Jeff Miles were having their duties rotated to the newest commissioned member of the Pacific Fleet—LPH-21: the *USS Capitol Hill*—a landing-platform ship for Navy helo's and Marine vertical-liftoff AV-8T Harrier jets, moored at the south end of the base. Fumo explained he was simply following orders from the Navy Department's chessmen in the Pentagon, to place a highly-experienced, flag-rank officer, along with his captain and exec from Pensacola, at the helm of the *Seven*. They would be filling in for Pratt and Miles. Admiral Fumo ended his speech by wishing everyone aboard the grandest carrier in the fleet a successful, peaceful deployment.

After a final round of farewells to his closest friends—Nieve and Jordan—Avery turned to Valentine with a firm handshake.

"I see they couldn't convince you to tag along."

"National security," Avery told him. "I'm exempt. Don't start a war out there. And keep the men away from lizard Saki and roasted pig testicles."

"I'd be stealing their virility." Four bells sounded over the 1MC, indicating 10:00 A.M. "Well, it's showtime. Wish it didn't have to be this way."

"Someone has to stand up to Korea and call their bluff."

"Forward Presence," Valentine said in agreement. "They'll back down."

Beneath Avery's feet, the *Seven's* mighty engines thundered through the steel deck. She was coming out of her long hibernation.

Valentine said, "If all goes well, we'll be seeing each other sometime next year."

Avery had a thought. "Six months is a long way off."

"We have the best fighting force in the world. We'll hang tough." He went to a couch, reached underneath the cushion and produced a Glock. He handed it to his nephew.

He recognized the weapon. "Why didn't you turn me in when you had the chance?"

"I transferred from Pensacola to San Diego. And for what?"

Avery stuck the 9mm where no one would see it. "What makes you think I still won't use it on myself?"

"I'll blow your head off before you can do it."

The young man felt the triumph in his grin.

With nuclear power surging through the ship like the adrenaline that rushed through his bloodstream, the big *Seven* rocked under the influence of its four, powerful, 40-ton brass propellers. She would be on her way, and soon, the 100,000-ton, six-block-long super flattop would be on the edge of the pitching horizon that loomed with the possibility of another war in Korea.

By the time one o'clock rolled around, Avery brewed in a poisonous concoction of enervation and fear. Stas and Jager were at the VSC supercomputer, busy doing what they had trained the serviceman to do: to carefully monitor the flux of radiation generated by the CTUs' uranium reactors.

Marcus swept across one end of the control station to the other, back and forth, gathering information from the army of monitors flanking him. With rows of green lights flickering from every instrument in every corner of the sealed laboratory, all signal panels indicated: *Go.*

Avery hoisted a duffel bag off the floor and approached the massive cylinder like a cosmonaut marching toward a launch pad. He climbed the negatron's platform under the whir and hum of engines and straightened his uniform. His jaw muscles twitched, a frown tightened his brow, and all warmth drained from his quiet features. No matter how many hours of shuttle practice he had gotten, for him, it was as though he were entering the tube for the first time.

Marcus stopped what he was doing and drew near. "What is it?"

His eyes rocked and he shrugged. "Nothing." His jack-hammering heart felt fist tight. He propped the duffel beside him. How difficult it was for him to relax and blink his eyes.

"Then why the grim look?"

He said nothing.

"Fear is to be expected," Marcus said. "We're dealing with a complex machine. One that has given birth to a constellation of unknown factors we haven't learned yet. Things only you'll be able to tell us about when you return."

Return. He would have to return for more tests, more radiation exposure. And who knows what else? he thought. He donned his wheel cap and Marcus motioned for Stas and Jager to step behind the control station in preparation for the big sendoff.

A rumbling sound filled the lab.

"Neil, there's something I neglected to tell you." Countdown flashed in the doctor's eyes.

"Oh, crap." Cold sweat dripped down his back.

Marcus pushed at his glasses. "We're sending you farther back than was originally planned."

"Whose decision was that? Jager's? Quinn's? Stas'? Yours?"

"All of us," Jules Ian said, gliding into the lab in a wheelchair. Quinn guided it to the control station and both men settled in. The rock wall behind them growled, closing with a shudder. "This is a joint venture," the old man said. "A rescue mission. We want Claudia back—alive. So we're sending you to a point in time ahead of her. No one's certain what will happen to you physically from such a big leap backwards. But be forewarned." He rose from the wheelchair on shaky legs. "The CTUs' C-graph has been synched with that of the Vector's."

Avery said, "Dump the jargon and talk straight."

With Ian coughing and shaking, Marcus took over. "It means you mustn't be away longer than what's computed in our system. You must return by the time indicated on the internal clock, or—"

"You'll dissolve like an Alka-Seltzer tablet in water," shot Jules Ian. "Causing instant death."

Marcus stripped Avery's watch off his wrist, unstrapped his own and made an exchange. "When that beeps, you'll have a forty-four-hour return window."

The face of the timepiece had three dials: Real time, Spectrum time, and an hourglass feature. He put it on.

Ian aimed bullish eyes at the Navy officer. "We have a lot of money invested in you, Captain. Don't let us down."

Marcus shot Jules Ian a look. It seemed the old man had divulged some important information. "Anything else you care to add, Dr. Ian?" His eyes rolled back to the serviceman. "I haven't figured everything out, but there's a chance someone might recognize you at Norfolk. If that should happen—"

"I wouldn't worry about that. People move around fast in the Navy."

"Don't argue with me. You mustn't let anyone you meet know who you are or what you do. It's pertinent to this project that you conceal your identity. That clear?"

"Clear as yellow piss."

Marcus would have kept on but time was running out. He lifted a small briefcase from beneath the control station and handed it to the waiting traveler. "Everything you'll need is in here: wallet-size snaps of Claudia Britney, a digital camera, ID, maps, lab keys, cash, and other items. Keep a daily journal. And when you find Miss Britney, don't send her back. Bring her back!"

Avery hated last-minute instructions but asked, anyway. "Anything else you haven't told me?" He prepared himself. What could be worse than the trip costing him his life if something went wrong, he thought.

"Yes, one last thing." Marc's face changed again, back into the person the naval officer had formed a bond of friendship with. "Godspeed, Neil Avery. See you soon."

In the protection of dark goggles, the stoic faces of CTU spectators were those of tired welders.

The transparent enclosure bolted tight over Avery, sealing him in. Air fanned his shoulders and lights flickered within the tube.

Jager began the countdown sequence.

The particle accelerator's green and red lights began to twitch, and every instrument in the lab hummed.

Within the tube, the speaker system clicked on and a voice came through: "Okay, everyone," Marcus said. "To your places."

A bulging knot wedged itself deep in the navyman's gut, and when the power converter over him whirred to life, his heart galloped with the hooves of a thousand stallions and his body shook without relief. Avery could not get used to being bottled up in the spinning cylinder as long as the horrible mishap lingered in his mind. He let out an excruciating yell when a crushing G-force twisted and squeezed his body in a viselike grip.

Marcus went to the humming unit with a broad smile and two thumbs up. Now that the rest of the complicated machinery in the lab clamored to life, the look of triumph readied his team. "How I love this job," Avery heard him say.

Ian's sickly face lit from the glowing cylinders like bright lightning shining on him at night. The technicians were ready and everyone gathered around the central monitor like surgeons huddled over a patient in an operating room. The skeletal traveler became engulfed in a swirling, bright-yellow mass of atoms and cells, and a wailing siren resonated in the lab. That's when everything went silent and black.

Chapter 20

Whirring engines powered down from a droning buzz to a roaring silence and Captain Neil Avery opened pinched eyes and found himself in a dark netherworld.

An overhead filtration system kicked in, air circulated within the tube, fanning his face, and ranks of halogen lamps flickered until the lab was bathed in its bright lights.

Across from him, the negatron cylinder stood like a mighty sentry with a row of green and yellow lights behind it coming to a twitching stop. Fifty feet in front of him, the control station's rear panel, damaged when the short circuit rained electrical sparks on it, now stood shielded with a protective Kevlar-coated Plexiglas. He scanned the remaining instruments he had seen everyday: the particle accelerator, the Vector 9800, the Van Allen Troubleshooter, the pulse magnometer, the bulbous, liquid nitrogen tanks. But as for Jules, Marcus, and the others ...?

The transparent tube Avery had been sealed in broke contact with the big O-ring and a rush of compressed air escaped with a deafening sound. The positron rose on its own, cleared the platform, and released the serviceman from its hold. A stillness hung over the lab like a fog. "Marc?" He waited for a reply. "Where is everyone?" he said out loud.

He moved around his familiar surroundings, checked each piece of equipment, and came to the control station. A row of computer monitors were still processing information, and in a moment, they would blink off and sleep until activated. He looked at his watch and Marc's final words came to him: Godspeed ... see you soon. It was now 1310—1:10 P.M.

Avery flipped a command switch on a panel, and with a rumble, the sealed lab opened, revealing a mineral-lit cave and the underground world beyond it. He sniffed at the stink of oil. "What the hell? I haven't gone anywhere."

He moved between the massive rocky teeth of stalactites and stalagmites, feeling like a runaway Jonah in the mouth of a hungry sperm whale. An unexpected breeze caressed his cheek and a frenzied sound followed. Something landed on the back of his hand and he shook it off. Whatever it was faintly buzzed, fluttered around, and landed on his head. He swiped it off his hair, and the faint buzzing returned, growing to a noisy drone of a thousand sheets of stringed paper flapping in the wind. He picked up the pace, moving in a sprint into the whining call ahead of him. Another one of those things landed on his face, then another, and another, converging into a blindfold—a shredded paper bag over his head. He yelped out a shout and ran blindly through the tunnel—slapping, swatting, clawing at the spindly, crawling, clinging, stinging mass of insects on his brow, eyes, nose, mouth. He crashed into a rocky wall and fell to a roll in an echoing scream, beating his face with the palms of his hands, putting out the stinging bugs like a man set on fire. When the ordeal was over he stood to his feet. He shook for a long time. One more of those things landed on his ear, whining angrily into the canal. He slapped himself there, and a pipe-like, boatswain's mate shrill deafened him. He spit a papery goo from his mouth, transferred bug-remains from his hand on a trouser leg, and staggered for a moment. The negative polarity from the strange trip was doing it to him again. He felt like he was about to pass out. He found a place to lean against and waited.

When he felt better he moved on, out of breath.

It took fifteen minutes of maneuvering through a deserted, subterranean maze—up the castle-like stairwell and past the demon-faced gargoyles of the main corridor—for him to find the elevator. This was the exact spot where the eeriness he first battled rushed at him from every direction, and where he and Dauerman stood on that first day. There was no mistaking the domed, marbled structure that rose majestically above him like the inside of an Arab mosque.

Something scampered by and he turned to look. A rat. He wondered how many more there were. If they traveled in packs and if they were hungry enough, he was in danger. How he hated being alone in a strange place. It meant he would have to figure things out on his own, including, why he had stayed behind while everyone else disappeared.

The elevator shot him to the building's lobby. Twelve floors up. There, he wandered along like a sleepwalker, surreal movements taking him to a back exit that led to the outside world. He inhaled and let it out. Living like a coney in a rock burrow was not what he bargained for when he signed up for Spectrum and was glad to feel the warmth of the sun kiss his face.

Bulwarks of armament berthed side by side reminded him why he joined the Navy in the first place. The frigates were sleek and stately, the destroyers were tall and imposing, and the carriers were cities of massive steel, all of them floating buildings, all bearing the names and hull numbers he had come to know. One of them was a combat-ready warship of radars, weapons, and armor. The *USS Essex*. CG-113: the guided missile cruiser that was jolted out of the water when a submerged submarine, rising like a rocket to the surface one dark night, slammed into the bottom of her keel.

Now something else struck him. It wasn't the moored *Essex*—its snapping flag with stars ablaze in a field of blue, or the mingling company of military personnel marching with purpose throughout the base. What caught his attention stood on the manicured grounds not faraway. The unmistakable sign that proved he had traveled a distance of three-thousand miles: Naval Station Norfolk—U.S. Atlantic Fleet

Avery drove to every motel, diner, bar, and rest stop he could find. He showed the picture he carried to anyone who would listen. Anyone....

"She's a dish," the potbellied, restaurant proprietor commented. "She your sister, wife, lover?"

"No, nothing like that." Pots and pans clanged in the background.

"Good. When you find this Claudia, introduce her to me."

He attacked an itch on his face as he turned to leave.

"Hey, mister," the proprietor called. "You should do something about those red pimples on your face."

A rough-faced man scanned the picture as though he wanted to keep it. "Got damn she's hot." He sucked on a cigarette and blew out a wispy cloud.

One of his buddies in a sleeveless stainless-steel-studded Harley leather vest, bearing Confederate and Nazi flag-patches, stomped over in combat boots, leaned against the crowded bar crowned with beer cans, steins and bottles, and snuck a peek at the photo. He reached into the back pockets of black, ripped-at-the-knee jeans and gave the stranger an unwelcome look. "Who is she to you?" He brought out a pair of brass knuckles and put them on.

Avery offered the buffed man a return stare, studying a plethora of tattoos on those muscular arms and chest: skull & crossbones, a bald eagle, an Aegis, Navy ship: *USS Argonaut*.... "She's a lost friend who's in danger."

"Danger?" The rough-faced man looked him up and down. "You undercover?" Someone whacked a pool stick over a billiard table and an argument ensued.

"Have you seen the woman or not?"

"Unless you're a cop, I ain't telling you squat."

Something told him he should have worn his Navy uniform that day. He might have gotten some respect. "Just give me the photo and I'll leave." He grabbed for it and came up empty.

"Hey, Elvis!" The man wearing the Harley vest, called over his shoulder. He snatched the photo from the first man and handed it to one of his cronies. "Didn't we see this broad?" A motorcycle roared outside.

Avery hoped he had a lead. "Where?"

"Downtown Norfolk. The Spade Nightclub."

A group of snickering older men approached, sporting wolverine sideburns and holding boot-shaped steins filled with foamy, piss-yellow beer.

One of them said, "That's a strip joint." He laid his beer on a bar stool and tightened a silver-spiked leather strap around his wrist. "She and a look-alike were wearing G-strings. I stuck a twenty in her sweet spot and she humped a fireman's pole." He cupped a hand over his crotch. "Wish she'd do me that way."

Avery pushed through a mahogany, obscured-glass door of the busy administrative building and marched to the North American Missing Persons Bureau Information Center. He had gotten a quick start by deciding to follow-up with NAMPB early in the morning, and hoped it would all end today. A short, plump man behind the sprawling oak desk in the rotunda, had finished talking with a client over the phone and hung up.

"Mr. Bremmer?"

"Ah, yes."

Bremmer was an odd-looking fellow. It was not hard to tell a rare disease had attacked every follicle on his face, stripping him of his eyebrows, lashes, and scalp hair. What irked Avery about him was that he wore a full toupee the way he wore his reading glasses: askew.

"Any luck?" he asked.

"Lady luck, Captain." The short, plump man pulled open a drawer, extracted a green file folder and laid it on the desk. "We've found your Claudia."

He was relieved the mission was almost over. "Where can I locate her?"

Bremmer looked flushed. "Well, we didn't actually find *her*. We simply matched the photo you gave—"

"Don't jerk me, Mr. Bremmer. I don't play by the rules. Just tell me where she is."

The phone rang.

"Captain, I understand your concern. But it's been five days of empty luck. Perhaps it's time you did business with the county sheriffs."

Avery decided to return to Naval Station Norfolk. Going to the sheriffs' office was the wrong thing to do....

"When did she disappear?"

"Who are you and what do you want with her?"

"Where are you assigned? Ship name? Hull number?"

"Why wasn't she reported missing in all that time?"

"What was she doing in NAS Norfolk, and what are those red marks on your face?"

Avery put in an uneventful smile. He wanted to say prickly heat.

The answers he gave put the deputy sheriff and assistant sheriff in attack mode, and that's when they tried to force him to admit to a crime he didn't commit. When that failed, a round-faced, stern-looking senior sheriff wearing a nametag (*Gatlin*), along with a gold, star-shaped badge over his left shirt pocket and a law-enforcement sleeve patch at his shoulder, took him to a private office for a polygraph test to make sure he was not involved in any foul play. With that done, he was kept locked in the room until an evaluator looked over the results....

The head sheriff, and another well-dressed man, came to the room that afternoon. There were spikes on the graph. Giving honest answers without revealing the truth had been a juggling act of trying to control his breathing, heart rate, and whatever responses the skin put out under pressure. After he was told a judge was called in, he was handcuffed, brought to another room, and locked up....

Later, Gatlin came to the door when a dusk-colored evening had fallen, and spoke to him through a telephone on a wall. His opera-deep voice was a sarcastic tone of an actor playing the part of a non-apologetic villain. The judge was on a fishing trip and would not be back for three weeks. By then, Avery thought, I'll disintegrate. The senior sheriff gave a smirk through a Plexiglas panel and said, "A bank was robbed this afternoon, and the description the teller gave matches yours. You'll be moved to a real cell in the morning...."

Night showed its dark face through a small, bathroom-like window near the ceiling. He had moved a wooden table against the wall, placed a chair on top of it, and climbed up. The window was still too high, so like a caged lion suffering from boredom, he paced the room back and forth. It measured 10-by-10, no matter how many times he paced across it, up and down it. When he tired, he lay on one of two sagging cots, hoping to find rest in the confinement, and a plan to get out.

Someone came to the door, the lock clicked, the door swung open, and Gatlin ushered a young, mannequin-white chick of a woman into the small room. The sheriff locked the door behind her and left. "Hey, sailor," she said. "What're you in for?"

He was tired of the questioning and itching bug bites. He raised his cuffed hands and scratched his nose while his tired mind raced. The woman, with too much boobs, too much lipstick, too much mascara, and too much hairdo, looked him up and down with appetite in her clear, jade-green eyes. Her riding boots, studded with blue cubic zirconia stones, her crotch-short pants and navel-length white top with a sultry Betty Boop in a Marilyn Monroe pose did nothing to put him in the mood. He said to her, "I'll trade you the story for one of your bobby pins."

Upon returning to the Navy base, Avery got out of the vehicle and left the door open with the engine idling. He approached a trio of petty officers at the main gate, flashed the worn photo at the keen-eyed sailors, and fired off one question: "Any of you seen this woman?"

"I saw her, sir," the first sentry said. "We all did."

"Yeah, spoke to us on the way out several days ago," the second sentry confirmed.

"Where could she have—?"

"Sir, you'll find her in Elmwood," the third sailor said with impassive eyes.

Avery parked a rented Dodge Neon at Elmwood's pristine, gardenlike entrance and started the rest of the way on foot. He followed a path of mulberry trees and studied the silent faces of those walking past him until he reached an army of gray gravestones standing in perfect rows like large, granite dominoes. A muffled sob nearby beckoned him to a well-dressed female kneeling in prayer on the clean-cut grounds. When she resumed her composure, she made the sign of the cross and stood. He removed his white wheel cap, pinned it beneath his left arm, and approached. "Excuse me." He looked at her profile again to make sure. "Miss ... Britney?"

The woman dabbed crimson eyes with a wad of tissues and turned fully toward the man in uniform. "Yes?" She didn't seem alarmed a stranger knew her name. She swiped at her knee caps, knocking off mowed grass clippings from her clear stockings.

The resemblance to the photo was amazing. "Claudia Britney?"

"That's me. And you are?" She waited for a reply.

"I was expecting to find ... never mind." Orange-breasted Orioles chirped in the background. "The sentry at the naval base said I'd find you here."

She looked in one direction, then another. "They're mistaken. No one knows me."

The wind blew, and Avery pushed back his dancing hair. "Miss Britney, I'm Captain ... Young. People are looking for you." He showed her the photo. "I was hired to track you—"

"Hired?" The woman appeared cautious but not frightened, giving Avery a cursory once-over.

"Don't worry, I'm not a hit man."

She took the photo. Looked at it. "Where did you get this?"

"I'm ... with the Judge Advocate General's Office."

"A Navy lawyer, huh? Has JAG nothing better to do than send you chasing salmon upstream, Captain?" She handed the photo back to him.

"Ma'am?"

"As you can see..." She motioned to the polished gravestone, then gave the photo a nod. "*That* Claudia Britney is deceased."

His gaze floated down past her striking legs to the big gravestone she stood beside. He read the name and inscription. "My condolences." The woman sniffled. Avery said, "Can you tell me where she was last seen? Who she was with? What she died of?"

"For a stranger you ask a lot." She dabbed her pretty eyes and blinked a few times. "But I understand, since those are the same questions I've been asking myself about my mother. I lost track of Claudia years ago. It's only now I've caught up with her. According to the local police, she was found yesterday in a deserted section of the Navy base."

Avery lost his breath. It was only yesterday he was at the sheriff's office. She could've been saved, he thought.

"The report from the medical examiner said she'd been dead twenty-four hours, and very little was left of her body. I find it hard to believe someone could decompose that fast. Anyway, DNA tests matched a database photo with the one she carried on an ID, and she was buried here. I received a call from the base chaplain after he notified the proper authorities and ...."

Avery fitted the eagled wheel cap over his brow. He extracted a digital Polaroid from his back pocket and took several pictures of the gravestone.

"May I ask why you're doing that?"

He put the camera away. The year on the gravestone made his head spin.

2051 .... "Just doing my job, ma'am."

"Well, now that I've answered your inquiry, Captain, perhaps you can answer one of mine." The woman turned to the fat gravestone as though beholding the face of a martyred saint. "The FBI is investigating this. Not because they think it's murder. But because they believe my mother was involved with something top secret. She was one of the nation's leading cell physicists who worked closely with Mitchell Braun and Marcus Weinberg.

Two big names at MIT with shady bioengineering backgrounds and no money to support their pet projects." She turned to face the Navy officer. "Is it possible they were building some type of … Captain Young?"

But Captain *Young* had just rushed away.

The tiring drive down Route 221 led Avery to Boone's Blue Ridge Mountain region where he found a Super 8 Hotel, made a stop, and stepped out of the Dodge to stretch cramp-tight legs. The scent of dewy foliage, brought on by the previous night's brisk rainfall, thoroughly revived him. He reserved a comfortable room overlooking a commuter railway station and unpacked.

He took a look inside the briefcase Marcus had handed him. Everything the doctor said was there, including a large amount of bundled cash in a side compartment that looked like he had pulled a small, bank heist. It was a lot of loot to simply use on hotel expenses, meals, and transportation…unless Marcus had something in mind he neglected to tell him about.

He called the attendant at the front desk on an old-fashioned rotary phone crowning the center of the nightstand and said he would be taking a nap and didn't want to be disturbed. But only for a few hours so he wouldn't fall asleep at the wheel when he resumed his trip. He told the attendant it was important he be awakened at six o'clock as he wanted to arrive in the next township, east of Boone, before sundown.

Avery dried up after an invigorating shower and saturated his underarms and chest in a cool jetting mist of Axe Phoenix body spray. He put on a clean pair of underwear, Calvin Klein tan shorts, and an over-the-belt tee shirt with the name Boracay—a tropical island of the Philippines—artistically displayed in dramatic, orange letters across it. His white Adidas sneakers were ready for him at the door when he got up, and a folded map of Boone, with car keys over it, were on a writing table. He laid down on the queen-size made bed without disturbing the velvety duvet, sheets, and pillows. But as tired as he was he couldn't sleep. He couldn't command his body to do what he wanted it to do. He couldn't even seduce his mind into conjuring up one pleasant dream. What he needed was a room hammock, which the hotel didn't have, or a sleeping pill, which he didn't have. So instead he rehearsed how he escaped from under the noses of the sheriffs, hoping it would cause him to drift away and gently rock in the soft arms of slumber ….

"Hey, sailor. What're you in for?"

"I'll trade you the story for one of your bobby pins."

"Just one? Shucks, I'll give you a whole handful." The girl, whom he decided to name Betty Boop, carefully plucked at her do, removing the bob pins one at a time. When she finished, her long dark hair had cascaded past her bare shoulders in sweeping curls and corkscrew locks. She handed him a fistful of hairpins and he took them, never taking his eyes off hers, wondering whether she'd take to his story, and how she'd look without makeup.

He bent one bobby pin open like a paperclip as he spoke, removed its plastic sheath from the tip of one of its twin prongs and worked it into the keyhole of the left handcuff. When it was in deep enough, he bent it again, away from him, pushed it down all the way, then pulled it back toward him.

Betty Boop let out a raunchy laugh, bathing him with her eyes. "A time traveler? You're turning me on."

Now he gave the hairpin a sharp twist, and the cuff's serrated latch fell open. He did the same thing with the right cuff and was free of the manacle. He showed her the evolved bobby pin. It looked like a skeleton key.

She applauded. "Nice trick. But we're still locked in here."

His face fell. But that didn't deter him from going to the door where he looked through the upper Plexiglas portion of it, hoping a well, thought-out plan would grow from the mustard seed that dropped into his brain from heaven. The corridor was clear of personnel and well lit. At this time the sheriffs who interrogated him earlier were no doubt gone, replaced by the overnight shift. He ran his fingers over the lock on the door and gave it a read: *Duo.* They made double-cylinder deadbolts that required a key for both sides.

He gave Betty Boop a look, his hand over the knob of the door, his mind a jungle of thoughts. He wished he had the key to the door. But thinking of it he didn't need one. Simple locks relied on one basic principle: internal pins and pressure to make them work. If tension could just be applied to the lip of the cylinder, it might manipulate the lock's components and….

It was a dumb idea but an idea nonetheless. He plucked out the fountain pen from his top pocket, removed the gold cap, and applied pressure to the lock by inserting the sterling silver tip into the lip of the cylinder. He guessed there were six pins within the lock, so with a strong grip on the pen, he leaned his whole body into it for six seconds. He then applied circular pressure, and the cylinder followed his move, rotating the tumbler within the lock and unbolting it. He grabbed the knob and slowly opened the door. He couldn't believe it had worked. Now if he could only control his racing heart.

He gave Betty Boop another look. It was impossible she could come with him, and she seemed to know that.

She lifted sun-kissed cheeks with an attractive smile. "Somebody's got to stay here and stall them." She blew him a kiss and wished him good luck.

Avery quick-footed down the hall, looking for an exit stairwell. At the end of the corridor he made an elbow turn and saw such a door with a red-lit exit sign over it. Just above the push bar was another sign: *Siren will ring upon opening.* He didn't want to take a chance of setting off the alarm, so he backtracked in the opposite direction, past the holding room he had been confined to. Betty Boop looked at him with those magnetic eyes through the Plexiglas as he swept past. At the end of that corridor he was relieved to find another exit. This one without an alarm sign.

Reaching for the door, it immediately pulled away from him, opening wide. There, the broad-shouldered Sheriff Gatlin stood, blocking the doorway.

Avery gulped down a mouthful of spit and air, regurgitating back as burning acid. The red-faced Gatlin was yelling profanities at someone on his cell phone as he pushed through like a horse wearing blinders, allowing the heart-sprinting navyman to fly down a flight of stairs....

He found himself moving down another hallway that by now should have been somewhere outside the Sheriffs Department Building. Ranks of lights shining through translucent fixtures shot over him as though he were being pushed along, flat on his back. Suddenly he took note he wasn't on his feet anymore. He *was* being pushed along, by two big men wearing blue scrubs and stethoscopes.

"He's coming to," he heard a woman say. He seemed to be on a gurney, being rushed somewhere.

The back of his neck throbbed like dynamite had set off a migraine and his left arm felt fat and numb. He wondered whether he was having a heart attack. He went to find the source of discomfort and discovered something with a sumo grip had choked off the circulation in that arm, from his triceps down to his fingertips, something that wouldn't let go. Now he heard wheels clattering and realized there was a woman in a white lab coat, riding beside him in a sprint. She was taking his blood pressure. "One-eighty over one-ten!" she shouted as they battled past occupied gurneys, hospital staff, and waiting patients.

Over the PA system a call came through: Doctor Pax, ICU stat. Doctor Pax, ICU stat!

Avery's right foot twitched as he studied the two scrub-dressed men, an Asian and a Caucasian, moving with Olympiad speed, pushing the gurney like a bobsled on ice. "Let's put him in that corner," the Asian ordered.

The gurney was guided past a sprawling desk, cubicles behind it filled with forms, gauze pads, gowns, bedpans. Nurses with unsmiling faces were attending walk-ins, and doctors with lowered brows were either busy talking on phones, treating sick patients, or writing notes in charts. The men in blue scrubs, jockeyed the gurney against a solid, plaster-shaded wall, secured the wheel brakes, and took off. Now the metal rings of the privacy drapes screeched like a shower curtain running on a rusty rail, and the woman in white removed the Velcro cuff from his left arm with a rip. He was startled by the tearing noise and grabbed the gurney's railing. Its ice-cold touch had finally awakened him. This was no bad dream. He was really there. I'm in a hospital, he thought. "What am I doing here?" he asked her.

But the woman who had taken his pressure, also took off.

A moment later the privacy curtains parted and a broad-shouldered small man with an abundance of curly brown hair, emerged. In his left top pocket he carried tongue depressors, a penlight, a patella hammer, and a black BIC. "Mr. Avery, I'm Doctor Banner. How are you feeling?" He looked at a clipboard, reading something.

Avery sat up. He was still in his Calvin Klein shorts and white Boracay tee shirt. Someone had taken the trouble of putting his Adidas sneakers at his bare feet, sweat socks stuffed into their opened mouths. "Why are they doing this to me? And where is this place?" His eyes felt big as hardboiled eggs out of their shells, jammed into the hollows of his skull. He cupped a hand over his face, shielding his vision from the lights that created curtains inside his throbbing head. Gooseflesh pricked every inch of exposed skin like acupuncture needles, and the cold filtered air made him bleed perspiration.

The doctor clamped the clipboard under an arm and grasped the neck tubing of his stethoscope with both hands. "You're in Boone Medical Center's ER. The manager at the hotel you were staying in called an ambulance. It appears you told the desk attendant to wake you at a certain time. When you didn't respond to the wakeup call, they entered your room and found you unconscious." He studied the clipboard again. "I see an EMT drew blood on the way." He clicked a pen and wrote something. "Soon as we find a bed for you, I'll take you upstairs where you'll be for the next few weeks."

"Few weeks?" Avery fought to get the railings on the gurney down but they wouldn't move. "I can't stay here," he bellowed. He ran a twitching hand up and down one arm, then the next, trying to assail the army of cold-induced goose bumps.

Dr. Banner looked at him with impatient eyes. "Mr. Avery, you're not going anywhere. We've got to run tests. You could pass out again. Are you diabetic?" He tossed the clipboard on the gurney and took the penlight out of his top pocket.

"No!"

"Any history of seizures?"

"Hell no!" Suddenly the accident at the lab, and what Marcus had said, loomed big over him. He had experienced a series of rolling seizures and had gone into cardiac arrest.

The doctor moved in close and shined a thin beam of light in the patient's eyes. "How's your vision? Any strange headaches? Nose bleeds?" The navyman gave a negative response. "Ever bumped your head hard?" Another no. "We'll do a CT scan of your brain and an EEG, anyway." He cut off the penlight, placed the stethoscope in position, leaned over the patient and planted the round, chest-piece on his sternum. "Hold still." He listened for a moment; eyes moving with slow suspicion. "Those look like bug bites on your face." Avery said nothing. The doctor straightened up, freeing himself from the U-shaped ear tubes. "Something's not right. You have a heartbeat of a ninety-year-old. Ever had an arrhythmia episode or cardiac arrest, Mr. Avery?"

Someone called from beyond the enclosed curtain. "Dr. Banner!" The MD excused himself and stepped away into a murmur of voices.

Avery got the railing to work and hopped off the gurney. The voices he heard were closer now, on the other side of the curtain wall:

"Blood results are in on that man," someone said.

Banner replied, "What've you got?"

The first voice again, "Strangest thing. His reds and whites—for lack of a better word—are *polarized*. Look at this."

Paper rustled and there was silence for a moment.

Banner again, "Where could he have been exposed to electromagnetism of those levels?"

"I'll tell you where." A third voice now, deep and threatening. "I'm Sheriff Gatlin. I understand you're treating a man named Neil Avery."

"He's inside," Banner answered.

"I contacted his commanding officer at Norfolk. Said there's another man with the same name that fits his description. Whoever *this* man is, he escaped my custody and I'll need to arrest him. He's a prime suspect in a bank robbery and linked to a missing woman."

Banner said, "He's not going anywhere without proper...."

Avery grabbed his sneakers and made a run for it, dodging past a heavyset nurse carrying an aluminum tray with pills in small paper cups. He flew past the sprawling desk where patients were waiting to be called and ran between the same two men in blue scrubs that brought him in. "Hey, where're you going?" one of them called.

A double-glassed door automatically opened for him and he scampered along, coming up on two security guards in short-sleeved blue uniforms and clean shoes. The older one was seated at a metal desk, giving directions to a young black male. The younger one leaned against a wall, gawking at a leggy woman as she went by. Avery stopped in his tracks. If he calmly walked past them without arousing their suspicion, he would be able to make a drama-less escape.

He switched gears and sauntered, whistling as he went.

"Hey, you in the shorts!" The young guard had shot him a look. "You're not discharged. Get back in there!" He pointed to something.

Avery realized he had pointed to the hospital wristband he was wearing. He wasn't even aware he had one on until now. "I gotta piss. Someone crapped their guts out on the bathroom floor back there. Got another can?"

The security guard's eyes relaxed and motioned down the hallway. "Straight ahead, past the waiting area. Make a left at the soda machine. Then, go back where you belong."

Avery drew in cool relief and breathed out hot anxiety. He hurried past a host of faces at the waiting area—an old woman with short, starry-silver hair; a fat-faced man wearing a Roy-Rogers' cowboy outfit and riding boots; an adolescent male holding an ice bag over his arm; a young girl with an adult female companion—all of them giving him a cold eye. A sleep-hunched hobo-looking man snored rhythmically in a corner seat with an old Cincinnati Reds baseball cap at his side. Avery spotted it and approached. He snatched the dirty cap and moved on quickly, past a baldheaded janitor swabbing a section of the tiled corridor with a stringy mop; its handle longer than he was tall. At the soda machine he heard a commotion behind him and gave a look. "Stop that man!"

Doctor Banner, Sheriff Gatlin, and a posse of medical staff had alerted the security guards and everyone rushed at him.

Avery flew down a main corridor, through one more automatic door, and danced around a charging gurney being rolled in by a team of EMTs. He took a swift shortcut between a row of idling emergency vehicles, legging past the toxic fumes that choked his throat. The thin padding of bare feet, slapping the concrete sidewalk, felt like he was running on bits of dull, broken glass, and this killed his hustle. But there was nothing he could do about that. There was no time to stop and put on socks and footwear. He had to make his tee shirt match the bummed Cincinnati ballcap. He stripped off the white tee on the run and tore into the cotton fabric with his teeth. He slipped back into a tattered tee shirt, having sprinted halfway across the street when he noticed he had dropped one of his sneakers. He doubled back ten paces and retrieved it, then jammed the ugly baseball cap over his brow. A speeding car blared its horn and shot past him so fast his bad knee buckled, his leg gave out, and he fell onto the hot pavement while he bled perspiration. Another rushing car approached as he struggled to get up. "Out of the way, you bum!" The driver—a big meatball of a man—swerved around him with a strident blast of the vehicle's horn.

The runaway patient answered back, "Fart hole!"

The woman in the lab coat who had taken his blood pressure, gave a look. "There he goes!"

He shot a hand over the hospital wristband, head bowed, raising only his eyes from beneath the cap's shadowy, curved visor lest they saw his face as they approached—doctors, nurses, security guards, and Sheriff Gatlin.

Avery wanted to jump to his feet and flee but the scalding heat of sun-baked asphalt burning through the injured knee prevented him from doing so.

He feigned scooping up a coin.

Gatlin unhooked handcuffs from his trouser belt, and the determined mob rushed past him, shouting as they went. "Somebody stop that man!"

Avery gave a cursory glance over his shoulder. His heart kicked and his mouth dropped a fraction. Gatlin had flagged down someone in a long white tee and tan colored shorts, half a block away; someone with the navyman's height and build.

A white and green car with a Boone taxicab logo on its doors, pulled up in front of him and two elderly women in long dresses got out. They walked toward the emergency room entrance, talking as they went. "Bonnie said she's being examined in room ten," one of them said.

He painfully rose to his feet and climbed in the cab's back seat, clutching the Adidas to his chest. The driver asked, "You got money, mister?"

His vision was beginning to clear. "You got gas, cabbie?"

Avery paid what he owed for his brief stay at the Super 8 and checked out. There was no time to comb his hair, take a shower, or anything else. So he threw his Navy clothes over the Calvin Klein's and Boracay tee: short sleeved whites, matching trousers, and rubber-sole shoes. From now on he had to think like a fugitive and move like a bandit. He couldn't afford to be caught by Gatlin or it was over. If the sheriff did his homework right, he would learn the ambulance had picked him up at the Super 8, and he and his men would backtrack there. If they looked in Marc's briefcase and saw all that cash, he would be locked up for a long time. Unless he died quick the way Claudia Britney did.

The fuel gauge needle had eclipsed the big letter E when he spotted a fill-in station. He pulled in at a pump and studied his surroundings like a sharpshooter looking for a target while the Dodge guzzled down regular. A man who kept his head on a swivel would never be caught with his pants down. He clattered the gasoline nozzle back on its hold and drove off.

The sign on the salmon-pink, two-story building's facade read: Days Inn. Its sloping, bronze-colored roof reminded him of the steep hills he snowboarded down in the township he was after. He felt he had traveled a safe distance, so he made a U-turn on the road and drove up to the hotel. He reserved a spacious sleepy room—with cable TV, two microwaves, a refrigerator, wireless internet, jacuzzi—and a moment later, was on the road again, making a quick stop at a pharmacy to pick up a bar of antibacterial soap for his face and a tube of medicated anti-itch cream for the bug bites. The severe discomfort in the back of his neck had lost its strength, and by that, he guessed his blood pressure had returned to normal.

Boone's small buildings and private homes were all behind him now, and up ahead lay a scenic mountainside that, according to the talking Garmin, was in Northern Watauga County.

To his left, as he drove on U.S. Route 421, the camel-shaped humps of Snake Mountain cradled a lush forest and a mist-clouded valley, and to his right, a clear, cobalt-blue expanse.

Sixty miles farther out and one hour later, the descending terrain led to a deserted, unpaved road where a valley, carpeted in earth-green tones, opened up for him. There were hiking trails, winding streams, and sandy-brown artery-like roads along the memory-inducing vista. "I love this place," he said.

He guided the car to a crawl, down from the summit of what was now Osborne Mountain, and rounded the last bend overlooking a two-mile dirt path. The land leveled, and there in the distance, a sprawling acreage of farmland came into view. He had arrived in Oak Leaf, North Carolina. A rural township of hills, sky, and towering, fair-weather clouds.

The dirt road ended, and over crunching graveled ground, he eased the Dodge to a stop and intimately studied a stone-grey, wood-brown house from afar. How long had it been? The answer he sought for came to him after a lost moment. Long enough for estrangement to set in.

Something whispered in the air and a moment returned: a harsh winter that blanketed the green land with several inches of powdery white snow. The familiar scene of a charcoal-black plume rising from a chimney, and the girls playing in the white fluff as they waited for Mama to emerge from the front door with a tray of warm biscuits, played back like an old, TV rerun.

Desperate legs summoned him to run across the open field like a missing child returning home after a long absence. But before he could twitch a muscle, a disturbing thought came to him: What am I doing here?

The question churned through the driver's tired mind until all he could do to keep from going back the way he came was to kill the humming engine, rip the key from the ignition, and grip the steering wheel with eyes brimming, heart aching, hands trembling.

The house. How many bedrooms did it have? he wondered.

Surfacing from lost thoughts, he found the courage to step out of the car. When he did, he closed the door, wiped moist eyes, and let his feet guide him. I rejected them and they rejected me, he thought.

Now a mournful conversation played in his head—the last one he had with April Gilchrist at her mother's funeral. She was moving to Boone, and when she gave him her new phone number, she told him her sisters would be joining her also. The entire property their mother had inherited, along with the dreams that came with it, had all been sold. Avery understood it was difficult living in a small, empty house strangely enlarged by cherished memories. He was forced to do it himself. It was the only way to defeat grief and keep living. But he resented not being informed until the last moment when the real-estate deal had gone through and the land changed ownership. It was another bitter pill to swallow on top of losing Roy. Now, as far as he knew, the farmhouse that stood before him belonged to strangers.

From up close, the house's stone and oak structure revealed its true age. It was old and in need of major repair. At one time, the land it stood on was a fruit and vegetable forty-acre farm. Beulah had said the house belonged to her second-great-grandfather when a big brown barn and pair of grain silos, like twin missiles pointing skyward, stood proud beside it. But that was before the Great Depression, and an excessive period of rainless climate, halted labor and caused extensive loss of crops. In time, the land's farming days were over and the once-fertile grounds were never plowed on again. A hundred years later, when four generations of farm owners passed on, Beulah inherited the weed-infested real estate and rundown house no one else wanted. As soon as she got someone to clear the land and touch it up somewhat, she relocated from her hometown in Warrenton, Georgia, and moved into that old house and the tender land that cradled it.

Overlooking a sun-filtered porch where he and Roy once played chess on a white, paint-flaked wooden table with the girls' carved-out names on it, a garden with an army of white daisies, pink geraniums, and lavender Iris perennials made him think of Beulah. She was good at growing things, too.

Draped in dirty-silk cobwebs, a stack of precut firewood lay piled against the side of a shed where three cars were squeezed into a small parking space. With bitter winters in Oak Leaf accompanied by snow, all anyone ever needed to warm the aged farmhouse was plenty of chopped wood and a good, old-fashioned fireplace.

Somewhere beyond the hills, a train's airhorn rekindled a smoldering memory. The familiar sound had a calming effect on the navyman, bringing back images of him and Roy bicycling along a stone-packed stretch of track.

A window with delicate drapes called to him and curious eyes peered in. Wonder who lives here now? he thought. Leaves on red-oak branches rustled their applause. "I'll soon find out."

He steadied his fast-paced breathing, opened the porch's screen door—a tear in its wiry mesh—and knocked.

Caught between crying and smiling, his heart quivered when the front door opened with a squeak and a short, plump woman greeted him.

It was impolite to stare, he knew, even with one's mouth closed, but he couldn't help it. He recognized the woman's chocolate dark eyes and the kindness that radiated from them. He was taken aback that she, like everyone he had seen and talked to so far, was ... real! This was no dream.

Riding a sudden crest billowing from within, he showed the woman no clue to the raging storm that tossed him. "Good evening, ma ... ma'am." I almost called her Mama. He doffed his wheel cap to her. "Is the Reverend home?"

He yearned to touch that black face—full and round—and throw weary arms around the woman who had been his second mother. But the lack of recognition in her eyes held him at bay.

"Sorry, young man. He's in Charlotte, attending a ministers' convention." Avery's shoulders dropped, heavy as a bag of packed sand from a levee. She said, "He'll be back tonight, though."

Her smile made him realize how much he still loved her. It also made him aware his white attire was unlike the forest-green uniform her husband Roy kept in the attic closet. Now when she looked at him with eyes of yesterday, he knew she had come to see he was not one of Roy's army buddies.

"Anything I can do for you?"

He loved her politeness. Smooth as homemade butter. "No, ma'am."

"You look disappointed."

"I was hoping to speak with him in private."

"Something important?"

The sentiments he estimated as having no importance suddenly became valuable. "Just stopped by to say ... to say...."

Beulah stepped out onto the beaten porch, and the air fanned her long, wide housedress.

McDaniel: For some reason her maiden name came to him. Someone from her church once mentioned she was a distant relative of the woman who played the maid in *Gone With The Wind*.

"You're not from around these parts. How do you know my husband? Does he know you?"

Avery hoped he could be as careful with his choice of words as he was with driving. He didn't want to sound strange but his appearance had thrown that into the air. "We met years ago. I doubt he'd remember me now. It's been ... so long."

"Roy never forgets a face. What brings you here?"

He had to make something up. Something he hoped was truthful. Anything to keep him from being a lying time traveler. But how easy would that be? he wondered. Marcus told him to safeguard his identity. "I've come because of a message he once preached. It did a lot for me and I wanted to thank him." It wasn't an out-and-out lie. It was a half truth painted over with a coating of despair.

"After so many years?"

He raced to plug up the obvious hole in the story. "He's been on my mind for the ... longest. Just wanted him to know how I ... felt." He hoped his sheepish grin wouldn't matter to her.

"That's so nice of you. But how'd you know where to find him?"

Did she forget who Roy was? "Everybody knows your evangelist husband." Suddenly he realized Roy was just another average man. The smiling preacher was still years away from reaching the pinnacle of God's calling.

Beulah looked surprised. "Evangelist? How flattering," she said with a dismissive laugh. "Roy'd be delighted to know someone took the trouble to visit. Would you like to come in and wait? I'd hate to turn you away. You look as if you've traveled a long ways."

"Yes, ma'am." He removed his wheel cap and tucked it under his left arm. "It was ... quite a trip."

"Then please, do come in. Supper is fixing." She reached out and touched him.

"Thank you, ma'am." He was hungry and tired, and Mama knew it.

The luring power of fried chicken, collard greens, black-eyed peas, and mashed potatoes, saturated the air and drew him into the small house behind Beulah, and with one hearty whiff, he fed himself off the tempting aroma of mealtime.

Past a staircase, a small dining area opened up where eight old chairs surrounded a fat-legged, cloth-draped wooden table. There, he and Roy once sat over many a hot, home-cooked meal, their growing father-son relationship nurtured to discussions of God, the bible, and classical music while the air around them was seasoned with the girls' laughter, forks and knives touching old china, Mama humming hymns. How I long to dine with the preacher again, he thought.

Everything in the house—an antique Calhoun-style Howard Miller grandfather clock against a wall with a chip in its door panel, the curling paint on the ceiling Roy said he would take care of with the help of his retired military buddies, and an oval braided rug that sported a funny little hole that looked like a mouse gnawed into it in a hungry frenzy—was as he remembered before the makeover.

In the family room, Avery sat in Roy's corner wingchair, herniated from constant use. His weight was to blame. Beulah made herself comfortable on a big firm couch across from him as he laid an oak-leaf decorated wheel cap on a piano and ran a hand on its smooth, fine wood.

"I've owned it since childhood. Do you play?"

Her gentleness opened his empty heart. If he could remember how the keys sounded at the touch of his mother's hands, he knew he would have smiled. But no smile came. No music played. "No, ma'am. Not inclined to tickling ivories."

On top of the upright were family pictures: Roy and the girls on one side, Beulah's sister Mae and her oldest daughter Hattie, on the other. Above that, a day, month, and year burned into his eyes: Saturday July 15, 2051.

The calendar confirmed why the house was in the condition it was in: a cracked windowpane, the faded wallpaper, and the porcelain figurines with sad dirty faces sitting on the fireplace mantel. He was in a different world, a fragile universe—twelve Spectrum years from the dreadful place he knew.

"Mama," called a girl from the busy kitchen. "Who's that you're talking to?" A diamond-shaped window-paned swing door gently wedged open and a whistling sound escaped the young girl's lips.

Avery couldn't see who it was from where he sat, but he recognized the voice: Taffi Gilchrist.

"Hush, child. Where're your manners?"

Taffi peeked from behind the open door. She had soft, honey-brown eyes and a taffy-dark complexion. "Oh. We have a guest."

"He's more than a guest. He's an old friend of your father."

She laid a keen stare on the stranger, measuring him with thought.

"Young lady," Beulah said with crossed arms. "Don't you have work to do in the kitchen? Like helping your auntie?"

"Yes, Mama." She coughed out a whistling wheeze.

"And please, before you run out of Albuteral, let me know. Last time you forgot and—"

Taffi disappeared behind the single, glass-paned wooden door, and within seconds, an excited murmur of female voices stirred in the kitchen.

"Lord, that child worries me. Last time she got so sick she could hardly breathe. I'm afraid one day another attack will come and her pump will be empty."

It's empty! Avery thought.

Beulah's cry must have cut through the turbulent air that day. It was nighttime when I-COM patched a call to the *USS Man Of War*. Taffi was in the hospital. She was intubated, pumped full of epinephrine, and put on an Aminophyline drip to keep her alive.

"Your cooking smells great." He wondered whether that was enough to help Beulah dislodge her worried thought.

"That's my sister and her daughter in there, cooking up a storm."

From the kitchen, the whispers and giggles died down. The door swung open once more and two young girls strutted into the family room like debutantes at a palace ball. Their even-toned faces were a picturesque blend of their parents: Roy's Indian cheeks, Beulah's Georgian smile. He had forgotten how much he missed them. How much he couldn't live without them. How much he hurt them. And what they had done that angered him.

"This is Daddy's friend," Taffi said to her younger sister April.

"Delighted." April extended a hand to him from a perfect curtsy as though he were royalty.

Avery played along. He pressed chaste lips on her hand and Taffi giggled. Their comical theatrics made him laugh, too.

Taffi and April were free-spirited and mature for their age. Sweet like their mother and intelligent as their father. They loved going to school, enjoyed having picnics, were thrilled when tending to the flowers in Mama's lush garden and delighted in singing to her piano playing. They also loved inhaling the fresh smell of her baked goods, wiping their sweaty brows when she wiped hers in the small, hot kitchen, and riding in their father's car with the wings of the wind flapping in their smiling faces.

And one more thing the girls shared. A secret fear.

"Now, girls ...." Mama halted their silly stage act and lowered the curtain. "Sit by me till supper's ready."

The two sisters invaded the seashell-beige couch, and their mother in the middle wrapped her large arms around her precious daughters.

"Oh, I'm so sorry." Beulah let out an embarrassed laugh. "In all the excitement, I forgot to ask your name." Her smile made him smile.

"Avery. But you can call me Neil."

"You mean we don't have to salute?" Taffi asked. "Daddy makes us salute."

He caught those flirtatious eyes playing with him. "I won't write you up."

Mama's smile was contagious.

"Can I call you Ave?" April asked with a big smile of her own.

"Hush," Mama ordered. "Gimme a chance to talk. This old house is big enough for all of us."

This old house.... I can't believe I'm here, he thought. Can I not hurt them this time?... The sun shone bright on the old farmhouse, but it might as well have rained. There were no warm feelings on the day they all flew to a funeral in Georgia, and there was little talk between them. Bitterness had set in like hardened cement, cremation became a profane word he hated, and the sweet bond that once held them together began to unravel like a piece of worn fabric. Taffi, April, and the youngest one were 22, 20, and 17 years of age respectively when their mother's casket was brought to a Warrenton cemetery. It was the second blow in a span of three months, more than he could bare, forcing the harsh silence to drag into years. But now the girls were preteens, all the bitter events had been postponed, and the youngest Gilchrist was in elementary school. Her bedroom filled with pretty dolls.

"What do you do?" Beulah asked with a smile. Something she was rarely seen without.

It felt so unusual no one knew him. Only Alzheimer's disease could do this, he thought. "I worked on a Navy carrier as an engineer at North Island in Coronado, California—"

April put in. "Mama, a carrier is a big, flat ship with a landing strip for planes. And an engineer—"

"Hush, child. Let the man talk."

"That's okay, ma'am." He gave them all a look. "Now I'm with counterintelligence at Norfolk. Keeping the bad guys from harming us with our own secrets isn't as easy as it sounds."

Mama and Taffi leaned in with eyes wide.

April's mouth dropped a fraction. "You're a spy hunter?"

Avery's laughter gave him away. "I wouldn't know a spy if he bit me. Hope I never meet one."

The girls groaned in disappointed unison.

Beulah tee-heed. "Children are a blessing from the Lord. Do you have any?" She had always been curious about the naval officer's personal life, and showed she was eager to learn more.

"No, ma'am."

"Well, it's never too late to get married," she said. "You're young—"

"And handsome," blurted Taffi. "Can I be your girl?"

Beulah looked surprised. "Taff!"

"I'm joking, Mama. I only wanted your reaction."

"That's what you say now." Her eyes returned to her guest. "But one day it'll be for sure. My girls will meet their soul mates and leave this happy nest."

Avery was impressed by the girls' level of intelligence. He always felt that way. He wondered where life would take them after they finished high school. He had no doubts they would go on to college and study great things; accomplish great things. "Your daughters are bright. They'll make you proud someday."

Footsteps clomped down the stairs, and a curly-haired cute little girl bounced into the family room with a skip.

"They ain't the only ones," Beulah said.

The child was a lifelike porcelain doll in a white-hemmed purple frock; her dimpled smile highlighted those carefree eyes.

"Mama, can I have …?"

At once the girl became mute in the presence of the uniformed stranger whose eyes were locked on her. With one glance she melted him, just like she did to him the first time they'd met. He couldn't deny the past had resurrected. The one Marcus Weinberg warned him about. The one Bill Valentine said would destroy him.

The child dashed to her mother on the couch and buried her small face in her large bosom.

"Mama," she muffled. "He's white."

Beulah smiled at the man, but it wasn't enough to mask her embarrassment. "Don't mind her." Mama knew how to excuse the young child in public, and when to scold her in private. "We don't get much white folk stopping off at the house." She pried the child loose from her tight embrace. "Why don't you tell the nice man your name?"

The youngster turned with hesitation and stared at the man for a measured moment. Her eyes were olive-black and button-round, and her nose was tiny as a fawn's. "My name is Olympia. I'm seven." Her thin voice wrestled with his heart and captured it. "But everyone calls me Pia because I'm small like a pea." She lowered her head with hands behind her back, swinging her dainty little body from side to side.

"Don't be shy, and don't be sad." He wanted to hold her on his lap the way he used to. "I have a gut feeling you'll grow tall like your sisters."

"Oh, they're not my real sisters," Olympia said intelligently. "I'm adopted. That means I'm loved." She examined the stranger with dancing eyes. "Are you a policeman?"

Taffi and April laughed.

"No, sweet pea. I'm a sailor."

"Like Popeye?"

Beulah and the girls let out a quick chuckle.

"Yes. Popeye. Minus the pipe."

Her pretty little smile widened, pushing away some of the shyness. "Wanna know what my Mama does?" She beamed with angelic pride. "She's a schoolteacher."

"How wonderful that must be."

Her announcement didn't surprise him, but it did jog his memory. Beulah Gilchrist worked in an elementary school in Boone, specializing in children with learning disabilities. Nothing satisfied her more, except going to church on Sundays, attending evening prayer on Wednesdays, and the end of the long school year so she could spend more time with her daughters.

"Dear Lord," Beulah exclaimed.

"What's wrong, Mama?" April asked.

"Forgot to offer our guest something to drink."

"Don't trouble yourself, ma'am."

"What trouble? Can I get you coffee, or would you like something else?"

"Raspberry ice tea would be fine, ma'am. A touch of honey would make it even better."

"How'd you know I had raspberry tea? Never mind, coming right up." She looked into Olympia's precious eyes. "And what was it you wanted?"

"Ice cream," she beamed.

"Can it wait till after supper?"

The youngster nodded with a patient face.

Beulah set an ice-tinkling glass on a small coffee table in front of her guest and dropped into a sit across from him. Her happy smile and pleasant demeanor put him in a relaxed mood. How strange it felt for his muscles to go limp.

"Hope you find the tea sweetened to your taste, General Avery." She wiped plump hands on a flowery apron and put on a wide smile.

"Please, call me Neil." He took a generous sip, allowing the liquid's descent to cool the parchness in the back of his throat.

"Mama," Taffi interrupted. "Generals are in the army. He's Navy. Even I know that."

"Well, I didn't. So hush."

"Taff thinks she knows everything," April informed her guest.

"Not everything," Taffi snapped at her sister. "Just more than you."

Olympia strode to the white, black-billed wheel cap resting on the piano and stroked its silver eagle, crossed gold anchors, and the lettering below it. "USN. That's a funny word."

"It means, United States Navy, sweet pea."

"I like the Navy," Olympia said. "But Daddy likes the army."

Army versus Navy. He felt he was being pitted against Roy. "Where did you get such a sweet, mousy voice?"

April joined her sister. She touched the four bands of gold stripes on the stranger's uniform, giving him a smile of approval. "I like your shoulderboards. What rank are you?"

"I'm a Captain."

Her face lit up and her eyes filled like full moons. "Like Ahab in Moby Dick?"

Ahab was a fierce hunter. A tyrant, Avery told her. His sole desire was to kill the great white whale out of revenge. "Not a good thing."

"But Moby got away. He's still alive!"

"April, you're a dunce," Taffi quipped.

"Am not."

"Yes you are."

"Mama, tell 'er to stop."

"Y'all hush now."

Taffi coughed, then pursued. "Moby isn't alive. It's only a dumb movie."

Avery picked up on Taffi's agitated wheezing. So did Beulah. It sounded more pronounced each time she coughed.

"April, hush. Don't excite your sister."

Mama brought quick order between the quibbling girls.

"Beulah, thank you for the tea. It was just right."

Her smile waned under a puzzled look. "How'd you know my name?"

Taffi leaned in. "It's embroidered on your apron."

Beulah glanced at the letters artistically sewn into the fabric and let out a tee-hee. "How silly of me. My daughter made this for my birthday last year."

Something squeaked in the kitchen and a woman entered the family room through the swing door. "Did I hear someone talking about me?" The floral, sweetheart-neckline-dress she wore highlighted her unblemished face and jovial smile.

Avery stopped breathing. Her hair was long. Nutmeg-brown. Highlighted with a touch of henna. Her skin was caramel downy and her legs were not bad-looking. She wiped hands on a white dish towel and a moment in time returned.

"Auntie said the cake needs more time, Mama. But dinner's ready." She walked past the Navy captain, and right away, the smell of food and her own natural scent swirled around him.

Avery found himself unable to blink or think. The woman sat across from him and the room grew quiet. She was more beautiful than he dared dream.

Almond-shaped eyes met his gaze. "Hello." Her voice rang like a door chime.

He knew it was impolite to stare but he couldn't resist it. How he wished he didn't have those red marks on his face. He would have to do something about that tonight.

Two older heavyset women with smiling cherub faces, swept into the room from the kitchen with a stack of clean porcelain plates in their hands. The young woman introduced them. "This is Aunt Mae, her daughter Hattie, and I'm Darah."

From across the dinner table, Avery was too afraid to look at Darah, guarding his attraction to her as best he could. What do I do now, Marcus? Your training didn't prepare me for this. Hell, I'm not supposed to be here, he thought.

When everyone finished the Sock-it-to-Me cake Darah and Hattie served—a pan-size, cinnamon-tasting loaf with three kinds of nuts: pecans, almonds, and cashews—they sauntered into the family room and sat. Olympia was the first to open up the after-dinner chat. She spoke of her many dolls in her bedroom, each with their own outfit and name.

Taffi and April raided their way between their adopted sister and their guest in the corner wingchair, each competing for his attention. They sat at his feet and asked him how many ships the Navy had, how long it took for him to make captain, what was the first ribbon he got. The questions kept coming, and each answer he gave charmed them. But when Taffi asked him for the name of his sweetheart, he scratched his neck and got quiet.

Mama reminded them it was time to do the dishes.

She got no volunteers.

Olympia said, "Wanna know what I'm gonna be when I grow up?" Her adorable eyes worked on him again. A healing balm for a wounded heart.

"Tell me." She always did like dinosaurs, he thought.

"A paleontologist."

All of a sudden he found himself in a dreamy setting, and what he was about to say next, he'd said before, long ago. "My, that's a big word for such a little girl." It was like rereading a surreal script of some sort. Every word written in stone. Every movement of the characters caught on film.

"I can spell it." She beamed with angelic pride.

"Impress me." Avery searched Beulah and Mae's smiling eyes. He turned to Darah. Her face was aglow.

Olympia stood to her feet and struck a spelling-bee pose: "P-a-l-e-o-n-t-o-l-o-g-i-s-t."

Beulah, Mae, and Hattie applauded, the girls cheered supportively, and Darah chimed out a song: Who's the best little girl in the world.

Avery enjoyed the praises for the little one. "You're brighter than a hundred-watt bulb." Everyone laughed for a moment. Its sound radiating warmth throughout the house. He took the child by the hand and drew her close to him. "Now, what does that word mean?" he challenged her.

She shrugged. "I dunno."

Taffi let out a burst of laughter, the others followed her lead, and Mama and Darah looked on in amusement.

"Yes you do, Pia," April said in her defense. "It's someone who digs up dinosaur bones!"

"Oh, yeah!"

"Sure you won't mind fossil hunting?" Avery asked. "It's a dirty job."

"Course not. Somebody's gotta do it."

In the contagious hilarity, Olympia covered her mouth with tiny hands and giggled. Avery had forgotten what he took for granted: family warmth, loved ones at a dinner table, a little girl making him smile until his face hurt. He snatched the child in his arms and sat her on his lap. "Pia, did you lose a dimple?" He couldn't resist looking into her precious, button-eyed gaze.

"I only have one."

"Some people have two."

She answered: "I heard those with one are smarter."

Mae and Hattie let out a chirp of laughter, and the child leaped onto the floor and climbed onto Mama's spacious lap.

From the corner of his eye he saw her. Any woman studying him with fixation always appeared on his radar, whether she was attractive or just plain looking. But this one was attractive, and he was familiar with every nuance of her face, every curve in her smile, every flicker in her eyes—and knew what it meant. Time was subtly repeating itself. Now, that part of his past, including her shortened life, strangely appeared before him like the spinning reflections on a revolving glass door.

Darah.

His heart leaped the day she told him her name. And when he entered her compartment and smelled her slept-on pillows, he knew she was the one. Now the dark memories that caused his heart to pump no blood, made it beat like that still.

Every fifteen minutes the grandfather clock in the dining room, chimed. Avery checked Marc's watch. Not a minute too fast; not a second too slow.

He was well aware it would go off when he least expected it, and that troubled him.

Darah's eyes lighted on him: his face, his hair, his uniform. "How long have you been in the service?"

What a career he had. "All my life." He served on a boomer, worked on a carrier, was deployed to the arctic circle, and later to Antarctica. He had visited France, Greece, Italy, Turkey, and Spain. The *Seven* had crossed the Atlantic twice, pushed past the Strait of Gibraltar, sped through the Mediterranean, crawled into the Suez Canal and sailed down the Red Sea. The carrier also journeyed across the Pacific, more times than he could remember, with ports of call to Australia, Hong Kong, and Hawaii. He had stolen a ride in a fighter jet, participated in naval war games in the Indian Ocean, and was there to observe the squadron launch its planes in support of Marine troops battling Communist insurgents in the mountain region of Makra in Pakistan. He had been to Alexandria, Egypt; Subic Bay in the Philippines; Port Elizabeth, South Africa; St. Petersburg, Russia; Rio de Janeiro, Brazil; and now—

"All your life? You weren't born dressed like that."

He threw his arms out and gave himself a look. "Sure feels like it."

At ten o'clock, Mae and Hattie bid Avery and the girls goodbye. Mae was disappointed the reverend missed another dinner with them and Hattie said to give Roy Nathan their regards. The preacher would eventually come. Beulah had said so. She was familiar with his schedule and knew he was on the way. There were no worried lines on her face that indicated otherwise. But when the time came, the serviceman wondered whether he would have the courage to speak the lines he had rehearsed. Hello Roy ….

At 10:30 his eyes followed Mama as she shuffled to her feet with effort from the seashell-beige couch and left the family room to go to the quiet kitchen. It didn't seem that long ago he strolled in after her, and to his surprise, found he had intruded on her privacy. Beulah was sitting at the table, injecting something into her upper-left arm. Eighty units, she said. Third injection of the day. She ran a glass of water from the tap and downed two pills: Atenolol—a beta-blocker for her pressure, and Triamterene—a water pill. She had been doing this for years and said she had to continue for the rest of her life.

Avery was entertaining the girls with his Navy stories when Beulah gently pried them away from him to prepare them for bed. "Tomorrow is church," she reminded them. "Your father will be preaching."

With Mama ushering her daughters upstairs, only two people remained in the quiet room: a young military man and a shy college girl. Beulah gave them both a look. "Why don't you two get acquainted," she suggested with a smile. "I'll be down in a moment." Avery knew she had witnessed the glances they exchanged earlier, and now looked pleased about it.

Darah gave him a certain smile, and a song popped into his head: *Strangers in the Night*. He moved from the wingchair to the long couch where she sat at one end and pretended he was at ease. His face felt warm and he knew he was blushing—or was it an angry surge of regret? She looked amused as her gaze wandered from his rank insignia, to his ribbons, to his zipper.

The downward descent of those eyes caught his attention.

She looked up at him. "I … like your uniform. Tell me about the Navy."

"Only if you tell me about civilian life in college."

"How did you—?"

"Hattie told me."

Darah crossed one leg over the other, letting a slipper dangle from a naked foot. With each word she spoke, her ankle danced and his eyes followed.

After a long, casual talk, he was aware she was beginning to feel comfortable with him. It was as though they had met years ago and were simply catching up on old times.

Darah told him of her second year at University of Virginia College and what her plans for the future would be: a master's in computer technology, then the corporate world of Microsoft, which impressed him. He in turn told her about the Recruit Training Command at Great Lakes, the Academy in Annapolis, and the boundless sea, which he saw intrigued her.

She also told him about her estranged boyfriend—a goateed black man studying toward a Bachelor's degree in Business—and of their interrupted relationship that left her in tears. It happened during the start of the fourth semester, she said. "If you love me, you'd let me, he told me over and over. And when I gave in, he stopped calling, stopped coming to the house, stopped seeing me. It's been months."

His face dropped and his pulse weakened. "Gerald Morgan?"

"Yeah!" She looked surprised he knew that much about her. "Did Hattie or Mae mention—?"

The clanging chime of the grandfather clock silenced her.

At that moment, Beulah came down. "Neil, I must apologize for my husband's absence."

"That's fine, ma'am. My overextended stay was an intrusion of your peaceful home and an imposition on your family." He fitted his Navy cap over his brow, wanting to remain longer yet needing to leave.

Mama drew close to him. "Nonsense," she said, touching his hand. "You're welcome here anytime."

He wore what he hoped was a smile, but wasn't sure it was that at all. It might've been a forlorn frown. "Thank you for dinner, and your gracious hospitality."

"I'll tell Mae and Hattie you enjoyed it."

Avery touched the black bill of his cap to Darah and tried that smile again. But it was a tense smile. There was no masking it. He was far from home, in trouble with the law, and would continue to run unless something or someone stopped him. Things were too heated up for him to return to Norfolk now. He would have to wait it out. But for how long? he wondered. And what would he do in the meantime?

"Why don't you join us tomorrow morning at our church?" Beulah invited. "Roy'd be delighted to see you there."

What would the minister be wearing? he wondered. A pulpit robe, or suit and tie? Would they shake hands or hug? "I can see it now. Old buddies reunited." He wouldn't even know me, he thought.

Darah rose from the couch. "Goodnight, Neil. See you tomorrow?"

A thought came to him like a stark vision: Godspeed, Neil Avery. See you soon. "Yeah. Tomorrow."

"Nice chatting with you." Darah's winning smile was the same one she wore the day they first met. Even her parting words were the same: Nice chatting with you.

He looked to Mama. "Goodnight, ma'am."

A pitter-patter of feet rushed at him from behind and a gentle tug on his trouser belt stopped him as he turned to leave. He looked at the child whose eyes sought his attention.

"Please say you'll come back," Olympia said in her winning, thin voice.

He hunkered to her level. Her little black feet showed beneath her ankle-length sleep gown. "Of course, sweet pea."

Everything in the room suddenly brightened with a momentary flash when a swerving car slashed its funneled headlights through the delicate drapery. The vehicle's brakes squealed, its engine quit, the headlights went out, and a door slammed. Someone marched to the porch and it creaked.

"Daddy!" Olympia would be the first to receive a hug from those oak, tree-limb arms of his. But what would Avery say to the preacher? He realized he wasn't ready to see Roy. I should've left earlier, he thought.

He opened the front door, taking a deep breath.

There, standing in the porch light with a galactic night as a backdrop, a young man in a gray, University-of-Virginia sweatshirt, stared into the face of the naval officer.

A grin curled his lips. "I want to speak with Darah. Now."

Chapter 21

The horn blast of a Piedmont train pulling into a nearby railroad station, stirred Avery out of sleep and out of bed. He barefooted across the woven Berber carpet to a double-paned, floor-to-ceiling window and parted thick dark drapes with a yank of fat tassels. Through gaps of black oak trees, silvery rails stretched into the distance. He wondered where they led and where time would lead him. In thought, he rubbed his unblemished face. The germ soap and bug cream had done its job, alleviating him of the constant itching and reducing the lumpy, red bites.

The crisscrossing, sunlit steel tracks seemed to have a hidden message. A meaning only the wisest of men could explain. The train pulled away, beating on its tracks. A moment later the Piedmont sounded like the rumble of distant thunder.

Avery guided the Dodge off Teaberry Road to a graveled area where other cars were parked under the hot, morning sun. Nestled among the leafy dark oaks, the bleached white, wood frame, sloping-roof building that survived the Civil War's cannonball blasts and Ku Klux Klan's arsonists, was considered a landmark, holding his attention the way it did when he first visited years ago. Drawn by it now, he wondered whether its gold crucifix, high atop the church's gabled steeple, had attracted more folks to its services. It was an odd thing in a religious town for people not to seek God. Although the building could comfortably occupy six-hundred persons, it never had in the past, and he wondered whether it was still so now.

In an elegant spacious vestibule, joyful hymn singing rose toward him, and each angelic black face that stared seemed ready to speak as he breathed in the scent of cedar and aged canvas oils. Around him, exquisite, pastel-tone paintings of previous pastors and clergymen of Faith Mission, reverently graced dark-paneled walls. Memorial Hall as it was called, had immortalized many a God-fearing man—ministers who prayed and had built the sacred sanctuary beam by beam from its foundation up; men who had become its patriarchs. At the bottom of each cherrywood frame, a golden tag bore the names—date of birth, year of death—of each lifelike face. It was on these same hallowed walls where he himself carefully removed an old portrait, and in its place, helped put up a new one.

Upon entering the main sanctuary, the Mozartian sound of the pipe-lunged organ and upbeat chorus of an old, familiar song, *Sign Me Up*—a hand-clapping, foot-stomping hymn of jubilee—enraptured him, bringing with it a time when his life came together like the distinct harmonic voices of a robed choir. That day, Darah Gilchrist was stunning in her billowy, ivory-white wedding gown. Its appearance was the creation of angels. She told him she was a recipe of emotions: euphoric nerves and rising tears. Roy told him this was the moment he prayed for, ever since he was ordained: to have the unique privilege of giving away the first of his daughters in marriage and performing the ceremony as well.

When the breathing pipe organ and excited tambourine rattle ended upon the last shout of praise, the Navy captain took a seat in an empty pew, settled in, and an offering was collected.

As soon as a final hymn was played by the organist, Faith Mission's senior pastor, Reverend Enoch Campbell—a cheerful-looking, chin-bearded, gray-haired man in white tab collar, clergy shirt and trousers—took the mike and made several announcements of upcoming events. He also reminded church members to continue in prayer for one of their faithful brothers, Elder Zechariah McKnight. The ailing minister, hospitalized with severe diabetic complications, would not be released as scheduled. The pastor urged the congregation to visit Elder McKnight. He told them God could change all things if they prayed.

Pastor Campbell announced the keynote speaker: a distinguished-looking man whose broad frame was hid beneath a violet-blue pulpit robe. When he was summoned, the big, cheek-boned, smiling cleric stood like a mighty oak and took to the sacred lectern with quiet strength and humble confidence. To Faith Mission, the peppered, gray-haired man was the assistant pastor, Reverend Roy Nathan Gilchrist. To Avery he was Dad.

Roy opened his big black bible, gave the scripture verse, and to the sound of pages turning, the congregation withdrew to a reverent lull. When everyone had the chapter, he read the verse and began.

"This scripture teaches us we need to pray. Not once in a while, but consistently. Everyday."

"Yes, Lord!" someone declared.

"Uh huh," said another.

"Praying is like breathing, eating, drinking. Sustaining us in our relationship with God."

Church members responded with affirmative amens and waving of hands.

"Did I ever tell the story about my mama and how she taught me to pray when I was a boy?" Avery couldn't get him out of his sight. He was good at holding the congregation in silent attention. "Well, I'm gonna tell it now."

The sermon. It was one he wanted to hear again.

"My mama," the reverend began in his distinct preaching voice. "God bless her, she's in heaven now. Anyway, my mama had a fiery temper. But it was she who helped me discover that anyone can call upon God in times of trouble. Yes, it was my beloved mama who taught me to pray."

"Praise the Lord," someone said.

"When I was a teen, I'd often come home late at night after hanging with the boys. You men know how it was."

"Amen," shouted some in affirmation.

The rest remained silent.

"My friends and I weren't out to harm anyone, you see. We just wanted to have fun by smoking and drinking the night away." The reverend paused to let some of the cackle die down. "But we were responsible drinkers, and therefore, knew when to stop. As soon as we felt nice it was time to go home. If we could find our way."

Laughter filled the building and reeled in the navyman. For the moment it calmed the swelling sea within.

"Then one night, I staggered home and walked on in. And by a dim lamplight, mama stood with a cross face, frowning lips, and a big ol' baseball bat over her shoulder. It was a Louisville Slugger. The kind Babe Ruth used."

The small crowd of worshippers tried to restrain their hearty outbursts, but the reverend wouldn't let them.

"There I was, locked in a staring game with my mama. Neither of us whispered a word until I opened my mouth and said, 'Hey, mama'. She got a whiff of that Thunderbird and went ballistic, swinging the bat at me with harmful intent."

Roy had everyone pealing with riotous laughter. "'I'll teach you to live holy'—my mama shouted as she chased me throughout the house. My old man and my brothers were startled from sleep when I leaped over beds, ducked the hammering bat, and fell down the stairs. Finally I crawled into the backyard; barking dogs inciting mama with more fury. That was the night I learned to pray: Lord help me. Stop this crazy woman. Save me God!"

Boisterous hilarity followed by loud applauses filled the sanctuary, spilling down the main aisle to the altar. "To this day," Reverend Gilchrist added, "I thank God for my mama. For it was she who taught me to pray."

Avery drank up the introduction to the message and the sermon which followed, appropriately titled: Crying out to God in times of trouble.

After the service, Avery spotted the dainty child Olympia, and their eyes met, like two, lonely stray dogs in search of friendship. She came to him with a mature grace for her years. "Does Mama know you're here?"

He picked her up. "I said I'd come. Where is she?"

The child pointed to Beulah and her sister Mae sauntering toward the vestibule—as Gerald approached Darah. Behind them were April and Taffi quibbling about something—while Gerald stood with Darah. Hattie smiled and waved at Olympia—as Gerald touched Darah.

Gerald Morgan ….

Avery clenched a fist.

Olympia hopped off his arms, and as soon as she took off, he went in the opposite direction—to the crowded altar of churchgoers that encircled the clergymen they were greeting. The swell had crested from within again with a force that propelled him forward. Not knowing where Roy had gone was like losing him again.

A tug on his trousers turned him around, and there, a small child stood proud alongside her tall, adopted father.

Avery fought back the sudden rush of tears not yet blurring his vision. He pinned arms to his side to keep at bay the urge to hug the man turned stranger.

The big black man introduced himself with a youthful twinkle in his eye and steel handshake. "Welcome to Faith Mission, young man." He had forgotten how strong Roy was. "My wife tells me you were at the house last evening." He searched his eyes. "Said we'd met before."

"That's okay, Reverend." He gulped down the heart lodged in his throat. "Wasn't expecting you'd remember."

"How about we get reacquainted?" He seemed to admire the navyman's service whites and gold-striped, black shoulderboards.

"I'd like that very much, sir."

April and Taffi joined their father, each wrapping a hand around his arms.

"My army days are over. You don't have to call me sir."

"Tough habit to break … Reverend."

"I understand. Why don't you join my family and me for dinner this evening. That'll give us a chance to talk and jog my memory."

Olympia patted the serviceman on the thigh to get his attention. "I'm so happy you're coming over." She turned to her father. "Can I show him my doll collection, Daddy?"

He put in a tolerant smile. "After dinner."

Roy had always been firm with all his girls. Even the little one.

Delighted with the news, Olympia skipped away, disappearing with Taffi and April through the chandeliered vestibule.

"If you're not in a hurry," Roy said, "I'd like to give you a quick tour of the church."

"That would be fine."

Roy led his guest to the ministers' prayer room behind the pulpit, the Sunday bible school area in the lower level, and up to the choir loft. "So, tell me about yourself, Captain."

He opened up as the two passed an old-fashioned, foot-pedaled organ where sixty-five ranks of polished copper pipes majestically rose to the heights of the rafters like an angel with spread-out wings.

Lastly, they stepped outside the building through a wide double-backdoor that led to a spacious acreage of flat, pristine land. The grass was immaculate, golf-course green; the trees were manicured, their limbs and branches clipped down and trimmed, the cobblestone walkways were clear of debris—and the standing gravestones, row upon row, were either marble white, granite gray, or smoky black.

"Those portraits in the vestibule—" Avery was anxious to fish Roy into the heart of the matter.

"Yes," the reverend interrupted. "They're all buried here."

Two centuries flashed before him. There were so many erect stones with so many names, each pointing to a moment in time. The older markers, dating back to 1855, were tipped at an angle. They were cracked, broken, and some barely readable; beaten by wind, heat, cold, moisture.

Avery followed Reverend Gilchrist as they passed between each gravesite like walking through a stone forest.

"And you?" Avery asked as an afterthought.

"What about me?"

"Where will you be buried?"

Roy came to a stop. "Right here, of course. But that won't be for a long time."

"Think so?" Avery swung the question at him much like the reverend's mother had swung the baseball bat the night he got home drunk.

"Okay, you and me both know we've never met. What's this about?"

"It's about you, Reverend, and the decisions you'll need to make before you die."

"Die?" He laughed away the amused look on his face, giving way to a frown. "Who said anything about dying? I'm not dying."

"Neither am I. But someday we will meet our maker."

Roy got quiet.

Blue Ridge sparrows chirped in the silence.

"Young man, unless you tell me who you are and what you want, this conversation is over."

Avery decided to take the Fifth. Saying things Roy could not possibly fathom would be equivalent to a criminal act.

Both men sauntered to the edge of the well-kept graveyard, reading tombstones as they went: *Pastor Jeremy Baines, born March 15, 1810, died November 11, 1858; Pastor Duncan McGee, born June 29, 1891, died January 2, 1946; Pastor Clive Dinwiddie, born August 21, 1954, died October 17, 2035.* Karyn was right. It was therapeutic.

On their way back they passed a leafless, twenty-five-foot-tall eyesore among the vibrant forestation. It was the Stayman tree. One look at it and Avery realized time was against him, growing shorter each moment, for him and for Roy. No matter how robust Roy appeared to be, sooner or later, Avery would have to go at him again before returning to Norfolk. Before a silent killer struck and stole the minister's health away.

He reentered the church building in search of a new approach. I can stop this, he thought with conviction.

Avery's earlier encounter with the minister seemed forgotten by Roy, now that he was home. But Avery was not fooled. Though Roy appeared to be enjoying his meal with his family, he wore a guarded eye against his two guests, especially the University-of-Virginia Business student—Gerald Morgan.

Darah and Gerald were the first to leave the table after they had eaten, followed by Mama and Olympia.

Roy looked to the serviceman with a yearning he had seen a thousand times. "Do you play chess, young man?"

For the longest, he had wanted to get even with Roy for losing two straight to him the first time they'd met. "Challenging me?" Now was his chance.

"Do I look like someone who'd back out?"

April and Taffi aimed gracious smiles on their father. Chess was his game. He played with such finesse, it was as though his fingertips had eyes, and no one knew that more than the girls. Avery understood why they had given up competing against him. They told their guest he was just too clever to beat.

Mama had outdone herself in both cooking and baking, and when dinner and dessert left soiled napkin cloths and full stomachs, Avery and the girls took over, carrying food-stained plates to the kitchen sink and placing them under running hot water and soapy mounds of Palmolive.

Darah told Olympia to hold on to her Raggedy Ann and Andy dolls as she worked on her hair at the table, while in the family room, the sound of a television station came to life.

Once the dishes were washed and dried, Avery went from the kitchen to the family room, where a brooding Gerald sat with athletic arms crossed over his chest, retreating with Roy to the creaky porch. Just like old times.

"Sorry to hear about Zack McKnight's illness." The two men pulled a pair of chairs away from the old porch table, the beaten deck boards put in a scraping squeal, and they sat. "You two close?"

"He's my chess mate, my fishing buddy, my best friend."

A ruddy sun beat on Avery's brow, painting everything in its near-setting glow: the porch table, the side of the house, and Roy—whose face looked lacquered from sweat. "What about Mr. Morgan?" The TV blared through the open window over his shoulder: Line drive, right field—

Roy said, "Gerald has a different agenda."

What he wanted to know was where Gerald stood with him. With Darah. He studied the reverend's unlined face. "Seems you don't approve his company."

Roy said nothing. He simply set up the knight-like pieces.

Avery made the first move. White pawn: e2 to e4. The preacher answered with his own pawn: e7 to e5. Next, Avery hurdled his knight ahead of the frontline troops: b1 to c3. Roy mirrored that move with his knight: b8 to c6. Now Avery: pawn, b2 to b4. He gave the preacher a long look. Those eyes, that had not yet looked at him the way he wanted them to, danced in strategy.

From inside the house, scraps of conversation distracted him.

"… Disappeared on me." Darah's voice. "Why?"

"Thought you were pregnant."

The TV: Ball four! That brings manager Abe Welco to the mound.

Roy broke the distraction. "So, what brings you to Oak Leaf?"

Avery's pulse quickened. He knew why he came. It certainly wasn't to watch Roy eliminate the first of the opposing army's eight pawns by a sly bishop: f8 to b4. Now the serviceman found himself on a thin tightrope of words. "Relatives of my father-in-law. Lived down the road past the church." He moved a knight on the board, hopping from g1 to f3.

Roy made a non-threatening countermove with a pawn: a7 to a5. "So what're you doing here in my house?"

He had a bad game going and he knew it. Working two fronts at the same time wasn't going to be easy. "Uh, there was no one home." He made a move, avoiding a confrontation with an intruding bishop at b4: pawn, a2 to a4.

"Should've let someone know you were coming." Roy did a peter-pan move with a knight, from g8 to f6.

Avery said nothing. What could he say? He studied the board, making note of the position of each piece. If he didn't start making some serious advances, the match would be over. He went for his first kill: knight, f3 to e5, and a brave pawn was removed.

Roy said, "Well, what's the man's name? Maybe I know him."

A haunted desire rose from within with frightening force. He blinked away the scene of a stately, cream-white hearse; pallbearers slowly marching toward a deep, six-footer. Roy eliminated yet another pawn with a knight: f6 to e4. Avery said, "He passed away." He followed the reverend's countermove with an absentminded one: rook, a1 to a3. "Died young."

Roy scored with a flying knight, c6 to e5, and the threatening knight was a goner. He never did much gabbing when he played, so Avery would have to keep talking to find out whether or not he was listening.

"Poor guy never realized how sick he was until the last minute, when it was too late." He bumped off one of Roy's knights with a twin, c3 to e4, and abruptly tossed it to him. The preacher snatched the piece in midair and gave the naval officer a pensive look. "Didn't mean to catch you off guard, Reverend. But life can be that way."

From inside the house, Darah and Gerald's pitched voices stirred the air:

"You don't want me. What you want—"

"Darah, please. Don't do this."

"What about what you did?"

Roy made a curious move with his king: e8 to g8. Now the rook at h8 stood at f8, body-guarding the king. It was a castling move, and Avery replied with his remaining knight: e4 to g5. The reverend pushed a loitering rook, from a8 to a6, and when Avery made a simpler move with a sleeping pawn, g2 to g4, Roy made a slide-step with his queen: d8 to e8. The young captain countered with a forgotten bishop, getting ready to do damage: c1 to b2.

"Too bad about your father-in-law." Roy nudged his bishop standing at b4, foiling Avery's rook from a major offense. Now the pope-capped piece stood at a3, waiting for the next move. "Where's he buried?"

Avery wished he could take out a big piece at this point but his forces were too far back. Then he saw an opening. His bishop at b2 could slice up the board and eliminate a confident knight at e5. But the queen lurking three spaces behind that piece would do him in. "He wasn't buried at all." A sore note hung in the air like a dark rain cloud. He settled for a less dramatic move, from b2 to a3, and one bishop bumped off another. "He was cremated without pomp or circumstance, depriving family and friends of a final goodbye and proper tears. The reason? He didn't want anyone grieving over him in a casket. Crazy, huh?" He wished he had never read Mama's letters to Darah about her father. Knowing too much killed innocent ignorance.

Seven pieces had been removed thus far. Roy had lost three and his guest, four. The game could still turn in Avery's favor, but the board clearly showed that Roy had supremely advanced, like Napoleon's troops had done in Alexandria, Egypt. Capturing the ancient seaport in a glorious defeat of his enemies.

Roy made his last knight dance from e5 to f3. Strategy kept him silent.

"My in-laws suffered needlessly for years because of his selfishness. While he was healthy, he had all the time in the world to open up a life insurance policy. It would've provided something for his loved ones after he was gone. But he never did. Didn't think it was necessary. He never imagined he would die young, after all, he was hardly ever sick and never went to the doctor. Said it made no sense to go when one was well. But my father-in-law deceived himself. He could've lived much longer." He attacked an idle pawn, pushing it out of the way with a leaping knight: g5 to h7. He made Roy look at him. "Some people are just hardheaded." He tossed the fallen piece to Roy in disgust. "What do you think?"

The cleric gave him a keen look. "I think you're trying to start that talk we had earlier at the cemetery. But as I said, the conversation is over. And so's this game." He pushed his queen straight down the board, from e8 to e1, knocking off his king.

Avery looked with open-mouth astonishment at the remaining black and white chess pieces and where each stood on the squares. There was no way he could have won without concentrating. "Alright, then promise me this …." Tension ravished every muscle in his body. He grabbed the deposed king and wagged it with a reprimand in the minister's face. "Promise me that when you die, you won't be cremated!"

"Say what?" Blood rose in the thunderstruck minister's dark cheeks. He knocked over several pieces he had scooped up from the conquest where they fell at his feet.

"Cremation," he repeated. "The legalized form of Hitler's—"

"I know what it means," Roy said. "What in heaven's name are you getting at?"

The captain put his hand down and held his silence, afraid of the next words he might have to say.

Roy barreled through like an army truck. "Ever since this morning you've been talking as if I'm gonna die soon. Well, I have news for you, young man. God has given me much work to do and many years to do them in."

He had forgotten how stubborn Roy could be when he wanted his own way, and how he wouldn't allow anyone to sneak a word past him when he disagreed.

"Yes siree," he said with sharp conviction. "I'm gonna have a good, long life."

Avery picked up the fallen pieces off the porch. He straightened up and willed himself to be defiant, despite the fact he loved Roy so much. "You don't seem concerned about your health."

"Not when everything's fine. Care for another match?"

"Yeah," Avery said. "This time don't quibble with me so I can do you in."

From within the house, something rattled when it hit the floor. The remote control.

"You would never survive without me."

"Don't give me that line about being a man."

Roy set up the pieces again and Avery set up another strategy. If he nudged all his pawns forward in one desperate charge, he knew he would be relinquishing them to their demise. "The bible states our lives are like passing shadows. Tomorrow is promised to no one."

"Don't preach to me, boy." Roy was adamant but let the navyman make the first move: pawn, d2 to d4. The reverend put his best pawn forward: e7 to e5.

Avery said, "I wasn't preaching. I was simply trying—"

"I know what you want," Roy said. "And I know who you are and what you do."

What did he know? he thought. Roy had thrown him for a loop and that made him shudder. He made a shaky move and wiped out the minister's charging pawn with his own: d4 to e5. This time he struck first. "Okay, who am I?"

"You're a slick insurance salesman. Should've known from the start." Roy advanced his queen from d8 to e7. "About a month ago, several of them came to Faith Mission, trying to coax me and Campbell into one of those fancy policies no one could cash-in on for another forty, fifty years. I chased them out knowing one day those whippersnappers would send someone else."

Avery placed a knight ahead of the pawny troops: b1 to a3. Roy balanced that move with a knight: b8 to c6. Avery moved the h2 pawn to h4, looking to get the rook at h1 out of the corner. The reverend's queen crept forward, from e7 to b4. Avery made a defensive move to keep his queen from harms way: bishop, c1 to d2. Roy's black queen at b4, descended on a white pawn defending b2. Now the game took on a war of attrition, forcing the navyman to take serious action. He moved a bishop, from d2 to b4, and paid for it when an f8 black bishop sliced diagonally down the board, intercepting him. Now he nudged a ready queen forward: d1 to d2, and Roy took advantage of a warring knight at a3 and got rid of it with his bishop at b4. With each piece Avery lost, a slice of patience went with it. An ounce of anger added. Now the two men were as serious as dueling generals in a war room.

The navyman made a spearhead move, invading black territory with a domineering queen: d2 to d7. The black king retaliated and put the white queen out of her misery: e8 to d7.

Avery decided it was time to move the rook out of its corner: h1 to h3.

"Checkmate," the minister announced.

"Where?"

Roy moved his queen from b2 to c1. He had the white king blocked really good. Chess was not a talker's game. It was a thinker's game.

Avery felt like he had just come up from holding his breath in an all-day, sea-training exercise. "Not my day." He toppled his king and looked away to the lofty treetops. He wished his fears were as the thin clouds: wispy and temporal; harmless as a dove.

Darah shouted at Gerald to leave. He blew past the porch and the wood-framed screen door banged as he marched to his car: a gold-colored Chrysler PT Cruiser.

"You'd better not be seeing anyone!" Gerald shot.

Darah stormed out to the porch after the irate black man, tailed by Taffi, April, and Olympia. "What if I am?"

Gerald climbed into his vehicle and slammed the door. He gave the Navy captain a look. "Don't let me catch you with her, sailor boy."

With the roar of the engine, the PT made a wide turn and gained speed, disappearing behind a row of black birch trees down the old, dirt road.

Darah's eyes landed on her father. "Sorry, Daddy. Won't happen again."

"That a promise?"

One by one, the girls reentered the house. Last at the scene was Olympia with a thin storybook cradled in one arm and eyes on the officer-sailor. He prevented her tender smile from working on him by not smiling back at the little farmer girl in perfect pigtails and denim overalls.

"Wanna read my book?" She showed him the glossy cover of a young girl climbing up a tree's leafy branches in search for a helpless kitten that had clawed its way up.

He turned away, cocooned in silent bitterness.

Olympia touched him as though she could cure him of his ailment. Her eyes darted from the chessboard, to her father, then back to him. "Daddy beat you, didn't he?"

Her gentle words pricked him and he frowned.

The child blinked.

"How about one more, General Custer?" Roy made himself laugh, his chest heave, and shoulders bounce. "Betcha I can win three straight."

"No thanks, Reverend. I've already lost."

"C'mon, I'll let you win this time." He laughed again.

"I've never known you to compromise."

Roy's laughter had been clipped to a sudden silence as though a thought had dawned on him.

Olympia chased away the quiet. "Daddy can beat anybody."

"Can he beat the game of life?" He snapped a stare at Roy, stepped off the creaky porch, and marched toward his car parked alongside the mailbox post. A choir of Goldfinch warbled a happy tune from the surrounding tall oaks, but Avery wished he could be oblivious to their song.

Olympia chased after him. "Don't leave. Stay and read my book. Sit me on your lap and tell me about the big ships in the Navy. Come back for dinner!"

But he never acknowledged her or said goodbye. Instead he left the sighing child where she stood, beside a chestnut tree that dangled an old rubber tire by a rope from one of its low, thick limbs. He opened the car door and slid into the vehicle like a felon making a getaway. It was time for him to hit the road and head back to the Days Inn Hotel in Boone, and from there...?

Roy stood fast to his feet. "Sorry for making you think we could hit it off the way you and my wife have."

"You won't even try."

"Drop that crazy notion about me and I will."

"Can't do that." He turned the ignition and floored the gas in neutral, revving up the engine. It countered the angry engine within him. He slammed the door shut.

"Young man," Roy pursued. "The thought of being cremated has *never* crossed my mind."

Avery fired back: "Neither has dying." He drove away, gripping the steering wheel tighter than usual.

Chapter 22

Mountain air rustled oak leaves and Avery followed its woody scent to a secluded area. He guided the Alpine-green Dodge over the graveled grounds and parked, wrestling with this thought: How much longer must I give in to voices from the past?

After a long sit, he adjusted his garrison cap the way he had seen the admiral do once, and went to the cemetery.

There, among the marble, granite, sandstone monuments and tombstones, he welcomed the perfect stillness. The cemetery resembled a peaceful state park. The only difference was that the markers, headstones, and memorial pillars had replaced the things one normally found in such settings: benches for visitors, ponds for ducks, playgrounds for children. The distinguished-looking trees were a pleasant mix of cedar, pine, oak, and birch—some tall with stunted arms, others grandiose and shady—all adding a gentle beauty to the wide open landscape. Whoever the groundskeepers were, they had done a masterful job of maintaining, not only the fresh spiky grass and robust trees, but also the sculpted shrubbery, and flowerbeds, abounding with red geraniums, blue lobelias, white daffodils, pink daisies. All was well in this garden of Eden, until his mind mechanically unleashed a torrent of thoughts: a white, blood-soaked carpet; the smell of acrid gunpowder; a Smith & Wesson at his side; a dead body sprawled at his feet. The past pursued him still.

Now he stood beneath the eyesore. Sunlight draped a shadow over him and fingers of grief began to strangle. Studying the diseased branches made him think of Roy. The way it would end. The way it would hurt.

The Stayman tree. It was a gnarly piece of stump when he first visited Oak Leaf. Yet there was a time when the noble tree's leaves greened and its fruit reddened. But all that was before they fell to the ground like dying birds.

The graveled roadside came alive, like corn kernels popping in a microwave. After a moment an engine stopped, a door closed with a gentle thump, and muffled footsteps drew near. He took a deep breath and let it out, rehearsing a line to himself: Hi, my name is Neil. What's yours? However, his pulse still raced to the sight of her.

"Didn't mean to disturb you." Darah turned her eyes away for a second. "What're you doing here alone?"

"Thinking. Praying."

"I believe God answers prayer. What ... what do you think?"

He swung his body away from her like tossing in bed from a bad dream. "I think being with me is making you nervous." He pushed against the dying tree with an outstretched hand. Above them, gathering clouds covered the sun. Now the shadow he hoped would darken his face like a widow's black veil was stripped away, leaving her to find the eyes he could no longer hide.

"You seem so alone." She took two steps toward him. "As though you've lost a friend."

He straightened up, staring at rows and rows of old and newer headstones. "Tell me something. Does your father ever see a doctor?"

"He's never been sick. Not that I can remember. And besides, he's a man of such great faith, that even if he were, he strongly believes God would heal him."

Old news didn't surprise Avery. But something else did.

"What about this tree?" He pointed to it with disdain.

"What about it?" Her voice was soft as silk.

"Why doesn't your dad take an ax to it? It's detracting the surrounding beauty."

"He can't."

"You mean he won't."

"Because it's his. Every year when its apples were just right, Mama would pick them and bake pies. Now it just stands there like an eerie sentinel guarding the cemetery. Dying before its time."

Before its time ....

He played with those words, making a connection to Roy. How he hated that tree. Had from the moment he saw it. Now he wanted to chop it down himself because he finally knew what it stood for. "But that still doesn't explain why he won't cut it down. It's going to happen eventually. Might as well be him."

She studied him with contradiction in those almond-shaped eyes. Her body language saying: No. "That will never be cut down. My father believes one day it'll supernaturally sprout back to life. He says God will perform a

miracle on that tree, much like Aaron's walking staff that blossomed with—
"

He cut her off. "Small branches, leaves, and almonds?"

"Why yes." Her lips parted and her mouth dropped a fraction. "Are you familiar with that portion of scripture?"

"Your father preached a sermon on Aaron's staff at Christ Church in St. Charles." What point he tried to make in saying that he wasn't sure.

"CCSC? That's one of the biggest churches in Maryland. Wait a minute." Suddenly her brow dropped with contradiction again. "Daddy's never been there."

Man, what did I just say? he thought. His mind raced to piece something together. "Maybe it was ... someplace else."

Darah drew close to him on slow, short steps, running her hands into the pockets of her denim skirt. She looked to the ground, then lifted unblinking eyes to him.

"You keep looking at my face like reading a map," he told her.

"Just wondering where you're from. Where you're going."

He wished he knew where he was going himself. "You fancy me, don't you?"

"Well, it's ... that uniform. Your military decorations."

"No it's not."

She huffed out a breath and shuffled her feet. "It's ... your eyes. They tell an unusual story of a journey. About a love story with a missing ending. A heart yearning for another chance. Is that the reason you have such a deep interest in my parents?"

Her warmth caught him off guard, but he decided to answer her, anyway. "Ever had anyone's kindness change your life?"

"You sound like my father preaching."

He bowed his head and let a tired laugh escape.

"What's funny?" Darah's face changed again. But each change was so lovely.

He smothered a silly grin. "You don't get around much, do you?"

"Just a simple home-girl on her college break."

He loved her silent charm. "Must be glad you have a summer stipend."

"How did you know that?" Her words sounded more like a deliberate attack than a curious question.

Avery knew too much and it was killing him. Lies, no matter how many he told, could never equal one truth. "Uh, Mae told me." His hungry gaze searched her face like looking at a lost photograph found—from those eyes, to her lips, to each pronounced nipple that pressed against her blouse. "You know, you're fortunate to have caring parents like Roy and Beulah. Not everyone does."

"Well, how about your folks? Your brothers, your sisters?"

She didn't mention cousins, aunts, uncles. It was just as well because he had lost touch with them growing up. Except one. "I'm like Pia."

"Oh, I'm sorry."

"For asking?" He was captivated by the thought of kissing her. Now the more he regarded her, the more he wanted—including moments life snatched from him with angry hands. "What else do you want to know?" He saw the burning interest in her eyes.

"The answer to my question. What is it about my father that causes you to well up with such emotion?" Despite his ability to keep things bottled up, Darah's magical gaze and tenderness were prying him open. "I've been observing you," she admitted. "Every time you look at my parents, I notice the admiration you have for them, and yet … there's a sadness, too."

Yesterday's tears rose, filling his head. But it wasn't Darah's fault. She simply had touched the chords of his heart, and like guitar strings, made them strum with emotion.

He knew it was too late to hide the look in his eyes.

"There, you're doing it again. Why do you feel that way?"

She had gotten to the heart of the matter and he found himself gradually weakening.

"Because …." His throat felt raspy and tight. "Because I …."

"Love them?" She looked surprised. "You don't even know them!"

It was clear Darah didn't understand. It showed on her face. But he had to tell her now. She simply wanted to know. "Ever lost someone you loved so deeply, so dearly, that your only thought, day and night, is to see that person again, just to hold one last time and say all the unsaid things you should've?"

"Like … I love you?"

His heart throbbed like a wound that refused to heal.

"I can't imagine what you've gone through." Her words were as her tears forming. "Whatever happened was awful, wasn't it?"

A thin pool shielded his vision and everything around him looked glassy.

Darah handed him a clean tissue from her skirt pocket, and together, they dried their eyes. She seemed to have another question ready on her tender lips. "Did you know my father before?"

"He's the reason I'm here."

"Were you close?" Her eyes, shimmering with interest, told him she had opened up.

"Close enough to know the family."

"Then ... why is it no one knows you? Why don't I remember you?"

He leaned back against the trunk of the failing tree. His heart had betrayed him. Her innocence had caused her to ask too much and his love for her had caused him to reveal too much. But it was too late. Too late to subdue his pounding heart that threatened to explode in his chest if he didn't come out with it. Too late to deny—to say things that weren't true. Now the urge to say more was on his lips. Things he was warned not to. The struggle with his conscience and emotions was as wrestling sumos—right against wrong—each trying to win.

"Please don't make me tell you things you could never understand." His voice had turned throaty, revealing more anguish than he cared to show.

"It pains me to the core you don't have a soul in the world. It's not strange to think you never had a family. What could you say I won't understand?"

He bowed his head to the frightening vision that billowed in his mind: the inevitable.

Darah laid a hand on his shoulder as though to comfort him. "You're trembling. What's wrong?"

Avery wiped his eyes and nose. He had run out of lies. "Your father has cancer but doesn't know," he groaned. "He needs to see a doctor—soon."

Darah looked like a gust of wind had clogged her lungs and stole her breath. "What? Who?" Her face told him he had alarmed her. "This isn't funny!" she cried out.

"Didn't mean to scare you." He drew a desperate breath to replenish what his emotions had sucked out of him. "I'm just trying to get you to understand."

"Understand what?" She looked angry but sounded fearful.

If he didn't say something quick, she would turn away, run to her car, and leave the same way she came. "That this world, this moment, is my past!"

Darah wheeled away, letting out a dismal laugh. "Didn't know you were a fruitcake." She started to retrace her steps.

Suddenly he felt vulnerable, abandoned. "Please don't go. I need you to trust me. To know what haunts me." He hated to think what he would do without her help.

She stopped in her tracks. "I don't know where you came from but I wish you'd go back."

He wished she wouldn't speak to him through the back of her head. "Not without completing the task I came to do."

Darah said nothing. She simply began marching away.

"Wait! What if I can prove what I've said?" Suddenly he realized: What proof do I have? He would have to think fast. No more pretty lies or counterfeit truths. "Someday, Roy's going to be a worldwide evangelist, sharing the simple message of God's love like he does at Faith Mission."

"Daddy?" She turned and faced him in a denying pose. "He's just a country preacher."

Avery slanted an omniscient eye at her. "Wait and see."

"No, that'll never happen."

He heaved out a sudden breath, raking fingernails through his scalp. The frustration was still there, though. "Stubborn like her father."

"What did you say?"

This was going to be more difficult than he realized. "I said: God help me, Father. How can I prove what I've told you?"

"Okay, mister." She crossed arms over her chest and flashed a dubious smile. "Tell me about my future. Will I ever get married?"

He was stunned she had asked that. Like being stabbed by a dart. "Let's leave that one alone."

"Why?" she laughed with mock. "Did I crack your crystal ball?"

What she had cracked was his fragile heart. "I knew you'd think that way." She looked at him in a way that made him uncomfortable.

"You said you could prove it. Now I'm curious to hear what else you'll make up."

He strung words together. But would that be enough for her to believe? he wondered. "Yes, you'll meet someone, and …."

She rolled eyes at him but seemed willing to hear the rest.

"And you'll marry. But not someone from church or college." He wanted to kick himself for saying too much.

"If it isn't Gerald, then …?" She studied his uniform. Her wandering eyes met his. "Who?" she asked. "Someone in the Navy?"

He stiffened. "What makes you say that?"

"I can't say. Don't know anyone in the Navy." She looked pensive. "Except you."

He hoped he could keep the secret from showing on his face, but he wasn't sure he could do that.

Darah's eyes looked like a gripping spell had been broken. "Okay. Who are you and what do you want with my father?"

"To save him."

"From what?"

Something dark came over him and he faced Roy's diseased tree. "I already told you!" He hoped she would take the hint and walk away.

After a long moment he turned and looked. Darah had not moved.

"Thought you left."

"Does my father really have cancer?" She held a hand to her stomach as though it ached from worry.

Her question had snuck up on him and shook him with fright. He nodded, but wouldn't look into her eyes.

"I don't believe you." She turned away as quietly as she had spoken, and as soon as she did, he rushed at her, seized her by the shoulders and whirled her like a mannequin. "What's wrong with you?" Her eyes were wild with thought. "Let go." He gripped her tighter. "Neil, let go. You're hurting me!"

Now he knew he would have to spew out the urgent thought. "I'm not sure when, but this might be the year of the accident."

"What accident?" Her caramel skin creased between her eyebrows. "What're you talking about?" she cried.

Darah squirmed loose from his grip and backed away.

"It's the proof—Pia."

She froze.

He had her attention.

"What about my baby sister?"

"She's going to fall from a tree and break her right humerus. If that happens that'll prove everything I've said."

"Pia's afraid of heights." She was close to tears. "What would make her do such a dumb thing in the first place?"

"It's that book she's been reading—"

"Stop it!" Darah cupped hands over her ears. "I don't want to hear your foolishness."

A fool is what he would be if he didn't warn her now. "I see there's no way to convince you, so I must tell you this …." He felt like the cowardly lion in the Wizard of Oz about to make a bold statement. "Unless your dad has a cancer-screening test soon, it'll be too late."

She lowered her arms, and with frightened eyes scanned the cemetery. People died young back then, same as today. But he wondered whether she could see that. She said, "Please, talk of something else. Let's go someplace where these headstones won't stare at us."

He and Darah walked around the church building, side by side. When they crossed the front steps of the tall cathedral-like doorway, a gold-colored vehicle with fiery decals on its side, cruised up to them. The grimfaced man cut the buzz-saw roaring engine, climbed out tall, slammed the door and approached, targeting the poised man in uniform.

"I warned you, mister."

"Gerald," Darah cried. "Don't!"

He took a swing, the serviceman weaved, and the momentum spun the college student into a vice-tight half nelson. In the struggle, conjoined bodies fell on the hood of the Chrysler with a pounding thud. He tried to throw the serviceman off his back, but he rode him, pinning him against the hood, causing it to give. "Dent this car and I'll dent your head," Gerald shot.

Avery grabbed the man's flailing free arm and jammed it tight behind his back like he was undogging a watertight hatch. The man grunted in protest, and got his legs kicked out, spread-eagle, to keep him from squirming.

"Neil, don't hurt him."

He waited until he knew the subdued college student could do no harm. "Where I come from, men talk first, not throw fists." He released him, scooped up his garrison cap, and dusted off the powdery, red dirt.

Gerald turned with a twisted face and massaged his neck and shoulders. He examined his nose and upper lip for blood. There was nothing. "You had it coming, sailor boy."

"Gerald, you don't even know this man. You owe him and me an apology."

"I didn't want it to be this way, Darah. All I want is for us to be together again."

"Well, you sure picked a stupid way of doing it."

Gerald kicked a gray jagged stone that lay at his feet. He opened the door to his car. "Is it ... over between us?"

"Nothing's over, Gerald. I just need time to think."

"Can't you think alone? Do you have to be with him?"

"Maybe I should leave," Avery suggested.

"No, Gerald's leaving!" Her eyes flared. "Aren't you, Gerald?"

He frowned like a sad clown. "Will you at least—"

"I'll call you," she said. "Promise."

Gerald ducked into the Chrysler and slammed the door. The vehicle roared to life, spat dirt in reverse, lurched forward in a wide turn and kicked up gritty dust as it drove away.

A moment later the young, college student was gone.

"I'm sorry," Darah said. "He didn't mean it."

"Could've fooled me."

She traced his form up and down. "Where did you learn that?"

"Learn what?"

"That arm thing you did."

"Every officer trains in hand-to-hand combat and Judo. Especially Navy pilots. Never know when you'll get shot down over foreign soil without a weapon."

He followed her across the quiet road, all the while looking at her legs. Around mid-calf of her right leg, she had a cute little, heart-shaped mole he had not noticed before—never.

She got into her car, a white Toyota Camry, like slipping into lingerie, and drove ahead of him.

After a stretch of towering oaks, verdant hills, and wide open sky, she pulled into a dusty dirt path and got out.

He swung his car around hers and heard it—the wail of brakes; the fatal crunch of metal; a windshield shattering in a mighty implosion. He stared at the front of her Toyota and a scene unfolded before him: rotating strobe lights flashing in the dark; EMS personnel covering a body; red flares igniting a glass-littered asphalt.

"Are you going to sit there all day?" she asked with arms folded.

He blinked away the hypnosis, unbuckled his seatbelt, got out of the vehicle, and together, they proceeded on foot, making their way through a secluded wooded area. They followed an old bridle path and he felt Darah slip her hand in his. He was spellbound by her touch, and the surprise intensified when they reached the end of the trail where the sound of rushing waters revived him.

"Where are you taking me? And what's this place?" He breathed in the scent of dogwood and magnolia.

"Dugger Creek. Daddy told me when he first met Mama, he brought her here."

"Now it's us." He walked to the crest of a short footbridge made of sturdy logs, and gave a look over the side. Clear water, sloshing over boulders and exposed tree roots, winked at him from below as finny denizens hurried by.

He and Darah crossed to the other side and sat on a large gray slab of rock that faced the stream. They kicked off their shoes, stretched their legs, and inhaled life into their lungs like newborn babies. He gave Darah a look. Her skin glowed like honey in the sun.

"How did you know where I was? Back there at the cemetery?"

Her eyes turned away from his and a gust of wind blew. "I followed you to the hotel. Then …."

Darah's behavior shouldn't have surprised him, for her eyes told him things he already knew of her. The air temperature suddenly felt chilly, so he ran a hand over the marching gooseflesh on her arms. "Hey, you're shivering." She seemed nervous, but warmed by the blaze in his touch. "Is there a reason why you tailed me?"

She let out a brief, embarrassed laugh. "Yesterday, I overheard Taffi explain to Pia what a crush was—an overwhelming, heart-fluttering, palm-sweating emotion for someone of the opposite sex. Pia repeated the word—sex? And this morning I found her Raggedy Ann and Andy dolls on my dresser, male over female. Looking at them made me think of you. Of us."

She leaned toward him and a lavender scent pulled him in. But when his eyes fell on her lips readying for a kiss, a rush of bad memories surfaced and he looked away.

"Don't," he told her.

"Then let me say it." The sun peeked over the racing clouds blocking it. "Neil ...." She melted him with that long-ago look. "I like you a lot. Actually—"

"It's much stronger than that, isn't it?"

Her delicate mouth dropped. "How ... how did you know what I was going to say?"

He shrugged. "Lucky guess."

"No. You read my mind."

"I can't read minds, that's absurd."

"Is it?" She looked into his eyes as though trying to read of some deep secret concealed in them. "I'm beginning to wonder about you."

The sun disappeared behind thickening clouds. He wished he could do the same with his emotions—hide them from her, from himself. "Sorry. This time I can't tell you."

"Tell me what?" Darah's brow dropped, her eyes narrowed, and her lips frowned. "Something else I won't believe?"

Avery knew she found him mysterious. First drawing her, then repelling her, only to draw her again.

"I don't want to hear about Pia, my father, or anyone else."

He liked the attention she gave his hands. His nails were trimmed and clean. She raised her eyes to the frolicking stream as though it had called her. She was deep in thought. Perhaps over things she wanted most, he guessed.

"Know what that babbling stream sounds like?" she said. "The sound of children laughing. Children I want to have someday. Three boys, four girls, and a dog." Her eyes met his. "May I ask a personal question?"

"Can't stop you."

"Why aren't you married?"

"What makes you think I'm not?"

"Don't see a ring."

"Takes more than a ring to be married."

His subtle way of saying things drew her to him once more.

"So ...." Her voice dropped and she sighed. "There is someone."

His heart skipped a beat. "There was. Once."

"Divorce?" She looked hopeful.

He felt fearful. "I'm a widower."

She looked wounded. Arrow-whizzing words had plunged into her. "Oh, I'm so dreadfully sorry for prying. I didn't mean to be so ...."

"You weren't."

"Doesn't anything good happen to you?"

He said nothing.

"Did you love her?"

This time he let her read his eyes, but knew she wouldn't find an answer. Yet he feared the more she asked, the more she would learn of him. And the more she learned, the more she would desire him.

"Love?" He deliberated over its meaning. "There can be no real marriage without it."

"People marry for many reasons," she said.

He looked away. "Mine was love. Only reason I ever had."

"So, you did love her."

He searched Darah's soft eyes; golden almonds in settings of pearls. How he wished he could've displayed the tears he never cried; spoken truth instead of lies. If he could do and say those things this moment, the slaps he once inflicted on her would now be caresses on her face, and long-ago bruised breasts would now be kissed. Her lips would never again be battered and blood caked. They would be as they were before they met: full instead of swollen, with a touch of lip gloss that would make him fall on them with sinful pleasure until she permitted him to invade her mouth with his lascivious tongue. Instead of punching her in the gut, his fingers would explore the padding of curly hair on her crotch. And instead of making her cry out in pain, he would make her moan with delight at the stroking touch of her spot. However, the guilt he carried still had not allowed him to do what she wanted him to do a moment ago. "I ... cared for her more than anyone will know. But ... I ... I should've...."

"I'm sure she knew."

"Knowing isn't the same as telling." He bowed his head, filled with thoughts that drained him. Only remorse weighing around his neck like a fouled anchor could make him stoop the way he did.

"What was she like?"

Avery wondered why he suddenly felt so lightheaded. He leaned back against the broad, flat rock; arms locked behind him. With reflective eyes on lofty treetops, he described a woman to the woman sitting beside him.

He was glad Darah Gilchrist had no clue he was speaking of her.

"I didn't deserve my wife. But thinking of her, forges me ahead to keep a promise I made."

Darah swiped at teardrops that had broken free. "I've never heard a man speak of a woman the way you just did."

241

The gurgle of rushing waters made him reach for her. This time I'll be tender, he thought. She was so beautiful when she wept. More so than when she smiled. "I was good at that," he said.

"Good at what?"

"Making you … never mind."

"Cry? I'm fine. It's … the way you spoke of your wife. I feel as though I know her. How long has it been?"

He studied Darah's right hand. The one she wore her Academy ring on with so much pride. Her ship had left port that night. The night that birthed ten-thousand more nights. Sleepless nights. Endless nights. Nights without the moon casting its light on the swaying bay, making it dance. "Long enough for me to get over her."

"No. Your tone is anemic. I can hear your heartbeat in your voice."

"My voice?" It trembled like a child's frightened voice. He couldn't deny it.

"She was special, wasn't she?"

"Never knew how much," he whispered. "Till …."

Crumbling from within, he slid away from her, not wanting to look into eyes that caressed him, yet aching for the warm touch he could only have in dreams. "What does my voice tell you?" He was afraid her concerned look would cause him to burst into uncontrollable, fresh tears.

"It tells me you never stopped loving her. Never stopped caring. That's the reason you've never stopped crying."

A gust of wind kicked up, and when its stirring stopped, it seemed to also stop time in its tracks.

"What was her name?"

Avery gasped at the pricking thought. He felt offended yet relieved she dared to ask such a thing. Then something squeezed him with such devastation, every dormant teardrop collected from within and rose to a mighty squall. He thought he could fight the surge, but it ripped at him, gathering strength. Once, her name flowed like two eighth notes from his lips; it was her identity. Hers was special: Darah. It meant compassion. Of which he had little of.

The sight of her turned him into a little boy with a twisted face, his mind filled with young moments of her. With all his might he willed himself to form on his lips the name of the first woman who had tried to teach him to love.

"Her name was …." He quivered with a sadness she was sure to feel if she touched him.

Unable to push her name into the air, he broke down and sobbed in Darah's arms ….

… And there he stayed, enveloped in her embrace, head on her lap, waiting for every ounce of crushing pain, every bitter teardrop to be drained out of him.

She fingered his hair the way she used to, until his head stopped pounding, and the darkening clouds warned them to leave.

He and Darah drove back to the farmhouse in the sudden rain, and when they rushed to the porch to escape the liquid pelting and opened the door, the smell of dinner was in the air.

Beulah shuffled from the kitchen to the family room, clutching a bloody finger with a thick gauze. Her face looked heavy, and her eyes were downcast.

"What's wrong, Mama?" Darah asked. "You look upset."

"Roy, he …." Her emotions choked back the rest of the message.

"Did you cut yourself? And where's Daddy?" She squeezed Avery's arm.

"He just called. Elder McKnight passed away. The funeral is in two days. Saturday afternoon."

"Where're the girls?" Avery asked.

"Upstairs crying." Mama's gauzed finger was blood-soaked. "Zack meant a lot to them."

"Let me look at that." She showed him the jagged pink path on her sausage-like index finger; the work a gleaming kitchen knife had dug. "Might need a stitch or two."

Darah shot up the stairs and returned with fresh gauze and surgical tape.

Avery dressed Mama's finger. Then, their eyes locked on each other for a quiet moment. She sank into the sagging wingchair's herniated frame with all the weight of grief she carried. Zechariah McKnight's name was etched on each line of Mama's tender face. The minister's long, hard battle against the dreaded disease, diabetes, was over.

A faint rhythmic sound came from somewhere in the room.

"What's that beeping?" Darah asked.

Mama looked up with sad-shaped eyes.

Avery stood there for a moment not moving. Not breathing. He pulled up a sleeve and his heart sprinted. Marc's watch was pulsating green. "Nothing. It's … just a reminder." A reminder he had forty-four hours left, or he would die. He pressed a tiny button on its side and silenced it.

Six days was all he had to work with—and how they flew away—the winged feet he walked in with when he entered the house, holding Darah's hand. Now what remained was a crushing, weighty emptiness that rose from within. All his life he felt like a failure, and now he was feeling it again.

Another defeat had slapped him in the face, leaving his soul to sting. What was just as bad, was that the revolving ride on time's merry-go-round was a familiar one, for he and Darah were falling in love—again.

Chapter 23

The view from the top of the woodland hill was superb. And floating over it, cumulus clouds were so big and so low, it seemed anyone could reach out and touch them. Heaven was an arms-length away, and everything Avery loved about Spring Mountain, lay before him, including the valley and the vista beyond it. This would be their picnic spot. A secluded area where he and Darah could eat and let a golden sun above a blue watercolor sky watch them.

From where he sat, the Dodge took on the appearance of a Matchbox toy. Everything seemed so miniature from up high, so insignificant. Even the problems that beset him.

He angled his head toward the majestic expanse—picnic basket at his side, finger sandwich in his hand, the strength of a mighty oak against his back as he calculated the hours he had remaining. Twenty-seven....

The uncapping pop of a Snapple distracted him. Darah wet her lips with a taste and dipped her finger in the glass bottle. She brought that finger to his lips and he kissed it.

"Passion Fruit," he said.

Darah recapped the bottle and put it aside. "No. It's your passion for me." She slipped her hand in his and they looked at each other. Her eyes swayed along with his like a pair of lovers locked in a slow dance. She nestled closer to him and kissed him on the lips.

"Wish I could tell you ...." he began.

"Tell me what?" She smiled as though she knew.

He fisted his chest like a repentant sinner. "How sorry I am for doing so many things."

Darah stood and stooped over him. "What things?" Her hair fell over his face like a veil.

He looked at her through the long mane stroking his face, dispelling all doubt this was a dream. "Want to know why I'm really here?"

"Isn't it obvious?" She kissed his lips, longer this time, then sat beside him. "To steal me away from my boyfriend."

"Hey, I'd like that."

"So, what're you waiting for?"

"He'll come after me again."

"Don't be afraid of him. Touch me."

His lips parted and he began to breathe faster, stronger. Is she joking? he thought. "If I did that, your father would come after me, too."

"He won't know." She undid the buttons of her blouse and unhooked her bra open from the center. "I know why you looked at me the way you did when I first saw you." She pulled his hand, guiding it where she wanted it to rest. "Are all navymen sex-driven as you?"

Avery looked away; her hand on his; his fingers on the soft flesh of her cleavage.

She said, "I want something to remember you by if you should go and never return."

Her whispering message made his heart race. She was right about him leaving. But is this what he wanted? Yes, he told himself. "No. Fornication without the commitment is not what I want."

"What do you suggest?"

"We could elope, but this isn't how I planned it."

"What guarantee do I have you'll return?"

None, he knew.

If he let another moment slip away, he would be denying the love he had for her, and later, no matter how hard he fought to get it off his shoulders, the distressing weight of regret would be as deadly as the poisonous bite of a rattlesnake.

Pushing aside intruding thoughts, hungry fingers traced long bare legs down to her calves, down to the curved arches of her childlike feet.

Now in each other's arms, time stood still and loosened its grip, granting them permission for their lips to touch and their tongues to meet. In that moment, the two worlds they were from merged into one: his past, her future; his hopes, her dreams. He tasted her lips, neck, working his way down to her standing breasts, stroking one and filling his mouth with the other, sucking passionately until she trembled with desire.

She lifted her pleated crepe skirt and delicately danced out of cottony-white panties like a cocooned butterfly set free. "I'm not the nice church girl you think I am."

"Doesn't matter. You're beautiful as ever."

"Ever?" She dismissed the puzzled thought he knew had come to her.

His fingertips throbbed from the rush of blood when she unzipped his jeans and searched inside. She teased it to full strength, then played with it for a while, a long while. Her hand felt small in comparison to the big, hardened flesh she held. To him, that part felt cruel, like a rapist's weapon. But in her fingers it was soft, as fruit to be desired. She undid his belt buckle as though unwrapping a gift ... exposing naked *cheeks* to the mountain air. She took the prize to her breasts and stroked herself with it, then brought it to her lips and kissed it, and when she did, the flesh beneath his hairy crotch tingled electrically.

She grabbed him by the neck, and willfully he followed, subdued by her passion. He fondled her moist spot for a long minute, and when she cued him it was time for the invasion; their bodies conjoined into one. Has Gerald ever stroked her like this? he wondered.

"Ohhh ...." she breathed with pleasure.

After the great rush they remained as they were: lying side by side in each other's arms.

"I have a secret." Darah aroused him to discover it. "Actually two." She slipped into her panties and dropped her skirt over it.

"You do?" He pulled up his jeans and fixed his belt buckle.

"Yes." Her mirthful eyes were shaped like those of an Asian-born woman.

The thought of losing her once more returned to assault him. "Well?" He smiled, and this time had gotten it right. But deceitful smiles were not the same as genuine ones.

"Last night I dreamt of us."

"You mean you aren't going to give me the details? Don't make me tickle you." Hungry fingers reached beneath her blouse where they had been before.

Darah chimed with laughter. "Please, anything but that." She caught her breath. "We were sitting alone, stargazing from the back-porch swing." He watched her lips move. She said, "You took my hand, drew me close, and proposed. Silly, right?"

"Not half as much as the dreams I've had."

"You dreamt of me?" She looked interested. "When?"

"More times than I can—"

Suddenly she lifted a hand to his lips and silenced him. "You seem to know my secret places. The way you do my thing. The way you kiss my breasts. It's like we'd made love before."

This is the way he wanted it. The way it should have been. But it wasn't the way it turned out. He had waited for the moment when he would make love to her for the first time. Marriage was a sacred commitment. Roy had said it often: at the dinner table; behind the pulpit. She looked striking in her wedding gown and ravishing in the nude. The minister's daughter was a virgin, the seal of her *vaj* not yet broken, and that thought pleased him. But when she opened her long bare legs and hugged his naked waist with them, he found to his utter dismay how easily he fell into her. Someone had been there before him. Damn! Now he would screw the preacher's daughter. Thrust himself like a rapist and make her feel pain. The moment was far from tender. It wasn't meant to be. What he wanted was the satisfaction of emptying his anger into her. But when the venom flowed, he found he was far from satisfied and felt the urge to inflict more pain. So he slapped her—until it became a habit.

"Yes, we slept together. Long ago."

"What did you say?"

The secret he owned churned within him to be disclosed. But a troubling thought interfered.

"You seem preoccupied about something," she said.

"I need you to believe what I said about your father. Even though I have no proof."

The smile in her vivacious eyes fled and her voice changed. "I don't want my family cursed by your prophetic tragedies."

Darah had never known tragedy in her life. Her world had never been turned upside-down the way his was. Losing a family friend in Elder McKnight was the closest she had ever come to tasting mental anguish and emotional devastation.

"What if I tell you something good. Will you believe?" She looked at him the way he looked at every facet of her silent features: the gentle curve of her nose; her apple-round cheeks; the contour of her collarbones. They sat up on folded legs and faced each other. A thick, large blanket lay spread out beneath them. "Yesterday at Dugger Creek, what I said wasn't a lucky guess. I didn't read your mind, and it wasn't déjà vu."

She seemed to taste every utterance that rolled off masculine lips. "What're you telling me?"

He would have to explain at the risk of sounding like a lunatic. "You spoke that line to me—before we were married: 'I like you a lot. Actually, it's much stronger than that.'"

Her lips parted and she forced herself away from him with a push. "You!" She stood to her feet and looked at him like a gesture-less mime.

"It sounds crazy—"

"You! You're just a smooth operator. Are there other women you've sexually preyed on?"

"Darah, please, I didn't rape you."

"How could I have fallen for your spicy talk and crocodile tears? What will I tell my child if I'm pregnant?"

"I wouldn't worry about that."

She threw her arms over her chest and pumped them crossed. "And why not?" She cut him to the bone with one sharp look.

He closed his eyes. A Navy gynecologist stepped out of the examination room. Darah waited inside. His hands went into the pockets of his white medical coat, and with one look, Avery knew what he would say.

"You'll never have children." Nothing had worked. Not fertility meds, not In vitro. Other means to achieve pregnancy also failed.

Her countenance was vandalized. "I'm infertile?" She clenched her fists, looking like she wanted to strike him. "All you do is steal my joy." Her cry disturbed the placid air. "When will you stop?"

He fought for something to say. "Soon as you realize I've spoken the truth."

"What truth?" Darah yelped. "You've proven nothing. All you're doing is scaring me!" She spun away and faced the slope of the evergreen valley below. A long time passed before she composed herself. "If you love my dad so much, tell him how you feel." She stood there with her back toward him. "Tell him you think he has cancer."

"Does this mean you finally believe?"

"I don't believe a thing." Her words fisted him. "This is between you and my father. You should do what you came here for and leave town—for good!"

"I'm through talking to him." His eyes sank beneath a fallen brow. "He's stubborn."

"Pardon?" she cried in defense.

"You mean you've never noticed?"

She wheeled at him, frown-faced. "I won't stand for you to speak of him that way!" She picked up a rock and threw it at him.

If he had not ducked it would have hit him. He was grateful she didn't have a gun. "Come on, how would it sound: Reverend Gilchrist, I—you have cancer …. Absurd, right? Are you listening?"

She looked like she wanted to scream again. She picked up another rock, but after a moment let it drop. She *had* been listening.

"You have to help me tell him, Darah, please. Roy's only chance of survival is an early cancer-screening test and treatment."

Darah leaped away like an injured fawn. The thought of Roy's death had been planted in her head and there was no dislodging it now. "I wish you'd keep bad news to yourself. All of it."

"Well, what do you want me to say?"

"Something that makes sense!"

Darah didn't speak a word to him the entire time they drove back to the farmhouse, and he didn't want to frighten her with more of his strange revelations. So he let her sit in the car the way she was: her body twisted away from his, strapped in a seatbelt.

When they returned to the house, late in the afternoon, Darah was instantly charged upon by Taffi and April who bombarded her with a simultaneous flurry of confusing chatter.

In the kitchen, Mama complained to someone about the manner in which the girls bolted down the stairs. She said she could never get them to move that fast on a school day when they needed to leave the house on time for the drive to Boone.

The girls' mixed volume of drawling clamor rose to a crescendo and Avery let a shrill whistle fly through the house. In the unsettled silence that followed, Roy and Beulah marched from the kitchen into the family room; beaded perspiration on their foreheads.

"What's this about Pia running away, Mama?" Darah's eyes looked like those of a scared child. "And why is it warm in here? Is the AC down?"

"Forget that." Mama explained what happened.

Darah gasped and cupped a hand over her mouth.

"Where is she?" Avery was relieved everyone looked tired instead of worried.

Mama looked to the kitchen. "Pia?" Silence followed. "Come here, sweetie." The single, diamond-shaped window-paned swing door wedged open and a nervous face appeared. Mama said, "It's okay. No one's gonna yell at you for climbing that tree."

"Tree?" Darah's mouth dropped from horror. "What made her do such a thing?"

"She thought she could find a cat, high up in a place like her storybook suggested," Mama said.

When Darah saw her shamefaced little sister turtling her way to the center of the room—plaster cast wrapped around her right-upper arm and dewdrop eyes lowered to the floorboards—she rushed into the protective arms of her father and burst into a flow of tears.

"Now, honey. She'll be fine. The doctor said she'll be out of that cast and running around in no time."

"That's not why I'm crying," Darah muffled into her father's shoulder.
"Then ... what?"

Mama and the girls looked on in silence. Avery's chest swelled.

Darah looked with adoration into her father's leather-brown eyes. "I'm ... worried about you, Daddy."

Chapter 24

Her voice quivered when she asked him when he was leaving.

"Tomorrow afternoon." He was too glum to make eye contact with Darah. Too upset to say goodbye. Beyond the red oaks and the old, dirt road, Mama, Taffi, and April sat on the front porch, cooling their faces with handheld fans while Roy doodled something on Olympia's cast with a pen. The central air system had gone down on what the weatherman said was the hottest day of the month so far, and the Gilchrists were waiting it out until repairmen from Boone arrived.

Darah's idle fingers stroked the fabric of his uniform, and he found her eyes, flickering like dying stars in a distant nebula. She was afraid of so many things, and he knew what those things were: Olympia's arm, Mama's diabetes, Taffi's asthma. And now her greatest dread, other than her father's undiagnosed cancer, was losing him to where he came from. If there was anything he could do to disarm her of those fears, this was the time to do it. But everything he said so far were predictions of tragedy, sadness, loss. She would hear no more.

"Guess you won't be staying for the funeral," she said.

"I can't." He turned from her, looking at that strange timepiece on his wrist, thinking of the hours he had left. There wasn't much time.

She grabbed him in a way that made him want to push her aside. "I told Daddy to see a doctor, but it's best he heard it from you. I need you with me. Please."

"I can't stay." It was over between him and Roy, between him and Darah. It was better to have something once, than to have it a second time, only to lose it again.

"No," she spat. "You mean you won't!"

Her anger surprised him, silenced him. This was not the girl he remembered dating, the one he married and abused. She had gumption, backbone, tenacity. She had put Gerald in his place, and now she was quick with the sword with him. But he couldn't blame her for the way she felt. The two most important men in her life were miles apart, and any hope of bringing them together seemed remote.

"If you really love my father the way you say you do, then you'd stay till after Zack's funeral. Are you listening? Talk to me."

He snapped her a look. "I ... I care for Roy more than you know."

"Prove it. Talk to him."

"He's too stubborn to listen."

"Not as stubborn as you think."

"I've tried, it's no use."

"Try again!"

His chest swelled with selfish pride, and he realized he, too, was stubborn. She was right. Somehow he had to find a way to stay and talk to Roy, to get him to hear his side of the story, to help him understand he needed to see a doctor regardless of how he felt. But with departure time drawing closer— twenty-three hours left on Marc's watch—he couldn't afford to squeeze in another moment.

"Remember when I told you I had two secrets?" Darah said. "I never did tell you the other." Tree leaves ceased to rustle and she stood farther away from him. "I've decided to enlist in the Navy."

Her practiced smile didn't please him one bit. He went from being forlorn to feeling dismayed. It must have showed on his face because she gave him a look that said she did not understand. "You can't quit school!" he said.

"I'll quit anything to keep us together."

"Oh, no—no, it won't work!" He turned away in hot displeasure, her plan pounding in his head. But there was nothing he could do about that. He was all too familiar with the power of the tongue and the nature of time. It created a past he no longer wanted to relive. Now he knew how things would turn out. Just as much as he knew her heart.

She pressed hands against his strong back, and immediately, he shrunk away from her tenderness.

"What is it?" she asked.

He took a moment to think: Annapolis. The boundless sea. A career with the Navy. He had recruited her without realizing it. "Don't force me to say something I can't explain."

"If I don't enlist, I'll never see you again." Her lips began to quiver.

"I'm sorry, but it has to be this way. It'll only turn out as before."

She clutched at her throat and heaved out a groan. "I know you love me." She looked grieved but sounded angry. "Why are you doing this?"

He had the mindset of a POW who repeated a tired phrase: name, rank, serial number. "Because it won't work. It just won't work!"

"You keep saying that. What won't work?"

Avery willed his lips shut, afraid to let out more than he had already said. But the damage had been done. I'll have to tell her, he thought. "The Navy won't accept college dropouts." He suppressed the dark memory of that last moment when his world came crashing down, burying him under a rubble of sorrow. "They just won't take you."

"You're lying." Her searching eyes had found him out and she lunged at him, grabbing him in a Judo-like hold. "The thought of joining the Navy never entered my mind till the day you came to Oak Leaf. You inspired me to do something better with my life. Don't squash it without telling me why I can't."

He wouldn't look at her.

She forced him to. "You said the military is the best thing that happened to you. And I can't think of anything better than being there with you."

He had to find a way to dissuade her. She was getting more determined to do what she had said. "There's no guarantee we'll be together with all the bases around the world."

"So, let's get married."

His chest tightened from within like strings of an old violin about to snap. "I wasn't proposing. Besides, if you enlist, I'll lose you for sure."

She gave him a troubled look. "What do you mean?"

He had no choice now but to break her resilient will. "I lived a hellish nightmare because of the accident. And the day I laid you to rest was the day I died!"

Darah squeezed eyes shut, fighting to hold back the force of rushing tears. Her delicate beauty was stripped away, and in its place, devastation ruled.

She screamed, and Blue Ridge sparrows were silenced. "If you're trying to discourage me, just say you don't love me! Why make up a crazy story?"

Her sobs knifed him in the gut and made him bleed. She's the love of my life, he thought. But if I tell her that …. "Darah, I don't love you. I never did."

Whatever it was she wore on her face—bitterness, rage, grief—the multilayered emotion made her look unrecognizable. She tossed a distraught glance at him and ran through the woods. In a moment she was gone. And now he, too, would have to leave. His mission plan had fallen to pieces and there was nothing he could do to right it. Now, alone he stood with a tortured mind of that awful night, dark as the printed words on the newspaper article he kept taped on the bulkhead of his quarters for over two years: Navy Investigates Tragic Collision

… Associated Press: Last night off Guatemala's Pacific Coast, just one week into the New Year, the *USS Essex*—a guided missile cruiser returning to North Island via the Panama Canal from Norfolk, Virginia—collided with the *USS Hammerhead*, a nuclear submarine rising from the dark ocean depths during a sea-trial emergency blow. Although the massive boat sustained heavy damage to its huge finlike conning tower, miraculously, there were no serious injuries and none of the sub's nuclear reactors were damaged. But the same luck was not shared by the *Essex*. Among the critically injured airlifted to Naval Medical Center San Diego, Ensign Darah Avery, wife of Lieutenant Neil Avery, was hospitalized with a cerebral hemorrhage, fractured ribs, collapsed lungs, and shattered femurs when the ramming force of the climbing sub's impact threw her over a bridge wing onto the steel deck below.

White road lines shot at Avery like arrows of a deadly archer. Why didn't more people come to the funeral? he thought with anger ….

Roy's face had gone limp when Sister McKnight plucked a pale rose off a nearby stand and wrapped its thorny stem in the stiff, black fingers of her departed husband's hands. Then, when Elder Zack's dark sickly features—nobody cared to see twice—disappeared beneath the shadow of the closing casket, a sound Avery hoped Roy would never hear again rang throughout the empty sanctuary, competing with the groaning organ; hymns that would not comfort. It was the stabbing noise of wailing; the agony of two women. Mrs. McKnight's adult daughters could not be quieted ….

The sun kept pace with the speeding car, skipping over the tops of whistling trees like *Elijah's* fiery chariot on its way to heaven. Now another moment surfaced: Mama blowing her sadness into a Kleenex tissue; Taffi defending her lungs from wheezing assaults with puffs from her asthma pump; April with hands pressed against trembling lips—swollen eyes exposed; and Olympia in her arm cast, repeating to Avery her adopted sisters' secret fear—losing Mama and Daddy. Being orphaned the way she once was ….

He ripped the key out of the ignition and shoved it into the pocket of his uniform. He had come to a grinding stop in a spacious parking area with his head pounding and the car's cooling engine ticking like a time bomb. Roy continued his crusade against the Navy captain, and the Navy captain made one, final, desperate attempt at converting the heavyset preacher with a message of his own. He told him that funerals, burials, were the ultimate gift a departed soul could give to their grieving loved ones. A sure cure.

Roy would have none of it ….

Avery sat numb, strapped into the driver's seat, eyes on the big, blue, white and yellow sunshine logo that read: Days Inn. The steel-gray sky uttered the same forecast as the weatherman's prediction the night before. It was the reason the funeral/burial had been moved up from mid afternoon to an early morning schedule.

He got out of the car. He had seven hours remaining. The drive to Norfolk was six. More if he ran into heavy traffic or some type of accident. He hoped not.

With duffel bag hoisted over his shoulder he went to settle his account.

At the front desk, he returned the cardkey to the attendant, and just as he was about to leave, he noticed the sketch of a man on a newspaper from a vending machine. *Wanted For Bank Robbery.* The face looked similar to his.

He headed back to the Dodge. It would be a long drive. But he would have to hurry. He couldn't move like every piece of clothing he wore were made of lead if he wanted to beat the torrent of rain and flashes of lightning the pregnant clouds threatened to release. The rhythmic action of the wiper blades had always created images of Mama and the girls on his windshield, and he wanted to avoid that. What he wanted was to remember the Gilchrists the way he last saw them. Especially Roy.

A sheriff's car pulled up at the service road and two men got out: a heavyset black man wearing an FBI jacket—and the gun-toting Gatlin. Avery ducked into the Dodge. Both men walked past the vehicle and went straight into the hotel. A moment later they marched out to the white car with darkened strobe lights on its roof and drove off. But how far? Avery wondered. There wasn't a moment to lose.

A tug-of-war pang jousted him as he fed his big duffel into the mouth of the car's trunk. And when he closed it with a firm clunk, he realized someone had been standing there all along: a heavyset black man.

Avery released a startled breath. But that did nothing to break the sudden tension.

"Slipped away before the funeral ended. What happened?"

He felt like getting in the car, driving off, and leaving Roy where he stood. "Couldn't stand the thought of saying goodbye to Beulah and the girls. How did you know I was here?"

"My daughter said I'd find you at this hotel if I hurried."

Darah …. "You must've drove like the devil."

Roy blinked. "Say what?" His face hardened.

"Sorry … Reverend."

He shrugged it off. "Call me Roy." He no longer looked like the man who wanted to beat Avery over the head with his obstinacy. He was calm.

"Okay … Roy." He wished he could call him Dad, but knew he wouldn't understand. "Why are you here?" Despite the simple smile, a teary rush rose.

"Heard you were leaving."

A sweeping breeze played with his hair and blew in his ear. "Uh, I … thought I was." The sheriff's car reappeared going in the opposite direction on the service road. Gatlin gave a look and kept going. "I mean, yeah. I am."

"Seems you haven't made up your mind." The preacher's hearty smile and lifted cheeks helped push away the hard feelings that pricked the navyman. Roy said, "If you stay, I'll whip ya at another game of chess."

"Not if I beat you first," Avery said. The minister laid a big hand on the naval officer's shoulder and the urge to leave abandoned him. "I suppose it wouldn't hurt to delay my trip for a while."

"Good," Roy exclaimed. "See you in church tomorrow morning, and afterwards, dinner at my house."

"Okay, but … I just checked out."

"You can stay with my family. We'll put you up."

Roy's offer was too good. Too tempting for him to pass up.

Avery and the three girls stopped off for lunch at Cape Hatteras in Buxton, then visited the National Seashore Museum, including the 208-foot, candy-cane-striped lighthouse tower that guarded the Carolina shoreline. He read the visitors' brochure that told the centuries-old story of towering Spanish ships that pushed through these waters, from South America and Mexico, on their return voyage to Europe. But the stormy coast—the Graveyard of the Atlantic—swallowed up many young seamen, along with precious cargo to the bottom of the deep.

He mused on what it must have been like to be a sailor in those days. The strong, north currents and adventures of the high seas were more than he ever experienced. For it was off these same waters where the infamous Blackbeard and his marauding pirates ruled, and where German U-boats torpedoed and sunk over seventy merchant vessels and U.S. warships during the early stage of the Second World War.

Now, with no more threats or ships being lost to the hungry coastal sea, peaceful shores ruled, thanks to the U.S. Coast Guard's fast fleet of rescue boats and the life-saving tower, whose bright, sweeping, Godlike eye rotated a beam of light that could be seen fifty miles away ….

The long trip had done to the girls what tears alone could not do, and on the way home they smiled away the pain that remained on their faces from Elder McKnight's eye-dabbing funeral.

Avery parked by the shed as the sun waited high above the western trees from a cloudless, periwinkle sky. April and Olympia launched themselves out of the Dodge and raced into the house, singing as they went. Roy smiled and waved from beneath the hood of an antique, maroon Cadillac Eldorado as Taffi approached. "Have a nice time?" he said.

She kissed him on the cheek. "We had a wonderful day, Daddy. Neil promised to take us to the Outer Banks again."

Taffi stepped into the house.

Roy removed an old radiator hose and attached a new one. He looked grateful Avery was willing to go the extra mile to take the girls out of their surroundings and out of themselves for a while, and it showed on their happy faces. Taffi, April, and Olympia would never forget their sweet *Uncle* Zack. But now that they were smiling again, Avery knew that somewhere in the great beyond, Zack, too, was smiling.

Avery approached Roy. His clothes smelled of motor oil. "Need any help?"

A big smile pushed cherub cheeks upward. "Almost done." Roy lifted a dead, bulky battery from its space and put in a new one. "I've owned this Cadillac for so long the ignition is showing signs of trouble. One day I'll take care of it." He wiped those big hands on an old, tattered tee-shirt, working the dark grime out from between thick fingers. "That'll do it." He tossed the stained rag into a nearby trash bin and brought the car's hood down with a firm clunk. "Come, show you my study."

Avery followed Roy into the house, past the upright piano in the family room, and into the small kitchen, where he snatched a big mug from a cupboard and filled it with his favorite, hot beverage. Mama always kept a fresh pot of coffee brewing whenever her husband was home. It kept the 270-pounder from overeating.

He snuck a fast kiss for each of the girls and lumbered up the stairs to the attic with his guest close behind. In a converted space above the pull-down ladder, the spacious office allowed the preacher the privacy he needed to read his bible, write new sermons, and pray without being disturbed.

Roy, dressed in old-looking jeans, worn yard sneakers, and a dingy, izod alligator polo shirt, rested the coffee mug on his desk, extracted a jewel case from a long CD rack, and fed a shiny disk into a GPX music system's compartment. Avery closed the attic's door and pulled up a chair. The bold-lettered inscription on the preacher's mug read—God is the answer—and the memories marched in.

Roy's favorite classical piece—a track from Dvořák's Symphony No. 9—filled the room with its distinct French horns, tenor trombones, oboes, bassoons, and fine-tuned violins; a rich sonata the serviceman had heard before but paid little attention to.

"Like my place?"

Avery made like he was in the attic for the first time. "Nice set up." He still admired Roy's craftsmanship and personal taste: the wood-knotted paneled walls, the recessed lighting, the henna-colored floorboards. "Cozy." This was better than any dream he could have.

A forest of book spines faced him on long, lacquered shelves. Roy's personal library, an impressive collection of scriptural study guides, ancient history, astronomy, travel, and horses, kept growing month after month. Roy disciplined himself to be a well-read man. Yet despite his intellectual appetite and much learning he lacked one thing: the ability to sit still and listen when he was wrong.

"Listen to those instruments."

Roy was the only person Avery knew who could give ear to classical music all day long. "Sounds like an ode to someone's funeral."

"A funeral?" Roy released a brief laugh. "That's a timeless piece, composed over a hundred-fifty years ago by the great Dvorák."

Avery sat back, folded his hands behind his head, and with a feeling of profound gratitude, reflected on everything he was brought back to: the father-in-law who didn't know him, Mama's warm hospitality, the girls' argumentative moments, the farmland he loved so much, the orchestrated sounds of each classical CD Roy played—and Dr. Weinberg's final warning.

A knock dissolved his train-of-thought.

April's quiet face peeked from behind the door and warmed his heart.

"Ave, Daddy. Mama said dinner will be ready soon."

He looked at Roy in surprise, not knowing how the legs of time had crept by without his notice.

"Ave, is Navy food good?"

Roy had just finished saying grace when April asked the question. His mind was on the minister—on the message he would soon have to preach to Roy.

"Never heard anyone complain." The house smelled of mealtime, with the Gilchrists gathered around a fat-legged, dining-room table, food spread out like a feast.

Taffi put in, "Is it better than Mama's cooking?"

"No contest. Beulah's fried chicken, cornbread, and collard greens can't be beat."

Mama's face beamed warm-red like a harvest moon over an autumn wheat field. "Roy, why don't you compliment me like that?"

He chewed like an ox. "Can't with my mouth full."

April let out a laugh. When no one joined in she excused herself and marched away.

"April?" Mama called.

"Leave her be," Roy said. He shoveled a forkful of mashed potatoes into his mouth. "Upset over something."

Mama's eyebrows curled in question. "What about?"

Olympia feigned clearing her small throat. "Why don't you ask Darah?"

Roy flicked a stare at Beulah. She traded looks with Darah, and Darah aimed eyes at Avery.

Everyone waited for someone to say something.

Avery blotted his mouth. "This is all my doing, Reverend. The last thing I wanted was to disrupt your family's peaceful way of life."

"If that's an apology for the soap-opera scene you and my daughter are acting out, you should be saying it to her."

But he couldn't apologize. He never learned to. Just like he never learned to love.

"Roy Nathan Gilchrist!" Mama pecked. "Can't you see the man don't wanna talk about it?"

Little Olympia sulked. "Must be nice having two boyfriends."

Darah let her fork clang on her plate. "Neil isn't my boyfriend!" She shot to her feet and walked away.

Roy shook his head with disapproval. "How I dread the stress I know will come when the younger girls grow up. Let's talk of something pleasant." He turned from Beulah to the serviceman. "Nice bunch of ribbons." The reverend fancied the neat uniform and colors of his military decorations. "Where're the Medals of Honor and Purple Hearts?"

"Those are reserved for heroes of war. Not a sightseeing sailor like me." He showed Roy the first bar he got and explained how the others kept coming as the years went by. For him, his uniform was like a calendar, marking a passage through his naval career that began long ago. "The rest are service and deployment ribbons. Except these two. There're for rifle and pistol sharpshooting."

Taffi let out an excited wow.

"What about the other one?" Roy asked.

"This?" He laid a finger on a foliage-green, gold-yellow, scarlet-red bar.

The preacher nodded.

"Navy-Marine Corps ribbon." Roy looked interested. "Had it pinned at Norfolk by the Secretary of the Navy. We call him 'SecNav'."

"I like that one. How'd you get it?"

He disliked being the center of attention. "Long story, Rev."

"I'm not going to bed anytime soon."

Olympia gave a giggle.

Beulah joined in. Said she was hungry to learn more about every aspect of his life.

"Well …." He gave it a second thought.

"Come, come, Lord Nelson," Mama said. "Don't be modest."

Coaxed into telling the story, he summoned up stormy images of that frigid, long-ago night. "It started with a Mayday…."

Avery was a lieutenant jaygee assigned to the *USS Polaris.* The sub was en route to the Arctic Ocean from Norfolk, where the boat's crew would spend six months training beneath the polar icecap. Roy said he'd go nuts in a sardine can that long. But the cruise was never completed. Submarine crewmen had a grim task to perform before heading back to the U. S: recover dead bodies and pick up survivors of a Norwegian Hercules C-130. Aboard the ski aircraft, a coalition of European scientists from every sovereign state, had planned to study glaciers in northern Greenland, when the Hercules—with fifty men and two-dozen Malamutes—came down too steep during a blizzard whiteout and was violently ripped to pieces upon touchdown.

Mama covered her open mouth with a plump hand, the one with the bandaged finger; her small eyes were big as quarters.

Avery said, "Some of the men made their way to sea while the others stayed behind to care for the injured. But when provisions ran out they despaired nobody would be found alive since no one knew for sure whether the plane's crash-jolted radios were working when the distress call was sent."

Taffi wheezed, then coughed. "This sounds like a legendary saga from the memoirs of Sir Ernest Shackleton!"

Everyone wanted to know what happened then, and he told them….

After tracking a weak distress signal, *Polaris* surfaced fifteen days later, facing a horizon of mountainous glacier peaks and threatening ocean waves. The sub's captain spotted the frantic-waving shore group through his binoculars and preparations to bring them in began. As the RAO—rescue assistance officer—Avery selected the men for the recovery, and together, they braved the harsh Arctic winds and turbulent subzero sea on motorized dinghies to the stranded Norwegians a mile away.

"My hero," Olympia chimed.

"Those who led us to the destroyed aircraft were the real heroes," Avery put in. "Their waiting comrades were exhausted, frostbitten, starving, but exuberantly happy to see us. However, the rescue wasn't a complete success. Nineteen of the fifty men and almost all the sled dogs died in the crash, and later, five injured men fell to hypothermia after a long descent from a towering glacier. While they had waited at the crash site, suicidal from fright, the remaining dogs were shot. According to the official report, it was the only way the men could stay alive."

Olympia grimaced. "Ooo, gross." She leaned in and listened to the rest.

Once all the survivors were on the sub, the Norwegian copilot, a strapper of a man, pulled a gun on his captain and blamed him for the accident. But before he finished pistol-whipping him, Avery grappled the weapon away and handcuffed him to the periscope railing. "You just can't beat up on people. I learned to become a vigilante the hard way."

Taffi and Olympia stared with gleaming eyes. So did Roy and Beulah. Avery would have gladly told story upon story of his experiences and journeys, indulging their curious minds about the massive gray ships and the men that sailed them: tales of troubled times in perilous waters. But the one thing he wanted to tell them most about, the one emotion that ached in his chest and begged release, he found unable to say.

Roy blotted his mouth with a cloth napkin and rose tall from his chair like he was about to preach. "Seems you've been everywhere, young man. Except outer space."

While Taffi and Olympia helped clear the table, Avery pitched in and followed them into the kitchen. "Anything I can help you with?" The word *Mama* fastened to his tongue and wouldn't let go.

Beulah took a stack of dessert plates from his hands and placed them in the sink under warm running water. "No, sugar."

He so much wanted to touch the smile that stirred his heart and bring back lost moments he had with his real mother. He also wanted for Beulah to call him son.

Mama said, "The girls and I will clean up. Why don't you join Roy?"

The heavyset preacher was behind the farmhouse, framed within the small, kitchen window over the sink. He attached a large, cylinder-shaped tube on a tripod, and when it locked in place, Avery let himself out the backdoor where smoldering colors of the twilight sky burned into the horizon.

Together, the two men stood side by side, patiently waiting, silently watching for the first signs of faint stars to gradually come into full view.

"Nice telescope." Venus, the tiny, diamond-bright star-like body, hung in the western sky over silhouetted oak trees in the distance. "Do this often?"

"Every chance I get."

From every direction in the open field, an orchestration of calling crickets and other chirruping night creatures filled the air with their evening song.

With darkness fully descended, a milky sliver of light parted a gray, cotton-candy cloud, and a crescent-shaped jewel appeared, 45° over the southern part of the sky: the moon. So unchangeable. So enchanting. So beautiful to behold. In the timeless sky it stood out like an ornament among the stars. Poems were written about it, songs composed to it, lovers kissed passionately beneath it, and man had gone there and returned safe to earth. Neil Armstrong, Edwin 'Buzz' Aldrin, and Michael Collins. He had always admired them for their outstanding courage. How he wanted to be brave like them.

Roy was like an ancient navigator charting the heavens. "There's the Big Dipper."

The emerald-speckled constellation of Ursa Major bedecked the sky. It seemed all the stars were out. The treasures of the universe put on display by God himself for all humanity to see.

"Saw that?" Roy looked to his guest with calm fascination.

"Sure did. Get many?"

"Now and then. Marvelous, wasn't it?"

"First time I've ever seen one."

"You've never seen a shooting star? You need to move out here someday, my boy." He aimed the telescope at a point of light and peeked in the main eyepiece for a moment. "Guess what that is." He pointed to it.

Avery stared with hungry eyes, head up-tilted; a gentle rush of blood pulsed through his tired neck. "No idea."

Roy nodded to the telescope. "Take a look, my boy."

The luminous orb was the exact sphere on the starry wallpaper in his childhood bedroom; the planet with the great red spot and wide bands of white, brown, and rusty-orange ammonium sulfide clouds.

"Jumping Jupiter," Avery cried out.

Roy's good-natured laugh was healing medicine.

They each took turns studying the giant, gaseous planet. The Navy officer was delighted they acted like young boys admiring a new toy—sharing it with each other.

"Got a riddle for you. If Jupiter were a piggy bank and the earth a coin, guess how many it would take to fill it?"

Avery was intrigued. "I'm not good at estimating astronomical things."

As long as Roy stood there by his side, he felt the protective presence of the father he yearned for as a child.

The answer to the question was 1,300. One-thousand, three hundred earths could fit inside the womb of mother Jupiter. Roy said it would take the same number of marbles to fit inside a giant beach ball.

Avery liked the fact that Roy loved spilling his knowledge on others. "Big planet."

"We live in a vast universe, my boy."

But Roy had no idea the universe ceased being vast the day quantum technology gave birth to something only the naval officer was privy to.

"I wonder." The preacher scanned the heavens.

"Another riddle?"

Roy shook his head. He was unusually quiet now. His face captured the same grave look as Auguste Rodin's famous bronze statue of a nude man in deep contemplation, sitting on a flat boulder with chin on his hand and elbow to his knee: The Thinker. "Can time slow down?" Roy asked. "Can the 'clock' stop?"

The moment he had been dreading had arrived. "That's Einstein's special theory of relativity." Avery willed his heart to beat slower. Instead it beat faster. "I call it time travel."

Roy threw the young serviceman a side glance. "Think it's possible?"

"Look at the stars. Each one is twinkling a million yesterdays down on us."

He seemed to be mulling it over. One by one, the bedroom lights in the house went out and everything became darker. "Sounds like you know something."

"Have a theory."

A broad smile pushed Roy's cheeks up like those of a Cherokee Indian. "Let's hear it."

Avery was confident he could tell it all. He had experienced it all. But would Roy believe it all? It was a chance he had to take. If time could be tampered with and its events changed, then this was the pivotal point, the moment of truth, no matter what anyone said to the contrary.

"Someday, maybe in our lifetime, men will not only hop from planet to planet, but also travel from one time period to another."

Roy studied the millions of stars in the distance of space, each one holding secrets to truths. Secrets only few on earth knew.

From a quiet profile, the preacher looked ready to speak. "Where're you taking me with this?"

Avery couldn't pull a fast one on Roy. "I know you're not going to understand what I'm about to tell you. Not sure I do myself." He placed a trembling hand on Roy's shoulder, and when he did, a moment flashed before him like a repeat episode from a poignant TV show he no longer wanted to watch. "Someday, you'll have a special friendship with a young man."

"What young man?"

"Your oldest daughter's future husband. One day she'll marry, and you'll finally have the son you wanted."

"Gerald?" He huffed out a disappointed laugh. "I don't want a son, much less him." An orchestra of insects hiding in the night, filled the silence with their rhythmic symphony.

"You used to pray about it. But stopped when you got Pia."

Roy grew quiet. "How'd you know that?" After the pensive moment passed he said, "Are you an angel? I've preached on angels."

"No, Roy. I'm no different than you."

"Then how did you know? Someone tell you?"

Avery fought back a rush of lukewarm tears and siphoned post nasal saline. Its alkaline choking him on the way down. "I just knew."

"But how?"

Something he could not describe replaced Roy's smile. He no longer looked like the gentle man he remembered. Everyone was multifaceted, he reasoned. Even the kindest of men. "The same way I know Beulah has high blood pressure and diabetes, and Pia will never break another bone in her sweet body, and you, become a famous preacher." Avery was aware his clever gabbing puzzled Roy.

"Who are you?" Now he knew the uniformed man was not who he thought he was.

"Suffice it to say I'm not from here." He sensed what the preacher could not grasp had flown away.

"I'm no Billy Graham," he said with determined defiance. "Don't aim to be."

"Not yet, but—"

"I'm just a simple man making a decent living as a country preacher. I don't plan to minister anywhere outside North Carolina. Except ...." Roy's eyes stopped blinking and his mouth dropped a fraction. "I was invited to teach at Christ Bible College in St. Charles, Maryland."

"That's just the beginning. In time, you'll be invited to speak in places you've never been. And eventually, you'll not only travel throughout this great country, but around the world. Preaching and teaching the same way you do at Faith Mission."

It seemed someone turned up the volume and the insect world around them grew louder.

"You have to believe what I'm saying. One day you'll be a great man. Mark my words. That's why being cremated would be a violation to who you are. Or will become."

He let Roy think. It was the only way he could be certain he was listening.

"What makes you think I want to be cremated when I die?"

"You believe no one will come to your funeral."

"And how do you know so much?" Roy said in a hot breath.

Avery sought the reverend's eyes under the sliver of moonlight. "You're wearing the same expression from Zack's burial. The turnout, or lack of it, depressed you. Admit it."

"'Course it bothered me. We can hardly get folks to fill empty pews during Sunday service, let alone a funeral. You were there."

"Don't lie to yourself, Reverend. That's not the only reason you've been contemplating cremation. You don't want your loved ones falling to pieces staring at you from an open casket." Avery let his voice rise. "Tell it like it is!"

"Young man, when I die—which won't be anytime soon—I want to be remembered the way I was. Not the way I'll look in a wooden box."

"That's not for you to decide."

"It's my body, not yours."

"Don't be selfish. Your family will need proper closure. Please don't make me go through this again."

"Go through what again?"

Roy wheeled from the telescope and stormed toward the dark house. He stopped, and with sudden abruptness faced his guest. "I never once thought about being cremated till the day you came to Oak Leaf." His bellowing army-voice returned to him. "You poisoned my mind!"

After a long, chirruping moment, the unsettled preacher bowed his head. "What time you got, sailor?"

His weary, stargazed eyes and the rush of anger that squeezed them made it hard for him to find the numbers. "Must be after midnight. Everyone seems to be asleep."

"C'mon, young man. Time to hit the sack."

He decided he would stay where he stood. "I'll be in shortly." He heaved out a breath of frustration. "You go ahead, Rev."

"Okay, but don't stay up long." His words were above a whisper.

Crickets ruled in the silence that followed. Blinking fireflies floated nearby.

Roy retired.

Avery shoved hands deep into his pockets and kicked up loose dirt. He shuffled around in the open for a long time until the crescent moon rolled from where it had been to its hiding place behind the trees on the opposite end of the field. But in all that time, the ink-black canopy holding a myriad of twinkling stars had brought no comfort.

I'll speak no more on the subject, he thought. It's over.

Chapter 25

The guestroom was tiny but cozy: a windowless hole in the wall Roy had built long ago from a blueprint in his savvy head. It was once a pair of walk-in closets, side by side, with a narrow walkthrough in between. But when Beulah decided the two closets would work better as an extra room, Roy took a sledgehammer and got to work. He gave the new sheetrock walls a coat of primer and went over them with sandy-beige paint. He hammered in the baseboards and crown moldings, put in a good solid door, added a dresser, nightstand and lamp, and picked up an old-fashioned fold-up bed from a thrift shop.

Avery lingered in the rollaway cot four hours after fingers of sunlight pushed aside the dark curtain of the night. It was not worth wrestling with fleeing sleep, so he got dressed, in Navy-issue sweatpants and sweatshirt, and barefooted his way into the small, quiet kitchen.

Beulah's invigorating presence opened his drowsy eyes. "Morning, sailor. Sleep well?"

He mumbled that he did, pulled out a chair at the table, and sat, releasing a catlike yawn. A phantom mugger had robbed him of sleep and he felt like he had a hangover and the flu, both rolled into one.

Beulah made him breakfast: brewed coffee, scrambled eggs, Jimmy Dean sausages, and buttered toast. She met his eyes as he ate. "Roy's up."

He packed food to one side of his mouth, wondering whether there would be another head-butting between him and the preacher. "He needn't bother seeing me to the door. I'll be leaving shortly."

"So will he. Plans to take you with him."

"You're joking. Where?"

Mama's round face bloomed with a smile. "Ask him."

"You mean he isn't angry?"

267

"At who?" She went to the sink, filled a glass with tap water and poured it into a big, dirt-filled flowerpot where a medusa-looking Aloe Vera plant sat on the windowsill.

Avery shoveled a forkful of eggs into his mouth as Roy lumbered down the stairs and turned toward the kitchen. The smiling preacher was dressed in old work boots, faded, denim farmer-john overalls, and a worn flannel shirt rolled up snug past his wide elbows. In one hand he held an old tackle box; in the other, a pair of Browning rod and reels.

"Where're you going?" Avery asked with a gawk.

"Where's it look? Not church. I'm going fishing. And you're coming with me."

Avery gulped down a slurp of hot coffee. "Sure you want *me* to go?"

Roy's smile fell. He looked apologetic. "Oh ... about last night—"

"What happened last night?" Beulah asked.

"Never mind." Roy dismissed her with a wave of his meaty hand. "This is between us men." His eyes returned to his guest. "The girls tell me you have nothing planned for today, so it's you and me."

"But ...." Heat rushed to his face. He hated being embarrassed over something so simple; something most kids knew how to do. "I'm not good at ...."

"A sailor that doesn't fish?" Roy looked to Beulah. "Have you ever?"

"Sugar, didn't your father take you fishing when you were a child?"

He looked at Mama. "He was the fish."

"Well, mister. You don't know what you've been missing." Roy's long-legged stride took him to the front door. "But don't worry none." His preacher's voice carried past the family room into the kitchen. "I'll teach you everything you'll need to know. You'll be a pro in no time. If you get outta those clothes."

Avery took one last mouthful of breakfast, slurped it down with sweet coffee, and charged up the stairs as two preteens and a child—Taffi, April, and Olympia—snickered past him on their way down.

"What's funny?" He stood at the top landing, hands on hips.

"Your feet," April giggled. "They're so white."

Mama let out a loud laugh.

The drive through rural Hodge town, brought Roy and Avery to Elk Creek. There were numerous fishing spots in the area where the two men could sit, relax, and cast their lines. But Roy insisted on going to his favorite place where he and Zack McKnight often frequented—in the waters farther south in Wilkes County, where plenty of wild trout and small, empty boats awaited them.

Under the soothing influence of the warm, Carolina sun, the preacher and the navyman launched out into the reservoir, selected a spot, put down the trolling motor, and something else they hadn't done since laying eyes on each other ….

"Roy, do you realize we haven't had a tiff all morning?"

"Do you miss it?"

What he missed was having quality time with a real father.

The sway of the fiberglass boat at his feet was like riding an oversized skateboard. Roy laid a hand on the young man's shoulder and showed him how to hold the rod, how to cast the line, how to use the reel—exactly like the first lesson he had gotten, with no deviation in the timeline. A moment later he reeled in his first catch from the teaming lake—an olive-colored Smallmouth bass, big enough for the entire family to feast on, and all it took was a five-minute lesson from Roy.

"An eighteen pounder, my boy."

Avery marveled it looked like the one he caught the first time with Roy, years ago.

At day's end, the two men, like happy boys, brought home their prize: a large cooler full of rainbow bass, steelhead trout, and other types of fish packed in crushed ice. The experience brought out the lost child in Avery. He had been in the Navy for so long, so used to being aboard a Titanic-size vessel, that the simple pleasure of slowly rocking in an old boat in calm waters seemed strange to him.

One leisurely afternoon replaced another, and a sun-filtered porch induced the two men into several rounds of chess. This time the match was friendly. Avery won three of four and the day was still fresh.

Roy brought out a pair of old mountain bikes from the cluttered shed and leaned them against the house. It had been years since he and Beulah used them, and even longer since they last exercised. Every now and then the girls would ride them, but for the most part, the bicycles were kept locked up and rejected, gathering dust and cobwebs. He inflated the tires with a hand pump.

Roy mixed work and leisure well. Monday and Tuesday afternoons he ran the church's soup kitchen. Wednesday nights he officiated the prayer service. Friday nights was bible study, and Sunday mornings, it was back to preaching from the pulpit. Saturdays were reserved for ministers' conventions, when there was one, he told his guest.

Avery let Roy coax him into bicycling through the countryside. He said it would get their juices flowing for dinner, and the day was perfect for it. They rode at a lazy pace, down a scenic stretch of road, passing gray-barked beech trees and their long branches of lush foliage. In and out they went, from under the dappled shade of each green canopy into the full strength of an unclouded sun.

Traveling farther than either of them anticipated—past the Super 8 Hotel in Boone, where Avery had stayed—clanging bells and blinking red lights halted the tired men at a railroad crossing. They straddled over their bikes, watching the long, red-and-yellow-striped, wooden crossing arms come down.

"Here she comes," Roy said.

A moment later, the blast of a pounding train blew past the two men like a controlled hurricane until the last streamlined, stainless-steel car swooshed by to the sound of a fading airhorn.

"And there she goes," Avery said. "Time to head back. Let's sit at the station for a while."

They dismounted and steered the bikes over the steel, silver tracks and broken ballast stones. Roy was so sorry he gave up bicycling, he said. Now his aching thighs and stiff back were berating him for it.

Darah and the girls prepared a sumptuous Southern meal that evening: Brunswick stew, hush puppies and fresh Cole slaw, followed by apple cobbler for dessert.

Mama capped off the family gathering by playing spiritual hymns on the piano, and Avery wondered how his real mother must have played. The rich sound of the keys at the graceful touch of Beulah's hands—rolling arpeggios and cross-hand inversions in major and minor chords—could not usher back lost memories, though. But it helped mask the nagging uneasiness that stood like a tall barrier between him and Darah. As long as there was music, there was harmony in the house, and it showed. Each time Mama brought the keys to life with dexterous fingers, the girls swarmed about her and sang along. It was good to hear their raised voices other than when they quibbled. And when they sat on the bench, two at a time, they cooperated, trying to play the way their mother did. But when the girls called it quits and Mama pulled on the brass knobs and covered the ivories, the atmosphere in the house changed and Avery was the first to feel it. He and Darah, so inseparable before the funeral, were miles apart. By hurting Darah, he also hurt Mama. The look on their faces were the same. Now he chided himself for bringing heartache into Darah's life. Yet sorrow, from whatever source, was an inescapable part of life. Avery overheard Beulah tell her daughters that evening that love was like a naked, long-stemmed rose in all its raw, thorny beauty. It made you cry with joy beholding it. It made you bleed to touch it.

Early the following morning, Roy and Avery were off again. This time, traveling to Lexington, Kentucky. There, at the Spendthrift horse farm, Roy had a preacher friend named Dusty Smith he had not seen in years. Roy told Avery they met in theological college, became roommates, and graduated at the same time.

Avery loved the sprawling, sixty-acre farm. And being there with the horses—petting them, feeding them—gave way to riding the tallest stallion among them. His first try. It wasn't long until the reverend also saddled up as he and Dusty Smith led their guest on an easy ride through a grainy trail.

On their way back to Oak Leaf, the serviceman hoped the long drive would revive the overspent preacher. "You look beat." It was the end of another day.

"My aching thighs from the long bicycle ride haven't forgiven me yet."

"You're not as young as you used to be."

Silence from a talkative man was odd.

"Guess I ... need to take better care of myself, my boy."

"That, and see a doctor." Avery loved driving Roy's big car. As far as he could tell, there were no problems with the ignition, the brakes, the steering, the air conditioner. The Eldorado was in great shape.

A moment later, the motion of the humming vehicle put Roy to sleep.

Avery was alone, sitting on the big slab of gray rock where he and Darah had been together, when the preacher came along. It was a long bicycle ride to Dugger Creek, and now *his* thighs were berating him also.

"My wife said you'd be here. I rushed out the house with a surge of energy I haven't had in days. Is it true, sailor?"

He turned a page on a pocket notepad; fountain pen in hand.

"Not used to seeing you in civvies," Roy said. "What're you writing?"

"Letter to a ... friend. I'm letting the babbling stream dictate the words to me."

"I'm no good at writing, either." Roy reached the crest of the wooden footbridge and stopped.

Avery's pulse raced. He was hoping to finish the letter before the preacher showed up. But time was too short—always fleeting. There never seemed to be enough hours in a day to do all the things one wanted to do. Never enough time to prepare the heart for what mattered most. In the back of his mind, Avery was aware some things were better spoken than written. It was just a matter of determined courage.

Rising with haste, he shoved the unfinished letter into the pocket of faded jeans and right away felt his head fill with a high tide. He knew he could not continue to conceal the message that pulsated in his chest. The only way to find relief from the ache of this kind of sentiment wasn't with the pen. It had to be spoken.

"Son ...."

The word squeezed Avery's heart like no other word could.

Roy took another step. "Does this mean goodbye?"

He nodded, not wanting to speak, knowing his voice would crack the moment he tried.

"I'd like very much to see you again. My family feels the same way, too. Especially Pia. She's crazy about you. She'll be so hurt ... when she finds out you're ...."

He struggled to look Roy in the eye. "I ... I'll be back someday, I promise. And when I do, we'll play chess, go fishing .... Heck, we'll have a great time."

Roy drew close. Avery turned away. The sound of the rushing stream made him realize the chances of him returning to the minister and his family were next to nothing: an iota of a possibility; a wispy cloud done in by the wind. He wished he wasn't such a hell-bound lair.

"Not sure why I want to say this," Roy said. Avery felt a hand on his shoulder. "Or why I'm feeling it, but ...." The yearning in his voice spun the serviceman into the reverend's face. "I love you, boy. Wish you were my son."

His throat throbbed with the message that begged release. "I am your son!"

Roy jerked the young man into a wrenching hug, and after the long embrace, Avery blinked back what should have been runaway tears. There was more he wanted to say; volumes. But he couldn't make himself speak the words he thought he would when the right time came. He also couldn't tell Roy of the silent killer: the cancer that ticked like a bomb from within.

Roy hitched the mountain bike to the top of his car and the two men drove back to the farmhouse at a lazy pace.

"By the way ...." Roy's attention was on the long stretch of country road. "Still fancy that medal bar of yours. What you say the name of it was?"

"Navy-Marine Corps ribbon." He knew the preacher loved the sound of it.

"Will you save it for me? When you retire from the service, that is."

Avery winked at him with a love that made his eyes smile. The first time Roy made that very same request, he answered the same way. "Will do."

"Thank you, son." He returned the serviceman's wink.

Avery masked the bittersweet heartache with an easy smile. He was glad that at last he had made peace with the country preacher. Glad he could make him happy at the simple promise of a military ribbon.

Mama was sitting on the front porch, talking to someone on the cordless phone, when they pulled up to the house and stopped. Both men stepped out of the car and Roy worked on loosening the bike. It was another day to get out and enjoy; to bask under a lemon-yellow sun and watch fat chiffon clouds roll across a periwinkle sky. But this time, Avery would not let Roy put him off again.

"What's with the big grin, preacher?"

"You'll be glad to know that when the Lord calls me home some sweet day, I won't be cremated. Behind Faith Mission there'll be a plot ready for me, along with a nice big casket and all the trimmings."

"Leave it to you to make a joke of something serious."

"Speaking of serious, I even plan to see a doctor soon. Then, get back to bicycling and taking better care of myself. Yes siree. I'm gonna have a good, long life."

Triumph rushed through Avery's veins like hot adrenaline. He had done it. Roy would live, and the added years would give them moments they never had. If he could return.

The preacher and the navyman spoke after dinner that evening, locked away in the attic while they listened to the classical masterpieces of Bach, Vivaldi, and Dvorák. Once more the Gilchrist family surrounded him. One more time Olympia's delicate face would add a lasting album of memories to the ones he already had.

That night, Avery stayed up late, watched TV with the girls, and afterwards kissed them goodnight and tucked them into bed. The long day had a perfect ending. An ending Taffi, April, and Olympia were none too happy about. He had told them, that in the morning, he would pack his things, place them in the trunk of his car and make the long drive to Naval Station Norfolk.

Avery spotted three, sleep-deprived faces peering at him through the parted veiled windows of their individual bedrooms. It appeared the girls were stirred into lethargy from a restless slumber when he closed the car's trunk. Now that the gas tank was filled up, he would be in the family room, waiting for them to march down the stairs, single file. He wondered who would be the first to lay eyes on him. The first to say goodbye.

Roy and Avery had already eaten and had their last chat over buckwheat pancakes, country fried ham, and hot black coffee. Nothing could keep the preacher from the boy he loved, he told him. But Taffi, April, and Olympia were slow in coming down.

As for Darah …?

Avery received a mother's hug from Beulah as Roy went upstairs to see about the girls. The buckwheat pancakes were getting cold. If the girls refused to leave their bedrooms, Avery would either come up, or say farewell from outside their windows. He decided to wait for them.

After a long moment filled with dreadful thoughts, he went to check the car's tires.

He walked past the house and noticed Darah spying behind the shed. She was breathing, yet dying. That faraway look said her breastbone thumped like his, and that a thousand racing thoughts fluttered in her the way they did in him—thoughts that would haunt him the rest of his life if he left without giving her any hope of returning, any sign that would hint he cared. I've got to return, he thought. All we had will be meaningless if I don't.

Dueling eyes were locked in a pining gaze—hers and his—and he realized the same act of bravery it took for him to make his first trip through time would take the same going back.

Estrangement flew into the air like frightened birds and they rushed at each other, meeting with impact. They clawed at their bodies in a knotted embrace.

He felt her shudder and lifted her dewy face.

"Does this mean you love me?" she asked.

"What do you think?"

"I was hoping you'd say—I'm sorry I hurt you. I didn't mean to. I love you so much …. But I don't think you can."

His brow hung heavy with the thought of losing her again. "I know this is a lousy way to say goodbye, but I've got to leave. I can't prolong this any longer. For me this is all a recurring bad dream."

"Was our love moment also a dream?" Her face twisted with anguish. "Didn't it mean anything to you?"

He couldn't answer. Couldn't find what she wanted to hear. No matter how tight he clung to her, he felt her slipping away.

"Will I ever see you again?" She blinked out fat tears.

He knew she feared him, yet her eyes said she yearned for one more answer, one more crazy explanation, despite the great sorrow they brought.

"You will!" He forced himself to believe his own speech. "One day I'll be back for you. I promise." They wrapped themselves around each other again, but Avery knew there were no guarantees. Claudia Britney was dead. What more was there to do with Spectrum?

When her trembling stopped, he pulled her away from him to look into liquid eyes. She smiled in a way that should have made him smile, but dread had taken over. In a moment he would be gone, and a shallow love would cause his heart to murmur until he could endure it no longer.

"I want you to do something important." An intense silence followed in which the breeze did not blow and the birds did not sing. Darah looked as though knowing what he was about to ask would take every ounce of resolve within her to make happen. "Promise me you won't be with Gerald—or anyone while I'm gone. Ever!"

"I won't do it. You can't make me. Soon as you drive off, I'll get in my car and—"

"Please don't. It's better this way."

"Then I'll join the Navy. I'll hunt you like a hound even if it means climbing every mountain—crossing every sea."

"That's not possible."

"Don't tell me what's not possible." She drove the point across by grabbing him by the shirt and trying to shake him. He was solid like a wall. "I can find you the same way you found me!"

"Not across the sands of time you can't. You'd die."

Suddenly Darah stopped fighting him. She was in a deep-absorbed trance. Her verbal onslaught had left her breathless, motionless, hopeless. "So that's what makes you such a mystery. You never meant to frighten me."

"Then you understand what I'm asking you to do."

She knew. He could tell.

"How long?" Darah croaked. "How long do you want me to wait?" She buried her grieving face into his uniform.

"Don't know." He was tired from lament. Sick of making lame promises. "I only hope if I'm right, one day it'll be clear to you."

"What will?" She began to tremble again.

The grip of her bitterness squeezed at his heart like an angry fist. She was frail with sorrow and all willpower had abandoned her. He could feel it.

He answered her question. "To have you all to myself. Sharing love till the end of time."

In that long moment, in which seconds were like minutes, and minutes like hours, he felt her beating heart no more.

He lifted her drooping head and brushed aside her long, nutmeg-brown hair. He looked into her like looking into her soul—past the hurt, past the tears, past her swollen, scarlet eyes. He pressed his lips on hers and the quivering stopped.

"Was that a kiss of promise?" She let go of him.

If but one last time he could smell the warmth of her breath, touch the nails of her fingers, feel her collarbones, it was this moment. Now that he had made Darah aware tomorrow she would not have him, he knew she would be left to wonder how many more tomorrows would march past her until she saw his face again, or until he reminded her of her own words: Kiss of promise.

Darah laid her head on his bosom where she withered into his strong arms. The lonely world he came from had beckoned him to return. The warning pounded in his chest, raced through his veins, played with his mind. Now the empty years without the woman he loved would tick away—one, heart-aching second at a time.

They trudged past the shed to the front of the house. What she felt was advertised on her face. What he felt showed in each step he took—that of a stricken sleepwalker stranded in an awful dream. Darah accepted her fate the same way she accepted a sealed letter he instructed her to give to her father. By then, she had composed herself. It was all she could do to make Avery know the long wait had begun.

A Chrysler PT Cruiser rolled down the dirt road to the house, kicking up a trail of red dust. Gerald parked the car and got out, rainbow bouquet in hand: roses, daisies, mums, lilies ....

Darah marched toward him, swiping stray tears as she went. Avery followed not far behind.

"Gerald, I said I'd call you!" Those saddened lips that hung in a frown a moment ago, now hardened into a straight line on her wooden face as though carved out by hammer and chisel.

"Got tired of waitin'." Gerald turned from her to him. Avery didn't like the look in his eye. The Gilchrist family now gathered around the serviceman. "Hey, what's with the scene? Is Navy boy leaving?"

Darah heaved out puffs of ragged breath and looked away.

"What a shame he's not coming back."

She spun at Gerald. Arms crossed.

He handed her the flowers and grinned.

She knocked them out of his hands.

Taffi was the first to say goodbye to Avery as she held his oak-leaf-fretted wheel cap over her heart. She gave it an impressive look, handed it to him, and with a wheeze on her lips, embraced him. A wispy smile came to her when he took her hand to read a message in those golden-brown eyes: I'll miss you.

Next was April. "Bye, Ave." She kissed him on the cheek with the same sheen in her eyes her sister had.

Mama's plump fingers held firm to Avery's hand, her eyes filled with affection. "You're welcome here anytime. Gimme some sugar." She threw big arms around him and pulled him into a hard squeeze. Warm lips smacked crisp on his clean, shaven face.

She stepped aside, and there, standing behind her was his darling Olympia. The child's eyes that danced each time she saw the tall military man were now drowned in sadness. She was already accustomed to the hard cast on her arm and not seeing Uncle Zechariah when he stopped by the house and at church.

But not having Avery beside her at dinner, like he had been doing for the past two weeks, was one more thing the youngster would have to get used to.

Roy clicked a picture of the cute girl in the pretty outfit. Her cast, which ran from her shoulder to the curve of her elbow, was scribbled over with names, well wishes, and colorful artwork.

"Please come back for dinner someday," she pleaded in a thin, injured voice.

Her fallen features and dewdrop eyes melted him.

"I will, sweet pea." He hunkered to her level, stroked her ropey braided hair and kissed her. Avery had made yet another promise he shuddered to think he could not keep.

A frowning Olympia bolted away from everyone, running into the house in a burst of tears. Avery wished he could have held her like she was his own; sit her on his lap and help her understand why it was he had to go. There, on bended knee, she could bury her small twisted face into the clean smell of his uniform and cry until she couldn't cry anymore. The thought of going after her came to him, but long shadows and rustling leaves told him his bag was packed, the car was waiting. It was time to go. And no one knew that more, no one felt it more than Olympia.

"She's gonna miss you," Roy said. His broad hand weighed on the young man's shoulder.

"Not half as ...." He strained to get the rest of the message out, but could not.

Avery read his departure in Roy's eyes. Breaking away from the only family he once had was one thing. Wondering whether he could return to them was another. Why have I lied to them? he thought. He went to the Dodge, opened the door, slipped behind the wheel, and buckled up.

When he closed the vehicle's door he rolled down the window and gave Roy a look. He stood poised to take a picture of him. He pressed the button but there was no sound. He gave the digital camera a strange look. "Won't click." Roy leaned in and touched Avery's arm. "Remember, son, you have my number. Call me. You have my address. Write me. You know where I am. Visit soon. God bless."

Avery said nothing. He simply nodded, turned the ignition, and instantly, a thousand yesterdays merged into one, solitary moment.

With the graveled ground crunching under the weight of the creeping car, Roy lifted a big hand and waved. A moment later, Avery was at the crest of the dirt road with a dwindled reflection of Roy in the rearview.

Now with the long drive back to Norfolk ahead of him, a relentless, single thought began to hammer at him: that of Mama, Darah, and the girls returning to their lives in his absence; and of his beloved Roy, marking the passage of time on a front porch where plastic game pieces on an open chessboard waited to be moved. Avery feared Roy would sit there all alone—days, weeks, months at a time. Yearning with a heavy heart for his boy to return.

Chapter 26

A hypersonic flight through a kaleidoscope tunnel, shot Avery into a deathly cold mist. An alarm wailed, and the clamor of instruments coming from outside the tube, brought him to a standstill. The elephant-weight of G-forces lifted and a cloud of swirling cells rushed to every part of his skeletal structure, converging into veins, tendons, and layers of muscles. Major organs filled the chest and abdominal cavity with a beating heart, breathing lungs, and snaking intestines. He was wrapped in protective skin and clothing, and when he realized he hadn't morphed into something grotesque, he heaved a sigh of relief.

The dazzling brightness of the positron lit Quinn and Jager's startled faces.

"Get Professor "J"," Quinn said through the cylinder's speakers.

Jager grabbed a microphone, clicked a dark button, and it lit red. "Attention. Event in progress. Event in progress. Team-A report to lab at once. Report at once."

The warbled message carried through the facility's PA system to Marcus and Stas, somewhere in one of the research spaces.

When the whir of nuclear engines stopped, Quinn and Jager abandoned their card game and approached the cylinder. The transparent, thermo-glass canopy ceased spinning, rose with a mighty hiss, and Captain Avery stepped through a subzero, silvery cloud.

"What's the matter with you nerds?" He didn't like the look in their cold, narrowed eyes. "Don't you know what goes on down here?"

Jager frowned. "*Dummkopf!* Do you realize what you've done?"

Avery threw a fat duffel and briefcase onto the limestone floor and the technicians backed up. "I've done nothing … yet." He climbed down the cylinder's platform as Marcus and Stas dashed into the transport chamber like ER doctors responding to a stat call.

The lab's rock wall behind them closed with a rumble.

Marcus gave the serviceman an unfavorable look. "So, you've decided to return. A wise choice. Where's Claudia?"

His mind spun like the swirl of glowing cells and atoms in the enclosed cylinder a moment before. "Dead."

Marcus pushed back his black glasses. "You'd better have proof, mister."

Avery popped open the briefcase, extracted a digital camera, and hurried to one end of the computer-cluttered control station. He connected a thin blue cable into the side of the camera, ran the other end behind a console, and plugged it into a serial port. When everything uploaded, images appeared on the screen.

Quinn stepped up beside the naval officer, maximizing each shot with a double click of the mouse: photos of Claudia Britney's gravesite.

Quinn was joined by Marcus, then Stas, then Jager.

"Sorry, Claudia." Marcus sulked. It looked strange for an adult to pout. "Now that makes two."

Jager gave him a dark look. "What are you lamenting about? The money meant more to you than she did."

Avery snuck away from the distracted men to the quantum computer at the other end. He punched in his access code and the system opened up.

The sound of anxious fingers striking the lit keyboard in hurried strokes filled the tense air.

"What're you doing?" Marcus said.

Avery ignored him, eyes on a submenu. He highlighted a program, hit select, rushed through the settings on a dialog box and the site blinked off the screen, followed by a request: *Apply?*

"I said, what are you doing?" The doctor's voice rang through the lab like a warning. He approached on quick legs and grabbed Avery tight by the wrist, yanking his hand away from the keyboard as the crew watched.

"Let go, unless you want a fat lip," Avery said. The stench of stale cigarettes wafted toward him, crawled up his nostrils and seeped down the windpipe. He coughed in the doctor's bearded face.

"Not till you tell me what you're up to, wise guy."

Avery clicked the apply response and the computer activated.

He and the doctor traded strained looks.

"What did you do?"

"Entered new info into the data link."

"You know I'm the only one authorized to do that. Delete it."

"Too late, already in."

"Then I'll have to undo it. Step aside."

Marcus nudged him back a step, and he shoved Marcus, landing him on the station's desktop.

Stas, Quinn, and Jager united as one, making a defensive move against the Navy captain.

Marcus called them off. He gave Avery that unfavorable look again. "What the hell's gotten into you?"

Avery went for the briefcase on the floor and kicked it out of the way.

The doctor motioned to his team to leave the lab.

The thick, rock wall rumbled open and they left.

"Not talking to me?" The lab wall shut, and the two men were sealed alone in the transport chamber. Marcus frowned and shot to his feet. "Spectrum's top CEO is ready to yank the plug on this project because of the boneheaded stunt you pulled. What the hell were you thinking?"

"Stop acting as though I committed a crime. I needed extra time, that's all."

"Extra time? So you could marry the love of your life?"

Now he knew he had to return back through time to save Roy—and marry Darah. "I didn't see anyone. I just lagged behind, okay."

"Your defense case won't help you," the doctor fired. "I'll have to make an official report. Why did you do it?"

"I don't have to tell you." Avery hoped the despair that could never appear on any document would also not appear on his face.

"I thought we discussed this? You can't alter—"

"Bringing back Claudia would've meant doing the same thing!"

Marcus paced back and forth. When he tired, he grabbed a seat. "You took a foolish chance with your life. Know that?" His face turned beet red.

"Save the power flash for the next shot."

"There isn't going to be any next shot. Not after what you did. What if something had happened to you?"

He gave Marcus a shifting eye. "Like what?"

Marcus launched himself from the chair like a rocket, toppling it over. "Like die, you idiot!"

The nonchalant serviceman scooped the duffel bag onto his shoulder and marched into his quarters with the irate doctor behind him like a pecking hen.

"Didn't you wonder why the forces of time didn't rip you apart cell by cell?"

"Relax." He tossed his gear onto the bed. "Your pet-theories were all wrong. Nothing happened. I'm okay."

"You don't get it, do you? You're still in one piece because of something *I did*!"

"This is all about you, isn't it? Professor "J" and another Nobel Peace Prize."

"If you weren't so young and cocky, I'd—"

"You'd what?" He waited for Marcus to stop threatening him with a waving fist and say what was on his mind.

"My job is to keep you alive. If I fail to do that, this project folds." He heaved out a smoker's breath and Avery turned away. "You're here because I figured out a way to override the internal clock's oscillator. The calibration was a gamble I had to take."

The navyman applauded. "Nice going."

Marcus yanked those fat, black glasses off his sloped nose, revealing raw, olive-green eyes. "Don't be a mule's ass." His hands began to shake.

"What you did paid off."

"That's not the point. Your overextension would've been fatal, whether it was five days or five minutes. That's the reason Claudia died. Not enough time in the clock's bank account. Wish the calibration could've worked for Claudia. Damn machine has a mind of its own."

Avery forced himself to sit, locked in an empty stare. He took a moment to think. He survived but Claudia didn't. Neither did Mitchell Braun. Were there any other white mice? he thought.

"Ah, has the truth bitten where the sun don't shine?"

He came to his senses. Someone's garbled remains had painted a gross picture for him. He didn't want to die that way. Not like Claudia: a compressed package of rotting flesh and exposed bones crawling with legless maggots and buzzing flies. He didn't want to die at all. "Sorry about the shove." A rigid-looking Marcus just blinked. "And thanks for saving my hide."

He fitted his glasses over angry eyes. "Forget it and I'll dismiss it."

But Avery could not dismiss the trouble he sensed he was in. "What else does the Corporation know?" Now that he learned the Corporation knew about everything, he was going to have to act like a model boy scout. Without delay he decided being decent would get him nowhere.

"There's only so much I can lie to them about. But not to worry." The hallmark phrase that had always steadied the young captain, didn't do its magic on him this time. "I've got your back."

"Who's got yours?" Avery noted each worried line on the doctor's sweaty brow. Someone—Jager, Quinn, or Stas—had gone behind his back when the time traveler did not return on schedule. If Avery did one more thing, Marc's head would roll. "Miss anything while I was away?" Suddenly he was interested in learning what had happened on the other side of the Spectrum world in his absence.

"Funny you should ask." Marcus pulled up a chair. "Quite a show." He plucked a cigarette from inside his lab coat, lit it, and took a tense drag. After a brief moment, his shaky hands relaxed. "Last week after Dr. Jules Ian died, the FBI came looking for me at my hotel room as though I could raise him from the dead."

"Did they question you about Mitchell Braun?"

Marcus gave him a surprised look, and in doing so, exposed the playing cards in his hand. "How did you know about him?"

The thick-whiskered doctor was up to no good, and Avery knew it from the moment he heard Jager say: 'The money meant more to you than she did.' If Avery turned in the fat man to the feds, he would have trouble clearing his own name. "I have my sources. Anything else happen?"

He plucked at his beard. He told him NCIS brought in two sailors for questioning and released them. Evans and Yancey. But the next day Dauerman had them arrested, along with a third man. An Ensign Hobbs. They were charged for participating in Black-Sunday's crime. It was great news, but they weren't the head honcho. The mastermind behind the scheme to bring down the U.S. Navy and the nation it protected, was still on the loose. It was only a matter of time now before they brought him in, too.

The motion of the rock wall rumbled in the background and Marcus put out his cigarette. "We've got company. Let's see who it is."

They stepped into the lab.

"Well, if it isn't the runaway captain," Dauerman said.

The doctor pushed his glasses back with a crooked finger. "I already discussed it with him."

"Get out."

Marcus stomped out, leaving both men to themselves.

Dauerman approached the Navy officer, slow and deliberate. "You were AWOL." He circled him, hands behind his back. "And in case you've forgotten, it stands for: Absent Without—"

"I know what it means, don't school me."

"In that case, it gives me great pleasure to notify you of your transfer back to active duty." Avery wanted to grab him by the shirt collar. "You're to report to the *Hill* first thing tomorrow morning. Pratt will be more than happy to sign all the paperwork."

"This project isn't over yet!"

"It is for you," the NCIS officer said. "I've been ordered to shut down the entire facility by the Corporation's top CEO in twenty-five minutes. Count them—twenty-five minutes."

Every time Dauerman grinned, the face of Avery's abusive father disturbed his thoughts. He hated the stocky man who menaced him all his life, and now, he hated the head investigator as well.

He let Dauerman have the final say. "As you know, I'm a busy man. Short on patience and no time for trivialities. You can turn in your keys to me in the morning—Lieutenant."

Marcus Weinberg was still brewing from the previous day when he stomped out on Dauerman, leaving Avery alone to deal with the agent. But the doctor hadn't gone far. He remained within earshot and was startled by the news. The open laboratory would be shut like a bank vault and he and his team sent back to MIT. What he needed was a plan—and Avery's help. He was living proof, the argument the scientist would use to persuade the Corporation's board of trustees that his work should continue. If Marcus won their favor, there was a chance Spectrum's CEO would change his mind, too.

Dr. Weinberg entered the elaborate transport chamber that housed the giant, glassy megaliths. He shoved a cigarette between tight lips and lit it to calm his nerves. Things looked and felt the way they did just before work commenced each morning. But an empty lab meant the rest of the schedule had been cancelled.

Touring eyes and deliberate steps led him to the army of monitors at the control station. There, at the helm of unspeakable power, history had been made when the clock's natural motion strangely reversed like a rolling altimeter in a falling jet. The doctor shuddered at the thought that all the hard work, the long hours at the lab, and Spectrum's marvelous technology would be thrown away. Now the possibility of every piece of equipment ending up in the Smithsonian Institute as an ancient artifact to entertain curious minds, ate at him. He would hate being among museum-goers, gawking at the awesome-looking machines that had actually been used.

Marcus loped past the positron, entered the captain's quarters and spotted that familiar duffel bag on the bed. "Neil?"

The room was cold and quiet.

He would wait it out until Avery returned.

Between tense fingers, Marc's cigarette burned down to the spongy filter. He dropped the smoldering butt on the floor, crushed it under his big shoe like a bug, and ran idle hands on the particle accelerator … the cylinders … the keyboards ….

Beneath the control station's massive table, a LED indicator light winked at him from the quantum computer's modem. Had the negatron unit gone into transport? No, he thought. He heard Shank clearly. Everything was to be shut down in twenty-five minutes. Everything.

He stepped around the long row of monitors, stood at the center of the floor between the mighty cylinders, and placed an open palm on the limestone floor. The area was hot to the core and meant only one thing. The nuclear reactors housed beneath his feet had gone critical within the last twenty-four hours.

He punched an access code into the quantum computer, and the answer he sought for came. Everything in the laboratory *had* been shut down. But nine hours later, the transporter somehow came to life. "So, that's why he shoved me." Marcus had put it all together and was thunderstruck.

His hands tightened into fists when someone marched into the lab. He was no longer alone.

"Where's Avery?"

He spun into their eyes—two, austere-looking Marine sentries—handguns holstered at their hips—and the top NCIS man dressed in a fine-tailored, three-piece vested suit. "Have you come to arrest him, too?"

"I haven't time for games," he croaked. "Where is he?"

"Gone!"

"To the ship?"

Marcus knew the agent wanted an answer fast. "I underestimated Avery." Indignation marked his tone. "I deceived you about him seeing his mother. Now he deceived me."

"What kind of talk—?"

"If you must know, he escaped last night."

"And you let him?"

Marcus pointed a crooked finger at him. "You drove him!"

Suddenly, there was silence. But even silence had a noise to it.

"I'm sorry, doctor. Didn't mean to accuse you." Dauerman calmed down. "Don't know *what* came over me. Just tell me where he is and you can be on your way. I only want him." He flashed an apologetic smile.

Marc's pulse pounded in his left armpit. "I told you, he isn't here!" He shoved back sliding glasses with a nervous finger.

The agent's face fell. "That's 'cause you showed him things you weren't supposed to. I don't have this place bugged for nothing."

Now the overweight scientist was really stunned. "What the devil's your problem?" he countered. "I'm no spy!"

Dauerman motioned for the sentries to wait outside.

"Let's talk." He lit a cigarette.

Chapter 27

It was the last Sunday in November, and the sixth floor was deserted, except for two employees going about their business: a middle-aged woman pushing a janitor's cart—carrying a wringer bucket, wet-floor sign, mop, broom, and cleaning supplies—through the long corridor, and a stout, blonde-haired man maneuvering a humming buffing machine from side to side over the interlocked crystal-gray tiles. Avery had given attention to the spotless, waxy floor only because of how slowly he walked: measured steps that led him to the private room where, a doctor at the nurses station told him, a visitor had been there since 8:30 that morning, and now it was going on 10:00. Avery had been stunned by the phone call, the name of the hospital, the moment he was thrust into against his will. The time machine's lock-in settings and analog destination system were still too complicated to grasp.

The urgent messages Beulah once relayed to him played in his mind like a disturbing recording. Only this time he was there ….

Roy's pain started two weeks before Thanksgiving, and for three days straight he said nothing. When he had trouble breathing, Beulah drove her husband to the emergency room in Boone. That was the night the tests were done. The night of the long wait. The night the reverend was advised to stay. The night the phone rang in his apartment. "Avery here."

Matt Tenpenny, the chief medical attending, was on call that evening. He assured Roy he would be given the royal treatment. But when the reverend objected, Beulah spoke with him, calmed him down, and with reluctance he changed his mind. He would stay. Only if discharged by Saturday afternoon so he could start work on his next sermon for the following day at Faith Mission.

Mama said ever since he became an evangelist, Roy traveled far and wide, taking longer journeys, tasting exotic cultures, and learning tongue-twisting vocabulary. His army days in Boeblingen, West Germany, could not compare to where he had been. Though he missed his family with each trip he took, they listened to his voice on the radio, saw his face live on Bible Network Television. But the little time he had for himself postponed promises he once made ....

Avery sampled a scent of antiseptic in the air and crept into the room to the hum of a respirator and beeping heart monitor. There, Beulah sat at Roy's bedside, holding his hand with an undistracted love-gaze fixed on her husband of thirty-nine years.

"Beulah?"

She turned from Roy's yellow, moon-slit eyes.

It pained him to command a sunny smile, knowing the effort behind it would quickly die in his facial muscles. She laid eyes on him, and when she did, a voice he hardly recognized replayed in his head: Is the Reverend home?

"Goodness!" Her mouth dropped open and she gave an exaggerated blink. "How are you?"

He sat beside her and took her hand. How he missed the warmth of her thick fingers; the look on her round, black face. "Same old me."

She studied the uniformed man carefully. "But ... you haven't aged."

How could he tell her he had seen her only yesterday? That a time machine was responsible for the rolling seasons: the rains of spring, the swelter of summer, the leaves of autumn, the flakes of winter.

He looked keenly at Beulah. No, not at her, but into her, searching her soul. Within those eyes that held his heart the moment they met, a prowling grief bore witness to the silent drama that unfolded on her dark face. She looked to Roy, then to him. "Let me tell you what happened," she began ....

Eight days prior, Roy had been sitting up in bed. He was upbeat and talkative with visitors from church, despite the nasogastric tube in his nose. By Monday afternoon, three days before Thanksgiving, the feeding tube was out and he sampled a bland diet. But when his most precious possession: a big, leather-bound bible became too heavy for him to handle, like the eating utensils that lay cold on the tray at his bedside with food he hadn't touched, the nurses rolled him into a small, private room; away from Pastor Campbell and the crowds he ushered in.

Beulah read to him after this, for hours on end, from the Old and New Testaments, even as he slept. And when she wasn't reading to him from the holy scriptures, she sat waiting, praying for Roy to pull through, hoping the new drug would be absorbed into his body ....

Avery inhaled deep and let out a ragged breath. But the sinking weight in his chest and gut refused to budge. "How is he now?"

Beulah shook her head with an unusual quietness. "Part of his pancreas was removed." She explained to him what Doctor Tenpenny told her: Pancreatic cancer was a stealthy killer; a difficult disease to detect. A person could have it for years, feel well, and not realize they were slowly dying. But Tenpenny offered one hope. At best, he believed Roy's immune system would not reject the drug that dripped into a dark vein from an IV bag on a tall pole guarding his bedside, and that afterwards, he would go on to lead a normal life. At worst, the most he would live would be six months to a year.

"He talked about you for months after you left. Making plans," Beulah said. "But when you didn't call, write, return ...."

An old pain rumbled in Avery's chest like angry thunder. He was so sorry he didn't spend the last remaining years with Roy before this. Now Avery returned from his absence to find Beulah had gained more weight, and learned from her that her blood pressure had risen and the diabetes worsened, even with an augmented regimen of insulin. Her thick, head of dark hair, now dull gray, revealed wide patches of pale scalp, and through fat lenses, her eyes appeared dim.

"Beulah?" He couldn't mask the thickness in his voice, and he couldn't do anything about his heavy eyes, full from a cistern of unwept tears. "Where're the girls?"

"On their way."

"I'm glad." They probably forgot about me, he thought.

10:25 A.M.

A young woman, topcoat draped over an arm, entered the private room on quiet steps, and immediately, the cardiac monitor beeping in the serviceman's ears seemed louder.

Avery studied her fall uniform and row of ribbon bars, all with a blinkless stare. The look of patriotism in the ensign's eyes—her professional appearance and military poise—never wavered.

She greeted Beulah with a hug and kiss.

"You look wonderful in cornrows, Darah."

"Thank you, Mama." She turned from her to him. "Well, hello. It's been a while ... sir."

She seemed to have forgotten the love they once had.

CG-113 marked the front of her service cap.

"The *Essex*. Isn't that the ship ...?"

"That what?" she asked.

"... Will be decommissioned after its last run?"

"Not without me at the ceremony. She departs next week for a month of battle-ready exercises with the Venezuelan Navy. Returning to North Island through the Canal sometime after New Year's Eve."

He heard people approaching in the corridor and gave a look. From the south end of the ward facing the private room, three females came: their frames taller, their hips wider, their breasts developed, their hair unbraided. The girls were older now. They had evolved from childhood into young attractive women.

Upon entering the patient's room, they kissed their mother and looked at him with vague eyes. "Don't we know you?" Taffi said.

It hurt him to hear her say that. "I was hoping you'd remember without having to ask."

Mama said, "He's the stranger that showed up one summer day at our door."

Avery added, "I was tired and hungry. And your mother, from the kindness of her heart, invited me in."

"Ave?"

He acknowledged April with a tired smile.

Olympia said, "Where have you been all these years?"

He said nothing. But Darah knew. She was aware of the strange secret her sisters did not know: why he came; why he left. It was only yesterday he told her frightening things—Roy's cancer; Olympia's fractured arm. How many lonely nights did she endure? he thought. How many tears did she shed on her pillows, all stuffed with broken promises? Wait for me, he had said. I'll return someday. Soon, it seemed. He convinced her of that. But when months turned to years, he wondered: Did her love remain strong? Did she wait?

11:00 A.M.

With the navyman at his bedside, Roy rested in the silence of another world while his family sat about with hope painted on their faces. The room smelled of flowers, fresh bed sheets, and a trace of urine.

Every twenty minutes or so, someone would get up to stretch tired legs and walk about the room. The girls found it difficult to stay in one place for so long, and eventually, they paced the long floors outside the ward by the elevators until hungry stomachs sent everyone to the lobby cafeteria. Waiting was hard on them, but Beulah stuck it out. She stayed by her husband and silently prayed. Avery could always tell when Mama was in quiet prayer by the fervent look in her small, round eyes.

11:45 A.M.

One of the doctors, a young white female under the direction of the chief medical attending, entered the room and drew a vial of blood from Roy's right arm. She explained it would be a while before results came through and encouraged everyone not to worry. CFD-180, the FDA-approved drug, had shown vast improvement in many with post-surgical cancer. The only drawback was that some, a small percentage of patients, did not respond enough to the treatment. Like the doctors, Avery and the Gilchrists decided to stay for the results.

1:15 P.M.

A short black nurse came by to look in on Roy. She checked the intravenous solutions that trickled medicated droplets into a metacarpal vein, then read the monitor for vital signs while Avery scrutinized her quiet, plump face. Every wrinkled fold on her forehead matched the diminished waves on the heart monitor. Pulse for pulse. Roy was breathing. He was alive. But it was all controlled.

He waited for the nurse to step out so he could tell Mama what was on his mind. "What if he doesn't make it?" He so much wanted to hear Roy speak. For him to say *son* one more time.

"Hush that talk," she answered. "BMC has the best doctors in this here county. They've given Roy a lot of hope. It's just gonna take more time for him."

Time…. He thought of all the opportunities he had. All of them now gone. "I had plenty of time. All the time in the world. I came to Oak Leaf because of something I'd left undone. Unsaid."

A calm smile came to Mama's wide, thin lips. She had the wisdom and ready answers to just about anything. "Talk to him now."

"But …." He tried not to sound frightened. "He's been in a coma four days."

"Use your faith. Tell him what's in your heart. Whisper it in his ear. He'll hear you. I know he will." The drawl in her voice lit the room like daybreak.

She pushed herself up from her seat with effort and held Avery's face in the cupped palm of her warm hand. "Everything's gonna be all right."

The girls stood to their feet and followed their oldest sister down the long hall. Mama had told them what it meant to want a moment; to allow the heart to speak words that throbbed at the throat, and they wanted the serviceman to have it first.

"If you need me, I'll be in the waiting room," Mama said.

She went out. The sound of footsteps at the end of the long hall, made the room quieter.

Avery was now alone with the preacher. This was not the special moment he planned for—just the two of them. Nor the second chance he hoped for. He was painfully aware he waited too long and now it came to this.

He moved into Beulah's seat. Her body heat had kept it warm.

Thoughts swirled in his head. Words—Mama's words: 'Talk to him now.' Beulah knew that the silence of a comatose mind could be penetrated with a message of love.

He pulled himself to the edge of the bed. "Roy, can you hear me?" The hand that once draped over his shoulder, was cold to the touch. "Dad?" A flame shot up his throat. "If you could see me trembling, then you'd understand how much you mean to me."

He grabbed an afro-pick by the phone on the bedside table and worked it into Roy's unkempt, flattened hair, trying to give it lift. But he couldn't do anything about his ghostly-gray features, or the endotracheal tube that tugged at his mouth, nor the ageless monster that invaded his lungs like a Nazi blitzkrieg, leaving the once robust man in a melted state.

With each second that passed, Avery's shaking increased like the rain-soaked air each time it thundered. This was the moment that frightened him most; a moment in which he saw for the first time the mountainous wall of emotions he had been summoned to scale. In all his life, nothing was as difficult as what he now faced—not the arduous eight weeks of boot camp he had endured, and not the dangerous challenges of a military career. Nothing, until now, could compare to a greater, more difficult task—exposing his own heart.

"I miss playing chess with you. Looking at the stars together. Going fishing. But most of all I miss that smile. Your touch. The one you gave me each time you called me son."

Roy's sunken face became a soft blur through standing tears.

With great effort, Avery pushed down what he wanted to say most. It roiled against him and pushed back. "I love you, Roy. Always did. Always will." He kissed a hollowed cheek. "Please give me a sign that you'll recover."

He lowered the bedrail and sunk his face into the foam rubber mattress. His eyes were on a pouchy bladder bag with cola-colored liquid inside. He prayed that the curtain to Roy's life would not come down on him like the end of a tearful play.

So he waited....

Someone's hand slipped into his. Fingers coming to life: moving, closing, relaxing, tightening again.

Avery opened sleepy eyes. Opened them wide. He was jolted erect when an arm curled over his shoulder and his heart sprinted with delight. Darah had now reentered the room—Beulah's arm over him.

Their eyes met. "Was that you who squeezed my hand?"

Her pumpkin-round face drove away the stubborn ache he felt. "That was Roy. He's slowly coming around. He heard you. I knew he would."

2:30 P.M.

After Darah and the girls had their turn to be alone with their father, a group of people gathered outside in the corridor; their voices filling the private room as they walked in. The young doctors, a team of them, were led by an older, distinguished-looking black man with a nametag over the top pocket of his white, hospital coat: Matt Tenpenny, MD. "We're waiting for blood results from this afternoon." They listened like first-year students at med school. "When the drug takes effect he'll come out of the coma."

3:05 P.M.

The white female doctor who had drawn Roy's blood, returned, holding an aluminum clipboard. Lab results. Her sudden presence made everyone in the room snap their heads her way. No one promised anything to anyone. Not the chief medical attending to his team, nor the ward nurses to the Gilchrist family. No one knew what the tests would yield until now.

The sound of crisp paper broke the stubborn silence and Avery looked about. Darah's knees shook. Olympia raised a hand to her breasts, the other on her bobbing throat. April looked to Taffi and grabbed her hand, fingers interlocking. Beulah found hidden strength and shot to her feet. Avery stood with her and wrapped an arm around her wide waist. Now the doctor was the center of everyone's attention. She pushed back a loose wad of chestnut-brown hair that tumbled onto her clear, apple-green eyes as they floated down a long sheet. She found it. Roy's name. He could tell.

"Good news …." Her drawling voice filled the room with joy.

The doctor explained that Roy's blood results showed the post-surgical anticancer drug was being absorbed into his immune system as she spoke, and would soon begin attacking every malignant cell in his body.

Avery released a sigh of long-withheld relief. He would take the tattered happiness. It was better than no happiness at all.

"Y'all waited wonderfully for this." The doctor's wide smile was a welcome sight. "He'll be monitored throughout the night. When he comes around, we'll call. Please, go home and rest."

Rest. The worst was over. Roy was out of danger. The anticancer drug would take care of what was in his lungs and soon he'd be breathing on his own. When he was feeling better, he would sign the discharge papers and be allowed to go home. He would look frail, even a little sick, but all that would pass when his appetite returned, and with that, gain some much-needed weight. When he was up to it, he would probably play chess, go for brief walks, begin laughing again and make his shoulders bounce. By then he would open the hood of his car and find out what exactly was wrong with the ignition. Mama was right. Everything was going to be okay.

From an open window a feathery breeze entered the room. Avery felt it and was certain everyone else did, too. But he couldn't tell by their tired faces. Each one of them were in their own world, seeking for a rest that would not easily come.

Roy's chest rose and fell to the rhythmic cadence of the humming, clicking, whirring, pumping respirator. Rose and fell. His fingers moved. Then came a sudden silence.

The feathery breeze was sucked out through the window and something strange replaced it, creeping into the room like a bandit as Darah stepped out in long, hurried strides.

Avery looked to Beulah.

She released Roy's hand.

Taffi, April, and Olympia were so remote in their quiet vigil, they had no idea the cardiac monitor stopped beeping.

Mama exited the room and returned a moment later with Dr. Matt Tenpenny. His flapping white coat pulled in a sudden chill and Avery shot to his feet.

The MD looked the way Avery felt: startled. "Who turned off the equipment?"

Now the girls knew.

"God did." Beulah's words were as soft as the flutter of wings that wisped by only a moment before.

The doctor stepped over to the bed and pulled the white covers over Roy's sunken face. "In all my years as chief attending, this is the first time I've gotten gooseflesh." His heavy-looking eyes fell on Beulah. "I'm so sorry."

A sense of wrongness swirled in the air like dark rain clouds threatening a family outing, and immediately, Taffi looked like part of the ceiling had collapsed on her. Olympia couldn't speak, bat her eyes, or even shed a tear. All she could do was stare with hypnotic horror at the long covered hump, slightly propped on the low, railed bed.

From the hallway, someone's sobbing cries filled the room, ripping the silence that held April. It was the young female doctor who had drawn Roy's blood. April leaped to her feet and shot a hand over her mouth that dropped open like a botched surgical wound. "He's dead." She twisted her face and circles of panic appeared around staring eyes. "Daddy's dead!"

Tenpenny removed a stethoscope from around his thick neck. "Sister Beulah," he said in a tired voice. "Someday we'll be able to explain why things like this happen." He took her hand. "Will you allow us to use the body for medical study?—after a proper funeral, that is."

Avery sucked in a ragged breath and blew it out. He was relieved Beulah would not allow her husband's body to be used that way. Roy was not a guinea pig. He was a decent man.

"No." Mama was polite but firm.

"Fine. We'll just take him away. Please receive my deepest condolences for you and the girls." But he didn't turn to look at the young women. He stayed focused on Beulah. "I know this is sudden. Have you made arrangements?"

A dignified look came over her. "Yes."

"Tell me what you want." Tenpenny's voice turned soft. "I'll need to call the morgue and inform them."

Avery waited along with everyone else. He was stunned but shouldn't have been surprised. Marcus said this would happen, he thought. He leaned against the wall, realizing he would fall if he didn't.

"My husband is to be cremated. Immediately."

"Mama, no!" Avery heaved out sobs and tears followed. "There must be some mistake!" He could hardly speak now.

She turned from Tenpenny to him. "There's no mistake. Roy left clear instructions as to his final wishes. It's all in his will."

Suddenly he felt dizzy. Sick.

"Will? What will?" He wanted to pound his fist through the wall and yell at her. But how could he yell at the woman who had become his second mother? "He promised me he would live a long time!"

Beulah looked puzzled. "I'm sorry but it's all been settled. This is what he wanted."

He fought to understand what she had said. "Are you saying Roy lied?" His cry filled the room.

"Lower your voice," Tenpenny said.

Avery discovered he could not recognize what he was feeling: Anger? Hatred? Suicide?

"Roy wouldn't lie to you." Beulah spoke above a whisper. "You misunderstood."

In that devastating moment, a weighty heartache brought him to his senses. He swallowed down a piece of throat-clogging grief and it regurgitated back on his tongue as acid-tasting bile. He admitted to himself he was still a coward. Afraid to love and be loved. I've lost, he thought. Marcus was right. The past can never be changed.

When Ensign Darah Gilchrist returned from her wanderings—hand in hand with Gerald Morgan—and saw that her father and the bed he was in had been taken away, she struck Lieutenant Avery full across the face with a head-jarring slap. A cold, fiery sting followed the firecracker-like sound.

"Why?" Her angry sobs filled the hallway.

People turned and stared.

A doctor shouted into the nurses station for someone to call security.

Darah went at him again, fingers balled into fists. She pummeled him in the chest and shoulders until her hands uncurled, until her flailing arms tired—until he was satisfied with the punishment he knew he deserved; the same blows he had once inflicted on her.

"Why didn't you tell him he had cancer?" Darah cried. "Why?"

All except Beulah, everyone arrived home walking in dazed. Darah looked like her Toyota Camry had stalled in the middle of a railroad track and a CSX freight train hit it, leaving her crawling from the wreckage of her mind in an angry state. She blew past Gerald Morgan, leaving him where he stood, and rushed upstairs. When a door slammed, Avery knew she would spend the remainder of the afternoon and dreadful hours of the night locked away in painful solitude—not wishing to talk, not willing to come down, not wanting for anyone to see her the way she really was: torn from grief, raw with hate.

4:35 P.M.

Avery dropped to a sit in Roy's corner wingchair as Gerald led Beulah past him into the kitchen. Someone threw their keys on the Formica-top table. "We have to go soon," Gerald said. "It's a long drive to Chesapeake."

"Why do you and Darah live so faraway?" Mama's voice.

"It's an easy drive to Norfolk," Gerald answered.

"I don't want you making a night trip. Wait for Darah to get herself together. Her ship won't leave till next week, so why the rush?"

"We'll be fine."

"You'll be sorry. You're tired, hungry—and stubborn like Roy was."

"I wasn't planning on staying here with ... *him*."

"He has a name. And you won't be sleeping together. You'll be on the couch."

5:10 P.M.

Taffi, April, and Olympia sat stranded on the big couch. Their blank stares and slumped postures spoke of a world turned upside down with the same devastation of a capsized ship. Now the contagious laughter that once filled the house had been replaced by something void. Something Avery could not describe. Instead, what claimed their sad faces was spelled out in one word: death; their death; creeping up on the young women with cunning stealth. Doing to them what the cancer had done to Roy.

"Praise the Lord, young man."

Avery heard Roy's voice and saw him lumber down the stairs to the family room. He was finely-dressed with a big bible in hand and a big smile on his face. He stood by the door, calling on everyone to hurry up. "I don't want to be late," he said with boyish mirth. He went through the front door without opening it, taking with him that mirth Avery sought within scraps of black and white memories—the things Beulah had said to Roy that made him laugh; a laughter he could hear through the armor of his sorrow; the same sorrow that left the Gilchrist girls in their pitiful condition. But Mama's prayers had already saturated the house. Avery heard her praying from the kitchen after Gerald left. The girls' fragmented hearts would not sink to the bottom of a tearful deep like the strewn remains of the Titanic.

5:26 P.M.

Avery was in the kitchen with Mama when the phone rang. She hit the hands-free button so that she could keep busy preparing something simple for anyone who cared to eat.

"Beu …?" Mae's voice.

"I'm here."

Mae asked permission to borrow Beulah's car while repairmen at a transmission service shop in Boone, worked on her vehicle. She asked about Roy.

Beulah told her sister what happened and said it was all right for Chloe to stay in Boone with her daughter Hattie. She was an excellent babysitter, and as long as the child was with her, she would be fine until things settled down. If Hattie dropped off the eight-year-old now, she would be overwhelmed by a grief-stricken household.

5:52 P.M.

Avery cracked open the bedroom door and heard Gerald say: "Your mother thinks I'm stubborn like Roy."

The navyman had gone upstairs to talk Darah into joining the rest of the family, but when he saw her on a made bed, facedown like a dying soldier in a muddy ditch, he decided against it. The light from a hatless lamp in the corner of the room, painted a ghostly shadow on the wall, and for a quick moment, Avery thought he saw Roy's motionless form.

Nothing Gerald said so far caused Darah to stir, to respond—until now.

"My father wasn't stubborn." She muffled a cry into a pillow.

"Of course he wasn't," Gerald said.

"Then why did you say it?"

"I was hoping you'd come out of your cell. You've been locked away since—"

"I like this funk hole, okay!" She raised her head and Avery caught those twisted lips, sunken brow, atrophied facial muscles. Her well of tears seemed to have been sucked dry by the searing heat of anger from within, while those eyes, narrowed and sharp, were stripped of the softness they once had.

Gerald said he was sorry, but didn't look it.

"What've you got to be sorry about? Daddy's gone and all you can say is he was stubborn."

"Okay, I'm guilt-sorry now!"

"You're sorry about lots of things. Walking out on me twice for six months; shoveling money into those stupid cars you own instead of your business; dicking me all these years with no talk of commitment. When is it going to stop?"

"A marriage license is just a crummy piece of paper."

"Not a ring. Not a promise."

"Okay, I promise not to break the seventh commandment with anyone but you. What else you want?"

She answered fast. "For you to leave me alone."

He snickered. "Seems I've heard that line before."

Her worn-out laugh filled the room. "Well, here's one you haven't …."

Avery closed the door and walked away.

6:03 P.M.

Night descended, and an unusually cold November air found its way into every corner of the old house. Beulah fed several quartered logs into the red-bricked fireplace and got it going while her lifeless daughters remained strung out on the couch. Those faraway eyes that could not blink or fill with tears were dark and quiet. Old beyond years. It would take more than the hearth's orange flame that radiated a warm glow to offer relief.

April was the first to show signs of life between the three women. She raised mournful eyes and found the serviceman sitting across from her in the corner wingchair.

"Ave?" Tears dropped heavy on her cheeks. Her voice squeaky-raw. "Did … d-did you love Daddy?"

A fresh desire to weep surged through his body.

"Yes," he said through weak vocal cords. "With all my heart."

"Then why didn't you come back?"

He welcomed the reprimand the way he accepted Darah's blows, hoping it would atone for his sins. But they had not. "Can't I just hug you and bury the past?"

"I'd rather bury Daddy. I heard it was you who poisoned his mind!"

April charged up the stairs, down the hall, and a door banged shut with such detonation he felt the shudder in his bones. Avery waited for the cries, the sobs, the sounds he hoped would resonate throughout the house and set off a mournful chain reaction between Olympia and Taffi; something to overshadow his remorse. But nothing. The numbing silence remained. Now it was up to the oppressive night to squeeze the girls back into reality.

He left Taffi and Olympia, and went to the kitchen to see about Mama. She was alone, wearing that flowery apron with her name artistically embroidered on it, standing by a mound-filled sink of soapy suds. Beulah was trying to take her mind off her heartache by washing dishes. She'd dry a porcelain plate with a clean towel, then alternate wiping her round face with the apron each time fresh tears flowed. It was the first time he had seen her cry since everyone stumbled back into the house, and looking at her from up close after they embraced, made him cry, too.

Gerald thumped down the stairs and charged into the kitchen. He cursed and snatched the car keys from the table. He moved like a man headed nowhere and was out the front door with Beulah after him.

"Gerald? What's wrong?" She was out of breath when she reached the open door. "Where're you going?"

Gerald jumped behind the wheel of a white vehicle. "Someplace your daughter won't see me for a while." Funneled headlights slashed bright circles of ovals into the night and the screeching car sped away.

7:24 P.M.

Avery responded to a knock at the door. It was Pastor Campbell. With him were a godly troop from his beloved sanctuary, along with several ministers from Charlotte and St. Charles. They had made the long trip to Oak Leaf as soon as they heard the news of Roy's passing. Beulah put on a pot of coffee and the best smile she could find. She would not be beaten down by sorrow. Her daughters needed her to give them fresh strength each time she rose from her knees in prayer. The same kind of inner strength Avery himself desired.

Beulah graciously accepted everyone's act of solace—the food, the flowers, the condolences—knowing it was their humble way of paying their last respects to such a great man as Roy. Especially since there would be no viewing, funeral, cremation service, nothing.

11:49 P.M.

When the long hours and the big crowd began to wear Beulah down, Avery politely asked everyone to leave. The grieving family still needed time to be alone; to pray, to cry. They all understood.

12:34 A.M.

Beulah had just come down from a long wrenching talk with Darah and sat across Olympia and their guest. Her shoulders went limp when her arms dropped to the sides of the corner wingchair. It was obvious she didn't want to retire for the night. No one did. Turning off the lights and going to bed was the last thing Avery wanted, too. It would be a double darkness he could not bear.

He met Beulah's drained eyes and sensed she saw his bleeding heart. "Neil, I know it hurts. But please, forgive Roy for the decision he made."

Olympia came to life and wept. She buried her face in her hands. She had painted her nails a rosy color as a reminder that Roy would soon be released from the hospital.

"But why?" he spat. "Why did he want it this way?"

Beulah looked torn. "We both know Roy was stubborn—even in death. All I'm asking is to fulfill his last wish. It's all I can do. All I have left for the man I loved."

Avery sought to bargain. If it worked, it would sooth the raging storm within. "If this is all a matter of money, let me pay the expenses." He felt his sandpaper throat constrict. "Roy was my father!"

Beulah pushed herself up from the wingchair, trudged across the family room, and plopped herself between him and Olympia. She grabbed their hands. "Roy never mentioned this. You see, he grew up with emotional scars. As the middle brother of three boys, his mother died just like yours. Before her time."

The glum serviceman listened. Black and white memories of an empty house flashed before him.

"It wasn't that his father was cruel. He just favored the oldest and youngest, making Roy feel unimportant. It's always the middle child that's left out, and Roy carried that for the rest of his life. Much as I tried, I could never convince him how wrong he was in believing no one would ever come to his funeral when he died."

Olympia emerged from behind her hands. In her scarlet eyes, Avery could tell she now had some understanding of the man she called Daddy, and that she, too, was terminal with depression. Now nothing could bring healing except Beulah's caring words.

"Son, don't be upset with me or Roy. He loved you, and knew you loved him."

"How could he?" He fought to curb his roiling anger. "I never told him how I felt till today—on his deathbed."

"No, he knew. Your message to him, that silent cry, was loud and clear. I've heard it. My daughters have heard it. But most of all Roy heard it, too. The things you two did together on your first visit showed you cared. He never forgot that."

Avery's head pounded from tiredness, from grief, from fear. His appetite had died the moment Roy did. All sure signs of major distress. He thought he had changed everything. Instead everything he did only made things worse. Like Olympia, he was silent and dazed and liked it that way. But Beulah had the remedy to heal. She always did. The problem was, he wanted her to keep it to herself. He didn't want a cure.

"Don't let your emotions dictate to you that it's over. If you really loved Roy, you'll find it in your heart to forgive him. And one day, you'll even find a way to honor the memory of your real father as well."

Roy's voice broke through his dark thoughts like a radio station transmitting an urgent bulletin: Forgive and you shall be forgiven.

He had a burning urge to battle back. "I'll never forgive my father. Never!"

A bleary-eyed Avery tossed in bed and grabbed his chest, searching for the gaping hole that brought so much pain. The blast of a high-powered rifle would have done it. But no one had shot him.

All night long, the endless hammering of the grandfather clock in the dining room, gonged in his ears. How I wish I had stayed in the world I was in, he thought. He knew the script and how the play would end. In the wee hours of the morning, from that tiny, lamp-lit guestroom, Avery decided, before the curtain came down on the last act, he would be gone. Never to return.

At four o'clock he went to the attic. Pain was a mocker and sleep was harassing. There was no way he could close his eyes and not see Roy's face; the way he looked in the hospital; the way he smiled on their fishing trip.

The study seemed uninterrupted, a room Roy would return to in a moment. Everything was neat and in its proper place: a black-and-purple vesture that hung on a hanger behind the door; the old upholstered brown leather chair, torn in spots but not beaten; and his desk, where a pair of half-moon reading glasses lay next to an open bible. Psalm 23 was the last chapter Roy had read before ending up in the emergency room: *The Lord is my shepherd ....*

Avery ran a hand on the CD player. A shiny disc sat in the compartment. He fitted the headphones over his ears, hit the play button, tilted back in the minister's chair, and with a blinkless stare, he let the melancholy music of violins, oboes, and French horns transport him to the wake he wanted, a funeral he ached for, a burial that would never take place.

Largo—the "Going Home" piece from Dvorák's 9th Symphony—seemed to speak of Roy's life like a biographical documentary. Its instrumental voices filtered into his weary mind, blocking out the sounds of Taffi's coughs, April's sobs, Olympia's screams, Beulah's prayers, Darah's silence.

Upon the last note of dying cellos, eyelids slammed shut, and the man with the perfect posture, folded over in exhausted stupor.

6:56 A.M.
Something bright shined in his face and he grimaced. A flashlight. "Hey, you all right?" It was a woman. Her voice was familiar. Through stitched slits of eyelids, he saw she was dressed in a sheriff's outfit. She asked him whether he had been drinking. It sure felt like it because his head hurt badly and his body was rigid like welded steel. He was told that tumbling out of a wrecked vehicle at night, especially in the middle of a deserted road, could make anyone feel that way.

Now she told him he was under arrest for stealing a casket, but he didn't care. He knew one of Gatlin's officers would catch up with him, and that made him glad. He fell back into the bog he crawled out of and he felt her shake him. "Ave? You all right?"

He jumped with a start from a disoriented state, dragged himself to attention, and forced groggy, stinging eyes open. He had fallen asleep at Roy's desk like a lost driver behind the wheel of a car with no gas, and found he was in a new day with the old pain.

"You locked yourself in here last night," April said, holding a key in her hand. Her voice was still raw. "Breakfast is ready."

Breakfast. What's it mean to eat? he thought. He studied April's empty eyes.

She looked the way he felt: horrible.

7:08 A.M.
In the bathroom mirror, the wild look of a popeyed stranger stared back. The extra growth of stubble that ruled his face like black iron filings, plus deep

lines that ran like scars, altered his appearance. Avery was too despondent to shave, to do anything. Like an illness, lethargy had taken hold of him. It controlled his every move, even the negative way he thought.

Dressed in civilian clothes, he shuffled down to the kitchen, unsuccessful at keeping the wooden steps from creaking, and fully aware he looked different from the snappy military image the Gilchrists had seen the day before. He sat next to his darling Olympia. Fallen shoulders spoke of the loss and of the weight she carried inside.

Beulah started him off with a brisk cup of dark-roast coffee while light conversation brought a weak smile to his face. She had come to understand the man hiding behind sagging features. There were no doubts. He was sure of that now. He had made it plain he didn't want Roy's ashy remains to be thrown into the air at Dugger Creek, or his empty urn to sit over a fireplace for time and eternity. He craved for a distinguished gravestone to lay flowers against. He wanted closure; an open casket so he could touch Roy one last time. He sought for a place to weep out all his sorrow until it either killed him or cured him.

Cocooned in silence, April and Olympia hardly touched their food. Taffi fared no better. In one hand she clung to a balled-up tissue, and in the other, an inhaler, readying herself in case a sudden wave of tears and breathlessness assaulted her.

The women's vacant, sleep-deprived eyes that once mirthfully danced were fixed on objects in front of them; the same things Avery had hardly noticed when the house was filled with laughter: the reflective napkin holder, the glass salt and pepper shakers, the red-and-white checkered cloth that covered the Formica-top table—and the big chair where their father once sat.

"Pia, aren't you hungry?" he asked carefully.

Quiet eyes answered. Everything she ever had was lost in a swift moment: a father, hunger, life.

8:32 A.M.

Beulah parted the thick fall drapes from all the windows and allowed beaming sunlight to cast out the stubborn darkness from every part of the house. Darah still had not come down, and by the way things were shaping up, Avery knew she would not. He had not spoken to her since her outraged assault on him at the hospital, and was certain no words of his, however sincere, could ever douse the furnace of her rage.

By the time 10:00 o'clock rolled around, Avery was ready to leave. He was disheartened by the series of events that led to the still-unwinding ordeal, and wanted to go—now. Why should I stay when the worst is yet to come? he thought.

At the foot of the door, Beulah halted him, shepherding him and the adult girls around the long couch. The yearning in her touch and in her eyes was for the family to remain strong and united, but there was no getting Darah to join in. Not even for a moment. She told him her daughter had decided to make hatred her ally.

"I know y'all don't realize it." Beulah's voice stirred the mournful air. "God was kind to your father. He took him before the cancer had a chance to bite down hard. The good Lord wouldn't allow Roy to suffer in a hospital bed all alone, painfully wasting away for who knows how long. So he quickly took him, sparing him from the agony that was to come."

The tall women took turns embracing their short mother. All they had now were each other, their void, and an uncertain future.

At the door, Avery let Mama wipe his teary face with a soft tissue, just like his real mother had done for him as a boy when he scraped his knees after a running fall. It surprised him he remembered that.

Mama cupped his long, unshaven face in the warm palm of her hand. But his fallen features, heavy from grief, did not respond. He was out the front door a swift moment later, waving a limp goodbye. He shot a glance at the paint-flaked wooden table on the porch where he and Roy played chess.

Checkmate!

It was a memory now. That's all it would ever be.

Another vision put the burly preacher behind the house. Roy wiped greasy hands on a dirty rag and huddled over the engine of his car to solve the problem he had with the ignition as he promised. No doubt the culprit was the distributor cap, or a coil gone bad, and Avery would have fixed it right there himself. But what was the point? he thought. The old, long-bodied Cadillac would still look abandoned.

Darah's Toyota Camry filled his mind with the sound of tires screeching, metal crunching, glass shattering, and a tarp-covered body on a debris-filled road. She was destined to die young and there was no stopping it. Death was ingenious. It had many tentacles it could use to slay its victims.

He examined the family cars closer—Roy's, Taffi's, Beulah's—and was chafed with curiosity when he discovered all the tires were flat. The crushing weight on his shoulders and chest made him feel like an airless tire, too. He walked away, imagining the vehicles were prehistoric turtles lying dead on the sod. Hmmm, Pia would love that. He huffed out a shortened laugh, dry and humorless, but it did nothing to dispel the silent grief that had churned into rage. He got into a rented Chevy Malibu and started the engine. He had reached the end of his journey, and standing on its rocky precipice he realized he could go no farther. He could no longer dream of changing things. Things were changing him.

Wrapped in a dark overcoat, Beulah stepped out past the porch, approached the humming vehicle, and leaned into the open window with eyes on him. The valley air was chilly. The girls crept out behind their mother but stayed at a distance.

"The moment Roy and I laid eyes on you, we loved you," Mama said.

Avery killed the engine, tossing a look at the farmhouse that would soon be sold. With a nod, he mentioned to Mama that the car tires needed air.

From an upstairs window, a peeking woman quickly disappeared behind the dark drapes. He got a glimpse of the grief-etched face and a stabbing thought came to him: Will she hate me forever?

Beulah broke through. "Please don't let another nine years pass before we see you again. I'd like for you to be part of us." She grabbed his face and kissed it. The feel of her thick fingers lingered. "Stay close."

He shot a look at the girls, then at Beulah's cherub-round face. "I … love you, Mama. Always will." The words tumbled out awkwardly, but nonetheless he was satisfied. "Tell … tell Darah I … said g-goodbye."

As his final act he placed a fresh wad of cash in the palm of Beulah's warm hand. She hesitated, and with mouth parted, began counting the crisp notes: all carrying the face of Benjamin Franklin. There were fifty of them. He revved the engine and drove off before she could speak a word.

This time there was no looking back through rearview mirrors; at the memories that reflected in them. He would wonder no more how things would turn out. He had lived through the heartache. Once was enough. Instead he would leave his family, and the memory of Roy, where it belonged—in the past.

'I love you, boy,' said a voice in his head. 'Wish you were my son ….'

"I am your son. Always, forever."

He no longer cared that Reverend Roy Nathan Gilchrist would be cremated later that day.

Chapter 28

Neil Avery dropped a ring of keys into the man's meaty hand: the ones that serviced the elevators, one to his office—room 413—and the big, lead, laboratory key. The lieutenant hated the thought of returning to active duty and wondered whether he would have to learn a new skill to stay in the Navy. "Where's Marcus?"

Dauerman took a sip of steamy coffee and rested the personalized NCIS black mug on his desk. He dumped all the keys, including his, into an open drawer, slammed it shut and locked it. Project Spectrum was officially over and the dreadful thought of it shaped itself around Avery's windpipe until he labored to breathe. Now with the laboratory sealed shut like a bank vault, no one could venture into the dark, underground labyrinth anymore. No one. "Mr. Marcus was no longer interested in working here. That's the reason the program was terminated."

"And the techs?"

"They followed him."

He would need proof. "They'd never leave."

"I have four letters of resignation to prove you wrong." The investigator grabbed four, nine-by-twelve manila envelopes from the top of his desk, waved them in the serviceman's face, and slapped them back down. "They were sick of this place like I'm sick of you. Now get out."

Avery mused on a thought that brought pleasure: One day I'm gonna ram my fist in his face.... He would enjoy the gnawing pain that would come with the blow, shooting through his arm with a bolt. His hand would start to throb, then his knuckles would disappear under swollen flesh and tendons. But satisfaction would dull the ache, especially if he flexed the joints in his fingers after the knockout punch.

"You heard me. Out!"

Avery massaged an uninjured hand, stormed out the office, and shut the heavy door with a bang.

One month. That's how long it had been since the *USS Man Of War* and its strike group were deployed. With no news coming from North Korea, the *USS Ronald Reagan's* flotilla of warships struck for the Yellow Sea, along with the navies of France, Great Britain, Japan and Australia. Avery read in the newspaper that this was how things would stay until two presidents—one Asian, the other, American—came to a decision to end their staring game over a political chessboard.

Aboard the tall LPH, the *USS Capitol Hill*, Avery hustled through busy passageways and over knee-knockers with his mind buzzing to the events that had taken place since the mighty *Seven* sailed over the Pacific's pitching horizon: his amazing journey back through time; his demotion to lieutenant; the arrest of three navymen by NCIS; Marc's abrupt dismissal; and the manner in which Admiral Fumo had averted him.

Avery rapped on a stateroom door with the bottom of his fist over the black stenciled name: J PRATT. There, a pair of Marine MPs flanked him while adrenaline prepped him for fight or flight.

"Who's that?" bellowed a familiar voice.

He switched a duffel bag from one hand to the other. "Avery reporting as ordered."

The fine-grain wood door unlocked and swung open like it had been blown by a hurricane.

Now he faced the tall skipper: head of graying dark hair and eyes peppered with animosity. "Ready to start?" Pratt snatched a nine-by-twelve manila envelope from the lieutenant's hand and fished the transfer papers out, looking them over with quick glances and a frown.

"Captain, permission to speak." He stepped inside Pratt's stateroom. The computer monitor on the desk was dark as a midnight sea. The skipper either had not turned on the system, or it was not functioning again.

"Denied." The senior officer wheeled away with an air of contempt.

Avery hoped he was wrong about the CO hacking into a naval network security site. But he wasn't too sure. "What's your problem?" he snapped.

Pratt spun with eyes that pounced. "It's standing in my quarters. Close the hatch."

Several khakis went by in the p-way and he closed the door, hoping this would not be another confrontation with the skipper. "So why am I aboard? Why sign those orders?"

The captain scribbled his signature on the forms and slapped the pen on his desk. The vibration deactivated the monitor's screensaver and the computer whirred to life. "If you must know, as a favor to Tex."

"What's Fumo got to do—?"

"To keep you from more trouble." Pratt broke eye contact, studied the collar of the young officer's khakis, and let out a breath of disdain laughter. "Got demoted. What did you do to piss Tex?"

Avery turned stone-face silent, eyes batting like spotlight blinkers.

"I'd be careful if I were you," the captain warned. "Heard NCIS have their eye on the admiral. Soon they'll be bringing him in."

He burned a stare into Pratt. Avery had no success in reporting his suspicion to the admiral. But suspicions were not facts and he was left with egg on his face. What he needed to do was report the skipper to Dauerman and let him handle it. "They're hounding the wrong man."

"Really? You're that sure it's not him?" Pratt waited until the uneasy silence between them passed. A message began to take shape on the computer screen: line after line; paragraph after paragraph. Message Traffic was texting information to the skipper. "Seaman Jordan will show you to your quarters. Get out of my face."

"Jordan? Captain, did you say Jordan? James Jordan?"

"Are you deaf, Lieutenant?" He pulled the door open and looked into the passageway. "Jordan, where the hell are you?"

In a flash, a tall, thin, young black sailor, in two-tone blue dungarees, rounded the corner of the p-way on hurried boon dockers to Pratt's stateroom. His ballcap had the silver silhouette of the landing platform ship, along with it's name and hull designation: *USS Capitol Hill.* LPH 21.

Upon laying eyes on each other, both men's jaws dropped open an inch.

"Caliber!"

"Slim! I thought—?"

"Get a move on, Lieutenant," Pratt ordered. "You're wanted in the dirty boiler room." He let out a humorless laugh.

Jordan escorted Avery to level three aft. B-town: Junior officers' section of the ship. By the time they reached the lieutenant's assigned quarters through the long passageways and down ladderwells, Jordan told him how he ended up back at North Island.

"Tuberculosis?"

The seaman coughed into the crook of his elbow for a moment. "Someone in berthing had it bad and I was exposed. My arm ballooned at the PPD site, but the chronic cough I have is the result of something else. A viral thing in the respiratory tract. Still gotta take meds, though."

Avery tossed the big duffel onto his rack, flipped his cover onto a fold-down desk, and began to change into his work clothes. He was used to having better accommodations aboard the *Seven*. Life was good there. Now this was his home.

Jordan told him he had spent the worst two weeks of his life quarantined at a military hospital in Pearl, then sent back to North Island to recupe. Simply put, that meant he would be recycled to CVNX-7 as soon as the medications had done their job and he was fit for action. "And all this time I thought you were kicking butt." A dark thought weighed on him: Nieve, Valentine, Davis, and the faces of dedicated men from the fleet. Who will die if a war starts? he wondered.

Jordan said, "Bad stuff going down everywhere. Including here."

Avery had forgotten what normal Navy life was like. "What've you heard?"

"Jarvis .…. Some, including me, think—"

"I know what some think. That he's behind it all. But that's absurd."

"Hey, Jarvis is the perfect busboy for the admiral. All he has to do is clean up the dirty table and make it presentable for the next customer. Like no one had ever used it."

Avery considered it, but an accusation like that would have to be proved. If someone had seen the admiral do something, news of it would spread like advancing cancer in a baby's lungs. Like Captain Jarvis, a man like Fumo had plenty to lose. He held a flag rank and was CO of North Island. Regardless of who it was, Black Sunday had not been done alone. Avery had a longstanding theory he had nursed to the point where it robbed him of sleep; the troubling thought hatching the moment Nieve told him that Jordan was spending too much time locked away in the electronics shop—alone with computers. Whoever else was involved, Black Sunday's main culprits had to be someone below flag rank, and someone from the Navy's lower echelon to help cover it up. Someone like—

"Okay, Columbo," Jordan said. "Who do you think the head honcho is?"

The investigation was taking long. Too long. Many said NCIS were sitting back, picking their noses. Now there was talk of certain naval officers about to take matters into their hands by launching their own private investigation. But who would dare and how would it be done? Avery gave Jordan a hard look. "Our Captain Bligh—and a certain seaman."

"You're full of crap. And stop looking at me like that. I'm telling you it's Jarvis and—"

"You're nuts. Fumo's getting ready to kick up his heels. He wouldn't pull an asinine stunt like this. Besides, he and that jerk agent are like two cups in a bra."

Jordan leaned in. "That's not what I heard."

Avery was cactus-pricked curious. The seaman seemed to know something. I have been away for a while, he thought.

Jordan told him that Dauerman showed up unannounced at the admiral's office the other day, wanting to question him. When Fumo refused to be brought in, the investigator grabbed a Navy briefcase and forced it open. The admiral blew a gasket and threw the agent out. But not before some rough-parting words. Now there was scuttlebutt that Captain Jason Elser of the *USS Trojan Horse*, and the *Hill's* new Air Boss, Frank Jarvis, were trying to get Dauerman reassigned. The ulcer prone Elser started to sweat piss when Dauerman went to pay him a visit. But the watch officer pulled a gun on the agent; pointblank. Close enough for him to smell the lubricant. He told Dauerman to shove off or he would blow his brains out. The OOW was under Elser's orders. No one wanted NCIS snooping around, asking questions.

Avery wanted his head to stop spinning. Jordan wouldn't let it. "Ask anyone and they'll tell you this: Elser and Tex have been out dancing late at night. And don't let that innocent look on Jeff Miles fool you. Our XO knows something. I say, that big cat Dauerman is sniffing out some fat rats and is closing in on them. Maybe that's why Tex, Elser, and Miles skipped town last week at the last daring minute on some so-called meeting of Navy bigwigs at Norfolk. You can run but you can't hide—so the proverb goes. Mark my word, Caliber. Before this week's over another arrest will be made. NCIS can't be shooed away for long and Dauerman's no chump."

Avery straightened the silver-barred collar of his work khakis, buttoned the blouse from top to bottom, and rose to his feet. "Sorry to cut you off, but duty calls."

"Hey, how come you're a JO now?"

"Promotions are hard to come by in today's Navy."

"So's a straight answer. When did you get demoted?"

Avery paused to think it over. "Soon as I check on the pit snipes in the hold, I'll tell you."

In the enlisted mess hall, Avery and Jordan pushed their empty aluminum trays up a cafeteria-style line. Today they would have their choice of meatloaf, stewed chicken or salmon, along with baked potatoes, brown rice, or carrots and green beans cooked in olive oil.

Jordan and a female galley seaman looked at each other and traded smiles.

"Hi, Slim Jim," she said.

Avery cocked an eyebrow. "Holding out on me?"

Jordan introduced him to the doe-eyed, nineteen-year-old black sailor named Cecilia Rice. "Met her two days ago…." He said her fast hands and love for food landed her a job with the Navy, and aside from being the newest members of the *USS Capitol Hill*, they both had a lot in common.

"Welcome aboard, Seaman."

"Thank you, sir."

Sailors in line behind them jumped ahead where other galley workers served them.

"Ceci here wants to make big someday. Culinary specialist."

"Come from a long line of cooks?" Avery asked her.

"Yes, sir. My father, grandfather, and great-grandfather."

"Ceci also has a friend at our weps lab. Trades good recipes to learn about handguns and rifles."

"My grandfather was a hunter," she said with smiling eyes. "Left all his game rifles to me before he died. I learned a lot from him. Including fixing up a mean dinner, like pheasant and venison. Perhaps one day I can prepare something special for the Lieutenant."

"I'd like that. How about you—Slim Jim?"

He and Jordan grabbed their orders and sat in a corner of the spacious mess hall.

"What do you think, Caliber?" Jordan looked back to find her smile.

"She'll probably make galley captain someday."

"No, I mean … you think I'm her type?"

Avery forked a chunk of baked potato and brought it to his mouth. "I think that venison was meant for you."

The two men conversed for a long time. But when Avery told him of his demotion, Spectrum's time machine, and the underground facility it was housed in, it kept the seaman from finishing his lunch.

A crisp, November breeze swept the deck from across the rolling Pacific; calm as the errant seagulls flying high above the ship's towering radars. Lieutenant Avery and Admiral Tom Fumo were at the forecastle where they conferred with a trio of BTs over the state of the ship's oil-fired boilers, all of them pissing superheated water through weld cracks, which resulted in flooded spaces. If the problem could not be fixed, the ship would need to be refitted with a new steam system. Since the *Capitol Hill* was a conventional ship, she relied on these boilers to serve the turbines for propulsion, power for the lights, water for the galleys and heads. If the *Hill* had a nuclear reactor, Avery thought, this would not have happened.

A dungaree-dressed female sailor ran across the deck with urgent speed and approached Fumo. It was Rice.

"Admiral, sir," Cecilia interrupted. "There's trouble below."

Fumo looked relieved he was being summoned. "Lead the way, sailor."

The admiral charged past the troop and headed below, barreling through a tight-packed crowd of enlisteds like a mad bull bolting from its holding pen. Tailing close behind was Avery, Jeff Miles, and a band of gun-toting, master-at-arms personnel. The moment did not allow anyone to snap to attention before their admiral. The tense air was to blame.

Violence rocked a cabin, shouts of profanity followed, and a moment later the cabin's fine-grain wooden door flew open. All at once everything became quiet. A strange unsettling kind of quiet.

In the murmuring crowd, latecomers craned their necks over men and women competing for a better look.

"Make a hole!" the admiral shouted. But no one moved. It was Grand Central Station during rush hour.

First to emerge through the cabin's doorway was a grim-looking man lugging a Navy briefcase. An authorized ID reflected light from the overhead.

Fumo locked eyes with him. "How the hell am I supposed to know you're conducting an investigation on my vessel if I'm not informed?"

"First of all, this isn't your ship. And second, I don't need your permission to make an arrest."

Avery stuck his head through the open door. The admiral moved past him and entered the cabin. A blizzard of papers carpeted the floor, a chair was turned over, and the rack had been stripped bare to the rubber mattress skin, sheets and pillows all thrown over the miniature metal sink. "What the hell?" He wheeled around and exited like he was going to the head.

Within the visibly-disturbed quarters, a disheveled man sat slumped on a settee: wrists conjoined in silver restraints and ankles clamped in long-chained cuffs.

"I want an explanation." Fumo and Dauerman stood toe-to-toe like two titans, each battling for supremacy.

"He resisted arrest then attacked me. I am trained to defend myself, Admiral."

Fumo grunted an order to the MAAs. "Get this p-way cleared."

They blocked the cabin entrance with their bodies and shouted the *make-a-hole* order to every sailor fore and aft. But the men and women would not move until the information they sought for came. Avery supplied it with a satisfied grin.

It didn't take long for the volume of noise to fall. And when it rose again, the news was carried to a host of itching ears:

"Pratt's been arrested. He's the hacker. Pass it on."

"Pratt's been arrested. He's the hacker. Pass it on."

Droning voices prompted Dauerman to reenter the stateroom and hoist the slumped captain to his feet and out in plain view. Only now did the senior officer's face show signs of bruised swelling from hammered knuckles that had connected against square cheeks while all Dauerman had to show for his struggle was dotted perspiration on his forehead.

Female sailors applauded the charismatic charms of the tall man dressed in the fine-tailored, three-piece vested suit.

"Our hero," hailed Cecilia Rice. She incited those behind her to join in.

The uniformed women cheered and whistled in unison.

"Make a hole," Dauerman ordered. A path was cleared for him and the prisoner squeezed through with a teetering shuffle.

Avery had not seen a gait like that since his early days as an ensign on liberty in Genoa, Italy, where a pair of strong-armed shore policemen hoisted a drunk buddy of his to his feet and escorted him back to his assigned ship.

Pratt turned puffed eyes upon himself and taunts from the ship's crew rang out. The huge crowd had peeled away in an endless single file, and now, with Dauerman's triumphant walk behind a shackled Pratt, the slow march to infamy began, one step at a time.

Fat leg chains rattled against the steel deck, and while all hands snapped to attention, Avery refused to do so. Behind him, someone in the crowd wept and sobbed. The senior officer of the *USS Capitol Hill*, the commander of the ship, was a prisoner. Gleaming pride no longer ruled his face, for a cocky stride was now a beaten man's gait. The former fighter pilot, a decorated war hero, was no more. His thirty-year Navy status had been reduced from that of a four-striper to a busted midshipman; a trudging spectacle for all to see. Now, inching past each of the ship's crew—men and women that had saluted him, feared him, hated him—there would be no more gestures of honor to be given.

Three young sailors pushed in front of Avery as Pratt began to pass their way.

"Schmuck!"

"Deep-six him!"

"Go to hell, bastard!"

At the quarterdeck, Dauerman halted the prisoner as a stray seagull cried in the sky overhead. Pratt raised cuffed wrists and swiped an enlarged bloody nose that dripped like motor oil, staining his khakis and oxfords. When he lifted his eyes, he broke the dark, coagulated seal that caked his lips and looked around as though he wanted to make some sort of speech. "Having the command of this ship was one of the damn proudest moments of my life." He sounded like a wad of gauze had been stuffed into his mouth. "But to my shame I threw it away. I regret what I did and admit my guilt for damage done to the U.S. Navy, our government, and national security."

Avery stood rigid in a swarm of disturbed servicemen, refusing to blink. Jordan stood at his shoulder.

Pratt seemed to look for an oasis in dark, stabbing eyes, and by chance, locked in on one with a red-eyed grip. The young officer studied the captain's battered face and disjointed jaw for the first time until it paralyzed him with fear.

Pratt shuffled toward him and raised cuffed hands. He pointed to the military decorations set over the left breast pocket of the man's uniform, aiming at one in particular: the tri-colored, Navy-Marine Corps ribbon bar.

A swollen eye rolled to him; the other was shut as though pounded by a heavyweight boxer. "Neil, my good friend." The captain flinched in pain when a blast of sea-salted air blew on an open wound above his brow. "We've known each other so long."

Dauerman nudged Pratt hard from behind with the confiscated briefcase and urged him to start down the brow. Whatever secrets were stashed inside that briefcase now belonged to NCIS.

The beaten captain turned aside and ejected a thick glob of blood spit. He laid cuffed hands on Avery's shoulder. "The day I pinned that bar on you was a proud moment for me, too."

Captain Pratt was taken off the ship and hustled into a waiting Buick LeSabre. With the luxury vehicle's doors now shut, the big, unmarked car sped away as Avery and a wall of servicemen and women watched from the vessel's roof.

Several hours later it was reported that Pratt was washed up and given a change of clothing—civilian. He was brought to San Diego's International Airport, escorted into a private jet by four armed federal agents, and flown to an undisclosed destination.

Chapter 29

Dauerman moved in on nine more servicemen an hour later and arrested them on computer-hacking charges: all of them young men, all of them whitened with fear, all of them accusing Pratt, naming him the leader in the cyber-theft ring. The news was announced throughout the *Hill* over the 1MC, and as soon as Avery heard it, he was surprised to learn that those who sided with the ousted captain were outnumbered by the ranks of men and women who had taken a liking to the officer they hoped would be his replacement—he himself. Avery mulled it over. Being skipper could restore loyalties among shipmates, but that wasn't enough.

Fumo approached Avery as he was about to enter his quarters. The Texan seemed hesitant about something. Their eyes met, and for a moment, the gray, windowless compartment felt like a tomb to the lieutenant.

"I need you to be the *Cap's* acting CO."

He felt uncomfortable with the request and sat on his rack to think it over. But there was nothing to think about. The admiral wanted a yes answer. "You know I'm not command qualified."

"You're not qualified to fly either, but that didn't stop you, so don't tell me what I can and can't do."

Avery realized there was only one way of dealing with the testy Old Man. "I'll take the job if the Admiral answers a simple question."

"Sound off."

"Do you have a personal beef against me, sir?"

"What makes you think—?"

"You've been avoiding me like a dead skunk since removing my shoulderboards. This would be a good time to clear the air."

"Lieutenant …." The admiral sat in Avery's chair with arms folded over the backing. His falcon stare was a deep, dark well. "I never avoid my men. But what's happened here these last few months has taken a tremendous toll on me. I should've left the fleet before seeing days like this."

"Sir, you demoted me for a reason. Was it personal? Because of Karyn?"

"I don't wield my Academy sword in acts of vengeance."

"Sir, just answer the question."

Fumo absentmindedly toyed with the blue, zircon-crested 10K white gold band he wore as though wanting to remove it from his long, rugged finger. Nothing could cause a naval officer to remove his Academy ring. Nothing except shame over something done. The admiral broke free of the distracted thought and said, "Karyn's doing well. Moving on. She loved you. But that's not the reason. Shank tells me you've been acting like an ass. Until you prove yourself worthy of being a commissioned officer in the United States Navy, maybe then I'll reinstate you."

"Then why hand me the command of this ship? What's wrong with the exec? The Combat officer? The senior lieutenants?"

Fumo huffed out a grunt. "I don't know them."

"You mean, you don't trust them farther than you can throw them." Avery aggravated him like a matador flapping a red cape at a bull. It showed.

"There've been too many arrests, Lieutenant. My hands are tied. I'm short of men and patience. Our fleet has more than twenty of its ships in the Sea of Japan, with another CVSG awaiting deployment to keep things from stirring in Korea. Now if you'll excuse me." He rose to his feet, tall and threatening.

"Begging the Admiral's pardon …."

"What now?"

"What do you keep stashed in your briefcase?"

"Dammit, Lieutenant, that's enough!"

Fumo rushed out of Avery's quarters the same way he entered—in a foul mood—and twenty minutes later, the lieutenant did the same. Making no mention to anyone why he was leaving the ship, or where he was going.

In an abandoned laboratory, a sole individual checked the zero-marked gauges of the PSI pressure instruments and gas-handling systems before he moved to the control station where he tossed a navy garrison cap. A chair, with Marc's lab coat draped over it, had been pulled away from the dark-eyed consoles, exactly as he had last seen it on the day a blue swirl of microscopic atoms and cells came together into a human form. His own form.

Avery had come upon the white coat and discovered a Quartz watch and ring of keys within its deep pockets—keys to the elevators, the transport lab, and room 411.

Tracing the doctor's possible steps was not as easy as he thought it would be. The young officer had snooped throughout the entire chamber, looking for clues, and just when the thought of giving up came to him, he found the crushed remains of an ash-black, gold-filtered cigarette. He dismissed it and moved on. He wondered why the particle accelerator, the liquid nitrogen tanks, and the Vector Supercomputer were left activated. Marc must've been in a hurry when he called it quits, he thought.

He pushed aside the coat-draped chair and snatched his garrison cap in one swift motion. He was scheduled to retrain BTs on the ship's sophisticated new boilers and would need to head back now.

Something stuck into the sole of his shoe. He checked it, planted his foot down and felt it again. Whatever it was came loose when he poked at it with a finger. What's this? he thought. He gave the chipped piece of something his full attention, turning it over in the palm of his hand.

Prompted by the find, he searched under the control station's network of tables and found another one just like it. The black object with a tiny strand of dark thread attached to it appeared to have been stepped on.

He donned the foldable navy cap. Now he had two things to figure out: Marc's resignation, and the secret the broken button held. He buried what he hoped was evidence deep in his trouser pocket, taking the thirty measured steps to the halogen panel where he slammed off the lights.

Suddenly he shuddered. It wasn't because of the dark. The florescent gleam of minerals in the rock cave offered him some light. It was a thought that came to him. Something Marcus once told him that gripped him with childlike fear.

He slammed the tuning-fork-shaped power lever to the on position, the circuits hummed, and the big lights came on again in a blinding crescendo. He wondered why he didn't think of it at first. The system would answer his question if he could remember what it was called.

Yes, that's it!

He rushed to the control station and realized the quantum computer was also running. A tiny indicator light winking at him from an obscure corner, confirmed it. He was right. Someone other than he had used the cylinder after the project was scrubbed. But who? he wondered.

He hit a button on the keyboard.

Within seconds, the dark monitor came to life and the lab's hydraulic system whirred. Without typing in a command, the negatron's transparent tube began to lift. As much as he wanted to run away, the urge to solve a mystery was greater.

He placed a chair under the descending canopy and stepped back. The man-size tube locked into the O-ring platform and the bright halogen lamps above him powered down, darkening the lab. A mechanical groan emanated from somewhere and an eye-shielding white flash shrunk his pupils tight, painting the lab in its intense afterglow. Burning spots clouded his vision with patches of bright colors, and when he could see enough through the fading glaucoma, the particle accelerator's lights had changed from blood-red to lily-white. There was no sense playing detective in a creepy place any longer, so he shut down every piece of equipment, having no desire to return—ever.

Avery's prying led him to HQ's fourth floor. He had to be alert if he wanted to avoid getting caught, so he went about like he always had. So far, no one had seen or followed him.

When he attempted to enter his office, he discovered the lock had been changed. He unbuttoned his uniform, breathed deep, and clenched the ring of keys into his fist as a pair of JGs walked past him to the elevators.

He waited an anxious minute.

Now a slow hand grabbed another oval-shaped brass knob.

Locked.

Dauerman always kept his office secured, and the pen trick wouldn't work this time. Not on these doors. All the locks' cylinders had no pressure pins. They operated on a system of computer-controlled magnets. What he needed was the key.

He turned on his heels and leaned against the wall, hoping to collect his thoughts. There was nothing more troubling than a blank mind. Nothing more perplexing than a room number, 411, and the name, Marcus J. Weinberg, which still appeared on the door.

He looked for the key on the ring and found it. He slid it into the lock and with an easy turn of the knob the mahogany door unbolted with a snap.

One by one, he opened Marc's desk drawers, adrenaline surging through riffling hands in hot bursts. Ever since Spectrum, the world around him was out of the ordinary, and that was the very thing he hoped to find. Anything that would speak to him.

In the last drawer, he came across a journal and flipped through its pages. Everything written was legible, concise, and in chronological order. The sketches of the time machine, including all the experiment results and statistics, brought him back to that first day when he set eyes upon that monstrous contraption. Marcus wrote how he dreamt of the day his fear would subside so he could enter the tube and be as the naval officer: a conqueror of modern technology.

He read the last section of the journal and learned Marcus had been hired by a secretive corporation many years ago after a lengthy private interview by their top CEO. He joined an exclusive club of scientists, the best the country had, and right away, got down to business: creating a spectacular machine.

This is what Marcus labored toward, what he was born for. It was all carefully written down; every line on every page shouted with triumph: *If only the great Albert Einstein were alive to see my work*, he noted. *How proud he would be ....*

What he read proved Marcus loved what he did.

He didn't just resign, Avery thought. He was forced to resign.

He closed the hard-covered journal and searched on, fishing several scientific textbooks out of a file cabinet. There at the bottom he saw it. It was made by *Locksmith Magnetics*, and had a number—412. It belonged to the office across the hall.

His breathing became ragged when he drove the grooveless, silver-colored key through the lip of the cylinder and unsnapped the deadbolt. Then, everything seemed to have stalled for a moment: his breathing, his heartbeat. He went for his wrist and felt the gentle throbbing as he sucked in and puffed out air like a pregnant woman in a Lamaze class. When he was ready he pushed his way in.

On a black, red-trimmed ink blotter, smiling faces stared at him from picture frames that crowned the oak desk. Wife and daughters, he thought. A fresh roll of Tums stripped open, and a smoldering, gold-filtered cigarette in a grimy ashtray lay side by side.

Avery pulled on the drawers. They were locked. His foot touched a cardboard box pushed under the desk and he lifted it out. He opened it, rummaged through a stack of papers, and found a batch of confidential file folders. He flipped through the first few, one by one: *J. Pratt, R. Hobbs, G. Evans, O. Rivera, P. Yancey, W. Lee, N. Avery ....*

He tried to breathe but it seemed he had no lungs.

The grave silence gave way to talking and approaching footsteps.

His mind raced with one thought: had someone been watching all along, waiting for him to make a move?

A loud knock on the door produced another chilling thought: Did I lock it? He couldn't remember. Everything he did, he did fast.

His chest kicked, and when Dauerman's name was called, his face burned and hot perspiration bled through his scalp. The knob rattled, but the men, whoever they were, left quicker than they came.

Gotta move fast, he thought.

He opened and closed file-cabinet drawers in rapid succession until something caught his eye: a perfectly designed gold button with an embossed anchor at the center. It was from someone's service jacket. He wondered how it got there.

He sank the object into the top pocket of his khaki and opened the last drawer. Under a ton of paperwork he discovered a fully-loaded ammo clip. Though he couldn't find the weapon, he settled for something less. He extracted two, brass, flat-point rounds from the long magazine and made a fast-footed exit, blowing past a chiseled gunnery sergeant rushing toward him in the hall.

The down elevator chimed at the same time an up elevator arrived. Its polished, stainless-steel doors opened, and Dauerman, along with two NCIS agents dressed in sand-colored Docker slacks and maroon polo shirts, stepped out.

Avery hurled himself into the empty elevator car with a surge of adrenaline and the doors slid closed behind him. A thought came to him during the descent. It stayed with him when he rushed out the elevator at the lobby and gnawed at him as he exited the building. Did they spot me?

Avery found Brian Mayo relieving James Jordan at his watch station on the *Hill's* bridge. With calm discretion he approached and handed the tall sailor an unspent round from the weapon he was hoping to find.

"Get a hold of Seaman Rice and have her friend run that through ballistics."

"What's this about?" Jordan held the slug between thumb and forefinger. Held it up like a front tooth had fallen out.

"I'll explain later."

"No, explain now."

"Slim, I promise never to bother you after this. I just need to know where that was manufactured." He had given the base of the casing a keen look in Dauerman's office and decided it would take a professional to interpret the engraved serial code on it.

"Let one of the gunner's mates do it," Jordan said. "Better yet, the armory chief."

"Too many eyes. This is on the sly."

"So why put me on the spot?"

"Because you and Rice have hit it off. You said she knows someone at the gun lab."

Jordan studied the projectile's ammo code. He was clueless also. "Fat slug. I'd hate to get hit with one of these." He dropped it in his top pocket. "Okay, I'll talk to her. She can keep a hatch dogged. Anything else?"

Avery had approached the whole thing without a definite plan of action. He was lucky Dauerman had not walked in on him while he was digging for clues in the agent's office. For a military officer, the crime of breaking and entering was punishable by court-martial. For him, it might have spelled imprisonment. "I need a real detective."

Jordan twisted his face with puzzlement, adjusting his ship's ballcap.

The copycat-criminologist navyman wanted to spill his guts. "Let's go to my quarters."

Jordan entered the cabin first and the lieutenant closed the door behind him.

"What's up, Caliber?"

Avery dropped to a sit on his rack, wondering whether or not Jordan would get it.

The seaman looked impatient. "Ever since the cap'n got his sorry ass dragged away, you've been acting wired."

"I've had a mind to do some serious investigating."

"Meaning?"

Avery summed it up with one name. "Pratt."

"So you lost your homeboy. Big deal."

"Jake and I weren't friends."

Jordan gave him a look Nieve once had. Pratt was an old, army boot. Hard and unforgiving. "Welcome to the club."

"Slim, he never pinned this bar on me." He shot up and pointed to it.

"So where—?"

"I got this at Norfolk, as a jaygee during my tour on the *Polaris*."

"What're you saying?"

Avery could not, nor would he ever forget Jacob Pratt's frightened face. That battered, bloody face. That swollen, empty eye fixed strangely on him. He had rehearsed Pratt's message over and over and was certain it had a hidden meaning. "Jake was trying to tell me something. Something only I would understand."

"Like what?"

"He was never involved," he blurted. "That's what he was telling me. He's not the Black-Sunday hacker. They've got the wrong man. He wants me to help him, Slim."

Jordan reeled like he was sucker punched. "Whoa, back up. This is nuts!"

"There is a way to find out if I'm right."

"How?" Jordan snapped.

"By getting into the database for ourselves."

"Hold up. How did *you* become *we*?"

Avery came up with a lightning-bolt plan even before he had it mapped out. "Because you're volunteering to help me."

"Like hell. Things aren't like before. Every frigging day the password changes. You gotta get authorization from Tex to peek into someone else's file."

Avery's face dropped. "Since when?"

The answer came fast. "Since Black Sunday," interrupted Fumo.

The lieutenant spun into the admiral's stormy features. What had he heard? he wondered. What would he do with what he heard?

"Forgive me for barging in, but I couldn't help overhearing your plot."

"You mean eavesdropping. You followed us, didn't you, Admiral?"

"Never mind what I did." Jordan went mute. "So what's this about accessing files behind my back?" Fumo glared at both men.

The lieutenant wanted to keep the seaman out of it. "Sir, call me crazy, but I have reason to believe Pratt is innocent."

"Is that a fact?" The admiral wasn't amused. It showed on his face. He crossed a pair of long arms over his big chest. "Since when did you become a gumshoe?"

"Sir, I'm serious."

"So am I," he countered. "NCIS have this damn thing wrapped up and I'm glad as hell."

"What if I can prove it?" He gave the seaman a quick look.

Jordan's eyes darted back and forth from him to Fumo.

"You already have." The admiral cocked those unruly eyebrows. "You sealed his conviction when he fessed to the crime."

Avery went stone-silent. His one-man sleeping quarters was as quiet as the electronics shop he walked into on the day he hauled Pratt's unit onto his shoulder. He had to admit it was a bold move. He had no reason to suspect the skipper was up to no good, but the computer Seaman Mayo brought in had cast a shadow that piqued his interest. Now he began to see he was contradicting himself. He *had* caught Pratt red-handed and he couldn't deny it. Unless the admiral interrupted him, he would sound like a fool for what he wanted to say next. "Sir, hear me out—"

"You can forget about getting into the system. I'm the only one with the password."

"Sir, I'm certain I can clear his name if you'll—"

"Flush the crap. Shank showed me what Pratt carried in his briefcase. Copies of the Navy's Project Black Files. Instructions on how to retrofit our Trident E-5s into any submarine in the world. This case is closed, Lieutenant."

"Then I'll have to reopen it. You leave me no choice … sir."

"I'm warning you, Lieutenant ...." Fumo pushed his hard face at the young officer. Their noses almost touched. "Don't give me an ultimatum and don't get in my crosshairs." He turned his back on the two men and slammed the door as he left. He belched a stream of curses through the p-way.

Jordan shot to the door, cracked it open, and waited.

The lieutenant discovered an unfamiliar look in the young, grimfaced sailor.

"Okay, you heard Tex. Case closed. It's outta our hands."

"Maybe yours but not mine. With the right plan, and a whiz kid, we can hack—"

"Hack? Are you outta your frigging mind?" He held up a thumb and forefinger like a pair of open pliers. "I'm this close to getting a crow on my sleeve—and you want me to do what?"

"I'm not asking, I'm ordering."

"Hell no, I won't do it!"

"Slim, if you go down, I'll go with you."

"No you won't. I'll be in the brig and you'll be feeding me bread and water."

He couldn't be coaxed, tricked, urged, forced. Nothing would work.

Jordan shuffled around the compartment like he was incarcerated. "I used to obsess over becoming an officer. My dream just took flight like a frightened bird."

"You, scared? You've got more backbone than—"

"Look, what makes you think I wanna help Pratt?" He jerked his ballcap off his head and threw it at his feet. "What makes you think I care?"

"Let me put it this way." Avery body-blocked Jordan to keep him from pacing. "What if that were you in Jake's oxfords? How do you know Dauerman won't come after the whiz kid next?"

"The bum deserves it."

He would have to drag out the same words for effect: "What—if—that—were—you?"

Jordan breathed quicker. "Do you want me to drag the Old Man back in here by the balls? What's it to you that Pratt's innocent? It's over with!"

The lieutenant dropped Jordan to a sit with one of his stares. He grabbed the back of the chair against his chest and squirmed.

"Got something up your six?"

Jordan gave him a sharp look. "Yeah, you! Big cat had me cornered." He told him when it happened and where it took place. "He's looking forward to doing business with me again."

"I'm surprised Shank didn't take you in on the spot."

"Look, I don't know the first damn thing about hacking," he told Avery. "So, tough nuts."

"Heard about your illegal tournament. How did you get those computers to behave like that?"

The seaman rubbed his face with long-fingered hands, but the worry was still there. He raised dark eyes. "What if I get caught, court-martialed, shot like a dog?" Avery had never heard him speak so fast. "I say it's over with."

Avery rebutted: "This could be the beginning. If Dauerman committed an error in judgment, I'll need to do something about it, Slim."

"Why, to get another stupid medal? So Rags can pat you on the back?"

He looked at the sailor without blinking. "It's called Navy pride. It's what I've lived for these past twenty years." He pushed hands into his pockets and paced to the plan stewing in his brain.

In the loud silence, Jordan jumped to his feet. "Why the hell do you want me involved?"

"Do you know what it would mean if the stolen Black Files could be traced and retrieved? Our nation would be out of grave danger." He studied the tension on the seaman's scowling face. Their friendship had been pushed to the edge of a towering precipice; a precipice that even now was crumbling beneath their feet.

Jordan's eyes flashed in the lieutenant's. "Know what guilt tastes like? Spiked sour milk!"

"Slim, this won't be a crime. Consider it an act of justice. Stop pissing on yourself."

"What's the penalty for grabbing a junior officer by the collar and shoving him against the bulkhead?"

He would have to make it sound worse than it would actually be to knock some sense into the sailor. "Captain's mast, followed by a nasty administrative sep—and court-martial. Let's not forget imprisonment with a bunch of foul-smelling inmates. Throw in some solitary confinement in a rats' den, too."

"Then I'll locate Fumo and let nature take its course." Jordan rushed to the door and opened it, about to make good on his threat.

"Where the hell you going?" Avery called.

The seaman froze, offering the back of his tall frame in hardened silence. If he left now and caught up with Fumo, the admiral would no doubt call on the chief master-at-arms and have Avery put in the brig. Then that uncommon camaraderie between sailor and officer would be over.

"Don't walk out on me, Slim. I need you."

Jordan spun at him with a sharpened look. When was the last time he offered his division officer a salute? Called him sir? Avery wondered whether the E-3 was losing respect for him. The seaman said, "The last nine men arrested all pointed a dick finger at the cap'n. What're you trying to prove? That you can outwit a crime-solving investigator?"

"The more you entertain the thought of turning me in, the more nerve you'll lose to actually do it." Avery hoped his theory was right. If the seaman did what he threatened to do, he would be sanding a rough piece of wood against the grain. Their friendship, he realized, had never been tested. Not once—until now.

Jordan closed the cabin door and faced the lieutenant. "Hack, huh?" Avery could tell he chewed on the thought like a leathery piece of steak. After a long moment the seaman said, "Okay, but we do this my way or no way—by cell phone."

"Takes two to tango."

"I'm not laying my ham hock on a chopping block!"

Avery stared into the steel bulkhead as though he could see through it while half-formed plans tumbled in his head. "You've put me in a tough spot." He wondered how long it would take for the clever seaman to train him to do what he knew about computers. "Alright, I go at it alone. Just guide me step by step."

Jordan looked relieved he was dismissed from actually participating in the task.

The lieutenant hated the feeling of abandonment, but would wait for the quiet seaman to give him a clear sign so he could proceed.

"How will you tackle your crazy scheme?" Jordan finally said.

"First things first. I'll need to know what kind of weapon that round's from. Then we'll take it from there."

"I hate it when you say *we*." He scooped the ballcap from the deck and put it on, getting ready to leave. "What do you expect a lousy slug to prove?"

The way things had gone for him lately he couldn't prove anything. "Don't know," he told Jordan. "Just following a gut hunch."

Avery met Jordan emerging from his eight-man berthing compartment on his way to chow. It had been a long week. They grabbed a corner table at the enlisted mess hall, had sliders and fries for lunch, and talked for a long time.

When the two men blotted their mouths and pushed themselves away from the table, Jordan told him he had a better theoretical understanding about Black Sunday, Pratt's arrest, the NCIS investigation, and Avery's course of action. Now, the eager seaman traded in the cell-phone scheme to help out in person—under one condition ....

A reluctant Avery agreed.

The clever seaman tinkered with the lieutenant's cabin computer. "Whatever we do is gotta be done outside this ship."

"How good are you at altering information from within the system?"

"Depends. Why?"

"You'll be walking into HQ." Avery's shrewd plan had the potential of putting Jordan in a deep hole if he was caught. But it was the only way he could be assured the seaman would be there, working at his side.

"There'll be hell to pay if this asinine scheme of yours doesn't work."

"Slim, stop worrying. I'll make it up to you someday."

"I don't want your counterfeit promises." He gave the officer a calloused stare. "Let's just get this crap over with."

"Okay. We'll start the day after tomorrow. That'll give me time to think things through while you take care of your end." The lieutenant sized-up the seaman with one look, taking measurements of his arms, legs, shoulders, waist.

"Man, I hope Tex doesn't catch me. He'll skin my black butt on the spot."

"If you run into him, just salute and keep going. Chances are he won't notice."

"Are you nuts? Old falcon-eye himself?" Jordan took in a ragged breath and huffed it out. The next few days would be tense. "Oh, by the way, that slug? Turns out it's from a military handgun—Russian!"

"Russian? You sure?"

"Got the report."

Jordan fished the document from the pocket of his work uniform, unfolded it, and flashed it before Avery's scrutinizing eyes: *One 46P3/212-10 type Brass Flat Point weighing 11.7 grams was examined by certified FFB on ....*

"Ballistics claim the weapon was manufactured over there. They also claim there's no such thing as an A-forty-six Barrington."

"I can read, Slim." He skimmed over the rest of the document with the blue USN logo on it. *Range: 1200 feet per second....* He had gotten the answer he wanted, except .... "Where do you suppose NCIS got a hold of those firearms?"

The seaman's starry eyes sparkled with an idea.

"Out with it, Slim Jim."

"Maybe they have friends in high places. Or perhaps those weapons were obtained in some kind of swap."

Suddenly, the lieutenant's stomach felt like a bag of rocks when he read the pulsating message on his flat screen: Warning ...Warning

Chapter 30

Neil Avery had a dreadful thought: If I can't convince Fumo of Pratt's innocence, what're the chances of convincing Dauerman?

Fumo gave Avery a direct command—restriction to the ship. The no-nonsense admiral called on the armory chief to arm all hands allowed to carry weapons: all MAAs, watchstanders, and gunner's mates. They were to shoot the lieutenant if the restraining order was not obeyed. This put Avery's private investigation on hold. But while he waited, he had an uneasy feeling ….

Dauerman suspiciously regarded the object in his hand and gave Secretary of the Navy, Ben Nobleman, and chief of DOD, Luke Driscoll an intense look. "Where did this come from?" He was hot and bothered, and loosened his tie.

He handed the *Locksmith* magnet key he found on his desk to another NCIS officer and immediately called North Island's Police Department. Dauerman had just returned to HQ after an unfriendly meeting with men from the Office of Naval Intelligence. They told him someone in ballistics leaked their findings on a Russian handgun to ONI, and when the suspicion spread to CINCPACFLT headquarters, they in turn reported it to the Security Enforcement Department at North Island. That was when ONI tracked Dauerman to his hotel room, grilled him like a foreign spy, and learned he was a CISSP—a Certified Information Systems Security Professional—investigating the Black-Sunday theft. When they also learned that a shipload of Russian Federation firearms were brought to the U.S. after a failed military invasion by Syrian troops in NATO-backed Turkey twelve years earlier—and that the handguns were given an American name, the A-46 Barrington—he was cleared of all wrongdoing and released.

A square-shouldered long-necked police sergeant, and his team, powdered, dusted, and cellophane-taped every inch of surface in every corner of Dauerman's office. There were fingerprints all over the place.

Nobleman and Driscoll followed the NIPD officers, drinking coffee from Styrofoam cups on their way out … and a short time later, the grimfaced policemen returned with Driscoll and Nobleman leading the pack. The lanky police sergeant said, "We have a positive on those fingerprints. Does the name Avery mean anything to you?"

The agent was satisfied. "I'll take it from here." He rounded up Marine sentries with one phone call and stormed out of his office in search of the wayward serviceman.

Avery read his watch for the fourth time. Its hands seemed to have stopped. What was taking Slim so long? he wondered. In the hallway a door slammed and trailing footsteps followed. "We'll get Avery," someone said.

He rushed to the door, cracked it open, and careful eyes paraded down the hall. Hiding out in Marc's office was not a good idea, he thought. But he had nowhere else to go. Despite the admiral's austere warning, he threw caution to the wind and felt energized by his rebellion. All he had to do now was wait for the seaman to arrive and the unlawful investigation of Pratt's arrest would be underway.

A car honked outside and Avery dashed to the window. He peered through strips of blinds and saw them: a troop of men, along with Dauerman, marching out of the building. They would be gone in a moment, but if Jordan didn't show up, his plot would not succeed. He thought about how the tense morning began, how he had been confined to the ship against his will, and the plan he came up with to slip away ….

It was 0613 and an explosive sun had risen, battling a fleet of dull-gray clouds trying to conceal it. A keen-eyed watchstander, pacing the quarterdeck, viewed the vista, while not far behind him, hidden from view, a POOW timed the light traffic-flow of men, waiting for the right moment to strike. When it came, he and a lieutenant approached the watchstander from behind. "You're relieved of your duties, mister."

The watchstander, under Admiral Fumo's command, spun into the face of the runty sailor. "Says who?"

Ragazzi pressed the barrel of a Beretta against the man's nose, flattening it. "Says me!"

The lieutenant motioned to the watchstander's firearm. "Give it up." He relinquished it and Ragazzi took it. "Lock him up in one of the machine shops before he's spotted," Avery ordered.

"Sir, UCMJ article nine-seven," Ragazzi warned. "Unlawful detention."

"Screw the justice code and do what you're told."

Ragazzi gave him a docile look. "Aye, sir."

Two brawny gunner's mates whisked the watchstander below deck.

"I should be back before Fumo sends a replacement," Avery said. "Oh, and thanks, Rags. This time I owe you one."

"Keep your head on a swivel. Tex has every Marine sentry on this base turned against you, too."

"It's not them I'm worried about." He had a volcanic image of Dauerman, and what he would do if he got caught.

"Get going, skip. See you later."

Avery scampered down the ship's brow like a skittish cat, moving with haste, leaving Ragazzi at the watch with hand over his weapon. Ready for whoever came along.

0651

Jordan made his appearance. The closer he walked toward the sharp-eyed POOW twitching a walrus mustache at him, the tighter he clutched a drawstring laundry bag he carried.

Ragazzi narrowed eyes on him. "Where do you think you're going?" His voice was bullfrog deep. "No one's allowed off ship till after overboard exercises. Skipper's orders."

"You're nuts. That was last week's drill." Jordan tried to get past the big sailor.

"Stand fast." Ragazzi body-blocked him. "The drill starts now. Get below."

"Don't bust my balls, Rags."

"Fine, I'll kick your teeth in, then."

Jordan grew cold. "Let me pass. I'm on an errand for the skipper and you know it."

"Avery told me squat."

"That's your problem." Jordan hustled past him.

Ragazzi grabbed the cotton laundry bag in Jordan's hand and forced it open. "Hey, what's this?" His bulbous nose flared.

"What's it look like?" The seaman snatched the bag, saluted the standing American flag, and hustled down the brow.

"You're going to captain's mast for stealing and insubordination!"

"Not in my lifetime," Jordan shot back.

Jordan's long sprint led him to his car—a fiery-red Jaguar he had left parked in the officers' section of the base, away from the *USS Capitol Hill*.

With clammy fingers he unlocked the car door and opened it as far as it would allow. The Jag was sandwiched between two other vehicles but he could still squeeze in. He looked over his shoulder to make certain no one was watching him.

"What do you think you're doing, sailor?"

Four men—Dauerman and three Marine guards—approached the tall seaman from behind an adjacent parked car and surrounded him like a pack of hunched hyenas.

Jordan's heart donkey-kicked. He tossed the white laundry bag into the passenger's seat and closed the door. But it was too late. The men's suspicions had piqued. The look in Dauerman's glaring eyes told him he had been caught.

Jordan's throat bobbed like a rubber ball in a rolling sea.

"Thought you could get away with it, huh?"

The seaman hoped that by playing it cool he could keep them from scrutinizing him further. "Something wrong?" He twitched a smile.

"Yeah, black boy." He adjusted his suit and tie, giving the sailor a smug look.

Jordan's tongue suddenly felt different. No saliva.

Dauerman leaned on him; hands now in his pockets. "Your damn car belongs in the enlisted personnel's area. Move it!"

He and the Marine sentries let the young sailor slip behind the wheel of the Jag. The engine roared and he zipped out of the parking spot in reverse without touching either vehicles on his right and left.

"Hold it!"

Jordan slammed the brakes. Dauerman approached. With one hand, the sailor grabbed the laundry bag; with the other, he gripped the steering.

The agent gestured for him to step out of the vehicle.

Jordan floored the pedal, the car spun 180° like a giant compass needle, and with a ripping screech, sped away.

In the sprawling marbled lobby of naval headquarters, Jordan moved quickly on the diamondized tile floor to a long, hotel-like front desk where a Marine Lance Corporal stood. The seaman loved the clean scent of a fresh-mopped deck. It made his rubber soles squeak like a classical guitarist tuning new strings on an instrument. To him, it seemed the spirits of every deceased admiral of the U.S. Navy fixed disapproving eyes on him as he placed his right hand on the visitor's palm-scanner and read the time on a mariner's wall clock. He was late, but was there nonetheless. The desktop glass panel was cool to the touch, and he imagined himself as the second black senator in history to accomplish such a feat—right hand held up in oath; left hand placed on Abraham Lincoln's 1861 inaugural bible as he repeated after the Chief Justice of the United States how he would faithfully execute the office of the presidency by preserving, protecting, and defending the sacred constitution birthed by the nation's founding forefathers. However there was no time to fantasize he was someone else, or play childish games. He had an important job to perform. A task, that if done properly, could very well spare his beloved country from being attacked by madmen who preferred power over peace; war over wisdom. He was sure this was a role the FBI and CIA were normally called to do, and suddenly, he found himself interested in finding out more about—

"I'm sorry, sir," the keen-eyed sentry said to him. Jordan returned from his musings when the sharp-looking Marine told him the system was frozen. He would have to wait ….

Avery peeked through slits of thin venetian, fighting the glare of the sun, the silence of the office, a carousel of thoughts. He realized how long his fingers were crossed when they began to throb.

How simple Navy life was before this, he thought ….

The seaman's name, rank, and last four digits of his social security appeared on duel computer screens and he entered officers' country. It was his first time in the restricted ops facility, and a moment later he strutted into Marcus Weinberg's office.

"How do I look, Caliber?"

He made sure the door was locked. The officers' uniform was pinstripe creased, a damn good fit. Anchor-embossed buttons ran down the service jacket like those on a double-breasted suit. His black shoes, at a forty-five degree angle, were buffed to a turtle-wax gloss, and he held the non-fretted wheel cap right were it was supposed to be: secured in his hand at the crook of the left elbow.

"Don't let the khakis get to you—Mr. Jordan." He should have warned him he'd get the bighead and was glad he made him an ensign instead of a lieutenant junior grade. "You're twenty minutes late. What the hell kept you?"

"Rags stopped me, the scanner froze, and big cat—"

"Saw him leaving. Which way was he headed?"

"To the *Cap*."

His abdomen went taut. He could run but not for long.

"You shouldn't have played 007 and broke into big cat's office. Was that lousy brass tooth really important?"

The grim officer answered with pensive silence. He was nearing a point of no return, but had no intentions of stopping. He was driven to be a renegade vigilante and amateur cop.

"My guess is they're looking for you," Jordan informed him. "To nail you the way they did Pratt."

"They?"

"Big cat and three jarheads."

"Son-of-a—" Avery squeezed lips tight to keep from saying it. He unbuttoned his service jacket and buried hands deep into its pockets. Thoughts were weighty when one didn't know what to do. He had run out of ideas and now he was running out of time, giving himself only an hour to do what he believed needed to be done—an act of justice.

"Soon as they find out I'm not aboard ship they'll double-back here. We'll have to move fast."

"Would've been here sooner if you hadn't gotten Alzheimer's over today's drill. We're due back in less than forty. Why didn't you square me with Rags?"

He wanted to kick himself for not thinking things through. He had rushed through the details and apologizing would not help.

Jordan pulled out a palm-size code prober and coaxial cable from his back pocket, installed it to the modem, and got to work. Avery hoped they could finish before someone discovered the system was being hacked into again.

As soon as the computer hummed to life, the seaman's speedy black fingers danced on the keyboard. The screen lit up, a desktop appeared, and the system came to a pause. There were twenty-five icons lined up on the screen, five rows, five icons in each row: *Stairwell Passage Security, HQ Elevator Power, North Island's Naval Net, HQ Magnetic Door System, CINCPACFLT Message Traffic....*

Now all they had to do was wait.

Jordan told Avery he had never attempted to do anything such as this, but he felt savvy enough and confident enough it would work. Once the narrow *enter-password* window came on, he would leave it blank, hit the Esc button and reboot the system which would re-modulate the modem to trick the computer to receive signals it would interpret as commands. Then he would press the appropriate keys and type in an algebraic-code phrase that would usher him past the intrusion detection system. From there he'd run a port scan and search for overlooked security holes. Once he found one and penetrated, a number of networks would be at his fingertips. If he chose to, Jordan said he could easily interfere with radar signals and radio transmissions in any air traffic control tower at any airport by shutting down their equipment, thus bringing chaos, panic, and loss of communication from ground to air, placing all incoming and outgoing flights in extreme danger. Or if he were ruthless enough, he could tamper with the city's complex power grid, just for kicks, and leave all of North Island without electricity, forcing a moonless night after sundown to plunge everything into a biblical plague of darkness.

With everything done, Avery checked the time on his watch. "What's the delay?"

"Let me handle this. Easy as ripping songs from a service unit into my laptops."

"That's what you've been doing behind everyone's back?" He was relieved the seaman hadn't done what he thought he had. "For a while there—"

"You thought I was one of them." He gave his division officer a disappointed look.

The computer screen flashed a warning: *Unauthorized Access*. The new, anti-hacking security system instantly activated and the code phrase bounced out.

"Any way of demodulating?" Avery's nerves felt like an army of clawing crabs had clamped tight to the skin beneath his uniform.

"Not with the damn firewall in the way. This is gonna be harder than I thought."

"Think of something fast."

"I'm trying."

A viselike tension filled the air, and each time Avery blinked, his head hurt.

Jordan selected the next access code, and with a touch of a few buttons on the prober, inserted it where the first one had bounced out. $E=mc^2$.

He said he hoped this one would pick up where the other failed without him having to exit the system and shut it off. There were fifteen, number/letter codes listed on the prober's review screen. But which was the current one? Avery thought. There was only one way to find out. The seaman would have to feed them into the system—one by one.

Avery didn't like the queasiness in his gut. Taking a harsh laxative for a gastro exam made him feel the same way once. Jordan told him they were back to square one and pasted another equation over the old one: $Y+25h=2.000$. Now there were just two codes left to play with—one on the prober, and a code Avery had given him. That was the deal. In the back of his mind he knew if all else failed, Jordan would be forced to use the ID number the reluctant lieutenant didn't want him to have.

He checked the time. "This should've been a done deal, Slim."

"Don't rush me. This was your idea."

"You said you could do this."

"You gave me a damn ultimatum, remember?"

Jordan worked against the silence ....

And the unyielding system continued to mock his expertise: *Access Denied*

"You're wasting too much time, Slim."

"I can't work miracles!"

Avery scooted to the window for a peek, rattling the venetian blinds. He spotted a security vehicle parked in front of HQ under the warming sun. How long had it been there? He turned to Jordan. "I'm giving you one last chance, Slim."

"Only one code left!" Jordan slammed it into the system, leapfrogged to his feet, and charged the lieutenant. He grabbed him by the collar and rammed his back against the wall. "Don't ever give me another damn order. I'm outta here!"

Avery broke free from the stranglehold—ready to strike Jordan square in the face—when someone banged on the door.

"Open up!"

The lieutenant stood poised with a big fist aimed at the seaman. He didn't move until his heart stopped kicking like the door.

"Shank?" Nobleman's voice. "You there? Open up!"

No one answered the door across the hall.

"Let's go, Dris."

Trailing footsteps filled the corridor with silence.

The tight-lipped lieutenant returned to his senses, then to a blinking prompt on the screen. "What's it doing?"

"You would've knocked my teeth out, wouldn't you?"

He realized how quiet the office had become when he heard Jordan breathing. "I said, what's it doing?"

"Searching for the database's password. But we're being tracked."

"How do you know?"

"Look!"

In the lower, left-hand corner of the screen, a nonstop flurry of jumbled letters flashed. "What's that, an encrypted message?"

"Negative. Names of every personnel stationed on this base. In a moment it'll lock on one of them."

They were in. But unless Jordan worked fast, the only *in* they were in was trouble. Avery understood that meant the seaman would have to beat the speed of the computer before it locked on a name.

A loud shout and smacking high-five by both men brought Jordan back to his seat. When the prompt stopped blinking, he selected the North Island Naval Net from the list of icons and left-clicked it. He checked the prober's rectangular window and typed that code into the command line: *06-876-ODF*. Another site opened up and he typed in a name: *Jacob Pratt*. They waited for a hit.

A reply came fast: *No Match Found*

"What the hell?" Avery's stomach turned rock hard as the computer continued to flash jumbled letters across the screen.

"Does he go by another name?" Jordan asked. "An alias?"

"Dammit, I don't know! No, wait." It came to him. "Warren. His middle name is Warren." He pulled up a sleeve and checked the time.

Jordan typed in the new data, and within seconds, everything they wanted to know on their former senior captain, filled the screen. Avery told the seaman to scan the profile for the Zyto virus barcode: cyber DNA.

After a long moment of searching, scanning, and reading through the detested officer's personal and military files, they stopped and looked at each other in awkward silence. Avery couldn't read anymore. He didn't want to. Now he had to come up with a way to stop the probing computer.

"We're in deep crap, Caliber."

The dumbfounded lieutenant had to agree, yet at the same time, he wanted to hold on to the possibility that maybe they had made a grave mistake. Perhaps they had gotten into someone else's file; another man with the same name. What were the chances? He tried joining the mismatched thoughts in his head, like splicing electrical wires together, hoping it would ignite a spark of understanding. But those thoughts were many, swirling as dust devils in a sandstorm.

"Still on the clay pot? Still on the clay pot?"

The lieutenant was awakened from his grim musings by Jordan's anxious, faraway voice.

"What did you say?"

"I said, still wanna play cop, or shall we get the hell outta here?" The tall sailor backed away from the unit as though it were about to detonate and positioned himself by the door. He grabbed the knob and waited for Avery to join him. But he didn't. The long-faced CO stayed staring into the flat screen. "Rereading the frigging thing won't make it change, Caliber. The damn file can't lie."

Avery hated to be interrupted when his mind was so worked up. He started again from the beginning....

Jacob Warren Pratt had received a non-judicial punishment through admiral's mast for surfing through USN cyber channels he hacked into as a commander. The report stated he was issued a forced, six-months leave of absence in lieu of jail time, a reduced paygrade upon return to duty, and a stiff warning if the transgression was repeated. Although no confidential files were deleted or burned onto disks, it was documented he did it for the rush it gave him. The report read he had many such vices. It was what he lived for. His first thrill was achieving a surge of orgasm over a Playboy centerfold when he was twelve, plunging him into a vicious cycle of unfulfilled pleasures.

Jordan said, "Didn't he learn his lesson the first time?" He looked exhausted from the strain of thinking and hacking.

"What a stupid man." Avery let out an audible sigh of disgust. "Why would he jeopardize his career?" The flurry of jumbled letters on the screen was slowing down. The computer was nearing the end of its search. There was no stopping it now.

"Sounds like something you should've asked yourself."

"Damn thing doesn't add up, Slim." Avery checked the time on his watch again.

"Will you stop doing that!"

He shot a look at the tall seaman. "You're UA, Slim. That alone will get you brig time. Not to mention what you'll get for impersonating an officer—when I turn you in."

"I'm not the one with his head in the toilet. Soon big cat will be hounding your six like a bounty hunter." He jerked the door wide open, anxious to take flight. "I hate to say this ...." Avery felt the coldness of Jordan's stare on his skin while his scalp stung from the acid perspiration that broke through. "You were wrong, Caliber. And if you don't get outta here soon, you'll be dead wrong."

Disorientation made him feel sick and his heart galloped. Dauerman had nailed the right man after all. Damn! The official report would keep him up nights no matter where he spent them. Now he and the seaman would have to run. But where?

He was jarred awake from his escape fantasies and realized who he was, where he was, and why he was there. He buttoned his service jacket, logged out of the system, and shut off the unit. But not without first catching a disturbing glimpse of the name locked on the screen after the computer ran through a list of every single person stationed at the naval base.

That name read: Avery, Neil. CO. *USS Capitol Hill*

When he learned of the news, he incarcerated himself in his quarters. The entire naval air station was in lockdown, prohibiting visitors, military personnel and ships from entering and leaving North Island. NCIS discovered the system's database had been penetrated for the second time, and until the individual responsible for the cyber break-in was in custody, and like Pratt, unceremoniously hauled away, the ban would not be lifted.

Avery felt something churn in his gut and rise to his throat. The fermenting started when his plans to go AWOL, change his identity and begin a new life, were dashed. His head felt heavy, then light, then heavy again. The last time it did that was when the *Man Of War* hurtled over a sizable swell during an ocean storm off Guam and pitched into the valley-trough below. The rollercoaster-feel was exciting.

Not this, though.

He hurled himself onto his rack, face-up, and with clammy hands crossed behind his neck, he stared into the overhead that seemed to close down on him like a compressor in a garbage truck. How many times did he find himself like this during the thousand sleepless nights he had endured, praying for the world to stop spinning so he could get off? This is what prison life must be like, he thought.

In a dreamlike state, he bolted into Weinberg's office and reenacted the whole troubling scene, forcing himself to read the bold-black letters on piercing-blue background that burned through the panel of the monitor. But no matter how many times he read the official report and the archives that followed, the old story remained unchanged ....

Yesterday, the *USS Sargasso*, a guided missile destroyer off the southern coast of Iran in the Gulf of Oman, was struck by two, remote-controlled miniature torpedoes which ripped holes in its hull and flooded compartments of the engine spaces. Though badly damaged and leaning twelve degrees port, the stranded *Sargasso* was towed away by sister ships of the Fifth Fleet Task Force before another strike could be launched. The ship's crew worked at a feverish pace to rescue endangered sailors out of neck-high seawater while stabilizing the vessel to keep her afloat. The courageous effort saved the listing *Sargasso* and many of its men, however, a handful of sailors were sacrificed in the deadly process of wrestling the DDG out of danger. One of the men, a nineteen-year-old seaman named Eric Pratt, was among those still alive after the mighty explosions rocked the ship. But when watertight hatches of the lower deck were ordered dogged by the ship's commander, and Damage Control refused to break Zebra, dedicated sailors were sealed in a watery grave ....

Avery put the lives of two men together—one dead, the other bitter—and came up with a tragic answer: Revenge ....

Over the 1MC, eight bells gonged in the passageway, indicating a high-ranking officer had boarded.

A moment later, someone hammered their fist against the cabin's door.

Avery squared himself on the edge of his rack and stood. "Enter." He stiffened. The ship's steel fortress no longer felt secure to him. The door cracked open and a narrow, black face appeared.

He threw himself back where he had lain. "Are they here yet?" Blinkless eyes refused to meet Jordan's. He preferred to stare at the overhead's fat pipes and snaking cables.

"No, but Tex just boarded. Know what that means?"

"It means get lost, Slim. I don't want him getting the slightest hint you were with me on this."

"What about you? What's gonna happen to you?"

He clawed into his feverish face; tense fingers hiding his eyes. Both his mind and adrenaline had worked overtime and he was dead tired. "I'm screwed." Suddenly a thought came to him and he sat erect. "Why the hell didn't you stop me, Slim?"

The seaman looked flabbergasted. "You blaming this on me?"

"Where's Ragazzi?" His jumbled fantasies had hatched, giving birth to another hasty scheme.

"Rags? Did you say Rags?" Jordan's voice pounded against the overhead. "What the hell you want with Rags? He a frigging godfather? A mobster with pocket full of favors?"

"I want to know where he is!"

"Tex had Marine sentries crawl on him like ants on a praying mantis, okay!" The seaman laid a scornful look on him.

Avery shot back a mean eye. "What's the matter with you?"

"You used to be full of respect for yourself. Know what you're full of now?"

"Hey, you forget you're talking to a naval officer!"

"And you forget you're dead meat. I saw Zyto DNA in Pratt's profile. Mayo told me he kept a defective computer stashed in his stateroom to cover up his act. The one with the problem motherboard. Now the schmuck's in the academy where he belongs."

The lieutenant closed his dropped mouth and clenched his teeth. "Why didn't you tell me that before?"

Jordan feigned a dumb look. "I dunno," he said with calm sarcasm. "Just came to me." He regarded the officer with dark eyes before grabbing the doorknob. "Enjoy the rest of your life behind bars … sir." He left Avery's quarters, laughing as he went.

"Dammit, come back!"

Somehow the cabin replayed the reverberating burst of its door being slammed, followed by a roar of silence which stripped his mind, leaving a horrible void of thoughtlessness. With no one to call upon—no Ragazzi, no Jordan, no Nieve, and no Valentine—nothing could change what was about to come. Not even a time machine.

Someone pounded on the cabin door again. It opened ajar but no one stuck their head in. "Should've known you were one of them." The man entered without being invited.

"Them?" The young officer sprung on the edge of his rack. The sweat on his back was cold like the cutting knives in the galley. "Whatever dereliction of duty you're accusing me of can be dismissed by—"

"You can forget about JAG," Fumo said. "You'll be in Leavenworth with Pratt. I have the scoop you two were the original conspirators of Black Sunday."

A sudden geyser erupted from within, shooting Avery to his feet. "Says who, dammit?"

"Says me," someone said from the passageway.

The admiral stepped aside and Hank Dauerman sauntered in. That unnerving grin said it all. He and he alone would take part in the last act of the Black-Sunday investigation. He would be the one to close the book on the nation's most boldest and dramatic cyber heist ever pulled off.

Avery looked at those eyes; eyes that blazed like the father he hated.

Dauerman said, "You're under arrest for computer hacking and espionage activity, Lieutenant."

The accusation struck him like someone had thrown a ball-peen hammer: I'm under arrest … under arrest … arrest ….

Finally it hit him. The seriousness of what he had done and what he was being charged with— conspiracy and betrayal against his own country— dropped him to a deadweight sit.

Dauerman had neglected to read him his rights. UCMJ's article 31.

Fumo stood over the prisoner and dared him to launch his body against Dauerman. But Avery decided he would not make a feeble attempt to defend himself the way Pratt had done. He would surprise them with his tameness in exchange for leniency. If that didn't work, then he would strike like an angry pit bull.

"I used to like this boy," the admiral said.

The threatening look on the agent's face disarmed the young serviceman of any action he had intended to take.

"I'll be back for you," Dauerman said.

Both the admiral and the agent stepped out into the passageway where a rigid-faced chief master-at-arms stood at attention. He wore a bronze enamel badge over the left breast pocket of his uniform with a raised law-enforcement star in the center and impressed MAA lettering below it. He also carried a firearm at the hip and looked anxious to use it. He and Dauerman were there for one thing and one thing only. To escort a hacker off the USS Capitol Hill and into a waiting, unmarked sedan.

The agent pulled the cabin's door closed and their talk died down to a whisper.

The indictment kept coming at him, forcing angry blood to course through shrunken veins: under arrest … hacking and espionage ….

Now the nasty throbbing in his head matched the pounding door. It flew open.

The admiral was the first to reenter the lieutenant's quarters, followed by Dauerman who sprang in like a lion-slaying gladiator. In one hand he held ankle cuffs, and in the other, shiny new manacles.

Avery hated the thought the king of cops was about to bring in his trophy. "I was never involved in Black Sunday!"

The agent approached. "You amuse me."

"You can't do this!"

"Watch me." Dauerman hooked Avery's wrists, and with grating snaps, cuffed them together.

He struggled to get free. "I've got my rights!"

"To what?" The agent pushed his jaw forward.

Avery searched for a reasonable answer, something he hoped would spring him. If he said the wrong thing, it would jeopardize his chances of ever getting out of prison and getting into a Navy uniform again. "To make one phone call." Damn, it sounded ridiculous. But if he could get them to let him use the public access phone at the end of the passageway, he could make an escape.

Dauerman ruptured into an obnoxious laugh fueled by the sudden request. "Who the hell you gonna call? You're in deep shit!"

"I want my call."

"Tough nuts, sailor boy."

"I said now!"

The NCIS officer's face went blank. "He for real?" he asked Fumo.

"Give it to him. It won't take long. Just don't let him use the public access phone. Keep him in here."

A two-way radio chirped from Dauerman's hip. When he looked at the ankle chains dangling in his hand and shifted disdained eyes on the handcuffed Navy officer, Avery realized he would grant the request. "Okay, mister. You've got ten lousy minutes. Make that damn call. But it's gonna be your last." He removed the biting cuffs from the lieutenant's wrists and rushed out of the compartment, giving the MAA some last-minute instructions.

Fumo stared Avery down with contempt. He stepped out of the cabin, said something to the NCIS officer, and the chief master-at-arms pulled the door closed. Avery wondered whether they would stand there waiting, or go for a walk. The admiral and the agent's voices died down, walking as they went. He guessed they would head to the end of the long passageway and wait. If not that, they would climb the ladders and proceed to one of the mess halls, lean against a pair of stanchions in supportive camaraderie, count down the time on their watches, and return. How he hated being a prisoner in his own confines without a new course of action.

Avery rubbed his wrists. He looked into the face of his Quartz. The watch's sweeping hand ate away the seconds like a ticking time bomb. Nine and a half left.

The phone on the bulkhead was not what he went for. NCIS would no doubt be listening, tracking whatever calls he made. Instead he opened the desk's bottom drawer, grabbed his cell phone and popped it open. "What am I doing? Who am I gonna call?" One thing was clear to him—the shape of a 9mm Glock.

Every twisted nerve in his body begged him to respond. His mind screamed at him to reach inside the drawer, lift the weapon out, and end it all.

Chapter 31

A tall, slim sailor skirted an unmarked sedan as the driver leaned against it: arms crossed over his chest, keys dangling from the ignition, a two-way radio sitting on the dashboard, a magnum-size weapon on the driver's seat. The big, gray LPH, the *USS Capitol Hill*, was an impressive sight: a bulldog version of the *Man Of War* with an Elm-tall mast equipped with sea-air radars and SAM missile launchers crowning the island's superstructure. In a moment, Dauerman would hustle a prisoner down the ship's brow and into the car's luxury backseat. Then the driver would slip behind the wheel, rev up the 200-horse-powered Buick LeSabre's six-cylinder engine and hit the gas, whisking a shackled Lieutenant Avery to San Diego's International Airport where a private jet, ready to depart, would take him, along with armed escorts, to an undisclosed destination.

Avery gripped the open cell phone in a clammy palm. He punched eleven numbers and waited for the intermittent burr to stop.

"Hello?" A woman's voice.

"Is ... is this April?"

"Who's this?"

"... Neil."

"Ave?"

"Yes."

"Do you know how long it's been? I gave up praying for you!"

"April, listen. I don't have much time. Get your sisters, it's important." He read his watch: Eight minutes to go.

"Wait a minute!" Her voice had hardened. "Aren't you going to tell me where you've disappeared to? What you've been doing all this time?"

He refused to answer. It was none of her business, he reasoned. But April was a smart woman. It wouldn't take her long to figure out that the silent treatment was nothing more than resurrected anger in a Halloween costume.

"If you won't talk I'll hang up."

"Please, April, don't. You have a right to be offended, but—"

"Pia and I are the only ones here."

"Where's Taff?"

A deaf silence followed. But he knew she had not hung up.

"Same place she's been since Daddy died. Remember?"

Her reprimanding message painted a dark scenario of what was yet to come.

"The ...." He could barely speak. "The hospital."

Within his tortured mind, a host of bad memories dizzied him: Roy cremated again, Mama's casket flown to Warrenton, the girls selling the farmhouse and moving to Boone, and Taffi ... dying.

"Why haven't we heard from you? I mean ... we used to be a family."

He spared her from a lengthy story filled with lame excuses. "It's all my fault." He felt somewhat relieved to admit he was wrong, but that was not enough to remove the sword of guilt embedded in his rocky heart.

"You never were the type to get over anger," she said.

He also wasn't the type to forgive himself for the things he should have said and done, and he let April know that. But he had to forgive. April said they both had to. The brick wall they had built would never crumble unless they started chipping at it now.

"Why did I wait so long?" he cried.

"Don't bang your head against a wall. We were all overwhelmed with grief. It took the life out of us. That's why things turned out the way they did."

The haunting cloud that had followed him all his life returned, darkening everything around him. He understood now with deep remorse what he did and why he had done it—mortally hurt those with trusting eyes and gentle hearts: those who wanted to be a family to him. The afflicted had learned long ago to be an afflicter, and when he made his last mark, he marooned himself like a remote-island castaway, hoping never to be seen or heard from again. Suddenly he realized the island of unworthy souls is not where he wanted to remain. There was a way to be found; to be rescued from all this. "Does this mean I'm forgiven?"

She gave him a true definition of the word: forgiveness was a groundbreaking process, and in their case, a jackhammer would need to be employed on the pavement of long-hardened bitterness. She sounded hopeful at suggesting it would help if he visited Oak Leaf.

"No, baby. You won't be seeing me for a long time."

For a moment he thought the battery power in his cell phone had expired.

"Oh...." The bottom dropped out of her voice.

"Sorry. Didn't mean to make you sad. That's all I'm good for. Take care of yourself. You and your sister will be the only ones left after today."

Her shrilled voice beat against his eardrum with a frightened tone. "What do you mean?"

"Put Pia on."

"Ave, what did you—?"

"Please."

The cell phone went silent. Then, a weepy voice called out: "Piaaa ...."

He checked the time. Five more minutes. The watch's sweeping hand seemed to move quicker, racing to fulfill what was to come: Leavenworth—if they let him live. Execution—if a JAG court found him guilty. He reached into the open desk drawer and lifted the firearm, bringing it over the turtle-green ribbon bars on his uniform, those he received for sharpshooting skills he possessed as a naval-academy midshipman. How he loved to aim and fire that M9 service pistol and M16-A3 assault rifle at a target 100 yards away with deadly accuracy. Now, sitting at his desk, cell phone in one hand and Glock in the other, his mark would be much closer. He had found a way out.

Olympia was long in coming. He lay the cell phone down, thumbed the weapon's safety lock to the off position, and checked the mag. It was loaded. He pulled back the slide, cocking the firearm into the single-action mode. One bullet would do it. He gave his watch a cursory glance. In less than four minutes Dauerman would return. If he wants me, he thought, he'll have to clean up mess. This was it. He pushed the 9mm's steel barrel against a throbbing temple.

He scooped up the cell phone and waited.

"Well, hello stranger." Olympia's adult voice carried into his ear, and with it, the years that had cemented between them.

"I don't want to be a stranger anymore. Not to you."

"Should've thought of that before accepting the lead role."

He huffed out a breath, making no effort to dress up his anger. "What's it going to take to end this?" He waited a pause for the answer.

"Time. It's ... going to take time to rebuild the relationship we once had."

"Yes. Time." But he had no more time, and he knew it.

"April wants to see you," she said. "And ... I guess I do, too."

He wondered what had happened to her voice. That child's mousy voice. The joyful trill she used that made him want to pick her up each time she spoke. Now she sounded vastly different. So much like a full-grown, mature woman.

"Neil, tell me you'll come to start over."

"How old are you, sweet pea?" Time was winding down. Two minutes.

"I'm twenty. You used to send me birthday cards. Now you have to ask."

"Don't be upset. It's been a while." He masked the burning shame in his voice with a declaration of her tenacity throughout the years. It took a lot of courage to survive losing two sets of parents. "What've you been up to?"

She blew her nose and sniffled. "I started college this semester. Decided to become a doctor. A children's doctor."

A parade of lost memories marched to the forefront of his mind: her ropey pigtails, a bedroom filled with dolls, a broken arm set in a plaster cast. Boone Medical Center's pediatric emergency room had left a lasting impression on her.

A bittersweet smile was all he could muster. But it was better than no smile at all. "I've missed seeing you grow up, falling out of trees, holding you on my lap. But I'm happy you're pursuing your dreams. Dad would've been proud. And Mama, too. God rest her soul."

He was getting ready to say goodbye—for the last time.

"Sweet pea, I must go. Please tell—"

"Did you know next week will be three years since Daddy died?"

"Seems like yesterday." He couldn't hold on to the lead-weight cell phone much longer. He felt weak and began to shake. "Listen ...."

But she didn't. She rambled on about what a good man Roy was: how he treated her; how he made her feel like a real daughter; how she became a Gilchrist. "... We leave flowers at the gravesite twice a year now. On his birthday, and—"

"What?" He tried to grasp her meaning. The strange silence made him think the signal had been lost.

Avery was distracted by the sound of hissing radio bursts carrying into his cabin. They were back—the NCIS officer and the austere-looking admiral. Now it would only take a second to slap the cuffs back on and haul him away.

A garbled message chirped through someone's walkie-talkie: *Oh, no! Shank, m'out here an... at.... O'er.*

"Driver?" Dauerman responded. "That you? Say again, over." A blaring hiss followed. "Something's up."

"Trouble?" Fumo's voice.

The same message came through again, clearer this time: *Dammit, I said come out here and look at this! Shank, you copy?*

"Who the hell's that?" the chief MAA said.

"Let's find out," said Dauerman.

"I'll go with you," Fumo said.

The two men climbed a ladder, one deck up. They went aft through the helo bay and arrived at the quarterdeck where an OOD and a POOW stood at the watch. Dauerman and Fumo ambled past them down the brow to the parked sedan. The pacing driver, hands shoved into trouser pockets, approached.

"What the hell kept you? And where's the prisoner?"

"You called. What the hell's the problem?" He plucked a folded handkerchief from his suit pocket, like a magician getting ready to perform a trick, and wiped the sun-induced sweat off his brow.

"I didn't radio you!"

The NCIS officer's angry eyes darted about. "Well, someone did!"

Dauerman smelled a diversion and slammed his two-way radio on the concrete pier. He stormed back to the ship and up the brow with Fumo and the driver not far behind.

"Are you there? Hello?" Olympia's voice brought Avery back.

"What did you say?" He put down the gun.

"April and I place flowers at Daddy's gravesite twice a year!"

A swirling thought took him to Dugger Creek, where Beulah emptied her husband's urn into the clear downstream; the remaining ashy cloud carrying downwind. "But ... Roy was cremated!"

"Are you all right? Daddy was buried after the two-day wake. Mama arranged the whole ...."

He put down the cell phone, picked up the gun, and fired it.

The MAA, standing guard in the passageway, burst into the lieutenant's quarters and immediately was met with a crushing blow between the eyes. The impact of the weighty chair knocked him out.

A two-way radio at his feet screeched again with that chirping voice: *Get out of there. Now!*

Avery tossed the chair aside, stuffed the Glock in his waistband, and pulled the door behind him. He made a beeline up the long passageway to the nearest exit.

Running footsteps at the far end of the p-way burned in his ears and he slammed on the brakes. The momentum sent him into a steel wall. He

U-turned on his heels and moved in the opposite direction like a skillful alley cat scampering through the ship's interior, one level up.

Emerging from ladderwell aft port at hangar bay two, he stumbled, and a sound receded behind him. The 9mm Glock popped out of his waistband and clattered down the ladder one level below. He belched out a curse and moved on.

Dauerman's chest was heaving when he got to the lieutenant's quarters. It was locked from within and the MAA was nowhere in sight. He withdrew his shoulder-holstered gun, fired two shots through the lock and kicked in the door. There, facedown, the semiconscious ship's police groaned in pain.

Fumo snatched a phone off the bulkhead and barked an urgent message. Within seconds the silent passageway rang with a series of loud bells and a booming announcement followed over the 1MC: Security alert, security alert. Away the security alert team and backup security force. All hands not involved stand down. Reason for alert, acting skipper, Neil Avery, is at large aboard ship. He is armed and considered dangerous. Deadly force is authorized.

The admiral stepped over the chief master-at-arms and lifted the Glock from its holster. "The barrel is cold." He handed the weapon to Dauerman, dark blood at their feet. "Avery shot him."

Dinging bells continued to ring throughout the passageway, and a long line of navymen with weapons drawn, rushed past the open cabin.

Dauerman picked up the scent of the discharged round. "Now he's wanted for attempted murder."

Avery scrambled across the vacant helo deck, sucking a rush of sea air into his lungs. Without thinking twice, he leaped over the side of the tall LPH, and with the grace of an Olympic diver, knifed into the flat blue bay, six stories down.

When he came up for air, someone over the ship-wide speakers alerted security: Man overboard, port midship. Man overboard, port midship! It sounded like Jeff Miles. Avery had been spotted from the pilothouse and now he would have to gulp down a deep breath and swim like a barracuda in order to escape being fired upon by ship's security as soon as they made their way to the roof.

The urgent, man-overboard call prompted Dauerman to contact North Island's Police Department on the MAA's walkie-talkie. "Alpha, Papa, Bravo: ten niner-eight. Code ten niner-eight." The code signifying an escaped prisoner would blare through every handheld radio throughout the base. He gave a quick description of the man. "Shoot to kill. I repeat. Shoot to kill. Suspect is wanted for attempted murder of master-at-arms chief!"

Avery rose to the surface of the deep bay in a breathless gasp. He swam to the pier, and there, a man with dark eyes and a gun pointed at him, fished him out of the water and ushered him into a waiting vehicle.

A two-way in the Buick responded: *Code ten niner-eight. Copy that!*

Avery gave the driver an order. "HQ. And step on it." Water pooled at his feet.

"Hope that machine of yours works." The driver coughed into his fist. "Or you'll be cornered like a rat."

"Not if I move fast."

"Your funeral," Jordan sang.

Avery asked the seaman how he managed to steal an NCIS vehicle from under their noses.

He said he snatched a two-way radio from the dashboard while the driver had his back turned. Dauerman took care of the rest and the seaman drove off. "Wait till he finds out the damn key was left in the ignition."

He floored the accelerator, sending the screeching vehicle speeding through the base. With one hand on the wheel, he grabbed the palm-size walkie-talkie laying on a laptop and pressed a button. "Attention all hands. Prisoner in stolen Buick heading toward main gate. Request backup. Repeat— request backup!"

Avery snatched the walkie-talkie from him. "What the hell's wrong with you?"

"Gotta plan. Open that laptop and boot it."

"What for?"

"Just do it if you wanna live!"

He did as instructed and was thrown against the door when Jordan suddenly veered around diving personnel before blowing past them in a noisy rush.

The laptop came to life. "Done."

"Click HQ's icon and wait for the prompt."

Avery fingered the screen's arrow over the appropriate position and double-clicked it. "Okay, waiting." The humming vehicle hit a speed bump with a jaw-jarring shake, causing a pen and pad on the dashboard to jump about. The lieutenant grabbed them and jotted down a series of numbers: 4-1-3-2-4-1. Into the seaman's top pocket the torn piece of paper went.

"What's that?"

"HQ elevator code. Don't lose it if *you* want to live." Suddenly an NIPD patrol cruiser screamed toward them. "Look out!"

Jordan fishtailed into a grinding crash, sending debris flying through the air. The sailor hit the gas again and took off in a screeching wail, leaving the police car with a snapped front axle.

Pop, pop, pop....

Shots. He and Jordan were taking fire by the policeman who spilled out of the wreckage. With each crisp, zipping pop, the seaman maneuvered the car to avoid being hit. Three bullets tore into the LeSabre's trunk and several more blew out the back windshield, sending shards of stinging glass into flesh like enraged killer bees. Another round was fired, and the slug found its mark in the seaman's right shoulder; dark blood spraying into the lieutenant's taut face.

Jordan zoomed out of sight from the deadly shooter. He spun the Buick in a wide circle, the passenger door flew open before the vehicle fully stopped, and with a shove from behind, Avery tumbled out. "Hey, where're you going?" A long arc of tread marks were tattooed into the asphalt.

"Never mind me." Jordan grabbed the laptop and typed in something at a site. "Do what you came for. I'll try to lose 'em." He winced from the biting, shoulder pain. "Get going, and good luck!"

NIPD cars wailed in the distance, and soon they would be upon the two men.

Jordan ripped the engine at hotrod speed and took off, leaving a stink of burning rubber to invade Avery's nostrils and parched throat. He crawled alongside the building, using its tall hedgerow of razor-cut shrubs to shield him from four white vehicles that flew by in deadly pursuit of the daring seaman. When it was safe, he bounced to his feet and bolted into HQ like a linebacker, bowling over the lone Marine sentry football style, flattening him cold on the hard floor before a round could be fired from his drawn weapon.

Now do the elevators, he thought.

Jordan rocketed through the main gate, shattered the lowered crossing arm into flying swords and scattered the Marine sentries who tried to stop him. More shots were fired. But the tall seaman gripped the steering wheel—hands bloodied, shoulder pounding, eyes stinging—and kept going, bulldozing over a chain-link fence and escaping into the outside world.

Dauerman, Fumo, and a detachment of Marine sentries hustled into HQ in hot pursuit of Avery. His objective made the head agent curse under his breath. He led everyone to a corridor behind the lobby into a stairwell and charged up, one floor after another. The fast-acting lieutenant, one step ahead of his pursuers, had cut service to all elevators.

At the top landing on the fourth floor, Dauerman and those with him found themselves unable to proceed. Someone had activated the stairwell passage system and now the NCIS officer sought for another avenue to enter. He ordered one of the Marines to check all doors on the lower levels and a moment later a reply bellowed up the stairwell. Everything was locked from within.

Dauerman stepped back, unholstered his gun, and drilled two shots through the lock. But the big, heavy, fire door refused to yield, sending everyone scrambling back down the long stairs to the lobby and out into the street.

Twisted with venomous frustration, Dauerman halted a vehicle as it approached the building. He dragged an 0-6 Navy chaplain out from behind the wheel, climbed in, and raced with demon speed to the far end of the base where the big, land-based USMC helicopters were kept.

Running through hallways with determined speed was like scrambling up the length of a football field toward the end zone. Avery reached room 411 and fumbled with Marc's keys. When he attempted to gain entrance to the scientist's office, he found he could not and sanity began to leave him. He shouldered the door, sending a screaming pain down the length of his arm. He donkey-kicked Dauerman's door, then bolted to the end of the hallway, checking other doors to no avail. That's when it came to him. Jordan on his laptop. That's what he was doing. The clever seaman had gotten into HQ's magnetic-door system before he could gain entrance to any of the offices. Avery was now boxed in the building with Dauerman locked out. He thought of reactivating the elevators, however, he had a hunch they were shut down. Now Spectrum's time machine called to him—louder. But he had no way of getting to it, or powering it up.

Dauerman brought the commandeered vehicle to a screeching stop and leaped out. He rushed into a four-story titanium-colored hangar, with weapon drawn, and pointed it at a knot of thin young men looking over a Seahawk helicopter with tools in their hands. They were in civvies. "Which one of you clowns is a pilot?"

Everyone turned. They looked like high-school kids. Wanna-be Marines on a tour of the base. Whoever their guide was had stepped away. They saw the weapon and threw their hands up. "Pilot?" said the youngest-looking from the group. "We were just dicking with the tools, looking around. Try the barracks."

He felt like giving the teen a head slap. Instead, he retreated with a departing eye on the boys. He should've known they weren't mechanics, or even pilots. They looked green from the get-go. Would they drop the tools and flee the hangar in pursuit of him, gun and all? The agent had no time to think of such things. He needed to keep moving and keep well ahead of them.

He galloped into the nearest building where he entered with his heart pounding faster than he could breathe. There he confronted a gathering of Marines in a chow hall. "I want a helo pilot!" He grabbed his belly and flinched.

The Marines stood solid to their feet, not making a move against the gun-toting agent who blocked the doorway.

"I said now, dammit!" Dauerman fired a single shot over their heads, flattening the young, clean-cut soldiers to the floor in a disciplined instant, except one: a first lieutenant.

He grabbed the Marine officer by the collar and forced him into a run while the hard barrel of a weapon was jammed into his ribs.

A minute later, a Bell UH-1D's four-bladed rotary easily came to life with a whistling roar, lifting the helicopter effortlessly over a crest of tall palm trees.

Dauerman gave an order to the pilot, and the stolen gunship headed to the naval complex. Below, the Marine pilots had stormed out of the barrack and scrambled across the tarmac. Though they ran fast, all they could do was follow the Huey's flight path from a distance and cause others to join their marathon.

High over the angled grounds, toy-like white vehicles and North Island's ant-size police force now gathered in front of HQ. It pleased Dauerman that the intense manhunt for the escaped prisoner had escalated, and as soon as he could get someone to unlock the building's stairwell doors, a careful, floor-by-floor, room-by-room search of the facility would commence until the fleeing officer's body was dragged out and tossed into a waiting mortuary van.

Avery located a red firebox at the south end of the hall. He smashed the compartment's breakable glass with his fist, yanked the lever, and activated a screaming alarm. Cold water sprayed from the sprinkler system, showering him in a steady hissing jet stream as a metallic clapping sound reverberated throughout the long hall. He ran back the way he came and realized power had been restored to the elevators when an OTIS floor-by-floor panel between them lit up. He grabbed one doorknob after another, pushing doors open as he ran by. It had worked. The firebox's built-in safety feature killed the magnetic circuit and unbolted every door to every office.

He cut off the blaring fire alarm and gushing sprinkler system, and hustled back to Marc's office, feeling energized with the success of making it this far. He thumbed the desk computer's on-button and waited for the unit to respond. "Damn!" He examined it and found it was waterlogged. It would be futile to go from office-to-office in the Sunday-vacant building, looking for a unit to work from. There were only two offices on the entire floor from which he could access his way to Spectrum.

Inside Dauerman's office, he peeled away the wet plastic covers from the hardware and tossed them aside. He thumbed the power button on the console box, and after a moment, realized the computer was not responding. There was no getting to Spectrum and there was no escaping HQ. He was as a chess piece on a game board. A king held in check. If he exited the building by way of the elevators or stairs, he would be charged upon, roughed up and handcuffed. Maybe even shot. However, if he went up to the roof, there was a chance he could monkey down the side of the four-story building by using the rainwater pipe. He had to admit it was a crazy risk. But he had done riskier things. Crazier things.

At the far end of the hall, he climbed up a wall ladder, pole-length high, leading into an unlit shaft in the ceiling. He reached the top rung and felt his way around. The roof's door above him was locked tight. He pulled on a rifle-like bolt with teeth-gritting might and the slide flew back, almost knocking him off the ladder. He got a grip on himself, and the ladder rungs, and with a handhold, pushed the horizontal steel door open, just a crack, just enough for a buffeting roar to deafen him and a whirlwind to slap his face. A Marine helicopter descended out of nowhere with a pounding thump, and Dauerman leaped from the aircraft's fuselage compartment. From under the oppressive beating of the cannon-toting Huey, the crouched, screwed face NCIS officer waved the big Russian handgun, and at the pilot's command, the screaming fighter craft rose swiftly, turned like a hang glider and sliced through the air, disappearing over a line of palm trees that stood like parade-rest sailors in the distance.

Avery slammed the hatch over his head but the long bolt wouldn't move. It was jammed. He unthreaded his trouser belt, looped it around the ladder's top rung and knotted the other end on the handhold, tying down the door. This would foil the intruder, he hoped. He had to move fast now.

Back in the agent's office, he discovered the computer screen was lit, prompting him to log in. He typed in a code.

A desktop with a bold USN logo in the center and list of icons beneath it appeared. He clicked a tab on the taskbar to get to the programs submenu and accessed his way into Spectrum's electrical system by highlighting the panel on the switchboard dialog box and clicking the OK button. He checkmarked all the halogen hieroglyphics on a toolbar with the mouse's arrow, feeling sure this had turned on all the lab's lights. Next, he commanded the laboratory's thick rock wall to roll open. Now it was time to awaken the mighty, thermo-glass tubes. He hoped this would be easy. Fast fingers danced on the keyboard. He bled sweat from everywhere and was done when he clicked one last OK button on a blinking prompt. All that remained was to run down the hall, reactivate the elevators, and—

A shadow appeared at the door and their eyes met.

"You're under arrest, Lieutenant."

Arrest ... arrest ... arrest ....

He couldn't get the thought to stop hammering at him. It was like being inside London's big Ben bell tower. Each deafening gong vehemently accusing him.

Dauerman entered his office like a hungry grizzly. He locked the door and flipped on the teakettle's hotplate in the corner of the room. "You're one hell of a slippery fish. But I still got you."

Now that he was cornered, the runaway serviceman knew his pursuer would savor the moment. The agent would indulge himself to a mug of instant coffee while the escapee squirmed. Dauerman would take care of his caffeine fix, then he would take care of him.

Avery twitched when the water-filled teakettle shrieked and a loaded weapon's dark eye stared at him. There were 10 rounds in each clip. How many shots would the NCIS agent fire to bring the lieutenant down? He ducked behind the fortress of the oak desk. "I didn't steal any classified info. You've got to believe that!"

Dauerman appeared to be enjoying a thought. "Why should I believe a hacker? With the evidence I have, you'll be put before a firing squad—after a kangaroo trial."

"Why don't you shoot me yourself and save taxpayers' dollars?"

"I'll take that as an admission of guilt."

"The only thing I'm guilty of is getting mixed with a scum like you."

Dauerman inched away from the teakettle. At pointblank range, the two men's eyes locked and a smell of hostile steam filled the office.

A sudden roar of helicopters turned the lieutenant to the window where he got a view of the innumerable crowd outside. A Marine assault team and North Island's Police Department were out in full force. All of them brandishing weapons. All of them shielded in body armor. All of them waiting for Dauerman to give the word that would send them storming mad into the building.

"You have quite an audience out there. Let's put on a show for them, shall we? Jump out the window. If you survive the fall, I'll let you go. Deal?"

The noise from the shrieking kettle grew louder and Dauerman radioed in a call. "Armed suspect in room four-twelve with female hostage. Approaching to negotiate. Standby for code-four response, over." He retreated to the coffee station with radio in hand and served himself a brimful of instant brew. A plume of angry steam rose with a swirl when he stirred sugar in. "Everyone thinks you're holding a hostage." He gave him a look. "Makes for an interesting standoff, doesn't it?"

The agent's two-way chirped a response: *NIPD. Ten-four, over.*

Now the office grew hot and smelled of stale coffee.

Dauerman took a hearty whiff of the black liquid and apologetic eyes found his prisoner. "I'm sorry. How rude of me for not being host." He pointed to the ceramic mug with the weapon. "Would you care for some?"

That uneasy smile froze the runaway lieutenant. His wet uniform felt like a frogman's rubber suit on his flesh: heavy and cold.

"Don't worry. I promise not to shoot you in the back of the head."

Avery knew he would die no matter what the agent promised. He rose from the shelter of the ambassador desk, and with stalking eyes on him, he snailed to the coffee station. Avery wanted something to calm him. Anything to stiffen his nerves. It didn't seem that long ago when his father drank tumbler after tumbler of the burning amber potion in the dark bottle to quiet him, only to gasp like a fire-breathing dragon.

The bitter smell of grind hardened his insides like a block of cement and would take an eternity to work its way out of his system. He offered his back to the agent and poured hot murky liquid into a mug but added no sugar. Nothing could sweeten venom.

He gave the NCIS man an over-the-shoulder look.

Dauerman surprised him when he lowered the deadly weapon to his side and burst into an annoying round of ill laughter. He abruptly raised the gun and pointed it at the navyman's head.

A shot rang—after a stream of scalding liquid was unleashed in the agent's face.

Avery bolted out the door past shrieking obscenities.

"Don't let him get away!" Dauerman howled. "He killed the hostage!"

The lieutenant scrambled down the long corridor, mazing right and left, all the way to the end. There he reactivated an elevator, waited a moment, and when the car arrived he jumped in. By now he was sure a horde of NIPD officers had rushed into the building and drummed past the lobby in search of a ruthless killer.

The ride down into the forbidden abyss took longer than he wanted. But when the elevator came to a stop and its stainless-steel doors split open, Avery's legs propelled him like a jaguar, rushing him past the demon-faced gargoyles of the underground world. He had not galloped like that since his football days in Naval Academy when as a Running Back he hurtled himself through an open field, dancing with amazing ease, faking turns and sprinting past the opposition that tried to tackle him. But this was no game. He had stopped playing games long ago. Today was the day he would either reach his last end zone or die trying.

He picked up the pace despite a twinge of knee pain and raced through tunnels, pounding the concrete with hurried shoes, descending deeper to a place he hated. Yet onward he went.

Something flared down his right leg and he came to a limping halt. A burning ligament, the old football injury, returned to assault him. His knee begged him to sit for a moment. But before he could squat, an old nemesis— the black monster—engulfed him. "Noooo …."

The dark. That awful, frightening void. It terrorized him as a child and its effects stalked him as an adult. His father would kill the electricity by tampering with the circuit box, then forcibly lock young Neil inside a bedroom dungeon. He did it to punish him. To destroy him because of who he was and what he stood for. The boy Avery was the last remaining memory a drunken man could not get rid of: the image of his deceased wife—the only thing that haunted him for losing her. He had never learned to deal with the raw thought of her death. He didn't want to. Someone had to bare the blame, he told the boy. In his father's twisted mind, someone was responsible for a dead, young mother. And that person was his son ….

With hands his only guide, the lieutenant groped on bended knees, creeping to the pace of a punishing heartbeat. He stopped when the torturous pain and the endless dark proved impossible to conquer. He tried to convince himself he needed to rest, but there wasn't time. If he didn't hurry, if he didn't proceed, his opponents would gain on him.

In haste, he surged to his feet, lost his balance and tumbled headlong down the steep, castle-like, cement spiral stairway.

A gunshot echoed, splitting his right eardrum with a wailing sound. The blast of the Russian weapon replayed like a 16-inch main gun booming from the deck of an old battleship, and the unconscious lieutenant awakened. He couldn't tell if his eyes were closed or open. Right now that didn't matter. What mattered was that he could hardly move. He lifted his head in a sit-up position, then passed out with a skull-smacking thunk.

To a reverberating cry, his eyes shot open when something crawled over his face and scampered away through the darkness. His body felt like it had plunged down an elevator shaft; every joint, every muscle, every bone erupting with pain. His parched throat felt like sandpaper. If he didn't drink something, even his own urine, he would pass out. His eyelids slammed shut and he thunked his head against the concrete floor again.

Awakened by his own groans he stood dazed to his feet and stared into the blurred florescent glow of his watch. He was puzzled as to why he saw only one of its arms. Avery was uncertain how badly he was hurt, how far he had journeyed, how much more he had left to go.

His pounding head felt fiery wet. He raised a hand to his brow and felt a gash. He was bleeding profusely. With a wall as his support he took his first drunken steps and felt more blood dribbling from the ear where Dauerman's bullet had nipped him. In the depth of his surroundings it was difficult to tell which direction he was traveling—the right way; the wrong way.

He rough-wiped his raw brow. The impact of the bone-jarring fall and the sting of sweat had set it ablaze. Time, and an entire naval police force were against him and he was keenly aware of it. He wished he could silence his screaming thoughts to pick up the pace, but burning calves and a throbbing knee wouldn't allow him.

He dropped to a crawl and something fell out of his top pocket. "What's that?" Sweeping arms and blind fingers searched.

Pain shot through his left leg when the object pressed against his shinbone, weakening him. It was long and round. Fingers examined it and the face of Commander Valentine flashed across his turbulent mind. It was Avery's last day aboard the *USS Man Of War*, moments before his farewell party. Valentine handed it to him as a going-away present and he kept it in his top pocket ever since.

He thumbed the pen-like device at one end, and instantly, a feeble beam of light traced a rocky wall. Although its glow offered little relief, he had a weapon to combat the blackness with.

With a limp, he stood to his feet and strained to see what lay only several inches in front of him. He stretched out a hand, laid it on the rocky wall, and step by step, the penlight led him through the incredibly long, incredibly dark passageway.

A heavy smell was a sure sign he was nearing that dreaded transport chamber. The putrid reek of petroleum, and whatever else stank, possibly a dead rat, steered him on until he realized with alarm the field of rocklike fangs he was in; the fossilized teeth of some ancient relic that had died before it could bite down on its last meal. That's what the hanging stalactites and standing stalagmites looked like: the open mouth of some monstrous great beast. He pushed onward, careful not to impale himself on a stony sword yet grateful that the florescent gleam of cave minerals was enough to help him see the lab's rock-wall barrier was wide open. He entered the laboratory, and with the aid of the penlight, found the electric lever and slammed it. The halogen lamps crescendoed to full strength, burning his skin like radiation, stinging his eyes with the glare of ten suns, shattering the cosmic darkness yet keeping him blind for a long moment still. When dilated pupils returned to normal and rheumy eyes adjusted, he got to work: turning knobs, rotating valves, flipping switches throughout the big lab. He still had difficulty seeing but he booted the quantum computer, and when it hummed to life, he quickly logged in.

He dashed around the computer-cluttered control station to the particle accelerator's data panel. He would need to adjust its three, graduated, safe-like knobs for speed, power, and control. Too little speed would only strip away his skin and organs, leaving a skeleton to float through a kaleidoscope portal like a dead man's bones for time and eternity. Too much power would char his skin, leaving him as victim of a Hiroshima blast. Not enough control, and the man-size thermo-glass tube would not lock with the platform's O-ring, thus blow away his remains like desert sand in the wind. He had to get the settings right.

A sound from behind froze him. Someone had waited for him in the blackout.

"Lieutenant, step away from the data panel without turning around."

If Avery resisted, he would be shot in the back.

With a careful, over-the-shoulder head turn, he drifted halfway between the strobing panel and the negatron cylinder. There, standing behind him across the lab, a hard-faced, helmeted Marine sentry with weapon drawn at arms length, waited. He recognized the man as having been with Dauerman on the day he broke into the agent's office: an up elevator had pinged like the *Seven's* engine room replying to the bridge, and when the cab's stainless-steel doors opened wide, three scowl-faced men in black shoes, Docker slacks, and maroon-colored polo shirts, stepped out with their backs to him. Did they spot me? he recalled asking himself.

"Sir, drop to your knees. Hands behind your back."

His mind raced and his legs felt energized with adrenaline.

The Marine cocked his gun. "On your knees!"

Avery leaped for cover, rolling with a tumble behind the wide glasslike tube in a hail of sizzling bullets. The noisy ricocheting shattered the chilling silence of the lab, sending echoing bursts rippling throughout the outside tunnel like a speeding freight train departing.

The navyman kept low, hidden from view behind the cylinder's ramp.

The armed Marine approached the goliath machine; his shoes clicking on the limestone floor.

It was too late to hide the blood on the floor.

Now the Marine was almost on top of him.

Avery groaned in pain.

He jumped out of hiding, and suddenly, four angry hands gripped the sentry's dark weapon: *Bang.* It discharged in the struggle but no one was hit. Avery scored with a punch, and the sentry's helmet hit the floor with a clack. He staggered for a second, swung a fist past the weaving lieutenant, and a return blow to the gut bent the armed man. Another punch landed on the sentry's bony face as he raised his weapon. He fell over a chair, landing on the floor with a thud; arms and legs splayed.

Avery dashed away from the bullet-riddled cylinder and snatched the loose gun from the scuffed floor. It released a mist of gray smoke in his hands. Now I can defend myself, he thought. Its hardness felt good in the soft flesh of his fingers. For the longest, Avery had wanted to examine the distinct Federation weapon up close; feel the bolt of recoil up his arm; breathe in its thick, burning gunpowder and experience the power of brass projectiles tear through the air at the speed of 1200 feet per second. The sleek, big, black handgun. Its beauty mesmerized him. It probably belonged to an army officer in charge of an elite Russian unit, he thought.

He wedged the weapon into the front of his waistband, feeling the warm barrel stroke his bellybutton. His uniform was in disarray. Shirt and tee hanging over his trouser belt. Necktie rumpled and tossed. Smudged service jacket falling off his back with the fat wrinkled folds of a Chinese Shar-Pei dog. Fighting was never pretty or neat. He tossed a pitiless glance at the injured Marine lying facedown in a dark pool of blood draining from his nose, and dashed back to the blinking accelerator panel. The impact of angry fists left the sentry stunned and disabled. But for how long? It didn't matter, he reasoned. It would give him the extra time he needed before the senseless NCIS junior agent, masquerading in a Marine uniform, even lifted a finger.

When Avery was certain he had tweaked the three knobs on the particle accelerator's data panel to their proper combination, he programmed the machine's timing sequence and waited for it to download into the system. Once that's done, I'll be safe in another world, he thought. Warm blood ran down his face and collected at the bottom of his chin, dripping to the floor like ready java dripping in a coffeemaker's carafe.

The lengthy wait tore at him. He wished he had something to wipe the stream now running down his neck, or a headband to stop the bleeding.

It normally didn't take this long for the quantum computer to respond. It usually ran smoothly; faithfully. "Come on. Start up!" He swiped a stinging, blood-veiled right eye with his sleeve as he dug through a rubble of anxious thoughts—thoughts of him making mistakes at the control station; of failing to transport himself; of dying where he stood.

Oddly, the system cleared when he broke out of what worried him most.

—Access Denied—
Screen Name/Password
*** Unknown ***
Zyto
Zyto
Zyto

"What the …."

He gave a look. The fallen agent stirred.

Avery typed in the antivirus code—Pheryl 13—as more blood streamed from his forehead and ear, down his neck, to his chin, to the floor. "Come on, dammit, work!" He slammed a swollen fist into a side panel over the same results: *Access Denied.* Now he would have to struggle to clear the system, but there wasn't time for his spinning mind to figure out what to do and how to do it. All he could think were those arrested by NCIS for stealing Project Black's Navy secrets: Pratt, Hobbs, Evans, Rivera, Yancey, Lee.

Another thought came to him like a sub's probing periscope-head breaking the ocean surface, and when it fully arose, the submerged thought was titanic in size: P-h-e ….

Strange how the first letter of each of those names and the number of folders he discovered in Dauerman's office—13 of them—created the same acronym as the antivirus code—Pheryl 13. My God, he thought. His temples throbbed with migraine strength.

Something ominous filled the lab, causing Avery's chest to ache and joints to stiffen.

Hank Dauerman, sweating and panting from overexertion, came into his periphery. Nothing would stop him until the long-barreled A-46, the dreaded weapon that pointed accusations, had done its duty.

Within red burn marks, critical eyes were those of an alley cat reflecting light beams of a passing car at night. He convinced himself that if he shot the psychopathic agent bent on killing him, it would be an act of self-defense.

He withdrew the hidden weapon, spun with arm extended, and easily pulled the trigger.

Click, click, click ….

His heart rate surged.

"What's the matter, Lieutenant? Out of ammo?"

With a grunt, Avery hurled the useless weapon at Dauerman. It smacked the wall behind him when he weaved and clattered to the floor.

A voice from within Avery spoke. Echoing. Haunting: You think I'd keep a loaded gun in the house? I'm not stupid!

The chilled air in the laboratory shrunk his wet skin against his aching bones. He was stupid to think he could kill his dead father.

Dauerman closed in on the dazed agent laboring to his feet and unleashed a chop, a kick, and a punch that sent him back to the floor on wobbling legs. This time Avery was certain he would not get up.

"I ordered you to kill him!"

From the motionless body, the NCIS man lifted burning eyes and aimed them at the Navy officer. "Now all I have to do is get rid of one more person." He stepped back, flipped the command switch on a panel and the rock-wall barrier rolled on its rails like elevator doors, entombing the two men in the transport chamber. A single blast from the agent's gun took care of the switch, assuring him that this time the runaway prisoner would not escape.

Avery wormed a finger into his taut collar and ripped the noose off his necktie with an angry tug. "Tell me something, Mr. CEO. How much did Al-Qaeda shovel into the Corporation in exchange for stolen, military info? Ten million dollars? Twenty million? Enough to run Spectrum?" He felt veins protruding from a throbbing forehead.

"Shut the hell up!"

"It's over, Shank. I know the truth. You, Luke Driscoll, and Ben Nobleman were behind this. The bogus corporation." He searched Dauerman's blistered face. "All others—the sailors, the officers—were patsies."

The agent grabbed his stomach. "You don't know a damn—"

"I know plenty. You set up Pratt for the big fall by creating a phony profile based on a past conviction and planted it in the database. Then you beat him to a pulp, threatened to kill him if he didn't play ball, and forced him into a false confession to cover your fat ass. You disintegrated Marcus, and now plan to kill me!" A thought came to him. Something else the navyman wanted to know. "What's your full name, Shank?"

He regarded the serviceman like a lion regarded its prey. "Henry—Joseph Henry." His eyes were filled with stormy vengeance. But after a moment, his hard features relaxed. "Not a bad synopsis, Lieutenant. However, you forgot one thing." He walked over to the corner desk, lifted a leather briefcase from beneath it and laid it on top with a thunk. It was monogrammed with a gold letter "J". "What you know won't help you a bit. You must die, and Spectrum's secret must die with you."

Suddenly everything seemed tight and small to the serviceman: his shoes, his uniform, the shrinking lab.

A patch of oily sweat on Dauerman's suit, and the place where a button used to be, were the fingerprints of a deadly struggle the NCIS officer had with a dedicated scientist.

"I tip my hat to you on your great detective work. But my job is done. The moment you made Spectrum a success, I repaid Al-Qaeda for the generous gift they up-fronted." He opened the briefcase and extracted several stacks of bills wrapped in mustard-yellow currency bands. He fanned the money in his face and breathed in its scent. "We got what we wanted and so did they—the Navy's stealth technology of its long-range submarine missiles. What a shame our haughty nation was too busy with a new, costly, space-defense system. They could've had a time machine."

"Our own radar-silent missiles turned on us. You're crazy."

"Crazy is doing nothing about it. All I did was even the scales to the monopoly. What could be wrong with that?"

Avery clenched his teeth like pulling the pin on a grenade. "Nothing. Until someone else steals our secret from Al-Qaeda."

"You're such a pessimist. Me? I'm a genius."

"Then how are you getting out of this godforsaken tomb?"

"I have a way." He looked calm; eyes plausible.

"And me?"

"I changed my mind about killing you. You'll be committing suicide, just like you always wanted. You see, you broke a strict protocol when you parroted about our little secret."

"In that case you won't be needing this." He ripped the top, nickel-size button off his service jacket and hurled it at Dauerman, striking him square in the face.

"My, what a nasty temper. But you're to blame for sewing that listening device on. Now that I know you can't be trusted, I can terminate you from the program. Literally."

He barked out a new antivirus code—Averyisdead—and instructed the lieutenant to feed it into the computer.

When the system cleared, he ordered Avery to type in another code, one he was all-too familiar with, and as he did, his hands trembled. He backed away from the control station at the threatening wave of the agent's gun—and from fear of the pulsating, plasma screen's message: Chill Factor …Chill Factor ….

"Now, Lieutenant, you're in for the ride of your life. A one-way ticket to a place of no return—oblivion."

Something activated, a whirring sound followed, and a twelve-foot, stainless-steel ram pushed through a narrow shaft in the high ceiling. The hungry negatron cylinder rose slowly until it cleared the platform. Everything was set. The lieutenant's heart pounded in his windpipe, choking him. He sucked in air, knowing what Dauerman's next command would be.

"In the machine." He waved that gun again.

Burning sweat dribbled from Avery's scalp and crawled like long worms down the skin of his paralyzed body.

"I said, get in!"

"I'd rather be shot than die in that genetic meat grinder."

Dauerman pounced on him and struck him in the face with a fast fist, flattening him on his back. He straddled over him, cocked the weapon, and pointed it at the serviceman's head.

Avery crooked a quick leg and knocked the agent to the floor with a swift kick. The weapon tore loose from his grip and slid across the floor, clacking into the other handgun like two disks in a shuffleboard game.

Dauerman rolled over and stood upright. Avery jumped to his feet and smacked a hard cheek with a swollen fist. Dauerman shook off the blow. Avery swung at him again. The agent blocked it and rammed an elbow into his opponent's gut, followed by a hammering backfist to the jaw that landed Avery on the floor for the second time.

Dauerman wiped his nose with the back of his hand. "Prick." There was blood. He clutched his stomach with a groan, spotted the weapons on the floor behind him, and went for them.

Avery launched himself to his feet, arm cocked high. He whipped a tight fist into Dauerman as he turned—a solid punch to the gut that left him wide-eyed and stunned. Avery followed with another jarring hit, then another and another, all in the same place, until Dauerman doubled over and fell to his knees.

Avery bolted after the weapons. The agent grabbed him by a leg, knocked him over and hammered a bent knee into his crotch, paralyzing him.

Dauerman leaped for the guns.

Avery uncoiled from the gnawing pain, crawled over the agent, and four hands fought to reach the weapons, each man snatching one. The two, huffing, angry men body-rolled away from each other and scrambled to their feet.

The Russian handguns were now locked in a duel of silence, ending when each man pulled the trigger. But only one gun flashed.

A Sea Knight helicopter pounded into a landing on a tarmac-black roof and the craft's huge rear loading ramp flew open like the mouth of a hungry gator. Royce Gold—a CNN reporter, along with a videographer, audio person, and lighting assistant—charged out of the helo's crew compartment behind two-dozen Navy-SEAL commandos as they rushed to the roof's access way where they climbed down a ladder, one floor at a time.

In the lobby's marbled rotunda, walls emblazoned with photo plaques carried the faces of immortal admirals from the Navy's inception to the present: Richardson, Halsey, Kimmel, Nimitz.... There, a pacing chief of police—a tall, decisive-looking man—stood padded in body armor.

The CNN reporter with slick black hair got his cue. "This is Royce Gold reporting live from North Island's Navy headquarters where the capture and escape of the Black-Sunday hacker has rocked the naval community." The cameraman moved toward the chief of police and Royce Gold followed. "Sir, any news of the fugitive's whereabouts?"

The brawny police officer ignored him and raised a walkie-talkie to his mouth. "Shank, what's your twenty, over?" He waited for a reply but with each urgent call to the top field agent all he got was intermittent chatter and a blaring hiss of silence. Now that NIPD and Navy SEALs had swept through all the floors of the vacant building, the keen-eyed chief of police called off the search for the weapon-toting assailant—and the NCIS officer who chased him with determined vengeance.

Avery grabbed his chest to lessen the pain while his adversary waited for him to crumble to the floor. The agent inhaled a breath of smoke seeping into the tense air from the round mouth of the Russian handgun, and grinned.

He leaned to one side, then the other. A jawbone clenched in anger was now locked in pain. He grabbed his chest, ripped his suit open and sent buttons clicking across the limestone floor like runaway dice. Dark blood seeped through the crisp Dior shirt, invading the dove-white and turning it wine-red.

Avery looked into those glazed eyes and tried to resurrect a haunting voice—the familiar mask behind the agent's rugged face—but nothing.

"Neil," he whimpered. "Help me!"

The navyman's jaw dropped a fraction. He felt certain it was he who had been shot. The pain he felt was actually a hammering heartbeat against his sternum that made his chest hurt so much. He managed to relax his grip on the Federation-made weapon when the agent grimaced with a moan and collapsed face first to the floor with a pounding thud.

Avery checked the time on his watch: twenty minutes. He had never stared at a motionless body that long without blinking.

He dashed to the control station with weapon in hand and exited Chill Factor's site. The bulletproof tube clamped down and rose again, waiting for a new command. He typed it in, and when he did, blinking instruments and glowing monitors filled the lab in a prism of splendid colors. "Soon I'll be home," he thought out loud. His surroundings no longer menaced him.

Shaclick

Avery spun toward the strange sound and an abrupt blast sent him tumbling over a chair. He was stunned by the joust-like mighty impact of an invisible lance, driven by an equally unseen armored knight on horseback. He swept a trembling gaze throughout the loft-size lab, and found him: Dauerman with head raised, weapon in hand, empty magazine at his side. He had reloaded.

The agent's skull thunked against tile, and a frozen, blank stare took over.

Slowly, Avery sat up and traced a trickle of crimson that led past his shoes and trousers. He found himself in a warm glob and placed a hand where a fierce heat crossed his chest. He pulled his palm away and looked at it. Fingers dripped with blood.

Behind the overturned chair—the computers, the glowing monitors—everything, was red-splattered. The round from Dauerman's weapon had punched a hole into his chest and out through his back.

He rolled over, coughed up thick fluid, and gasped for air. He yanked on a dangling cord and a keyboard clattered on his head. Why he had done that he wasn't sure. He forced his mind to think.

When it came to him, he pecked out a series of letters and numbers with shaky fingers as life gushed out of him. Did the bullet strike an artery? He had no idea, other than what the blast from the magnum-size weapon had done: it left a devastating sucking wound in his chest which made his stinging lungs gurgle. No matter how hard or how fast he inhaled, it was like breathing with a plastic bag over his head, tied around his neck.

Sweat crawled into his eyes, burning them like battery acid. He smeared a garnet-red hand across his face and coughed. He coughed again, volcanically this time, jumpstarting an arrhythmic heartbeat back to normal. Now his chest felt heavy and he began to wheeze. He peeled off a soaked service jacket, ripped open a soiled blouse, and tore through a bloody tee. The ugly hole would require emergency medical attention. But fifteen floors down in the secret world of Spectrum, no one would be able to hear his groans for help. No one could reach the dying man sealed in an underground laboratory.

With hand pressed into his chest, he moved on his belly like an old turtle and paddled onto the negatron's ramp, activating the tall cylinder into a slow descent. The gunshot wound leaked like a fractured concrete levee, and all efforts of an anxious Dutch-boy did nothing. There was no stopping the flow, the fear that assaulted him, the boney chill that seized him. In an attempt to climb over the O-ring's threshold, he lost his grip, slid down the blood-slippery ramp, and a death sleep came over him.

He awoke to find the thermo-glass canopy near the end of its descent stage and fought to crawl into the machine he hated. If he failed to do so, his brain would shut down without the unit being reprogrammed, and he would die.

Despite his depleting strength, he pushed his deadweight forward, inched up the ramp and squeezed himself in between the platform's threshold and the standing glass tube. The magnetic plate under him came to life and glowed neon yellow as the heavy enclosure clamped down on his legs with a crush. He gave a yell and pulled in one leg, folding it into his throbbing chest. Now he would have to work on getting the other one free.

Under the gnawing bite of the angry negatron, he coughed up a dark clump of blood, pulled in his other leg and heard the loud snap. The cylinder and O-ring became one and he was sealed in.

Two bodies filled his blurred vision: that of the Marine-like sentry and Hank Dauerman—weapon in a frozen grip as though he could fire it one last time. The serviceman was relieved justice had been served. But no one was there to witness it.

Avery upped himself with a wheeze, a grunt, and a gasp, and wobbled to his feet. Smeared handprints on the bullet-riddled enclosure streaked bloody rivulets, changing into strange shapes: a deformed turkey; the fleshy, red comb of a proud rooster. Funny how the mind played childish tricks. He thought he should laugh at that but was too weak to breathe, to wheeze, to stand. He teetered, trying to maintain his balance between life and death, and collapsed.

Chapter 32

It was dressed in a kaleidoscope of sunlight that fell upon it through stained-glass windows—a bronze-handled, six-foot-long, stately casket surrounded by lavish floral arrangements at the foot of an altar. The man lying in the upholstered interior looked comfortable, until the visitor remembered what the bible had to say about those who had departed: the dead know not anything.

The man's life had been cut short; snatched away by warring angels bidding for his soul, and they had triumphed. The forces of good over evil always won. That was the message the stream of filtered air carried with the smell of sweet blossoms, wood lacquer, potpourri-scented rug powder and fresh paint as a formidable line of men and women of all ages cast long looks upon the deceased individual: deflated hands folded over his chest and pigeon eyes closed in perpetual sleep. Rest well, someone murmured from behind. Rest well.

Throughout the long service, an overweight black woman with thick prescribed spectacles, kept a close eye on her young charge, holding her small hand in solace. Comfort was a powerful tool; a weapon to defeat fear and anxiety with; a balm to keep one from unraveling while infusing courage. But the eight-year-old could not be persuaded. She remained paralyzed, afraid of the open casket and the motionless man within. She preferred to sit far from the altar, away from things her mind understood so it could not touch her, yet close enough for her to remember. Yes, the child wanted to remember the man. It was in her eyes; the way her mousy voice sounded; it was in the way she held on to the old-looking woman's hand.

With every seat and pew in the 600-person capacity church filled from front to back, dozens of extra folding chairs were brought out for additional seating. Ushers sat as many as possible. But they could not accommodate the multitude that packed the large vestibule, or the thousands that thronged tireless outside the building's cathedral-style doors—a wide line of faithful lamenters that stretched over a country mile on the last day of tribute.

Earlier that morning the somber visitor, seeking refuge from the crowd, sat silently cocooned inside a window-tinted towncar as a canopy of creeping clouds devoured what little sunshine there was. The weather forecaster on the radio predicted rain, on-and-off all day, from chilly drizzle to locally heavy downpours. Although many came prepared, dressed in dark-colored raincoats and toting black umbrellas, the sadness they brought with them called for nature to reflect it: heavy clouds, heavy hearts. And when the winds increased and the temperature dropped, the umbrellas went up, and the raw, miserable, misty rain came down, blanketing everything and everyone.

On the pulpit, a gathering of clergymen looked on in pale silence by two inscriptions among the botanical flowers.

One read: *We will miss you.*

And the other: *Him whom we loved, God hath taken to himself.*

Hymns of the faith were played by the organist while everyone, in reverent contemplation, listened to the graceful words of the young female vocalist, supported by a choir of voices and quartet of fine-tuned stringed instruments. Someone told him it was the first time during a funeral service at their beloved sanctuary the woman sang for two hours straight, the second day in a row. Now he wished he could have gotten there sooner.

Pastor Enoch Campbell took to the lectern and gave a moving eulogy—words Avery had written; ink that flowed from the pen like blood from a fatal wound. Beside him Beulah sat, looking dignified in black. The huge turnout had strengthened her and it showed in her eyes. Her courageous smile also displayed her thanks that nothing—not even the inclement weather—had deterred aching hearts from traveling near and far. Wherever Roy Nathan Gilchrist went during his years of ministry, however far he had gone in service to God, the same distance was journeyed by a great host who came to see his pious face for the last time.

The big backdoors were swung wide open, and Avery moved past a waddling Beulah, arm-in-arm with her two oldest daughters, Darah and Taffi, dragging behind the pallbearers who led the way out of the church building into the private cemetery grounds.

He felt a female's comforting touch and their eyes met for a warm moment. It was Olympia. She was no longer the dainty little girl with ropey pigtails and a shy smile. She was now an attractive, mature-looking woman, fully developed, cascaded hair over her shoulders, drawing the attention of potential suitors in the crowd. She slipped through the clustered mourners ahead of the escort and laid a hand on the wet surface of the closed casket.

The brutal pain on her face told the story: she had discovered what it was like to lose the dearest person in her life. Roy was the only man the adopted young woman treated as a father. No one had to tell Avery there would never be another.

Joining the pallbearers, a familiar grief weighed on him, heavier than the casket he helped shoulder. When it was laid by the dead apple tree, he thought of all the birds that once rested on its branches before it refused to blossom. But it was Roy's tree. This is where he should be, he thought. The preacher planted that tree by the cemetery's edge long ago with a small shovel and a big heart, and now, it was there where he would rightfully come to rest. He convinced Pastor Campbell that was the thing to do.

Now Avery stood alongside Beulah who dampened corners of sagging eyes from beneath a delicate veil with the soft tissues Olympia fed her as they trudged along. A moment later, the big church bell, high atop in the white steeple, sounded for two minutes—sixty-two times: one, slow, monotone gong for each year of Reverend Gilchrist's life until the last one rung like a final heartbeat in a dying man's chest.

The pastor opened his bible and spoke: "Scriptures tell us death is not the end. It is the beginning ...."

Avery traded looks with Darah whose sheltered long face emerged from Dusty Smith's embrace. Roy's long-time seminary friend.

"Why?" he asked her as Enoch Campbell spoke. "Why didn't you hit me harder at the hospital? I deserved that and more."

She looked away to the mahogany-red casket he had picked out and paid for, her head finding refuge on Dusty's spacious shoulder once more.

Cold thoughts mingled with the pastor's message: "Except a seed falls to the ground and dies, it amounts to nothing."

My Roy will be laid to rest.

"But if it dies, it brings forth life."

But not the unborn memories.

Avery wanted the funeral to be a private affair. But every newspaper in every country in the world already carried the face of the smiling minister on every front page. Every TV and radio station had announced a national hero was gone.

Pastor Campbell finished preaching and closed his fat bible. He approached the serviceman and took him by the arm. Avery took Beulah's hand, and together, faced the long casket. Light droplets of chilled drizzle had become fat raindrops, softening the ground they stood on.

Just before the casket was lowered into the hungry red earth that waited with mouth open wide, a breeze whimpered through the leafless, arthritic-like branches of fall trees and Avery turned in that direction.

A distinguished-looking, elderly black man slipped through the crowd and made his way to the front. He stood by the casket and those nearest it: Dusty Smith, Pastor Campbell, Roy's army buddies, Beulah, her daughters, and Chloe, who gripped her long ropey pigtails like they were safety lines on a whaleboat being hoisted into a bouncing sea.

Avery witnessed an unspeakable peace in the old gentleman. The look he gave was strangely wonderful, for his eyes spoke of a place beyond the great expanse; a world he knew he would journey to one day. He was convinced now that heaven was real; more beautiful than all the sermons he'd heard described it to be.

With head bowed and eyes closed, the gray-haired man invited those around to join him in a moment of silence. When it was over, he raised a golden trumpet to his mouth and pressed it light upon his lips. Then pointing the instrument skyward, he exhaled the beloved hymn, *Amazing Grace.*

The sweet clarion call showered on Avery the comfort that huddled people together in the relentless rain, a thronging that created a canopy of black umbrellas covering every inch of the park-like cemetery. He lifted his hands in worship and whispered a prayer for Mama, for her daughters, for himself: Lord Jesus, come into my heart….

When the tender notes ended, the elderly man lowered the trumpet to his side, and with great ease, slipped through the overwhelming crowd the same way he came, disappearing with the cold breeze.

With the exhausting funeral service over and the incredible multitude gone, a lone, tall man remained hunched over a gravestone. Since sunrise, even before he stumbled out of bed, the navyman longed with angry mourning to have this moment all to himself, with nothing and no one surrounding him except bare trees and churning memories. How easy it was to wish a venomous snake would bite him. Death would be quick.

Earlier after the downpour, it was a downcast Pastor Campbell who stood alongside the fresh gravesite with several, slump-shouldered young men from the congregation, all staring at a dead tree while Avery listened from afar. "Why did God cut down the life of such a pious man before his time?" No one dared to answer the hard question the grieving pastor put to them. "Tomorrow," he said to the grim-looking, black men, "first thing in the morning, this tree will also be cut down. Its stump, a reminder of what God did to Reverend Gilchrist."

All day long, Avery fought against a grief that rose like a surfer's tide. While he waited for it to wash over him, for its waves to pull him down and knock him senseless to his knees, he read each line of inscription on the newly-made granite gravestone.

> Forgiven by grace
> Forgiven by grace
> All my sins are forgiven
> I can now see his face

He reached into his peacoat and pulled out a one-time-use Kodak camera he purchased at the Norfolk NEX. Diminishing sunlight was long in coming, so he thumbed the film-advance wheel until it locked. He squinted through the viewfinder, getting ready to press the shutter-release button.

Roy's gravestone. Click.

"Thank you for wrapping your arm around my shoulder."

Fallen, wet leaves. Click.

"For calling me your son."

The lifeless tree. Click.

"And for teaching me to say: I love you."

A steel-gray sky. Click.

"Soon, sweet closure will cure me."

A trampled rose from a wreath. Click.

"Because I buried you."

Click, click, click.

Avery had sat for over an hour on the muddy, leaf-strewn lawn; his back touching the face of the cold gravestone; his trousers and coattail soaking up what the ground refused to drink. Above, a sliver of watercolor blue began to split the clouds wide.

From beyond the hills, a sound transported him to another place.

He straddled a bicycle at a railroad crossing—bells dinging, tracks humming, wheels clanking. Here she comes. Roy's voice. At the rising blare of the approaching behemoth, the earth rumbled at his feet and a gust of wind hit his face, making his hair dance. The tonnage of long-bodied stainless-steel cars thundered with a diesel roar until the blast of the train's distinct airhorn trailed away. "And there she goes," he whispered. "Bye, Dad."

He pointed the camera upward and found what he was looking for in the viewfinder. Faith Mission's tall steeple.

He centered on it. Click.

The big brass bell. It was silent now.

The film-advance knob tightened and a zero appeared in a small, round window.

Avery studied the red-and-black plastic camera and the army of trees flanking him. He thought of where he would put the pictures once he had them developed. Some he would enlarge and frame. The others he would slip into the vinyl sleeves of a photo album. The knifing memory had to be kept razor sharp. If he let it go dull it would cease to cut.

With calm acceptance he rose to his feet. He had confronted grief and rising tears, and felt better for doing it. He placed a hand on the smooth gravestone, lowered his lips to it, and kissed it. "It's a new day."

He hurled the pocket camera like a football where it landed beyond the trees in the distance.

Avery sped down a winding road, flanked by stately trees and rolling hills; a shortcut to the parking lot where he abandoned a Honda minivan on Teaberry Road. Together with the Gilchrists, he rushed past the church with the gabled steeple, and dashed into the noisy cemetery behind it. He knew full well that nothing would stop the slashing teeth of chainsaws: not Mama's pleadings, or the glum faces of the adult girls, each ready to sob out tears as soon as they witnessed their father's twenty-five-foot-tall, lifeless tree topple over with a crash.

Soon the stump would look exactly as the serviceman remembered it.

Avery spotted Pastor Campbell looking at the spectator-workers from his rectory-office window. A moment later, the pastor stormed out the church building's backdoor and marched toward the eye-goggled men; roaring power saws in hand. He moved his arms in big circles, palms up, urging the tree cutters to get going. But it looked more like he was trying to fly.

"This should've been cut down already. What're you waiting for, the rapture?"

The tallest black man among them fired back: "Are you angry at us or God?"

"Never mind," Campbell said. "Just get to work."

"And if we don't?"

In the noisy commotion, gasping wheezes turned Avery around. Taffi had fallen to her knees and her Albuteral pump had dropped out of her hand.

Beulah scooped up the fallen inhaler, gave it a vigorous shake, and shoved its nozzle into her daughter's gaping mouth. She gave the pump a squeeze. "Someone help. It's empty!" The cry cut through the turbulent air, turning everyone around. "She can't breathe!"

"Call an ambulance," Darah pleaded.

"Give her mouth-to-mouth," April said.

"There isn't time," cried Olympia.

The tree crew joined the girls in one knot as they gathered around Taffi, and Pastor Campbell battled through. He looked to the clouds. "Father in heaven, help us!"

A crow cawed a reply from the treetops.

Avery's quickened pulse jogged his memory, and the moment that would follow resurfaced like a phantom submarine. If he hesitated a hair's second to scoop Taffi in his arms, rush her to the van, and race to the nearest hospital, it would be too late.

A hot, buzzing current beneath his feet froze him where he stood.

Beulah dropped to her knees beside Taffi and turned her daughter's bird-open mouth to her. She closed her frightened eyes tight as she prayed.

Another surge of current buzzed beneath the ground where Avery stood, and all eyes met his. "Did anyone feel what I just felt?"

The workers turned off their power saws and the dying roar gave way to silence. It stayed that way until muted birds released a burst of chirping praise. The power cords on the wet ground were checked by the men, but there didn't seem to be anything wrong with them.

When the strange moment passed, Avery realized the color on Taffi's bleached face had been restored. She inhaled deep and let it out. Her eyes popped open and her mouth dropped wide. "I can breathe," she announced. "I can breathe!"

She jumped to her feet and let energized legs take her for a run. And with each inhaled breath, she made the same declaration over again. "I can breathe. I can breathe!"

Beulah stayed on her knees, lost in a lip-parted stare while her shouting daughter ran in endless circles, throwing her arms in the air. "I can breathe!"

Avery stood alongside Pastor Campbell whose silent eyes darted about. Everyone had all experienced the same thing.

A swirling wind rustled bare branches, turning everyone in its direction.

Avery approached Roy's tree. Pastor Campbell followed. They were everywhere. He plucked one of them off a branch and examined it. In unison, the tree-cutters moved to help Beulah up, but she waved them off as her awestricken daughters circled the tree.

"Pastor," pointed one young man. "That's a sign from God."

Another said, "It's best we leave it be."

The crewmen put away their cutting equipment.

Avery showed everyone what he had in his palm—a tiny green leaf.

"Dear God." Pastor Campbell's eyes refused to blink. "We've just witnessed a miracle."

Beulah was caught between crying and smiling. "The first at Faith Mission." She rose to her feet with effortless moves.

For the first time since Roy's passing, Darah looked to Avery and snapped that long estrangement; tears spilling down lifted cheeks.

April, draped in her father's favorite pullover sweater, covered her mouth with its long, oversized argyle sleeves and released a deep, joyous laugh.

Pastor Campbell snatched the empty inhaler from the cold ground, looked at it, then aimed eyes at Roy's tree.

The cutting crew threw their hands up and thanked God for what they witnessed.

Mama grabbed Taffi, Olympia, and Chloe. Nobody wanted to move an inch from Roy's gravesite.

Avery blinked away tears, his happy gaze on the sign from above—a tree of life.

Avery sat alone in the family room by the warm orange flame of the red-bricked fireplace. He loved cold, quiet afternoons in December. He wore a red flannel shirt, blue corduroy pants, and white Adidas running sneakers. In his hands he held an open book—one of Roy's pictorial bible dictionaries. He fancied the thought he was turning out to be like the father he loved and vowed to read every bible commentary the minister kept treasured in his library. Each day, he sat beside a stack of books. Hours of reading. Hungry fingers turning wordy pages. However long it would take, he wanted to learn what Roy had learned. All the things that made him great.

Someone emerged from the kitchen, ushering into the warm room the smell of biscuits, pies, and muffins. He paused from reading. The passion in Beulah's eyes was as bright as the flame in the hearth.

She handed him an envelope. He gave it a quizzical look. The unopened letter had Darah's handwriting on it: *From Neil to Roy*

His eyes found Mama's, and a thought mushroomed in his head. It swept him away like the wind-raked leaves that skipped over his feet each time he went to lay flowers on Roy's gravesite.

Her light touch brought him back. "Thought maybe you might want it." She sank into the couch beside him. "Seems Roy never read it."

That day at Dugger Creek, he was alone, surrounded by the beauty of oaks, birch trees, and the splendid waters that hurried past him like streaking pods of dolphin. There, on a big slab of gray rock, he held a ready pen, and in the other, a frightened child's heart. His head was filled with aching thoughts and the notepad before him with fast-written words; sentiments he knew he should have said.

"Where did you find it?" he finally asked. He regarded her carefully. It had been a while since she wore those thick-lensed glasses, the ones that made her eyes appear dim. Now he wondered how thickening hair regrew on the bald spots of her scalp.

"I found it behind his empty dresser. With most of your father's clothes at Boone's Goodwill, I came across it moving the unneeded furniture out the bedroom."

The envelope was old, dirty, and folded out of shape.

"Son …." She laid a mother's hand on his shoulder. "I'm sure Roy didn't just throw it aside. But with the clutter in the room and his busy preaching schedule, well … he probably forgot."

Mama made her way back to the safe haven of her small kitchen to tend to her baking, leaving her son in a moment of long silence. An invisible hand came to his throat, strangling him. It fell loose when he tore into the sealed envelope.

He fingered the old letter like a frayed dollar bill. He unfolded it, and when he was certain he wouldn't cry, he read the ink-blotted words written twelve years prior:

Dear Roy,

I hope as you read this, you and your family are well. There's much I wish I had the courage to say, but here, I'll share the two most important. First, I want you to know I love you with all my heart. The way a son loves a father. Second, it's important that you see a doctor soon for a full health screening. Cancer kills over 1,500 people in this country everyday and I don't want you to be one of them. A timely checkup can mean early detection and treatment. Caught on time, you could be healthy for years to come. Years you and I can spend together. Please don't try to figure out how I know about the cancer. Just do as I say and you'll be fine.

Looking forward to special moments with you. Your only son, Neil

Chapter 33

Neil Avery was in the roof-sloped attic, sitting at an office-type desk, reading a lengthy article in the morning newspaper about a long-sought-after fugitive. The sunlight by the window was neither strong nor weak, even when he parted the lengthy drapes every few minutes to watch a sheriff's car pace up and down the old dirt road behind the naked birch trees dancing in the breeze. Avery wore a Van Heusen plain white shirt, a pair of *Dickies* dusty-olive colored slacks, and his favorite footwear, those old boon dockers he had owned for so long. He reread the bold-printed caption for the fifth time: *FBI's Most Wanted Man.* He studied the male's features for the umpteenth time: clean-shaven face; trimmed dark hair; well-defined nose; wide, somber mouth; soft, keen eyes. A picture of the same man appeared in the papers the previous year—just ahead of the comic section. The year before that the face appeared on page five, moving up gradually, until today, when he appeared again on the front page, grabbing the headline story. The man in the photo never seemed to age. But time and certain people were catching up with him.

Beulah came up two minutes later, swiffer mop in one hand and feather duster in the other. In all the time since Roy's passing, she was still cleaning up after him.

"Mama?" He motioned for her to come to him, and when she did, he stood, draped an arm over her neck, kissed her warm round cheek and whispered in her ear. It wasn't a brief sentiment, though, or a timely word of encouragement, something from the bible. It was a rather lengthy explanation, and she listened with the patience of *Job*. He knew she understood, even though she never said she did. Now he had what he wanted from Beulah: her blessings, a private moment with her, for them to look out the window together at the white carpet of snow, and for him to express the thoughts his mind held so that she could leave him alone for a while. She had all day to clean.

When he finished packing his scant belongings he went to the window again. The sheriff's car was long gone, so he let his eyes follow a pair of baby prairies playing a game of tag in the snow. If it was safe for them he knew it would be safe for him. He headed down the stairs to the family room.

At the front door he laid a beaten suitcase down and faced them: Beulah, Darah, Taffi, April, Chloe. "It's a long drive. I ... should get going." He tried to work up a smile but could not. He had stopped practicing long ago.

"Don't stay away too long, son." The gentle strength in her embrace was as the morning sun, calling him to complete a journey. "You have a family that loves you."

He studied her clear, chocolate-brown eyes. They looked like the soft prairie-dog pups he had just seen: small, huddled, round; side by side; resting in the open field of fluff after they had chased each other for a long time.

Behind them in the corner of the room, a beautifully-decorated, six-foot-tall Christmas tree blinked every few seconds with green, yellow, red, and orange lights. But the bulb within the cherub that crowned its top had gone out.

Taffi whimpered a wheezeless sob and threw her arms around his neck, pulling him in for a kiss. April did the same, holding on to him for a long time. "I wish you wouldn't do this," she whispered as Darah looked on.

Darah's discreet eyes rolled to him for a nanosecond. "What's wrong with him, Mama?"

Beulah gave him a forlorn look. She seemed to know that some broken hearts never mended. "I suppose part of him never fully recovered."

Now it was Darah's turn to stand before him. "You're so near, yet so far. When I met you, I rediscovered love. Now I've discovered an ache I can't get rid of."

There had to be a better way of saying goodbye, but he frowned when he couldn't find one. "I made you wait for nothing."

Her eyes melted into shimmering pools, and when her lips met his, time stood still. She reached for his hand and held it. "Pia won't come down." She swiped wet cheeks with a balled-up tissue. "She wants to say goodbye to you in private."

He pulled away from her chiffon touch, wanting to leave as soon as possible. But when she grabbed him by the arm and held him where he stood, he saw she understood that things were different between them.

"Neil, there's something you should know." She regarded him with a look he had never seen before. Secrets always sharpened her eyes, turning them from golden brown to a glassy sheen. "Chloe—"

He turned away. Chloe looked nothing like Darah. She had a slight resemblance to Gerald. A love-child from an outside relationship, he thought. He climbed the stairs and walked down the hall where the crooning voice of Nat King Cole, singing *Don't go*, came over Olympia's multi-disk CD player. He tapped on her bedroom door.

"Come in."

As soon as he entered, her face said it all. Olympia's button-round eyes, that smiled so warm and bright, were sharpened on him. He closed the door behind him with a *clink* of the lock.

"You're always leaving!" She sat up on the edge of her queen-size bed and crossed arms over her heaving chest. A ruffled cream blanket was pushed to one side. "When will you stay forever? And why won't you marry my sister?"

He knew he'd be wasting his breath explaining incredible things, so he kept it short. "Because this isn't my world. I don't belong here."

"Yes you do," she cried in a raspy voice. "In case you haven't noticed, Mama and my sisters love you. But you can't feel it b'cuz you're dead!"

Avery sat beside her on the bed. Dead things still haunted him. Perhaps they always would. "I'd like to be your big brother. Honest. But I'm the victim of too much hate and abuse. It's all I know. Plus, I'm on the lam for killing a man, I'm on the FBI's most-wanted list, and sheriffs in Virginia are after me, too. Not a good recipe for a lasting relationship."

"Don't gimme that crap, I'm not a child. Every four months for the last two years you've been ducking somewhere, and now this." She berated him with her eyes.

He groped for a long time, in search of something more reasonable and less remarkable to say. What would she say if he told her the truth? *I'm a lost time traveler who needs to find his way back home....* He slipped into some kind of trance fantasizing what her answer would be.

She told him, "Know what you are? You're just a big turkey who's afraid to love!"

He thought he heard her say: pig jerky. "What did you call me?"

"A turkey!" Olympia broke down and buried her face in his lap. But he understood her tears. She no longer had a father. And the only man who brought comfort through her awful loss was about to leave also.

Nat King Cole's mellow voice trailed away and the CD player switched disks. A melancholy tune on a piano came in and another voice crooned through the stereo speakers. Barry Manilow.

Avery stroked her hair, long and thick, taking in its fruit-scented smell while she sang along with the CD: *I'll be seeing you ....*

When all the songs on the CD played, the unit switched off and she sat up. The silence in the room calmed her the way Mama's voice often did. "That a girl." Things would be all right, even without him. But he ached with wonder what she would do with her emptiness.

"Will I ever see you again?" The pain of his departure was etched on her tender face.

"Of course, sweet pea."

"But that'll be a long time from now," she whined. "I'll miss you."

He knelt by her bare feet, holding her baby, powder-soft hands in his. "I promise. This time I won't be far."

She studied him as though wanting to believe.

"Whenever you want to see me, all you have to do is visit."

"Where will you go?"

He rose to his feet and leaned over her, getting ready to plant a kiss on her forehead. "Right there. *Muah!*"

He had not gotten her hopes up, and he had not saddened her more than she already was. He saw that in her eyes. It was the only way he knew to say goodbye and she accepted it.

She wiped her nose with the edge of the bed sheet and sniffled. "I'll remember you forever, too."

"Does that mean I'm not a turkey?"

Olympia let a smile lift her pretty face. Under a stack of pink pillows, she pulled out a wrapped box with a cheery-red bow on it and offered it to him. "It's from all of us. Merry Christmas."

He peeled off the snowflake-designed wrapping paper, opened the flat box, and there, a pair of brass, ivy-wire photo frames made him smile. One carried a picture of the Gilchrist family with Roy Nathan in the center, and the other displayed a ten-year-old Chloe, standing by the chestnut tree Olympia had fallen from as a little girl.

He shook his head, adding a brief huff of amazed laughter. Chloe was developing breasts. "Thank you so much," he said. She laid her hand on his. "Your touch is another gift I'll take with me wherever life's journeys lead."

He stood at the front door in his wool peacoat and Navy ballcap: LPH 21. With a brown suitcase in hand, he grabbed a dented metal knob, opened the door, and a rush of cold air entered the house. Like music, it set the fireplace's orange flame to dance and a scent of fresh pine swirled around the room.

"Isn't anyone going to race me to the car?" he said.

Taffi and Olympia sat by the tall Christmas tree as though the colors of its winking lights had transported them to a world of make-believe: a place where no one shed a tear and loved ones stayed close by. Avery knew the girls would not watch him walk out the door. He had made it clear he was not coming back, so he couldn't blame them for not facing him. In fact, he expected they would offer their backs to him. He stepped into the December cold and turned up his coat collar against the air that nibbled at his neck with icy teeth.

April and Chloe dashed from a frosty window to the coatroom. They ran back bundled up and rushed out to the porch after him; their eyes twinkling with the holiday spirit.

"Merry Christmas, Ave." April put on a brave smile. She handed him a long, red plaid box. "It's from Mama."

He stripped open the box and wrapped a lengthy, handmade, red-white-and-blue scarf around his neck like a world-war-one flying ace. He breathed out a swirl of breath and stepped off the icicle-decorated porch to his Nissan Altima dusted with virgin snow. Frost crunched beneath thick, black boon dockers, and he turned around. "Merry Christmas, everyone." He smiled, feeling his cheeks burn from the cold.

He slipped behind the wheel of the gray, four-door, started the engine, and waved.

A moment later he was gone. Happy. Free.

Merry Christmas, Uncle Neil ....

Chloe's pouting face was the last image on his mind. He studied her honey-brown eyes for so long, he was sure he had seen them before—in someone else. Perhaps a young movie starlet, he thought. Avery was glad the child had no idea where he was going.

Neither did he. Loners never knew.

Epilogue

Rousing cheers and vigorous applauses resounded throughout the Criminal Investigations Division for a tall black man in a dark pinstriped suit and flashy red tie as he loped from the elevator corridor to his Maplewood desk in one of forty cubicles that filled the open-space floor at the J. Edgar Hoover Building on Pennsylvania Avenue in Washington, DC. The standing ovation which lasted a good five minutes came from fellow plainclothed agents, those from the finance department, the legal staff, the labs division, and other bureau employees, including the assistant director-in-charge, Morton Downs, an averaged-height individual with an eyebrow thicker than the other and whose hardy torso was longer than his legs.

Downs led the well-dressed black man to a boardroom in the north wing where another knot of welcoming people broke out in cheers, applauses, and a rehearsed song: *For he's a jolly good agent....*

A big, lavish cake—square, tall, and wide—was rolled in on a stainless-steel cart, and Morton Downs began his speech: "It is with profound mixed emotions that I announce the retirement of an officer and a gentleman. One of the best FBI men I've had the pleasure to work with, and still an eligible bachelor—our own, Special Agent Jimmy Ames."

Ames ran a hand over rows of tight short coils of afro hair as he masked his humility and displayed his delight. The speech was followed by good, old-fashioned banter and hearty bursts of laughter, all aimed at the young-looking man everyone had worked with and admired for almost three decades.

When the FBI building-shaped white cake was devoured down to the first floor level, Downs presented several gifts to the SA: a gold Rolex watch, a glazed teakwood plaque—his name in silver at the foot of a proud American bald eagle clutching a quiver of arrows in its menacing claws over a blue, gold-trimmed Department of Justice logo—and keys to a brand new car: a BMW. Someone in the festive throng said BMW stood for Black Man's Wheels.

Back at his work desk in the busy office, the agent cleaned out all of the drawers and put everything in a one-foot-deep, two-foot-wide, three-foot-long U-haul box: past commendations, old awards, more honors. He knew the new man replacing him was left-handed when he answered the phone and right-handed when he wrote, so he arranged a banker's style lamp at the head of the blotter, the phone to port and a one-inch-thick file folder with a clean yellow pad and fountain pen on top, to starboard.

Port and starboard.

He had not thought about those terms since he was in the Navy thirty years ago, and now that his career was ticking to an end, he wondered with intense interest how far he would have gotten if he had not been dismissed from the military.

With great satisfaction he mused on an assignment he had solved early in his career, regarding a vehicular accident in North Carolina. The man, whose last name escaped him—no, it was Morgan—was involved in a head-on and took off, leaving the body of the other driver lying on an unforgiving, dark road. Years later, when the fugitive was found in a foul stinking hideaway of excrement and piss, Ames was there to cuff him and read him his rights. A mangled, white Toyota Camry was excavated from a nearby site and the manslaughter case was closed. But not before agents found out what else Morgan had done. On the night of the fatal crash, he returned to his girlfriend's mother's house and slashed tires of three cars in an act of retribution. Then he cut the telephone line, and after attacking a thorny rosebush, he crabbed into an opened window and stole the occupants' cell and iphones, leaving everyone in an Amish world. He then made a call to Norfolk and claimed his navy-girlfriend had deserted after killing a man in a car wreck. By the time JAG lawyers arrived at the woman's house and sorted out the story, they called in NCIS who advised her to remain with her family until the perpetrator was in custody. Local police staked the premises for a week, hoping, with the woman as bait, the dangerous man would return. But when there was no encore, and the police felt the household would be safe, they left. Why Ames thought of that day just now was unclear to him.

Fingering through the contents of the thick folder on the desk, he regarded each wordy page, including strange pictures—scientific in nature—with cursory glances and a dose of disappointment. Every case he handled in the last twenty-seven years were solved because he attacked each one with persistence and tenacity: insurance fraud, rightwing extremist felonies, illegal firearm sales, drug trafficking, money laundering, terrorist bombers, espionage activity within the government, moles within the FBI branch, and one investigation he aided the CIA in—the capture of top Al-Qaeda insurgents in an underground bunker in Pakistan, along with all their computers and all the U.S. Navy's Project Black Files in its databases, which led to the whereabouts of three Russian subs loaded with American stealth missiles in the sea caves of Karachi. But all that did nothing to remove a smudge on his pristine record regarding a high-profile case he had never cracked—that of an American serviceman missing for thirty years. What the Special Agent knew of the secret undertakings the man was involved in was that all official documents found in a file cabinet had been burned in a bonfire and the project's sophisticated machinery, photographed and filed in the folder, were destroyed so that the world would remain oblivious to Spectrum and its underground facilities in Norfolk, Virginia, and North Island, California. Now the whereabouts of the missing individual would forever be hid from the government, the military, and general public because people in high places, including the Pentagon and DOD, had worked hard to cement a missing man's identity in secrecy and deceit.

The agent decided to do one last act as an FBI man: shred the entire file, one page at a time....

He had just fed the last piece of document into the giant cross shredder's slashing, piranha-like teeth and switched off the hungry machine when Morton Downs approached with what appeared to be a flat cookie box dressed in a brown paper-bag wrapping and tied about in feet of worn hairy twine.

Downs raised those eyebrows, cocking the thicker one higher than the other. "It's been in my office for the past two days. But with all the goodbye preparations, I'd forgotten it."

Ames handled the box and gave it a discerning eye. *Return To Sender* was stamped and crossed out with a magic marker in several places, and more than five different addresses, along with thirty dated postage stamps, were tattooed on the tattered wrapping. The sender's name and faded return address, scribbled on the box's top-left corner in red ink, looked like it read:

Rev Alln C. Lien
17#9 Blck Crk R
Wlsn, N 27897

He, whoever the man was, had taken great pains and numerous dealings with the postal service to make sure the original package was delivered into the right hands.

The agent said his thanks, offered Downs a handshake of dismissal, and together, marched down the corridor to a pinging elevator light.

Parked down the block from the stately government building, a sapphire-black BMW glistened like a polished looking-glass under haze and sun. Ames gave it a two-noted whistle. A shapely young woman walking by looked back, supposing he had whistled at her. He unlocked the 750i's luxury vehicle's door and got in slowly, deliberately, making the seat's smooth leather creak and pop. The interior smelled of fresh deerskin and clean carpet, and the wrap-around, self tint windshield had the dark cool shade of UV sunglasses. He ran a hand over the leather steering, giving the spacious dashboard and gleaming speedometer gauge an exuberant once-over. His buttocks and spine were supported by the contour of the seat, and when he tested the horn, gratification bubbled inside him. She was built like a Navy fighter jet, and from the inside, looked like one, too. He tossed the wrapped box next to him and started the engine. She growled like a hungry tiger cub.

"Listen, Jimmy...." Downs said from the opened driver's side window. His judicial eyes had dark crescent pockets beneath them. He had mentioned about retiring himself once, when he was ready. Now looking at him, Ames realized that day was a long way off. "If you don't open that package, I swear I'll do it myself."

He put in a clipped laugh, picked up the box, and gave it a vigorous shake. Something bounced around inside. "Mort, thanks again for the humiliating sendoff. Talk to you soon."

Downs gave a satisfied grin. He sauntered up "E" street on Pennsylvania Avenue and retreated into the sprawling, eleven-story, dolomite limestone building through a court-like entrance.

The retired agent opened the U-haul box; the DOJ plaque with the gold lettering sat on top. *Jimmy Ames*. He laughed with triumph over the name. Past transgressions were pardoned because he started afresh. Had someone he'd once known do the same?

He began to undo the strange-looking package.

Underneath all the biting twine, wrinkled paper-bag wrapping and dark box cover, he discovered another box. Within that one he found two, Hallmark-type envelopes: one was flat and bent around the edges; the other was partially torn open from the bulge it carried inside. He went for the stuffed envelope first and ripped it open. Its contents slid out like a glossy new deck of playing cards.

Pictures. A lot of them. All four-by five's. Of faces he didn't know. Black people.

He regarded the face of a woman in the first one. Her honey-colored skin and charming good looks infatuated him. The next few photos had the same cheerful-looking woman, along with three other females, all approximately in their 50's and 60's, surrounded by younger male and female adults, and children, too, all standing in front of a picturesque, colonial-style house. A yellow Labrador Retriever lay panting at the women's feet, and behind the grand house, several tan and brown horses grazed safely within the confines of a white-logged fence. In the background, tall leafy trees abounded beneath fat-bellied clouds and pastel-blue skies. More pictures revealed the same group of people gathered around a dining room table. It seemed to be a family reunion during a recent Thanksgiving holiday.

He moved on to another set of snaps showing the same four adult women, all finely dressed, all apparently standing in age order, taken in what looked like a church vestibule. Leveled at their shoulders a fabulous lifelike oil painting of a pious-looking clergyman, graced a cedar-paneled wall. The resemblance of the man was mirrored on the women's delicate features, except for the youngest one with button-round eyes and a dimpled smile.

Now the agent understood that the pictures were part of a mosaic; a puzzle meant for him to put together.

He shuffled through the remaining ones, all taken in a monument-filled cemetery. In these, a white baldheaded man sporting a clergy collar, Civil-war-style beard and a thick over-the-lip mustache, stood at the foot of a dark granite headstone. A closer shot of the large headstone carried the names of two individuals. A man and a woman. A husband and wife.

The remaining two photos were of the same silver-bearded clergyman: one holding a faded colored object in his hand, and the next showing the bald man on his knees, poking something into the ground at the gravesite. He flipped that photo over like he had done with the others. It was the only one with a message written on its backside: *Ribbons are for heroes*

The clues were of no help to him, so he tore open the second envelope with the nail of his index finger and plucked out a letter. Within was one last photo of a happy-looking couple: that bearded Caucasian embracing one of the four women; the one with the honey complexion.

He read the letter:

I married the woman of my dreams, and now I live at the address below in Wilson. Visit soon,
Your longtime friend, Rev Allen C. Lien

Ames was stumped. Who is Reverend Lien? he thought. He studied all the photos of the clergyman again but had no idea who he was. He flipped through the rest of the photos and saw one he had somehow missed. A tree in a snowfield. A tree with green leaves and red fruit in a snowfield. He started to put the letter away when he noticed a postscript on the reverse side:

P.S. Hey, you still single? Have a daughter about your age I'd like you to meet. Her name is Chloe. Laura Chloe. I'm sure you'll flip when you see her, Slim Jim.

About the Author

Nelson Riverdale is a science/military enthusiast having studied astronomy, genetics, history, and writing. His military love began with war comic books, then war movies, evolving into writing short war stories. Nelson holds a black belt in martial arts. He lives in New York with his wife Ann and their cat Lollipop.